*Marshfield
October 3, 198?*

Betrayal

Dirk wanted to cry, but his anger was too great. Lying out of sight, he was seeing proof of her infidelity. She was taking her lover to his secret place, a place made sacred by her love for . . . him!

He watched as they entered the bower, waited in agony, and breathed a sigh of relief and increased anger when the two emerged. Marietje's hair was in disarray, but what he noticed was how brightly she moved, how high she held her head. Was this the behavior of a woman who wanted to be rescued! No. Willem was right. Marietje had betrayed his trust. She belonged to the enemy now . . .

Also by Iris Bancroft:

DAWN OF DESIRE
RAPTURE'S REBEL

ATTENTION: SCHOOLS AND CORPORATIONS

PINNACLE Books are available at quantity discounts with bulk purchases for educational, business or special promotional use. For further details, please write to: SPECIAL SALES MANAGER, Pinnacle Books, Inc., 1430 Broadway, New York, NY 10018.

WRITE FOR OUR FREE CATALOG

If there is a Pinnacle Book you want—and you cannot find it locally—it is available from us simply by sending the title and price plus 75¢ to cover mailing and handling costs to:

Pinnacle Books, Inc.
Reader Service Department
1430 Broadway
New York, NY 10018

Please allow 6 weeks for delivery.

_____Check here if you want to receive our catalog regularly.

The Passionate Heart

IRIS BANCROFT

PINNACLE BOOKS   NEW YORK

This is a work of fiction. All the characters and events portrayed in this book are fictional, and any resemblance to real people or incidents is purely coincidental.

THE PASSIONATE HEART

Copyright © 1983 by Iris Bancroft

All rights reserved, including the right to reproduce this book or portions thereof in any form.

An original Pinnacle Books edition, published for the first time anywhere.

First printing, September 1983

ISBN: 0-523-41892-2
CANADIAN ISBN: 0-523-43028-0

Cover illustration by Norm Eastman

Printed in the United States of America

PINNACLE BOOKS, INC.
1430 Broadway
New York, New York 10018

9 8 7 6 5 4 3 2 1

THE
PASSIONATE HEART

Chapter One

"In here, quick!" Dirk Hendrik caught Marietje's hand and pulled her behind him into a natural bower. The rain was expected, it always fell in the late afternoon during the monsoon season. But in his pleasure at being alone for the first time with the girl he loved, Dirk had forgotten the time. Now they were trapped—unless they wanted to return to the house dripping, broadcasting to everyone that they had strayed from the shelter and the company to be found near the plantation houses.

Marietje laughed gleefully as she ran, feeling the freshness of the air that greeted the beginning of the rain. What a wonderful adventure! In the years since she was ten and her father had appointed two youths as her teachers and guardians, she had never been alone with either one. That circumstance was her father's doing. Together he considered them trustworthy.

He had assigned Pieter Daan and Dirk Hendrik the task of guarding and educating his daughter only after years of failure in his first choice—to get a proper nursemaid and governess to come from his homeland. Not that he had been unable to locate women willing to take the journey. One after another had sailed over the seas, seemingly anxious to assume the duties he had described, only to succumb to the heat sickness and die soon after arrival. And so, at last, Hans had been forced to admit that Sumatra in 1772 was not the place for most European women. His sturdy wife, Johanna, was unique.

It was then he decided to assign the task to Pieter and Dirk. Two youths—not only to protect his daughter, for even as a child little Marietje promised to become a beauty, but also because their talents complimented each other, thus assuring his daughter of a well-rounded education.

Now, at seventeen, Marietje had more than fulfilled Hans's expectations of her. She had grown into a slender, well-formed creature, with flashing green eyes and red-gold hair that cascaded over her shoulders. Her features were fine, not at all like her mother's, and yet something in the quiet sincerity of her glance and the determined set of her lips made their kinship undeniable.

As she stepped into the shelter Marietje shook her head, still laughing from excitement, and glanced around at the welter of leaves that protected them from the downpour. "When did you find this place? I never knew it was here."

"No one knows of it but me." Dirk turned to face her. "And now you. Please, promise me you will keep my secret? I come here, sometimes, when you are resting, to think and to plan for my future."

In the dim light, Dirk seemed more handsome to Marietje than she had ever felt him to be before. His dark, wavy hair was ruffled from the wind, and the slight dampness had teased the ends into tight curls. A strand, unwilling to follow the dictates of his comb, hung loosely over his forehead. She stared at him in silence, drinking in his dark beauty. As long as she could remember, she had wanted to grow up and marry him. During those first years when he was assigned as her tutor, she had tried in many childish ways to charm him, but he had always remained aloof, as if he saw her as nothing other than a sometimes-naughty girl he had to protect and instruct.

Now, alone with him for the first time she could remember, she wondered again if she could ever be more to him than a pupil. "Will Pieter find us?"

"He isn't looking. Remember, my dear child, we left him tending to an emergency."

Marietje felt a rush of anger. Why was he always so right—and she so stupid? Of course she remembered. One of the workers on her father's coffee plantation had been bitten by a snake, and Pieter had first lanced the wound and then carried the injured man on his horse, anxious to reach the house where better medical aid could be administered.

She was angry at herself for her temporary forgetfulness, but she was also annoyed at Dirk. This was not the first time he had shown his disdain for her. She drew herself up, her chin abnormally high, as if she wanted to look down on him as he so often looked on her. "I'm not a child, Dirk Hendrik. I would have you remember that."

"You are a child to me. I am your teacher."

"Just because you're a few years older . . ."

"Ten."

"And just because you happen to be assigned to teach me numbers and reading and—"

"And manners, and how to play the harpsichord, and how to sing, and—"

"That's enough! I didn't come out here with you so you could preach to me. I thought . . ." She paused. What, exactly, had she expected? The dream was there, where it always lurked, waiting to draw her into a world far more pleasant than the one in which she was forced by circumstance to live. She had dreamed, as she rode beside Dirk, that he was taking her to some secret place where he could speak the words she longed to hear him say.

But Dirk had shown no inclination, either on the ride or since the start of the rain, to speak of anything except the suddenness of the downpour and the geography of the land above the plantation. Still, he had directed their horses toward this bower. Had he planned all along to show it to her? To take her inside and . . .?

She saw that he was laughing at her, and she stamped her foot on the soft dirt. "That isn't fair! I certainly am not to blame for your being made my teacher. Besides, lesson time is over for today, isn't it?" The last was more a plea than an order, and she looked up at him, her eyes wide. She saw the glint of amusement in his dark eyes, and she remembered she was angry at him. Impatiently, she lowered her head. "You must never, never call me a child again."

He had been laughing, but now, abruptly, his expression grew serious. He looked at her in silence, his gaze seeming to penetrate to her very heart. "I must, Marietje. It's my only defense."

"Defense? Against what? What harm can I do you?"

"You can make me forget . . ." He paused. ". . . that your father is my master." He grew silent again, but the thought, once admitted, seemed too strong for him to repress. "And that I love you."

She stood rooted to the spot, staring up into his strong face. Had she heard right? Had she slipped once more into a dream? Instinctively she reached out and touched his arm. He was real. "Say it again, please."

He grimaced. "Why? So you can laugh at me?"

She barely whispered. "No. Please, Dirk, I have to know. What did you say?"

He seemed angry now—at her as well as at himself—but he faced her stubbornly. "I said I love you. I'm sorry. I know it isn't your father's wish that I be more than a servant, even though I lack not for breeding. Still, I know he has plans to wed you to a landowner. Yet, sometimes a man cannot control what should and should not be."

She spoke softly, as if only now facing truths she had known all her life. "My father will not decide whom I wed. When I am a woman . . ." She looked up. "I'm a woman now, am I not?"

His smile was sad. "You are not a child, though I call you one. Forgive me. I did not intend to destroy our friendship."

She shook her head slightly. "You have destroyed nothing. Say it again. Say you love me."

"I must not. I beg your forg—"

"Do not beg to me!" Her eyes flashed. "If you love me, show me. Kiss me." She saw him hesitate, and she clenched her fists. "If you don't, I'll tell Papa."

He laughed, in spite of his obvious worry, and bent his lips to hers. It was clear he had meant it to be a light, almost brotherly kiss, but before he could pull back, she caught him around the neck and pulled him to her, lifting herself onto her toes. She had wanted this for too long to let it pass quickly.

For one moment he resisted, and then his arms circled her, pulling her close against his body. She felt the hardness of his jacket buttons against her breasts and squirmed to ease the pressure, and it was then she felt something else, hard and demanding, pressing against her stomach. She moved again, and she felt the hardness grow. Fascinated, she shifted her body once more.

He moaned, his lips pressing against hers so forcefully she feared he was bruising her. "Oh Marietje, I love you. God, how much I love you."

She moved again. A new sensation flooded her body, starting deep in her abdomen. Was it stirred to life by that hard something that seemed to want to tear through his breeches and push into her belly? Why did a kiss on the lips stir her there?

For the first time since she changed from child to woman, Marietje felt herself growing angry at her mother. There was, she sensed, something she should do. There was a reason for her strange ache. But she had no guidance. All she could do was wait for Dirk to do something to her. That—and press against him with wild fury, for in so doing she was obeying the inner compulsion of her own desire.

She shifted again, and once more he moaned. Had she hurt him? She opened her eyes and looked into his. But she dared not look long. Never before had she seen him look quite as he did now. His lips rested on hers. His eyes were half closed. There was a transparency about his features, as if he had dropped all the barriers men usually hold before them to hide their emotions. She had seen her father look that way once, when her mother was very sick. But Dirk had no reason to be worried. What, then, was the meaning of his expression? Why did he hold her so close and yet refuse to respond to her slight movements?

Would she learn now what it was that men did to women? Her mother had hinted at it, that first day when she began to bleed. "You must bleed." Johanna had spoken grimly. "It is God's curse on all women. Yet, it is also God's blessing, for it is the Lord's way of letting you know that you, like Eve, will bear children."

There had been so many questions Marietje had wanted to ask that day, but something in her mother's face had silenced her. Yet from that time on, she had suffered from strange dreams. Strange dreams—and an unexplainable compulsion to search for meanings. Yet there was no one she could ask. A faint hope stirred in her breast. Would Dirk be the one to answer her questions—and to still the ache in her abdomen?

"I love you, Dirk Hendrik."

His body seemed to shudder, and his voice came from a distance. "Thank God that you do." He moved his hands down, pressing her buttocks. She felt the hardness push against her, and she thought that never before had she experienced so sweet a sensation. She wanted to move again, but he held her too closely, and suddenly she was thankful that she had worn a light summer dress and had left off her petticoats. She wanted him close, wanted the pressure. She inhaled, aware of the sweet, musky scent that emanated from his pores.

Had she loved him before? She had thought so. But now she knew there was more to love than an innocent child could possibly imagine. More, even, than she could experience in this close embrace. There was more. And she was willing to accept it all. Whatever her love for Dirk might bring upon her, she was eager to taste it all.

A cool breeze, wafted in by the falling rain, touched her back, and she shivered.

"Are you frightened, my love?" What gentleness was in his voice!

"No." She could say no more. His nearness left her breathless.

He remained silent for a while, as if considering. She felt his arms tighten around her, felt his hands push her buttocks forward. And she waited. He would know what she had to do.

Abruptly he drew back, letting the cold air push between them. When she tried to close the gap he had created, he held out one hand and forced her to stay. His expression had changed. Now he seemed angry, and his look was hard.

"Dirk, what have I done?" She tried to push his hand aside.

A gentle breath passed over his features, and then the coldness returned. "You have done nothing. Thank God. Nor have I." Why, she wondered, did he seem so frightened? "Dear God, that I should come so close to destroying what little happiness I have had."

"I don't understand." She was hurt—too hurt even to

be angry. "How can our loving one another destroy anything?"

"Believe me, my darling. What I wanted to do could have ruined our love forever. Your father would have had me shot."

"Why would Papa shoot the man I love?"

He was in control now, and Marietje felt a new sadness. She could see the strange hard thing that had pressed against her stomach still pushing against the tightness of his breeches. And suddenly she was possessed with a longing to touch it. Her hand moved forward without conscious will.

Once more, Dirk retreated. "No. Please, Marietje."

Confused, and still hurt by his sudden change in behavior, she drew her hand back. Why, she wondered, did he act so strangely? Why one minute holding her so close she could barely breathe and the next pushing her away? She looked up, the question in her eyes. "You do not love me?"

"Oh, believe me, I do." The force of his words left no doubt of his sincerity. "More than anything, I want you to be my wife. But we must wait. I will speak to your father as soon as you reach your eighteenth birthday. And then, if the English do not come, and my plans work as I wish them to, we will be married." The gentleness had returned again to his face and voice. "There will be times, my darling, when you may think I have forgotten what has happened here, but that won't be true. It's just that I dare not speak to your father too soon. He will want proof that I can give you all you have learned to expect in comfort and happiness. Do you understand?"

She shook her head. "No. But I will try." She put a hand out and touched his sleeve with her fingers. The material felt wonderfully masculine, and when she brought her hand to her face, she smelled the musky odor that had been so strong before. "May I touch you—sometimes?"

He laughed again, and the lightheartedness had returned. "If you are very good." He held up a hand to stop her rebuke. "Forgive me. We can't return home looking so sad-faced. I want nothing to cause your father to send me away—not when we know . . ." He caught her in his arms and smiled down at her. "Oh, little Marietje, there is so much more to my love. I want to hold you in my arms as you sleep and feel the softness of your hair against my arm. I want to stroke your body, and . . ." He touched her lips once more with his, and she trembled with a renewed longing.

She wanted more, even though she could not say what that meant. Yet for the first time in years, she felt a peace. Now she could put uncertainty behind. The day would come when she would be Dirk's bride, and then all the dreams and unknown longings that had tormented her for so long would be explained.

When they stepped from the bower, the rain was ended. A ray of sunlight touched her hair. She turned and looked back at Dirk. *How wonderful*, she thought. *One rain—a few moments in a hidden shelter—and my life is changed.*

I'm a woman, she repeated silently as she mounted her horse. *I'm a real, grown-up woman. And soon I will know—everything.*

As Dirk spurred his horse and led the way down toward the distant houses she thought that no one in the entire world could possibly have as wonderful and handsome a husband-to-be as did she.

Chapter Two

"I know I have no money, sir." Dirk Hendrik's military stance belied any humbleness in his words. "But I am prepared to prove my worth. I have knowledge of the spices most sought by traders, and I know where there are large stands of valuable woods." He glanced quickly at Marietje. Her birthday celebration had taken place almost a week ago, a month after their talk in the arbor. He knew she had wondered why he delayed. She did not realize that once he voiced his intentions to her father he could no longer serve as her guardian. Hans Koenraad was too protective of his daughter's honor.

Hans studied the young man who stood before him. Dirk was certainly handsome enough to satisfy the romantic natures of both his wife and his daughter. And there was no doubt that Marietje was fond of the lad. But the weight of his decision hung heavy on Hans. Was Dirk the right man for bright, effusive, glowing Marietje? True, she might be safe with him. The letter . . . He touched his pocket. He had not shown the letter to Johanna yet. Maybe he never would. It had arrived only a day ago, and it told of war between the Netherlands and England. A threat that might already have become a reality. The letter had been a year in coming. And the date, February 1780, had been inscribed with careful precision in his son's hand. Fall in Sumatra, if that tropical island could be said to have any seasons.

He glanced at the young man once more. What was it Dirk had said? Oh, yes. He obviously wanted permission to leave for Palembang. And, as had been expected, he wanted Marietje to become his wife.

Dirk, standing so straight before his master, ran a hand through his dark hair. He was growing uneasy. Never, when he thought of this moment, had he considered that Hans Koenraad might be undecided. From the first, he had expected to be turned down. True, he was of noble birth. His father had large holdings in both the Netherlands and on the island of Java. But he had no claim to the estate, for he was the youngest of five sons.

Maybe Hans was willing to consider him, after all. Why else did he pause so often and study the matter with such care? Dirk felt his courage grow. He had been right, after all, to bring the matter to a head.

He had been uncertain at first. How could Hans Koenraad even consider marrying his only daughter off to a man who had been his servant? Yet . . . If he did not ask, he would never forgive himself. And Hans Koenraad had never seemed upset with the closeness that existed between his daughter and her two teachers.

He glanced past Hans's imposing figure to where Marietje stood beside her second guardian—Pieter Daan. Pieter was a common man, the son of a tradesman who had died years ago killed by a trader. Pieter had never raised his hopes to Marietje, though it was clear that he loved her, too. Always, even when she was but a child and it was his responsibility to protect and, to some degree, teach her, Pieter had always treated her with a quiet respect. The correct reserve to show when dealing with one's better.

"You inherit none of your father's property?" Hans was thinking of the large warehouses that lined the docks in Batavia.

"No, sir. I am the youngest of five sons. My father gave me nothing but his will to succeed. And that I have in great abundance. Sir, I beg you to consider my request. I am exceeding fond of your daughter."

"Of that I am aware. As I am also aware that she finds you to her liking. Yet I must not decide lightly. You have done naught so far to improve your fortune. And my possessions will go to my son, Johan, who is presently in Amsterdam, at the university."

"Yes, sir. I understand. Yet, do not think me slothful because I have obeyed your orders. It was you who appointed me, along with Pieter Daan, as dual tutors for your daughter. I trust I have obeyed your instructions in that matter to your satisfaction."

Hans smiled grimly at the reminder. It did not endear Dirk to him to know that the lad recognized how invaluable he had been. Yet he could not deny the truth. "Aye, you and Pieter did well. I was wise to divide the duty between you, for Pieter has taught my daughter the simple honesty of a man of labor. And you have done well in instructing her in the arts and the dance. She is well prepared for the society of her homeland."

Dirk felt a growing uneasiness. "You intend to send her to Amsterdam?"

"I intend to *bring* her to Amsterdam. Johanna and I are planning to return there within the year. Marietje has a full life waiting for her in the house of her grandfather."

Dirk hesitated before voicing his next question. He feared that he knew the answer already, for any provident father would consider his daughter's future by the time she reached the age of eighteen. "She has already been promised?"

"Aye." Hans watched the expression on Dirk's face with sharp attention. If the lad resigned himself too quickly to his loss, he was not worthy of any woman's hand.

Dirk inhaled. His jaw was set tight, and his eyes narrowed. "I have not heard of him before."

Hans repressed a smile. "Nay, that you have not."

Dirk's chin went up. "I think you are not certain that her pledge should be honored. Else you would not have permitted me to speak so long, nor would you have given ear to my plea."

"You are perspicacious, Dirk Hendrik. What you say is true. I am not certain that the man I chose for Marietje when she was born is the man she should wed."

"Then there is hope for me?" Dirk's eyes brightened, and he glanced swiftly toward Marietje, who stood a distance away, pretending to be in deep conversation with Pieter.

"Aye, there is hope for you." Now, at last, Hans dared to relax. Dirk had passed the test. He had not given up his dream too quickly. And he saw through the small subterfuge with ease. He was, as Hans had suspected all along, an intelligent lad with strong ambition. Now was the time to spur that aspiration into reality. "But the hope exists only if you follow your intentions. You cannot win my daughter if you remain here. It is time, my boy, for you to leave and make your fortune."

A shadow passed over Dirk's face. "I cannot go with her pledge?"

"Nay, I think not. If you do not succeed, I will not be held to any promise. But I can assure you that she will not be given to another until a year has passed. A full year. At that time Johanna and I depart for home, and if Marietje is not wed, she goes with us."

Hans Koenraad glanced to where his daughter waited. "Now I suggest that you go with Pieter and tell them both of your departure. I recognize that your time is short, and I will not hold you to your contract with me any longer."

Dirk bowed as Hans turned and crossed the yard. He waited until the portly Dutchman had vanished inside the open doorway to the study before he moved. Then he hurried to Marietje's side. "Do you think he meant it? He will not send you off to the Netherlands while I am in Palembang?"

"My father is a man of his word, Dirk. You know that."

"Then you will be mine!" He swept Marietje into his arms and danced around, crowing with delight. She kicked in mock fury, laughing with him all the while. Pieter watched the play with a smile of happy amusement. He was accustomed to seeing his friends behave like happy children. Nor was he in any way jealous of the love Marietje and Dirk shared. They were not common folk, as he was. He recognized that they honored him when they treated him as an equal.

At last, Dirk put his lovely bundle back down on the ground, but he did not release his hold on her waist. "You will wait for me?"

"Of course I will, silly!" Marietje laughed with glee at his obvious discomfort. "I would go with you, were it possible." Her expression grew serious. "I love you, Dirk. I will be no other man's wife."

"You won't have a chance!" He picked her up once more and swung her around in a circle. Then, abruptly, he put her down and caught her around the waist with one arm. "Come, let us go for a ride before I pack."

"No." Marietje planted her feet solidly. "Let's pack first. I want to be certain you take the right things with you."

Dirk knew what Marietje meant. There was no question about his clothing; he had only the suit he wore and one other—a hand-me-down from Hans Koenraad himself, that Johanna had ordered a servant to alter to fit the slender young man. No, it was not clothing to which Marietje referred. She was anxious lest Dirk forget to bring her picture with him, a sketch that he had drawn himself one afternoon as they rested after a ride through the forest. He had said at the time that he wanted it to remind him of her when he went off to make his fortune.

There was one other item she wanted to be certain he carried with him. A scarf she had knitted of yarns imported from Amsterdam. There had been much amusement when she began to create the heavy wrapping, for warmth is provided by the sun in the island of Sumatra. But Marietje refused to be teased into dropping her project. "It grows cold in the mountains, doesn't it? He might need my scarf when he travels." She had dared Pieter and Dirk to continue their teasing.

"Yes, certainly." Pieter was quick to defend anything his mistress might do.

"Well, I will not take it." Dirk had looked solemn at the time, but then he burst into laughter. Life was good. Who knew when he would have to leave the plantation to seek his fortune? Why prepare for an unknown future?

But the unknown was known now. The future was upon him. And he knew that even without Marietje watching him to make certain he packed it, he would never leave her strange gift behind. "I have drawn another picture—for you." He picked up a sketchbook he had dropped on a bench when Hans Koenraad called him. From it he removed a single sheet of paper and pushed it into Marietje's hands. "This is to keep my memory fresh while I am gone."

Marietje glanced down and squealed with delight. "Oh,

Dirk! How handsome you look!" She held the drawing up for Pieter to see. "Look. He is wearing the uniform of a soldier." A shadow clouded her face. "You are not planning to become a fighter, are you? Please, say you will not." She caught at Dirk's sleeve. "You promised you would never become a soldier when my cousin Jon was killed fighting the British."

"Of course I will not become a soldier, silly. I just drew the uniform because I think I look good in gold braid. Anyway . . ." He shrugged and glanced at Pieter. How like a girl to fail to see the obvious. "Anyway, I would never become a general—at least not before I grew to be an old man." He caught her face between his open hands and turned her toward him. "You will be true to me, won't you? There are many handsome men in Padang—and Thomas Hannsvaal has a full plantation already, though he is only two years my senior. You are sure you have no wish to wed one like him?"

"I am sure." Marietje laughed and caught one of Dirk's hands. "Come along. You must hurry. The sooner you depart, the sooner you will return."

Dirk followed Marietje docilely, glancing back once in a while to see if Pieter was also following. When the three reached the servant's quarters where both Pieter and Dirk had rooms, Marietje paused. "I have not been into your room." She drew back. "Maybe I will wait here for you and Pieter to return."

"How will you know that I take your scarf?" Dirk smiled teasingly.

"Pieter will see that you do what is right." Marietje turned to face Pieter. "Won't you?"

Pieter nodded. "Yes, mistress."

All three burst into laughter at the propriety of his response. They made a charming trio. Dirk Hendrik, close to six feet tall, with a fine slender body and strong shoulders. His dark hair hung in loose curls that almost touched his shoulders, and his sharp, brown eyes seemed to see everywhere at once. His lips were most generally curled up in a smile, and his eyes seemed to sparkle from an inner joy. His long slender hands were those of an aristocrat who had never worked at hard labor, but they bore calluses from too much swinging of a scythe, for he refused to ask the native workers to perform a task he could not do himself.

Besides his duties as Marietje's tutor, he also supervised a few of the native hands in preparing the spices for shipment, and he took both of his responsibilities seriously.

Pieter seemed just the opposite of Dirk, both in appearance and temperament. His yellow-blond hair stood in contrast to his sun-darkened face. His build was stocky, with broad shoulders and a thick chest and thighs. His arms were sturdy, with muscles that bulged when he flexed them. A peasant, he would be certain to announce were he asked, but proud of his ancestry nevertheless, for his father had had a thriving trading station before he died of the heat sickness. And though Pieter seemed content to serve Hans Koenraad, he had dreams of one day reviving the business that had died with his father. All that kept him now from joining his friend and departing for Palembang was his loyalty to the man who had taken him in and fed him when others would have left him to die.

Marietje completed the threesome—complimenting both of her teacher-guardians. Her red-gold hair fell in long curls over her shoulders, catching the sunlight like burnished copper. Her green eyes met Dirk's, reflecting the twinkle that seemed to dwell permanently in his. And the fine line of her lips curled up, as did his, into a smile of good humor.

She was slender, and tall for a girl, with delicate features that her mother claimed she had inherited from an aunt. Her slender arms and tapering fingers moved with a grace that would have been admired on a princess.

Hans Koenraad, watching them from his study window, nodded his appreciation. He had done well to trust his daughter to these two young men—and he would do equally well to give her hand to Dirk. He let the curtain fall and returned to his desk. Dirk would return before the year was over, of that he was certain. And he would justify the faith that had been put in him. Marietje Koenraad would be wed to a good man.

"God go with you, my boy." Hans spoke to himself as

he drew out a sheaf of papers and laid them before him. "You have passed every test I could devise. You will make my girl child a good, dependable husband. To you, I will give her hand with pleasure." He picked up the first paper. Now that the business of his daughter's future had been settled, he had work to do.

Chapter Three

"I wish Papa could have been here to say good-bye." Marietje glanced for a moment away from the receding figure of Dirk Hendrik. It had been difficult for her to let him go, yet she knew his journey was necessary. Only if he succeeded in Palembang would she be permitted to marry him. "Papa has business in Padang all the time. He could have delayed his trip there for one week."

"Your father knows the importance of Dirk's departure. I'm sure he had good reason for rushing off to Padang. A message came . . ."

"I know a message came!" Marietje hated when Pieter was so sensible. "But he still shouldn't have rushed off. He's never been in such a hurry to reach Padang before." She spoke swiftly to keep Pieter from interrupting her, as she had interrupted him. "I know he said something important had come up. But Dirk will be gone for at least a year."

"Yes." Pieter stared at the path down which Dirk had vanished.

Immediately Marietje was contrite. "You wanted to go with him, didn't you?"

"Yes, I did." Pieter turned his horse around on the narrow path and waited until Marietje's mount stood beside him, facing toward the plantation. They moved then, slowly, both young people reluctant to leave the place where they had said their farewells to their friend.

As they approached the clearing of the Koenraad plantation Pieter drew his reins tight. His horse paused, its nostrils flared. Marietje, behind him, frowned. What was he doing now? When he did not move, she raised her voice impatiently. "What's the matter, Pieter? Why stop now? You were most eager to see Dirk on his way."

"True." He spoke almost in a whisper. "But that was

17

because he has a long journey ahead. He will be a week reaching Palembang—if he encounters no problems."

She felt the tension in his voice, and she blanched. "What's the matter? Is he in trouble?"

"I don't think so. But something is wrong ahead."

She tried to move around him. "Then we ought to hurry. Maybe Mama is sick again. Or maybe Papa had another attack of dysentery and has come back from Padang."

Pieter blocked the path. "No. Don't rush out yet." She heard the sounds that had caused him to stop, and her eyes widened in fear. "Don't be too alarmed, either. Just wait here until I see what happened. It's probably nothing." His voice gave her no reassurance.

"Pieter! Don't frighten me." Marietje tried to conceal her uneasiness under a cloak of anger. "Why should I be in any danger?"

"I don't know." He dismounted and led the horses back into the woods, where they would be sheltered from sight. "You must promise me you will wait here until I return."

Marietje shivered, despite the muggy heat. Pieter was carrying the joke too far. "Did you and Dirk plan this before he left—just to tease me? Well, I can see through your little fun, and I don't think it's amusing at all."

Pieter refused to admit anything. "I am serious, Marietje. You must promise me."

"Is it some present Dirk arranged for me, to remind me of him while he is gone? Oh, Pieter, is it a new foal?"

Pieter seemed only annoyed by Marietje's questions. "I tell you, I don't know what it is. Something's wrong. I can feel it. I want to see what's down there before we both go barging in."

Marietje smiled. "Well, if you insist, I'll play your little game. Yours and Dirk's. But I'll get even with you both—someday. Just you wait." She settled back on her horse and did not protest when Pieter tied both reins to a nearby bush.

Silently, as if he really were afraid he might be heard, Pieter crept through the underbrush. Very soon, he was lost in the thick growth, for Hans Koenraad did not waste the labor of his workmen on clearing forest he could not cultivate. Around his plantation the native growth was thick with vines and strange flowering trees and bushes. An entire army could be concealed in the forest, and no one on the plantation would see that anything was amiss.

Dirk had remarked about that one day when they were riding the perimeter of the cultivated ground, checking for encroaching jungle. Pieter and Marietje had gone along, as was their usual custom. At the time, Marietje found the remark amusing. Now she recalled it with distinct uneasiness. Was that what Pieter had detected? Signs that one of the wild native tribes from near Lake Toba had come down to raid the plantation for food—and God only knew what else?

Despite her father's and both her tutors' attempts to reassure her, Marietje had always feared the savages that lived in the mountains to the north. She had learned of them by accident, when a seaman turned explorer stumbled into the neatly cultivated lands of the Koenraad plantation to die. He remained alive for a full day, and during that time he was barely quiet to sleep.

He told of the Tobas, the Mandailings, the Karos, and at least two more tribes of cannibals who lived in the mountains. They had caught his companions. Only fortune had saved him. Johanna had him carried to the servants' house and made comfortable, but she could do nothing to save his life. He was too much overcome by the heat sickness and exhaustion. So she sat with him until he died, listening to his ravings and sponging his brow with cool, damp cloths.

It was only when she finally rose to leave that she saw Marietje. The child had followed her into the room when they carried the dying man into the house, and she had crept behind a great chair, where she remained, her eyes wide with fear, listening to the tales of horror.

"Oh, Marietje, my darling! What are you doing here? You should be out with Dirk and Pieter, doing your studies."

"Dirk is back checking the perimeter." Marietje could not take her eyes from the dead man. "Are the Tobas and the Mandailings going to follow him here?"

"Of course not, darling!" Johanna bustled from the room, half pushing the girl before her. "What nonsense!

You must not worry about such things. That was just the ravings of a very sick man. Dreams. Nothing more." She tried to speak reassuringly, but the tone of her voice was angry. "You must never do a thing like this again. Do you understand? There are some things a little girl does not need to know."

Marietje understood the true meaning of Johanna's words—and her anger. Despite her protests, what the man had said *was* the truth. There were cannibals up in the mountains. And though she pretended not to be fearful of them, Johanna was, in fact, terrified that they could come and destroy her.

Marietje heard Johanna's words—and clutched her own fear closer to her breast. She lived with it as she grew up. Dirk, always teasing, recognized the terror his charge felt when she heard mention of the Tobas and used her fear to keep her near him when he rode about the plantation.

As she grew older, she realized that Lake Toba, around which the cannibal tribes had built their villages, was far to the north, and that the hunters would not risk traveling into the territory occupied by the Dutch to search for their victims. Yet the fear still remained to haunt her if Dirk was gone too long on an errand—or if Pieter, sent on a journey to another plantation, did not return as scheduled.

And now, unrealistic though her fear might be, it returned to set her trembling. If the savages had come at last, what would Pieter find? And if they caught him, too, then what would she do? Could she catch up with Dirk? He had insisted upon taking his horse with him, though they all knew he could not ride through the jungle. Most of the way, the beast would be a handicap, for he would have to chop a path for it. But when he reached Palembang, the horse would again be an asset. His only possession—a proof that he was not a common man, but a man of property. That, and the letter he bore written by Hans Koenraad, might procure for him a position as an overseer in one of the factories.

But if the savages had reached the plantation, might they also have followed Dirk? Marietje pushed the fear back. She was being foolish again. Letting the unknown frighten her.

She slid from her saddle, landing lightly on the moss-covered branches that blanketed the ground. She was accustomed to such sponginess underfoot, and she knew that most of the matter on which she trod was half rotted and eaten through by insects. This was the material that created the rich soil in which her father planted his coffee trees.

The path Pieter had hacked as he departed was easy to follow. Nevertheless, she moved slowly, searching ahead for signs of wild beasts or snakes. She brushed moss from her shoulders. It was not her habit to walk through the forest alone. Hans was strict, demanding that Pieter and Dirk be with her whenever she left the clearing.

She glanced over her shoulder, afraid she might see the face of a wild native. But the woods behind her were empty of human life. The sight of the winding path reminded her of Dirk's lonely trail down into Palembang. She would say special prayers for him, that he remain safe and come back successful.

He was uniquely suited for the role of adventurer. He had arrived in Padang on one of his father's ships, cabin boy to a captain his father trusted. But he had learned that the man was sadistic in his treatment of his men. An attack of the heat sickness had saved the lad from sailing when his ship left port. Marietje had once heard her father remark that the captain had been glad to leave the lad behind.

Nevertheless, Hans Koenraad had filed indenture papers for the boy and had taken him in as a servant. Marietje did not fully understand all of the legalities of such an act, but she accepted what was done without question, since all of it had occurred when she was an infant.

Pieter had come from different circumstances. When his father was killed by a disgruntled trader, he was alone, for his mother had died at his birth. Other merchants took the business, legally and by subterfuge, leaving Pieter penniless. And Hans Koenraad took him in out of pity.

Neither act had Hans ever regretted. The boys were ten years old when Marietje was born, and they loved her as if she were a sister. Johanna often remarked that God had sent them both to her, so her little daughter would have good protectors, for from the first, they accepted the responsibility of watching her. They cared for the baby when the first nurse sailed from the Netherlands. They resumed Marietje's care when the woman died. It was not until Marietje reached the age of eight that their position as guardians and teachers was confirmed. Yet she thought of them more as brothers than guardians, except for her knowledge that they were not true family. And that knowledge had fed her dreams when she began to grow aware of Dirk as a man—and herself as a budding woman.

A sharp noise brought Marietje to a halt. Fighting the damp chill of fear that she always felt in the forest, she turned to study the path behind her. In the dark jungle, she could see nothing. Overhead, monkeys chattered. A small furry body came hurtling down from the treetops, catching at an overhanging branch as it fell. Nothing unusual. No sign of cannibals stalking her—or of a tiger on the prowl. With a small sigh, she resumed her walk. Ahead lay the path she and Pieter had been following—actually no more than a narrow line through the underbrush, made by animals on their way to a nearby watering hole.

She paused, uncertain as to whether or not she should continue. Pieter had told her to wait, and she was disobeying him. Would he be angry if he returned and found she had left the horses? She looked back to where they stood, munching at the abundance of greenery that filled the jungle floor. They were in no danger—nor was she.

It's just a game Dirk put Pieter up to. The thought gave her a feeling of confidence. She didn't have to play the game, no matter how determined Pieter was to see it through. Still there was comfort in the knowledge that Dirk had thought to work out such elaborate details before he left.

I'll prepare a better one for him! She smiled. Pieter was not very good at making up funny jokes to play on his fellow guardian, but she was sure she could get his cooperation in any plans she might make. That, she decided, would be the way to make Dirk feel at home again. Maybe she would have Pieter greet him with some story about her being captured by the cannibals! That would frighten him! Maybe he'd realize he should never leave her alone again. Yes, that's what she'd do—on his return.

A sharp retort drew her attention back toward the plantation. That was no twig snapping. It was gunfire!

Forgetful of danger, Marietje lifted her riding skirt and ran along the narrow path toward the clearing. But before she broke from her hiding place, caution overcame her. No one fired guns on her father's plantation. Ever. He permitted hunting in the forest, that was true, but out of deference to Johanna he banned firearms around the house. Or, at least, their use. And these shots—for more followed the first—came not from the woods on another side of the coffee trees, but from the cluster of buildings.

Wide-eyed, Marietje pushed a leaf aside and gazed down at the scene below. Soldiers were everywhere, and though she was not well versed in military uniforms, she did recognize the colors they carried. The English flag!

A scream shattered the air, and a female figure appeared at the door of the house. Marietje recognized Anna, the only Dutch servant who had survived the climate long enough to become a part of the Koenraad household. Though she had lived on the plantation now for many years, she had not yet grown accustomed to the weather—or to the restrictions of the manor. Marietje had hoped, when Anna first arrived, that the young girl might become her friend. But Anna's strict upbringing permitted no close relationship with "the gentry."

Anna screamed again, and now Marietje saw the cause of the maid's distress. A burly soldier ran close behind her, and as the two reached the clearing between the house and the milk house he caught her in his arms. Anna fought wildly as he tugged at her clothing, tearing it when it would not come off easily.

Marietje gasped. Never before in her life had she seen such brutality. When Anna kicked at the soldier in an attempt to stop his attack, he swung his arm wide and hit her soundly on the side of the head. The blow seemed to kill any fight left in the frail woman, for she dropped limply to the ground. The soldier did not bother to concern himself with her condition. Instead he ripped open his trousers and fell upon the supine figure.

Marietje stood transfixed, unable to turn away from the sight. It was then she realized that the screaming had stopped. "I think she's dead, thank God." The voice came from behind her, and Marietje jumped in surprise.

Pieter stepped quickly to her side. "I've been all around the plantation. Soldiers are everywhere. I came back because I feared you might try to get to the house."

"Mother." The word was little more than a whisper. Marietje turned to face Pieter. "Mother's there." Her voice rose higher. "Pieter, we must save my mother!"

He caught her in his arms and held her firmly. Angry at the restriction, Marietje struggled, hammering her fists against his chest. "Let me go! I must save my mother!"

"You cannot save her. No one can. There are too many of them."

With a sudden jerk, she broke free. But she did not head for the clearing. Instead she ran back to where the horses were tethered. Tucked in its holster on Pieter's saddle was a gun. No man traveled in the jungle without one.

Pulling it free, she brandished it wildly. "If you won't go, I will." She was crying, and she brushed the tears aside with the back of her hand. The gun still waved before her. "I mustn't let them—do that—to my mother!"

She broke then, and dropped the gun on the ground. It was hopeless. She knew that. If she ran into the clearing, she would only provide the rampaging soldiers with one more victim.

Pieter picked the gun up and returned to his horse. From his saddlebag, he removed lead and gunpowder. Silently he loaded the instrument and checked the hammer. It was ready to fire now. He hesitated a moment before he spoke. "I will go." He touched Marietje's arm. "But you must promise me to stay here until the soldiers go." He paused. They would not leave so rich a plantation without first looting it of its treasures.

He pursed his lips as he thought. It was not easy for him to make decisions. That had always been Dirk's privilege. "If they stay, you must promise to take both horses and go carefully to the Johannson plantation. It is farther up the mountain. The soldiers might not have gone that far."

Marietje frowned. "Why are you telling me to go? I can't leave my mother. If you save her . . ." Her mouth fell open, and she stared up at her companion. He did not expect to return. Nor did he consider the possibility he could rescue her mother.

A new scream tore through the air. It was beginning again. Pieter dropped Marietje's arm and ran toward the clearing. She hurried behind him, unmindful of the brambles that caught at her sleeves and tugged at her skirt.

He stopped at the edge of the jungle. Once more he faced her. "Do you promise?"

The scream drowned out any answer Marietje might have given, and Pieter broke into a run. Marietje watched as he plummeted down the hill toward the house. Fearful of what she would see, she searched for the source of the strident cry for help. She clutched at a branch to steady herself. The same man who had killed and raped Anna was dragging Johanna across the yard. The woman was resisting wildly, but Marietje knew there was no chance that she would break free. This man was mad with his power. And none of the other soldiers seemed the least concerned with his actions. They were too busy removing food from the larder, and gems and valuables from the house. A number of them had harnessed horses to a wagon and were loading it with their loot.

Suddenly Marietje realized that Pieter had managed to reach the cluster of buildings without being seen. Johanna saw him, too, and she pulled back from her captor. "Kill me, Pieter. Save me from this horror."

Marietje heard the words clearly, and she gasped in alarm. How could her mother ask such a thing of her friend? But Pieter took no time for thought. He raised his gun and took aim. The soldiers were moving toward him, their guns in their hands, but as one after the other stopped to load, Marietje realized they had been too busy looting to follow simple army procedures.

That oversight alone gave Pieter the time he needed. He fired, and Johanna fell to the ground. Running swiftly, he reached shelter behind the milk house. Marietje could see that he was reloading. Tears obscured her vision then, for the full impact of what she had seen overwhelmed her. Her mother was dead!

And Pieter had killed her.

How could he do such a thing? Why hadn't he tried to rescue her? At least he should have tried!

A volley of shots drew her attention back to the clearing. Pieter had reloaded. He stood concealed from the soldiers' view, his gun ready. Some of the soldiers had shot at him, and they were once more reloading. Others advanced toward the place where he hid.

Her heart aching, Marietje looked up to where her mother's body lay. A cry escaped her lips. The soldier who had violated Anna's body was approaching Johanna. And then, with sudden insight, Marietje knew what Pieter intended. She held her breath when he stepped out from hiding and aimed his gun not at the men who threatened him, but at the lone soldier who stood over Johanna's crumpled body. There was a puff of smoke, and Marietje closed her eyes and prayed that his aim was true. When she opened them again, the soldier had fallen beside her mother. Pieter had accomplished his mission.

He achieved his goal with no time to spare. Now the other soldiers were approaching. One, seeing what Pieter intended, knelt and took aim at the youth's head. His gun went off only a brief moment after Pieter's own, and his aim, too, was true. Pieter fell to the ground. As he dropped, other guns were aimed in his direction. They fired until there was no doubt that the intruder was killed.

With a moan, Marietje dropped to the ground. "Mother." The word was muffled by her tears. "Pieter." She cried for them both, for she knew Pieter had done the right thing. An animal like that had to be stopped.

Even as she wept she knew why Pieter had not tried to escape with Johanna. They would never have reached the clearing. He, for certain, would have been killed. But her mother might have survived. And then, after attempting to get away, she could well have become a victim of more than one of the British looters.

A voice nearby startled her into awareness. "He must have had a horse. You go that way." The language was foreign to her, neither Dutch nor a native tongue. And the speaker was male. She froze. Would she be found? The soldiers seemed to be on both sides of her hiding place. If she was lucky, they might pass her by. She could hear them shuffling around in the forest behind her. Then a cry brought all movement to a halt. "Hey! I found it. There's two, and one belongs to a woman."

A voice from the other side of Marietje responded. "A woman, eh? Well, then, let's flush her out."

Marietje prayed as the rustling began once more. What if one of these men was like the beast Pieter had killed? There was no one now to save her, as Pieter had saved her mother. Her fingers closed around a loose branch that had been cut when the plantation was enlarged. She held it tight. If any man tried to harm her, she would at least put up a fight.

"Hey! What have we here?" The soldier stood over her, a smile of triumph on his face. He bent down and caught her arm, pulling her to her feet. "I found her!" A call from nearby let Marietje know that her captor had been heard.

"She's a pretty one, isn't she?" A second man appeared, leading the two horses. "And a fighter." He caught her upraised arm just in time to keep her from swinging at his companion's head. His fingers closed on her wrist and he twisted sharply, pushing her hand open. The branch dropped harmlessly to the ground.

"Let me go! I hate you. I hate you all." She barely realized that she was talking, because she was crying, too. These were the men who were responsible for her mother's death—and for Pieter's sacrifice.

"A feisty wench." She understood the language now. Her father had insisted that both she and her brother learn English and French, as well as their native tongue. "Better talk English, lassy. We don't speak your heathen language."

"You are the heathens. You kill and rob. I hate you." She saw them smile as they realized she had slipped into their own tongue. They found her amusing! The thought angered her more, and she kicked at the soldier closest to her.

He snarled and caught her wrist. "Mind your manners, woman." In one easy motion, he pulled her toward him. His free hand moved over her body, stopping to cup her breasts. "She's a smooth one, she is." His expression changed, and a cold fear brought a gasp to Marietje's lips. There was no friend nearby to save her from shame.

"Bert! Frank! Commander's coming!" The call caught her captor in mid-motion. He glanced toward the clearing and cursed. But he did not delay. Instead, he swept Marietje into his arms and stepped from the forest.

The heat of the sun encompassed them both. Automatically Marietje reached up to pull her hat over her face, but it was gone, fallen, no doubt, somewhere in the woods behind her. Then the incongruity of such a concern dawned upon her. She was about to die. She was certain of that. All she could do was pray that she died quickly, as Anna had.

Bert, for that appeared to be the name of her captor, moved swiftly down the slope, stumbling only once over an unevenness in the ground below him. She felt the leaves of the tiny, newly planted coffee trees brush against her head, messing up her hair, but she did not concern herself with such inessentials. She barely saw the grove of trees through which she was passing.

How could she save herself? The question burned into her mind. How could she prevent the debasement of her body that lay ahead? Escape—freedom—was obviously impossible. She was surrounded by soldiers. But if she tried to run, if she got free of these thick arms and ran toward the forest, wouldn't some eager marksman shoot her?

She struggled against the restraint of Bert's hold. "Let me down. Please. I can walk."

"Yes, I've no doubt you can. But will you behave? I've no mind to race after you on this half-tended ground."

She felt the sting of his words. Why was he maligning her father's standards? "My father is a good landowner. His groves are among the best cared for in all of Sumatra."

A smile broke the harshness of his features. "Aha! So now we know who you are? Have you sisters?"

"Let me down!" Marietje increased her kicking.

"Bert! Do you want the commander to find you wandering off on your own? Move!" The command came from a young-looking officer who stood near the door to Marietje's house.

"I've found a prize, sir." Bert increased his pace. "This wench claims to be the daughter of the landowner."

The lieutenant slapped his leg impatiently. "Lock her up, then, and help clear up the mess. Are you beasts, that you cannot see women without killing them?"

"It was James, sir." Frank hurried behind Bert, leading the two horses. "I think he's dead, sir."

"I know he's dead. Fools!" The lieutenant snapped his sword with the flat of his hand. It hit his leg with a sharp crack. Bert hurried to stand at attention before him, but he did not release Marietje. "Put the woman down!" The order was shrill, and Bert dropped Marietje so suddenly she turned an ankle and fell to her knees. Before she could recover herself and break away, he caught her wrist and held her firmly.

"Let her go." The lieutenant's voice was hard. "There are corpses to be buried."

Marietje had already buoyed herself for flight, but now she paused. "Please, sir, is my mother to be buried without clergy?"

The lieutenant flushed. "We have no chaplain here." He stared angrily into her face. "Damn it, woman, we are at war."

Something in his behavior gave her courage. "Do you carry on war against women and slaves?"

He turned in anger. "Get to the burial detail! Now!" Bert and Frank both jumped at his shouted command.

Marietje, too, was startled by his harsh command, but she held her ground. He had given no order to her. She waited until he turned once more toward her.

He bowed slightly in her direction. "My apologies, madam, for your treatment. It is not possible to command the troops and serve as aide to the commander. You say that one of the dead women is your mother?"

The cold strength that had supported Marietje throughout her ordeal began to collapse. She was not prepared for kindness. "Yes." She pointed to where two bodies lay. "That man was trying to . . ." She realized she could not continue. The vision of the chase, the attack, and the single shot that had ended Johanna's torment was too vivid.

"Did others assist him?"

The tears she had held back began to flow. Speech was impossible, she knew that. Helplessly she shook her head. She had seen no others. Only that one man whom Pieter had stopped.

"And the man?" The lieutenant pointed toward Pieter's body.

Marietje rubbed the tears from her face. "He is my friend." Her voice was muffled and thick with tears.

"Then we owe you an apology. He was not a soldier?"

She shook her head again, too overcome to speak.

"Commander Scott will not like this at all." The young lieutenant tapped his sword lightly as he spoke. He stared at the two bodies in silence, his lips pursed. "We cannot keep them long. This climate . . ." Abruptly he raised his voice. "Put the bodies of the women and the man in the barn. And get to burying James before the commander sees him. Idiot. To let himself be killed by a stupid farmer."

Marietje took a step toward him. "Pieter wasn't a . . ." She paused suddenly. Kind as this man might be, he was the enemy. She would give him no information he did not demand.

Would he be as considerate of her mother's body if there were no observers? She was certain he would not. Her presence was all that assured her mother and Anna and Pieter decent, Christian burials.

She glanced up toward the woods. She dared not try to escape yet. She would wait until the burials were taken care of. Her mother's soul was more important even than her own honor.

Chapter Four

"Attention!"

Around Marietje, the soldiers scrambled to present themselves. The six whose job it was to dispose of the corpses paused in confusion and then, seeing someone on the road behind her, dropped their burdens and stood up stiffly, their hands pressed against their sides.

She could see that the two men preparing the grave for James, the soldier Pieter had killed, were well along in their task. They stood with little more than their heads showing aboveground, his body immediately behind them, wrapped in a blanket someone had taken from one of the bedrooms of the house. Her mother's body, and those of Pieter and Anna, were yet where they had fallen.

She moved swiftly to where her mother lay and, dropping to the ground, lifted her mother's head into her lap. Now, at last, the full impact of her mother's death broke through her defenses. With a cry of "Mother!" she began to weep, stroking the still features she loved so dearly.

She paid no heed to the bustle around her. Her entire awareness was centered now on her loss. Cradling the still form in her arms, she relived the terrible moment when Pieter raised his gun and fired the shot that had ended Johanna's torment. The shock of the sight had protected her from pain. Now, suddenly, that shield was gone. She could no longer pretend that the body belonged to a stranger. She could no longer comfort herself with the thought that she had had a nightmare—that her mother was safe in the house and the soldiers were part of an unhappy dream.

Her moment of self-renewing grief lasted too short a time. The odor of a horse and the trampling of hooves close to where she crouched forced her to look up. High above her, mounted on the largest horse Marietje had ever seen, was a tall, graying man. His portly build filled the saddle, but yet he rode with ease that spoke of years in the cavalry.

He stared down at her in silence, and then he turned to look around. She could see him pause to study first the body of Anna, and then, some distance away, that of Pieter. At last he looked toward the gravediggers. He snorted angrily, and his horse shifted, one hoof coming perilously close to Johanna's gown, which spread out over the ground around her. Then, abruptly, the tall man returned his gaze to Marietje's troubled face.

"What is that?" He pulled at the reins of his horse and faced toward the luckless lieutenant. "Since when did we wage war against women?" He swung his whip around to point at the two men in the grave. "And who is that? Are you ashamed to admit that you killed the landowner and his entire family? What insanity possessed you? The next thing you do, I suppose, is burn the trees."

"No, sir." The lieutenant spoke quickly, hoping by the speed of his retort to quiet the anger of his superior. "Sir, I found things like this when I arrived. The men . . ."

"The men are your responsibility! I have other aides, yet I saw you at my side as your men departed. Your assignment was not one of danger. The fighting took place in Padang. Sir, I will speak more of this with you later." He whipped his arm around once more. "Now tell me—if you can—what occurred here."

"Sir, I have been led to understand that these people resisted the takeover. Unprovoked, that young man fired at my troups, and the women rushed to his side. Understandably, sir, my men fired back. It is unfortunate that the women died, but . . ." He left the sentence incomplete.

"That is not what happened." Marietje was barely aware that she spoke. "The soldiers—one soldier—tried to violate both my maid and my mother. My friend stopped him."

Dirt sprayed over Johanna's gown as the horse swung around. Once more, the commander stared down into Marietje's face. His eyes were narrowed, his lips pursed, as if he were considering whether or not to believe her words. "You accuse my lieutenant of permitting his men to loot and kill?"

Marietje stood up, her chin high. "I accuse him of nothing. I do not know if he was here at the time. But I know that he is lying to you now. My mother is not—was not—a violent woman. She permitted no guns in the house. But that man—" She pointed toward the wrapped corpse beside the open grave. "That man broke my maid's neck when he tried to make her be still while he took her. And he would have violated my mother in the same manner had not my friend"—her voice broke as she spoke of the scene—"stopped him."

She saw that the commander was listening, and she felt a return of courage. "They were going to force me to submit to them, but then they were warned that you were on the way."

"Is that true?" The commander turned back toward the lieutenant.

"Not quite, sir. We found her skulking in the woods, and we felt it wise to keep her from riding off to warn others of our arrival."

"That was wise. But you have not answered my question. Obviously this is the daughter of the landowner. What were your intentions regarding her?"

The lieutenant hesitated, and the commander turned away from him. He gestured toward the men who stood near the bodies. "We will bury all of them. Go to, men. Dig deep. One hole should contain them all."

"No!" Marietje heard the shrill sound of her own cry, and she gasped in alarm. Would she be shot, now, before she could finish?

No one moved. Even the commander looked in her direction without speaking.

"Please, sir, don't do that to my mother. She is a good Christian woman, and it is not right that she should be buried with the body of the man who tried to shame her. Please." She knew she was weeping, and she silently cursed her own weakness, but she stared up at the commander, without recoiling, even when she could see that her words did not please him.

He studied her in silence. Then he looked first at the body of Johanna, and then from Pieter to Anna. At last he turned again to face Marietje. "We will do as you ask. It is the least we can do to make amends for what has happened." He gave the appropriate orders to the lieutenant. Immediately more men were dispatched to dig graves, this time under the great oak tree that sheltered the burial grounds for the plantation. Marietje's infant brother lay there, as did the two nursemaids who died so shortly after their arrival on the island. There, Marietje knew, her mother would want to lie, next to the place already reserved for her husband, and close to the tiny grave of her dead child.

Pieter and Anna were to be buried there, too. The commander allowed Marietje to decide the placement of all three graves, and only when she was satisfied with the arrangements did he dismount from his horse and politely hold out his hand to her. "Come now, my dear. We will say a proper service when the holes are dug." He waited until she rested her hand on his. "Are all your servants fled?"

"I don't know. They might have hidden in the milk house. Or in the cellar. Anna would have remained with my mother."

"I regret sincerely that this has occurred. There is little I can do to control the men unless I am before them all the time. And I find that is impossible." He stepped forward, and Marietje realized why he had remained so long in the saddle.

He had a bad case of gout. His boot had been split up the inside and tied over his leg to protect it from branches that might scrape at him as he passed. He used a cane that was handed to him by an aide as he dismounted, and with its help, limped up the path to the front door of the great house. He turned once to speak to the lieutenant. "See to it that we are called when the graves are ready. And do not think that this matter is ended. I will deal with you—and any men responsible—later."

When they entered the parlor, Marietje felt the same glow of pride she had felt the day the fine pieces of furniture arrived. It had been a gala occasion. Piece by piece, the new furniture was uncrated and put into place, and when the last item was put where it belonged, the entire household stepped back in awe. Now she saw the same admiration in the commander's face. "You live a good life here in the jungle, do you not?"

"My father sent for these things from Amsterdam." Subtly, as they entered the house, their roles had changed. She was now in charge—the hostess. And he was her guest. She hurried ahead of him and pulled the footstool aside from in front of the great chair so he could sit. Then she lifted his sore leg and slid the footstool under it. Only when he appeared to be as comfortable as she could make him did she settle on a chair across from him.

The position brought a wave of nostalgia. This was just how she sat with her father, when, at the end of a day, he chose to talk with her about her activities and her lessons. Many a time she had struggled with questions of theology or fine points of some piece of literature he had set her to read. And always, though she felt pressed to respond as her father demanded, she also felt his love. He wanted her to learn because he loved her. And she paid close attention to her lessons not only because she wanted the knowledge they offered, but to please him—her father—the rock on which her life developed.

Now, all that was over. The soldiers had come from Padang. And both the lieutenant and the commander had spoken of the battles that had taken place in that city. Her father, she was certain, was one of the strongest resisters. He would not sit passively by when foreign soldiers invaded his land.

So Hans Koenraad was almost certainly dead, too. She had to know. "Sir?" She leaned forward, her eyes pleading.

"You must call me by my name." He struggled to his feet. "I am Commander Byron Scott, at your service, ma'am." He bowed and then, with a grunt, dropped once more onto the chair.

She bent forward and lifted his leg back onto the footstool, then smiled weakly. "Thank you. My name is Marietje." She accepted his nod, and continued. "Was there much fighting in Padang?"

His eyebrows went up. "You have family there, too?"

"Yes. My father. He went into Padang this morning early, to see to the loading of his crop. Sir, that is what I wish to ask you. I do not know if he is dead." The word came easier now—like an old friend. "Mother would want to be buried beside him. There is a place for him next to her, under the tree."

He ran a gnarled hand through his graying hair. "And you want me to find his body—if he is dead. Is that right?"

"Oh, yes. Thank you! I did not dare to hope."

"Well, you were right. My dear young lady, that is impossible. Thousands of men were killed this day. Are we to sift through the piles of dead in search of one man? Have you any idea what a distasteful task that would be? By now they are all tossed into the sea, no doubt."

"Please, can you not at least try? My mother will not rest peacefully unless my father lies beside her."

Once more the commander's eyebrows went up. At last he sighed. "Call Lieutenant Nelson, then." He saw her indecision, and he continued. "Lieutenant Nelson—the lieutenant you showed up to be a liar." He smiled a crooked smile that contained both amusement and a wry acknowledgment of the uncomfortableness of her situation. But he did not speak again until she rose and headed for the door once more. "Tell him I want him immediately."

She did as she was told. Lieutenant Nelson scowled at her as he passed into the room, but he did remove his hat, and he waited respectfully for her to lead the way across the room to where Commander Scott waited. He stood at attention then, to get his orders.

Commander Scott stared at him in displeasure. "Sir, repeat for me the events that led to the death of this young lady's mother and servants." His voice was cold.

"They resisted my men, sir. The man fired upon us."

"Yes, that I can understand. But why, if, as you say, the women were killed accidentally in the assault on the violent resister, were they both some distance from the man. Closer, I could see from the amount of blood, to the man Frank, whom your men seemed so eager to have underground." He paused. "I have been a soldier too long to misinterpret the signs. However, it appears that the courageous youth carried out the execution for us." His voice deepened. "Can you assure me, on your honor, that there was only one man who waged war on women?"

"Yes, sir!" The lieutenant seemed relieved.

"Then let us be certain that you understand me well. You and your men may take what you will from the houses in Padang. We want nothing there but the factories, and the slaves who work them. But we are not prepared to replace the landsmen who operate the plantations. They are needed. Need I say more? You and your men have a sensitive task—to subdue the Dutchmen, and yet to keep them working. To take over their plantations without disrupting the operations. And you must treat civilized women with respect." His voice rose. "Have I made it perfectly clear?"

"Yes, sir!" The lieutenant saluted smartly, turned on one heel, and marched from the room.

Commander Scott turned back to Marietje. "I know you cannot forgive me for the damage my men have done this day. But I can assure you that I regret it at least as much as you. And I guarantee that you will be unharmed from this time on."

Marietje looked long into the soldier's dark eyes. He was, she felt, the kind of man who could be trusted. Much like her father in appearance, with graying hair and rugged, sunburned features. He was beardless, of course. She remembered her father remarking that the British suffered more in the tropics because they insisted upon shaving daily.

"Thank you, sir." She dared speak only because she trusted him at last. "And my father? Is there any chance . . . ?"

"Ah, yes, the graves. I don't know. It is not an easy task you set me to, my dear."

She lowered her head. He was right, of course. How could strangers recognize his body among so many? Yet she gained courage from the knowledge that he was truly sorry for what his men had done. He had spoken of his regret. Did he not, then, wish to atone for what had been done? And what better way than to grant the most sacred wish of a dead woman? "I could go with the men who went to search for him." She saw a shadow cross his eyes, and she knelt at his feet. "Please, Commander Scott. I will do anything if only I can fulfill my mother's last wish."

For one moment his eyes brightened, and then he smiled a gentle, paternal smile. "My child, it is hopeless. But if it pleases you, you may try."

She leaped to her feet, her face aglow. "Oh, thank you! Thank you!"

He barely altered his expression, yet the spark appeared once more in his eyes. "I may remind you of your bargain—someday."

She did not bother to heed his words. Eagerly she crossed to the windows and gazed out on the grass where her mother had fallen. Far to her left was the great tree beside the small chapel. She could see two men busily digging the graves. Color drained from Marietje's face, and she turned abruptly. Why was she so happy? She should never be happy again—now that her mother was gone.

"Thank you." She spoke soberly. "First, however, I must see to my mother." The memories returned unbidden. "And to Pieter and Anna. It is getting dark. Please, can we . . .?"

"Immediately." Commander Scott pushed his chair back. He groaned as he stepped down on his sore foot. "Damn! Will this discomfort never cease?"

"Papa has me put compresses on his foot when he has the gout."

"Aha! Well, then, you shall do the same for me. Now give me your arm. I will do your mother honor, since it was my man who ended her life. But I will need your support."

The graves were ready. Marietje had located her father's book of ceremonies, provided by the church to all adventurers who might, at some time, be isolated from proper religious leaders, and she read the service herself. More than once her voice broke, but she persisted, noting with satisfaction that Lieutenant Nelson had lined up all the men out of respect for the victims of their companions' excesses.

She winced when the first shovelful of dirt was dropped into her mother's grave, but she caught at Commander Scott's arm for support and stood her ground. This, she knew, was the last duty she had to her mother. She was determined not to shirk any of her responsibility.

And then, at last, the painful chore was ended. Slowly, out of deference to Commander Scott's gout, she returned to the house. Once more she found the footstool and placed it carefully beneath his outstretched, swollen leg. But she sat dumbly before him, unable to respond to any of his questions. Suddenly, as if her body had taken all it could endure, she was overcome with the need to sleep.

He chuckled when, in mid-sentence, her head bobbed, and she jerked herself awake. "Enough is enough, my dear. Go to bed. I will have my aide care for my needs until morning. Are you an early riser?"

"Yes, sir."

"You must call me Byron. I am your protector now."

She spoke quietly, overcome with shyness. "Yes, Byron." The familiar name felt strange on her lips. Her father would never have permitted her such a privilege. And Commander Scott was at least as old as Hans Koenraad.

"Good. Lieutenant Nelson will be taking a contingent of men down to Padang early tomorrow. If you wish to go with him, you must be ready on time. We cannot delay our duties, you understand."

"Yes, si—Byron. I understand." Marietje curtsyed. She curtsyed once more when she reached the doorway to the hall, and then she hurried to the stairs.

Her native maid Mai greeted her as she entered her room. "Mai! I thought you had gone." Marietje slipped easily into the native dialect.

"No, mistress. I hid under your bed. The men were too busy tearing the curtains from your windows to look for me."

"Oh!" Marietje stared at the bare framework. "What can they possibly want with such things?" For one moment she considered rushing downstairs to complain to Scott. No. Not now. He might become angry at her if she showed too much impatience with the soldiers. At least they had left her bed intact. "We will see what can be done about it—tomorrow."

She removed her clothing slowly, thankful that the servants had been left to go about their duties unmolested. Mai had even managed to have water drawn for Marietje's usual bath. "You did not come down for my mother's burial."

"I did not know when it happened. No one told me. And I did not dare go out. The soldiers are everywhere."

"Maybe it is just as well." Marietje was too tired to worry about her maid's absence. She was only thankful that the girl was here now—and that she seemed willing to quietly go about her duties.

The water, as usual, felt soft and silky against Marietje's firm young skin. She trailed her hands over her breasts and let them rest on her thighs. Somehow, thinking back on the events of the day, she felt none of the pain she had expected. It all seemed unreal—a bad dream. She leaned back, letting Mai rub her scalp, ridding it of the dust from her journey. Surely the horrors of the past hours were all a bad dream. Everything was so normal in the peace of her own room.

Taking some soap, she began to rub her own body, feeling its firmness, responding, as she had so often before, to the smoothness of her own skin. Surrounded by familiar things, immersed in the water Mai had had heated for her, Marietje found the peace her troubled mind needed. Once, the vision of her mother's grave floated into her consciousness, but she rejected it. Her loss was too great. She needed time to grasp it all—time to accept the terrible change that had forced itself upon her.

And then she considered Mai's response to her remark about the burial. Mai did not know! That proved it, certainly. It had never happened! In a moment, her mother would come in to reprimand her gently for delaying her bedtime, and then, together, they would say the evening prayers that she had been taught when she was a child.

As if relieved of a great burden, her thoughts moved eagerly to the plans of the past. She had celebrated her eighteenth birthday just before Dirk's departure. Her papa, who was right now in Padang, would be sure to bring her some special gift. Maybe something he had ordered from Amsterdam. She smiled to herself—a secretive, tiny smile. Papa always called Amsterdam "home." But to her, this was home—the only home she had ever known.

Engulfed in her dreamworld, she rose from the bath and

stood quietly as Mai dried her. Then, with a fresh gown brushing softly against her legs, she crossed the room to her bed. "I'm so very tired, Mai. Why doesn't Mother come, so I can go to sleep?"

Mai showed no surprise at the question. She had been prepared for some sign that her charge had suffered enough. And now she knew. Marietje would be able to face the world when morning came. But not now.

Now she needed sleep—and she needed the very forgetfulness her own mind had provided. "Don't you remember, Marietje? Your mama went with your papa. You must say your prayers by yourself."

"Oh." No vagrant memory disturbed Marietje's temporary peace. She knelt silently and folded her hands, her lips moving in silent prayer. Then, with a smile, she slid inside the netting that protected her through the night from the bites of insects. Mai stepped beside the bed and carefully tucked the netting under the mattress, so no stray creature could disturb her mistress's sleep.

"Good night, Marietje."

"Good night, Mai." Marietje's voice was already muffled. Sleep, that precious relief from the trials of life, had brought its gift of peace to her at last.

Chapter Five

One moment Marietje was lost in dreams. The next she was wide awake, staring up at the ceiling of her room. The loss of memory that had allowed her to sleep peacefully was over. Every terrible detail of her mother's death and burial pressed against her consciousness.

Yet tears did not come. She felt removed from the bed on which she lay. She saw Mai, sitting in the light across the room, and stared at her in silence, like a ghost observing the living.

Abruptly Mai rose. "Good morning." She advanced toward the bed. "You must hurry now. Commander Scott is expecting you down for breakfast."

Marietje stirred uneasily. Now she remembered. This was the day when she was to go to Padang to search for her father's body. Automatically she performed her morning duties, and then, dressed in a sturdy gown Mai chose for her, she descended to the dining room. Commander Scott sat stiffly in the chair that had always been reserved for her father. He half rose as she entered, but he did not dislodge his foot from the chair on which it rested. She noted with satisfaction that the swelling seemed less than it had been.

"Good morning Marietje. I trust you slept well?"

She nodded, and then, aware that his respectful behavior required equal politeness from her, curtsyed. "Yes, thank you." She took her regular place at one side of the table.

Scott seemed about to speak, but then he took up his fork and resumed eating. The kitchen servant brought a dish of food in and placed it before Marietje.

"I trust you are ready for the journey? Or have you decided to remain here, after all."

Startled by his voice, Marietje looked up. "Yes. I mean no. I do not wish to stay home today. I must try to find my father."

"I understand." His expression did not reflect his words. "Lieutenant Nelson will be ready to depart shortly. I suggest you hurry."

Marietje did not answer. Instead she resumed eating. When Mai appeared at the door to the kitchen, a basket over her arm, Marietje put down her spoon. "May my maid accompany me?"

"If you wish. That is food she is carrying?"

Mai nodded and bowed. Scott beckoned her to approach. He rifled through the basket and then, satisfied, waved her back. Once more he turned toward Marietje. "You must stay with the lieutenant. A young girl like you is not safe in the town alone." She made no response, and he continued. "Do you understand? There are many soldiers like James who see in war an excuse for any excess."

The vision of her mother, begging Pieter to shoot her, flashed into Marietje's mind. "Yes." She barely spoke above a whisper. "I understand."

"Good!" He struggled to his feet, leaning heavily on the back of the chair. "Well, then, you had better leave. I have instructed the lieutenant that he is not to stay the night in Padang. Are you a sturdy horsewoman?"

Marietje shook her head. She knew her limitations. After a few hours on horseback, she grew very fatigued.

"Well, then, you shall take your carriage. I suppose that is better, at any rate, since your servant has probably never mounted a horse."

Marietje did not bother to respond. Instead she led the way onto the wide veranda that extended across the front of the house. She stood there, in the shelter of the overhang, while her carriage was being prepared. And then, with Mai behind her, took her seat. Mai settled next to her, placing the basket on the floor between them.

Commander Scott reached up and took her hand. "Until tonight, then. Do not be too disappointed if you do not succeed in your mission."

"Good-bye. Thank you for permitting me to make this search." Marietje wanted to say more, but the carriage was already moving. She felt Scott's hand slide away from hers, and she turned to look back.

The old house stood as it always had, like a monument

to civilization in the middle of a wilderness. That was how her mother had once described it. Now, looking through wiser eyes, Marietje understood how her mother had felt.

The commander waved, and Marietje waved back. He, too, was a monument to civilization. Her only protection against the beasts who called themselves soldiers, but who were actually little more than pirates on land.

When Marietje was a child, she had sometimes resented her father's ever-present protection. She had been pleased when, totally by accident, she learned of the savages who lived up in the mountains and far to the north of her plantation. She felt for the first time that her home had a location. That it was not just floating in a never-never land of trees and heavy undergrowth that supported it—and also kept it isolated.

It was shortly after that secret discovery that she was permitted to go down to Padang with her father for the first time. She had learned then that Padang was much like the plantation. There were a few Dutchmen like her father. But mostly Padang was filled with natives. And she saw for the first time a ship ready to sail for "home."

Dirk, who rode his horse beside the carriage that held Marietje and her mother, had laughed at her surprise. "Where did you think the Netherlands was, little Marie?"

She shook her head, unwilling to take her eyes from the great ship that rocked gently beside the dock. "I don't know. No one told me there was so much water."

"Sumatra is surrounded by water." Dirk laughed again.

She looked past the ship to the expanse of ocean. On land, if she rode to the top of the mountains, she could return in one day. "Does it take a whole day to get to Amsterdam?"

"It takes months." Dirk shook his head. "I will speak to your father. I think you should learn something of the world in which you live."

It was after that trip that Marietje began to have formal lessons in geography. Also, at Dirk's instigation, she studied some mathematics, and he spent part of her lesson time teaching her about the many kinds of people who occupy the earth. She found the lessons exciting. Now she realized that they were also valuable. She knew how isolated she was, and she realized that any attempt to escape would result in disaster. Lulled by the rocking of the carriage, she leaned her head on Mai's shoulder and soon fell asleep.

"Marietje. Wake up. We are here." Mai nudged her mistress gently.

Immediately Marietje was alert. She looked about her with growing apprehension. "Do you see any bodies?"

"No."

"Maybe he isn't dead. Oh, Mai, do you think he might still be alive?"

Mai let her hand rest on her mistress's arm. "You must not let yourself be too filled with hope. Your father is a brave man. He would not let soldiers take his business without a fight."

"No." Marietje leaned forward, searching the streets. Mai was right. If her father fought, and the English won, then he was dead. But where should she look?

Lieutenant Nelson slowed his horse until he rode beside her. "Where was your father's factory?"

She pointed ahead. "Up there, close to the docks."

"Yes, I know. But which one?"

Would she be able to pick out the right building? She hesitated only a moment. "I will point it out to you when we reach it."

She recognized it immediately, even though she had not seen it in over a year. Gesturing to her to remain in the carriage, Lieutenant Nelson dismounted and ran up the steps. A soldier, lolling against the railing, jerked to attention as he approached.

Marietje stared impatiently at the door until the lieutenant reappeared. What little hope she had that her father was still living faded when she saw that he was alone.

The lieutenant stood beside her carriage. "He is not here. The soldier says he was killed in the fighting." He waited, as if expecting a response, and when she did not answer, he continued, "I have to complete my orders before we return. You will be safe here. I know this man to be reliable."

Still Marietje did not move. He held out his hand to assist her. "Please, mistress. The commander will be very angry if I do not care properly for your welfare."

She seemed to wake from a trance. "Wait here? But aren't we going to search the place of burial?"

"We cannot do that! It is not a sight for a woman."

A stubborn line formed on her chin, and she looked directly into the officer's face. "Byron Scott said I could search for my father. This is the beginning—not the end—of a search. Take me to the burial place."

With a grimace, Lieutenant Nelson turned and mounted his horse. He called an order to the driver of the carriage, and then he was off. Marietje settled back, the look of determination still etched on her face.

It was needed in the hours that followed. Marietje gasped when she first saw the graveyard. Natives were set to digging, but they made little headway, for they feared cutting into the flesh of the earth with their shovels. The few soldiers spared for the duty were sweating copiously and swearing as they worked. Bodies lay where they had been dumped by the carts that still rumbled in, carrying more from outlying parts of the town. Even as she approached, Marietje could see that the corpses were divided into two piles: soldiers, and the defenders of the town.

When the search was over, Marietje could not remember what she had done. All she knew was that she had found him. She crouched on the ground, holding him close, until the lieutenant approached, followed by two strange soldiers. "Let them have him. They will put him in a box for you."

She did not immediately release her burden. But then, when Mai took her by the shoulders, she rose. "We can take him home?"

"Yes, of course." The lieutenant sounded impatient. "It is what the commander would want."

"Thank you." It was a breath straight from her soul.

"Come along now. I must accomplish my tasks before the sun is gone and the rains begin again."

Marietje climbed back into the carriage. She watched as the soldiers put her father's body into a wooden coffin and tied the box to the back of her rig. She wanted to have it placed inside, but she knew there was not enough room. "It will not fall, will it?" She looked anxiously at the bindings.

"No." Lieutenant Nelson spoke more kindly now. "It is resting on the ledge where a footman might stand. It will not drop, even if we go over bad road."

"Thank you." She touched the ropes tenderly. "Thank you. You have saved my father's soul."

The lieutenant nodded curtly. He had had more than enough of Marietje's sentimentality. He turned and rode swiftly to the headquarters, where superior officers waited for his report. The driver of Marietje's carriage flicked his whip, and the carriage moved slowly behind.

When they reached the headquarters, Lieutenant Nelson was already inside. Undecided as to what she should do, Marietje sat for a time without moving. She wanted desperately to look once more on her father's face, but now that his body was sealed in a coffin, she felt a new and unexpected fear.

Ashamed at her reaction, she turned abruptly to Mai. "Come, let us see what is left of Papa's town house."

Mai shook her head. "Oh, no, Miss Marietje. You promised the commander that you would stay with Lieutenant Nelson."

"Well, I have tried, and he managed to evade me." Her feeling of annoyance at the lieutenant seemed to purge her of her unnatural fright. "Come along." Before Mai could reach out to hold her back, Marietje slid from the carriage. She looked back at her maid, silently commanding her to follow, and then she moved away, turning her steps toward the street where the Koenraad town house was located. Mai hurried behind her. Neither girl noticed that the soldier who drove the coach trailed some distance behind.

At the first corner, Marietje paused to permit her servant to reach her side. They continued together, walking swiftly, for now that she had launched herself on this new adventure, Marietje was beginning to have second thoughts. Already she had passed two soldiers who leered at her, shouting things to her that she had never heard before, yet somehow she knew their meaning.

"We must go back." Mai tugged at Marietje's sleeve. "Please. We are not safe on these streets."

"No! Lieutenant Nelson had no right to leave me alone—

unless he knew I'd be safe. So, I see no reason to be afraid." Was she trying to reassure Mai—or herself? Marietje clutched at the comfort of her words and at the strength provided by her anger. "Hurry. We're almost there. We can see Daddy's house and be back before the lieutenant even knows we're gone."

She turned another corner, and there it was. For one moment, Marietje was overcome by a strange impression that nothing had changed at all. The street was empty, except for two natives who seemed intent upon some important business. Lights shown through the windows, though it was barely past noon, as if someone was bent over ledgers in the semidarkness of the interior.

Marietje hurried forward. Before Mai could stop her, she was up the steps that led to the house that had once contained her father's offices and town residence. Mai called out and ran forward, but before she could reach her mistress the door burst open. Two soldiers, both obviously drunk, stepped onto the landing. Their voices were raucous, their words were unintelligible. They caught Marietje by both arms and pulled her inside.

Terrified, Marietje screamed. "Mai! Help me!"

Mai was already at the foot of the steps, but she was not fast enough. The great door closed, muffling Marietje's cries, and when Mai reached it, she found that it was locked.

It was then that the soldier-coachman appeared around the corner. He had failed to see which direction Mai and Marietje turned when they reached the second corner, and he had been delayed when he chose the wrong direction. But he had heard Marietje's scream. He mounted the steps two at a time. "Where is she?"

"Inside." Mai spoke only her native tongue and Dutch, but she understood the soldier's question, and his concern for her mistress.

The young soldier raised his hand and hammered on the door. "Commander Scott demands entry!"

There was a moment of silence inside, followed by the sounds of a muffled argument. Again, the coachman slammed his fist on the door. "Open up for Commander Scott!"

Inside, Marietje was aware of the indecision of her captors. They released their tight hold on her wrists, and she drew back, free from them, her eyes focused on the door. Had Commander Scott really followed her to Padang? And if he had, what miracle brought him to this door when she needed him the most?

The order was repeated, and this time one of the two who had dragged her inside the house moved. The argument that was started by the first demand for entry continued, but it was clear that at least one of the men feared the results of disobedience more than he anticipated the pleasure of pursuing his desires toward his intended victim.

The argument continued as the demand for entry was repeated yet a third time. Now, abruptly, the second man stopped his protests. He turned and caught Marietje's wrist once more, forcing her to face him. His fingers were hard, bruising her skin, and bending her arm so that he drew her face close to his. "You listen carefully. You are to say you came here of your own accord."

Marietje was too frightened to answer.

"Do you understand? If you get us in trouble, I'll kill you." His grip tightened, and she cried out in alarm.

Roughly he pushed her toward the door and assumed a position behind her. The other soldier unlocked the latch and pulled the door open. His expression changed when he saw only another private on the stoop. A single soldier—and a tiny native woman. Reversing his movement, he tried to close the door again.

But the coachman-soldier was too quick. Throwing his entire weight against the door, he forced it open wide. At the same time, he caught Marietje's arm and threw her outward. As she whirled past him she saw that he held a gun in his right hand.

His voice, when he spoke, was a snarl. "This woman belongs to Commander Scott. Had you harmed her, you would now be dead men." He did not wait for the two miscreants to respond. Instead he slammed the door, caught Marietje's arm, and hurried her back to the street.

Marietje was too stunned by the suddenness of her

rescue to say anything. She had been terrified when she was thrown out of the house—almost as frightened as she had been when she was dragged inside. She was confused, too, for she did not recognize the man who came to her rescue. How did he know about Commander Scott? From where had he come?

He offered her no explanations. Silently he guided her up the street, around the corners, and back to the carriage. When they stood once more in front of the building that had been commandeered by the English to serve as headquarters, he released her arm. "You must say nothing about this to the lieutenant—or to the commander."

Marietje had recovered herself, and though she still felt the shock of her sudden capture and release, she was no longer shaking. "Why not? You saved my life."

"No. I saved mine. Have you any idea what would have become of me had you come to harm? I was dozing when I should have been alert. Never before have I failed to guard a prisoner. The commander would have had me shot—if the lieutenant failed to do it before he left Padang." He held out his hand. "Now get back in the carriage. The lieutenant will be out any moment."

Marietje did as she was told. When the lieutenant appeared at the door of the headquarters, she was sitting primly in her place, staring ahead, as if she had been waiting for a long time and was very, very bored.

He gave the signal to move on and, with a tip of his hat to Marietje, assumed the lead in the small procession. At the first opportunity, he commandeered a cart and horse and had Hans Koenraad's coffin transferred from the carriage. "We can move faster, if it is more secure," he explained, when Marietje protested. "Do not worry. I didn't expect that you'd find him, but since you have, I do not intend to lose what has been recovered."

"Thank you." Marietje's appreciation was as much for his respectful treatment as for his words. For only one part of the coachman's scolding hung in her mind. He had called her a prisoner. And he had said that she belonged to the commander.

A prisoner. She repressed a shudder. But the reality

would not go away. She glanced back at her father's coffin. Maybe, after all, she would be better off if she, like her mother, had fallen, killed by a bullet shot from Pieter Daan's rifle.

Chapter Six

Despite her apprehensions, Marietje felt a new peace when, at last, her father's body lay beside the grave that held her mother. It was as if a period of her life had ended. Before the arrival of the English soldiers, she had been a child, dependent upon her father for protection. Now she was a woman, responsible for her own security.

She could not forget the soldier's description of her as a "prisoner." It stood between her and Commander Scott whenever they met. She studied him carefully as they sat at breakfast, waiting for him to make a move that would prove her worst fears to be true.

But Commander Byron Scott seemed unaware of her unease. He greeted her gently each morning, aware that she was still in mourning for her parents and acutely conscious of the part his men had played in her mother's death. Yet he never spoke of the past. Outside of ascertaining that she had, in fact, found her father's body, he made no inquiries regarding the trip she had made into Padang.

He was, instead, completely preoccupied with the task of returning the plantation to full production. He spent his mornings in the fields, talking with the overseers, and his afternoons in her father's study, reading everything he could find that dealt with the cultivation of coffee and with the camphor trees that Hans Koenraad had recently planted, in hopes of adding the export of camphor and camphor oil to his profit.

He greeted Marietje each morning more as a father would than as she assumed a master would greet his prisoner. When she entered the room, he rose. "Good morning, Marietje. Did you sleep well?"

She curtsyed. "Yes, thank you. And you?"

Then he would sigh and shake his head. "Not too well, thank you. I am still bothered at times by my gout."

"Oh!" She felt real concern for his trouble. Her father

often had had great pain caused by his gout. "Maybe I should massage your legs again."

"Yes." He settled back in his chair as she took her place. "Maybe you should." A troubled expression came over him, and he turned his attention to his coffee. "You and your parents lived very well here."

"Yes, I suppose we did." Marietje had never thought about her style of living before. "This land is very bountiful."

"It is very dangerous, too. Few civilized people survive this climate for long. Were you born in Amsterdam?"

"No, s—Byron. I was born here, on this plantation. A native woman cared for my mother when I was birthed, and her daughter is now my maid. Papa never was able to find a maid in Amsterdam who could live here without getting sick."

"Aye. Maybe it is the water. Though I suspect the food." He saw her frown, and he continued quickly. "No, not that which is served by your domestics. They have learned to cook food fit for a civilized stomach."

"Mama taught them, after Katrina got the heat sickness. Katrina was the last nursemaid to come here from Amsterdam. She lived for almost a year. Mother hoped that she had overcome the curse that seemed to visit itself on any servants we brought from home."

"Yes, it must have been disappointing." He paused, staring first at his dish, then at his cup, and finally across the table to where Marietje sat.

Sometimes, when this long silence occurred, Marietje would break in, at last, to speak of her plans for the day. But most often Byron Scott himself was the one to finally resume the disjointed conversation. "What have you planned for today, my dear?"

Always, whether he asked her or she volunteered the information, Marietje had the same schedule. "I will go first to pray at my parents' graves. And then I had thought to ride a bit."

This morning he surprised her. "Would you care for a companion? I have a thought to see the perimeter of your estate."

Not sure whether she was pleased or not, Marietje still

dared not object. "I will leave shortly after lunch." She paused. He always had lunch in the study.

"Maybe I can join you at noon, then."

She nodded, confused by his unexpected interest in her companionship. In the weeks since his invasion of her home, she had come to expect him to ignore her.

She went first to the garden, cultivated with great care by three natives especially chosen for the task by her mother. These men seemed to love the flowers, and they had always, when her mother was alive, provided her with a large bouquet to be placed on the dining table. Since the invasion by the English, the bouquet had appeared in Marietje's room, ready to be placed on the new graves.

This morning, Marietje, following her custom, divided the blooms into four parts, placing one on Pieter's grave, one where Anna lay, one near the rough headstone she had had carved for her father, and one on the mound under which her mother was buried. Then she settled down, seeking a quiet time close to the ones she loved. Always, she prayed at such times. Sometimes she spoke to her mother, half expecting some guidance from the dead.

"Is it wrong, Mother, to feel kindness for Byron Scott?" She barely whispered, for she knew her mother could hear her thoughts. "He has been a gentleman. Sometimes when he talks I could almost believe it was Papa speaking."

She sat quietly for a time, not really expecting an answer yet not willing to ask for help without allowing time for it to be given. Deep in thought, she continued. "No, I suppose, if I had an uncle, I would feel toward him as I feel toward Byron Scott. He has been kind to us. It was he who helped me find Papa and bring him home. Yet there are times when he looks at me so strangely, as if he wanted to speak but dared not." Even to herself she could not admit that at such times he reminded her of Pieter. That recognition would have forced her to think of something she had known—but never admitted. That Pieter loved her, too, as Dirk did, but never overstepped the limits imposed by his rank to speak to her.

Had she loved Pieter? In a way, she knew the answer was yes. She had loved him as a pupil loves a dear teacher. As a child loves her brother. But only Dirk had stirred in her the longing, which, she knew not so much from herself as from what Mai had said, meant much in a relationship between a man and his spouse.

What troubled her—and what she dared not yet mention, even to herself—was that when Byron Scott studied her in his odd, quiet way, she felt that same stirring. And often a blush would come to her cheeks, which she would hide behind her hand, thankful that at the distance provided by the table, Scott could not be aware of her discomfort.

Now her thoughts went to Dirk. Was he safe? Or had the English invaded Palembang and killed him? She considered the possibility of sending a message to him, but always, before she actually called a servant to send on the errand, she reconsidered. The commander would not want her to make such a move. He might, if he was angered enough by it, kill the messenger—or have him shot by a guard. And she had no wish to cause another person to die.

Another consideration made her avoid a message that might bring Dirk rushing home. She knew the plantation was guarded. What if Dirk stumbled into a sentry and was shot for his trouble? Then, certainly, her last hope would be gone.

Yet with each passing day, she longed more for news of her fiancé. Was he alive? How was he succeeding? Now that her father was dead, would he have to fulfill the demands that Hans Koenraad, in his concern for her welfare, had placed upon him?

She had touched his body once. Had pressed her own against him, longing for more and yet not knowing what it was she wanted. Remembering that day, she felt an ache that threatened to consume her body. With a cry, she knelt down, resting her head on the grass that was already covering the mound of her mother's grave. "Dirk, my darling, why did you push me away?" Her tears flowed, more for herself than for her mother, and then, relieved for the time, she sat up, wiped her eyes, and returned to her room.

Byron Scott appeared as he had promised, in time for lunch. In honor of his presence the food was served in the dining room and not in the kitchen, where Marietje had grown accustomed to eat when she was alone. This time, however, she was waiting for him, and she half rose, uncertain as to how she should behave.

"Please." He held up his hand to urge her to remain seated. "I hope you still intend to go riding."

She nodded, suddenly shy in his presence.

"Good! Then let us make it an adventure. I understand there is a small lake on your father's plantation."

"Yes. But . . ."

"When I was a child, I lived near a lake in Scotland." He took his seat at the table, lost in private thoughts. Marietje watched in silence as the kitchen maid brought out a tureen of soup and rice cooked with peanuts. This was her favorite lunch. She wondered how Byron Scott would take to so novel a repast.

He paid little attention to what was served. "I went fishing there often, with my grandfather. Are there fish in your father's lake?"

"I . . . I don't know. I don't think there are. Did you fish with nets?"

"Oh, no. We used a rod, and we rowed out to the middle of the lake in a small boat. Do you have a boat on your lake?"

"Yes. D—" She stopped herself in time. In the weeks since the English invasion of her home, Marietje had managed to avoid any mention of Dirk. She had no real reason for such secrecy. She could not imagine any way that such knowledge could be of benefit to Byron Scott. Yet somehow she was aware that he preferred to think of her as unattached.

There was, however, more than that to her reluctance to speak of her affianced. Deep within her dreams was the hope that he might appear and rescue her, for though Byron Scott treated her with great kindness, she could not forget that he and his men were responsible for her parents' death—and for the killing of Anna and Pieter. Dirk Hendrik remained her only chance for deliverance.

And now Byron Scott was demanding that they visit the lake that in her thoughts belonged exclusively to her and Dirk. As her companion spoke longingly about the cold waters of the lakes of Scotland she waged an inner battle.

Should she lead Scott astray, and then pretend that she had forgotten where the lake was located? Would he accept such an explanation for a fruitless search?

What harm lay in taking him to her lake? He would not be able to tell, just by looking at its smooth surface, that it held special importance to her. They could ride over, maybe have a light snack as they sat on the shore, and then ride back. In her mind, she could see the innocence of such an afternoon. But her heart protested. The lake, its shore, its isolation from all that represented her father's control—all of it was part of her love for Dirk.

"Have you ever been to England?" Byron smiled as he spoke, but his voice held an edge that told Marietje that she had ignored his first query.

"Me? Oh, goodness no. I have never been far from the plantation. My father does—did—not permit me to travel alone."

"I am speaking of England. It is far away—across the ocean. Across two oceans. You have not been there?"

She relinquished her private soliloquy reluctantly. "No. I have not even been to the Netherlands, though Papa is—was—going to take me next year."

"Would you like to go? Maybe not to the Netherlands; I doubt that they would welcome an officer in the English army. But I could take you back with me to England. In some ways, the climate is similar."

She decided to follow him in his fantasy. "Papa said that Amsterdam was covered with snow in the summer."

He burst into laughter. "No, my dear. In the winter. You must not forget that when we have winter, it is summer to the north. And when we have summer, they are having winter."

"Oh?" She was really surprised. "How could that be?"

He rose, suddenly impatient. "Some other day you will get a lesson in geography. Now, if you are finished with your lunch, we should be on our way. I have ordered our horses saddled and waiting." He held his hand out to her, and she rose to take it. "Shall we go?"

Suddenly she did not want to ride with him—or ride at all. Uncertain as to how she might avoid a visit she had seemed to anticipate before, she turned toward the kitchen.

"I must get our lunch." She laughed awkwardly. "A small snack, for us to eat when we reach—our destination." She had determined, now, that she would lead him away from the lake that reminded her of Dirk.

But her subterfuge to delay their departure did not succeed. Just as she reached the door to the kitchen the maid appeared, a basket in her hands. She opened it, to show Marietje its contents, and then, without a word, crossed the room to the door that led into the courtyard. Scott stepped ahead of her, and Marietje, unable to think of any further cause for delay, came behind.

The horses were ready, as Scott had ordered. Though Marietje attempted to carry the basket herself, he insisted that it be tied behind his saddle, and then, without asking her for directions, he headed across the yard toward the road.

They had gone only a short distance when Marietje realized that all of her plans were useless. Byron Scott did not ask her to lead the way. Either he had received directions from one of the servants, or he had located the hand-drawn map her father had made of the plantation, for he went unerringly in the direction of the lake.

When they reached a clearing, prepared for new trees but not yet planted, he drew his horse up and leaned toward her. "Shall we have a race? I have seen your filly run, and she is very fleet of foot."

She nodded and, leaning forward, whispered a command to her horse. The light-footed beast sprang ahead, as if it had been waiting for such an order. Byron let out a shout of glee as he spurred his horse behind her. For most of the distance, he remained there, just out of her line of vision, close enough so she could hear his animal panting and feel the heat of its breathing against her bare arm. Then, just as she felt the race was hers, she was aware of a noise behind her. Byron Scott was speaking to his horse, urging it on, and as he spoke he plied it with his whip.

Now she could see the stallion's nose beside her. Then his withers, and then the smiling face of her guardian. The stallion was moving more quickly, passing her as if she had ceased to race. Angered, but excited as well, she urged her filly to keep the gap from closing. But the little horse was stretching its endurance as it was, and slowly it began to fall behind. Suddenly aware of the beast's need for rest, she pulled up on the reins, slowing her mount to a trot. The race was over. Byron Scott had won.

Yet, now that he had the victory, he seemed not to want it. Abruptly he turned his horse and made a wide circle, coming up behind her once more. When he reached her side, he was laughing. "A good race! Had we a bit more room, I might have won it."

"Oh, but you did win."

He shook his head. "I do not consider it a win when my opponent reins before we reach the finish line."

She wanted to speak of her concern for her horse, but she felt somehow that, kind as Byron Scott was to her, he would not understand such an attitude toward a mindless beast. "I grew tired of competing. I thought we came up to the lake for a rest."

He was contrite, but the smile remained on his lips. "Yes, we did, of course. Are we not almost there?"

"It is just past that grove of trees ahead."

"Good. Suddenly I know that I will enjoy whatever it is you had the cook pack for us. I have not had so much fresh air in weeks."

"But you spend every day with the overseer."

"Aye, watching slaves prune trees, or dig holes for new plantings. That, my sweet, is work—especially for a man accustomed to the free life of a soldier." He looked up as he spoke. "Here we are! My dear, how could you have for one moment considered staying away from this? It is not like the lakes I remember from my childhood, but it is lovely in its own way. Is it a natural body of water?"

"I do not understand."

"Did your father dig out the land to make this lake?"

"Oh, no. There are many lakes as we reach the mountains." Digging back into her memory, she continued. "There is one lake far to the north and high in the mountains where cannibals live."

He chuckled. "You have seen those cannibals?"

"Oh, no. But I saw a sailor, once, who had escaped from them. He died in D—in Pieter's arms."

Byron glanced up. A cloud had moved from the water

over the land. He held up his hand. The wind was brisk, from the ocean. "Damn! I'd forgot the rains!" He glanced about. Was there any shelter to be had so far from the forest—and the plantation buildings?

It was then he saw the clump of forest growth, standing like a gazebo beside the lake. Had Hans Koenraad, in the natural wisdom of an old-time resident of this godforsaken island, left that small bower for just such an emergency as this? "Come. I think we can hide from the rain in there." He caught Marietje's reins and headed for the shelter.

Marietje had seen the rain cloud, too, but it had not sent her hunting for protection. A wave of nostalgia swept over her. This had happened before. She had been with Dirk, and they, too, had sought shelter in the bower.

Almost in a dream, she let herself be helped from her saddle. She moved behind Byron as if in a trance. All the emotions she had felt that day so long ago returned with a rush. She could not enter the bower with another! This place was sacred to her love for Dirk.

"No." She pulled free and stood staring at the dark shelter.

"What's the matter with you, Marietje? Can't you see that the rain will be here any moment? Do you want to get all wet? And ruin the nice lunch you brought?"

"I can't go in there." She barely whispered. "We must not."

"Surely you do not believe that the spirits of some dead natives haunt this bower. Come, now, my dear, you are far too bright a woman for such foolishness." Inexorably she was pulled behind him until, at last, she stood in the special place.

Dirk had kissed her here. He had held her body close against his. She had wanted so much from him. More than he had been willing to give, for it was he who had put an end to their pleasure, and though she had no knowledge of what it could be, she had sensed that there was much she had not experienced.

And now she stood here with another man. A strange man who was both her captor and her friend—her father and . . . And what? Only in his eyes had she seen a hint of something more in his affection for her than that shared by father and child. Or, possibly, uncle. She had never had an uncle. Maybe this was how an uncle would act—like an odd blend of father and suitor.

She felt suddenly free of her worry. Here she stood, and the presence of Byron Scott did not interfere with her memories of Dirk. She laughed gaily, hoping to hide her emotion, and stepped farther into the darkness. Already, through the sheltered entry, she could hear the patter of rain.

A moan from her companion startled her. With one stride he closed the distance between them and caught her in his arms. She fought as his lips closed over hers, but her struggles seemed useless.

And then she was free. Thrashing her arms to push him away, she stepped back. "What are you doing? I belong to another."

His voice was very quiet. "No, my dear one. You belong to me. Everything on this island belongs to me. It is only your youth and innocence that has kept me from taking you before."

She understood him without explanation, yet she was not willing to accept his word. She had kept her promise to Dirk a secret before. Now it was time to speak. For Dirk would not let this man harm her without seeking revenge.

"You have a young man somewhere?" There was amusement in the deep voice. Amusement—and an edge of irritation.

"Yes." She was feeling stronger now. "He is in Palembang. And if you harm me, he will kill you."

His laughter was harsh. "Do you believe, my dear one, that we would destroy Padang and leave Palembang untouched?" He seemed to grow as he spoke. "For far too long we English have permitted the Dutch to wander at will among these islands. The spices here are important to us. From now on, the wealth of Sumatra and Java are ours."

She barely understood what he said. Over and over his first sentence was repeated in her brain. "Do you believe that we would destroy Padang and leave Palembang untouched?"

Destroy Palembang. The English had destroyed Palembang

—as they had destroyed Padang. The vision of the dead lying side by side, waiting for burial, sent a shudder through her body. Palembang—a city she had never seen—was familiar to her now. If Scott was right, its streets were littered with the corpses of its defenders. And one of those bodies was Dirk's.

A sob racked her, and she covered her face with her hands. "No." Her reply was so muffled that Byron barely heard her. "Dear Heavenly Father, please don't let it be true."

"I fear that God has little to do with the fate of man—at least when we are at war." He drew close to her again, and now she was too broken to repel him. "Is this defender of your honor supposed to be in Palembang?"

"Yes." Her voice was thick with tears.

"Ah! Now I know why you were not among the victims of my soldiers' stupidity. You had gone to see your lover on his way." He put his one arm around her shoulders, drawing her close, so that she could lay her head on his shoulder and weep. Sensing the change in his approach, she let herself be moved. He was her guardian once more.

He waited until her sobs subsided. "It is strange, my dear, how fate conspires to keep me from claiming you. First it was the killing of your mother. How could I ask a child mourning the dead to respond to my affection?" Her hair tickled his cheek and he brushed it aside. But he did not release his comforting hold on her shoulder.

"Then it was your father's funeral. And then . . . I am not a beast, like the soldier James. I want no woman who fights my embrace. And so I have waited, watching the sadness leave your face. Waiting for that moment when I knew you were ready. And this bower . . ."

She shook her head, but he did not wait for her to speak. "This bower seemed so perfect for my overture. We are alone. The rain is whispering outside, singing a song of nature. This is the place for love. It was made for two passionate bodies. It is a love bower. How could I resist its charm?"

She sensed the controlled passion in his voice, and she knew she dared not look up for fear he would kiss her. He inhaled, and then he spoke again. "And now there is yet another barrier. Do you believe me when I tell you the man—whoever he is—must be dead?''

"He cannot be! Please, he cannot be dead. How can you know for certain? I do not believe it." She spoke through her tears, and she hated herself for her weakness.

"Have I lied to you before?" He sounded so sad, she looked up into his eyes. She could barely see his face in the dim light, but she could tell that he, too, was weeping.

"No." She did not wish to give that answer. If only she had some good reason to distrust this man.

"Yet you do not accept my word now. Is it because you do not want to? Or do you feel that my desire for you makes me unreliable? Whichever it is, my dear little one, you are wrong. Surely you have seen my soldiers leave the plantation and others arrive. I have sent messengers to Palembang, and they have responded. The city is under our control. And if the man you believe is still alive in any way resembles your father, you can be sure that he was among the casualties. I think this is one of the reasons for my fondness toward you. You would not love a man who showed no spirit."

She did not reply. She felt the color drain from her face, and she swayed in his arm. Dirk was dead. There was no doubt left for her to cling to. Dirk was dead—and her life was over before it had a chance to begin.

Byron Scott moved unexpectedly. Releasing her shoulder, he lifted the basket and placed it on a tree stump. "Sit here, my dear. Have a date. I will not touch you now. I have waited this long, I can surely wait a bit longer."

When she did not move, he took her by the shoulders and moved her gently to where she could sit beside the basket. He dug for a moment in his vest and pulled out a kerchief, which he folded and used to blot her tears. "Forgive me for the hurt I have given you. I did not know that you had a lover."

She sat quietly, her hands still covering her face, blocking his tender ministrations. Around her, the memories of that afternoon seemed to crowd close. Here, Dirk had told her of his love. And now, in the same place, she had learned of his death. The circle was complete. "I wish I could die! Why have you let me live?"

"Because it is not my way to wage war on women. And because . . ." He took her chin in his hand and forced her to look up at him. "Because I have grown most fond of you. I regret that I have been the one to tell you of the death of your lover, but I am relieved to know that you are not quite as innocent as I believed. Later, when your tears are dry, I will prove to you that your life has not ended because one man is gone. I, too, can show you the pleasures of love."

She shook her head, dropping her chin once more into her hands. His fingers moved gently to her hair, stroking softly.

They sat, thus, until the rain no longer rattled above their heads. A bird chirruped near the door to their bower, and a ray of sun cut a line of light through the darkness that surrounded them. Byron Scott rose, lifting her gently to her feet. "Come along, my darling. I will ask nothing of you today, though I had hoped for the consummation of my desire. Maybe, after all, it is for the best. I am not so young that I enjoy the feel of damp dirt under my knees. Nor, I imagine, do you find the ground as comfortable as a good mattress. I will come to you in your room. It is more fitting for a lover of my years."

She did not reply. There was nothing she could think of that would not rouse his anger. For reasons she hated to face, her captor—for now she knew only too well that this was what Byron Scott was—had delayed his intended action.

But he would not delay forever. He had given her almost a month to mourn her mother and her father. Would she dare to expect as long a period to be given her to grow accustomed to Dirk's end? And when Commander Scott grew tired of waiting?

She let him help her to her horse and lead the way back down the hillside. She would have some time. Time she would use to plan her escape. For now she knew that she did not want to remain any longer as a guest—no, as a prisoner—on the plantation that once had been her home.

Chapter Seven

"Do you feel better this morning?" Byron Scott rose as Marietje entered the dining room. As usual, as he gazed on her delicate features and her slender body he felt the tug of desire. This requirement he had set for himself was becoming intolerable.

"I'm fine, thank you." Her voice was soft, rich with overtones of passion unfulfilled. He felt his body tense. There was a limit to the endurance of the most noble of men, that he knew. And he was fast reaching his.

Marietje took her seat, her eyes downcast. The food that was set before her might once have stirred her appetite. Now she wanted only to push it aside and return to her room, where she could mourn her dead and plan for her own escape. Most of all, she wanted to avoid further conversation with Commander Scott, for she felt certain it was he who was responsible for her misfortunes. His men had killed her mother and father. And now some of them had murdered Dirk as well.

The week of mourning she had entered into following the news of the invasion of Palembang had affected her more than she knew. Her cheeks were pale from long hours of weeping, and her eyes seemed always wet from more tears. Deep hollows had formed under her eyes, and she looked out onto the world with a lackluster gaze, where once she had smiled with joy at the breaking of each new day.

To Byron Scott, these changes served only to increase his desire for her. He studied her closely, observing her disinterest in food, and considered what a boon to her appetite it would be if she surrendered to his longing. "You must eat, Marietje, my dear. You are too young, too passionate a woman, to mourn for long the loss of one lover."

"He was not my lover." She felt the tears start down

her cheek, and she wiped them away, suddenly angry at her captor. "We were to be married. He is . . . was . . . my fiancé."

Byron inhaled the fragrance of the rich coffee that was set before him. There were many good aspects to being the commander of an occupying army. But this, certainly—this recalcitrant, sad-faced girl, was not one of those benefits. He let his mind wander to the short time he had spent as a captain in the fighting army during the battle with the colonies. There he had found women aplenty, all eager to charm his nights. He had regretted the promotion that moved him from such affluence to this poverty.

One young, beautiful woman. He had determined that. Not that there weren't other plantations. But the women there were mostly older—or, in the one case where the female was young, she was also pregnant. This was the best of what was available to him. And if she would stop her weeping and abandon her useless mourning, she would be completely satisfactory. More than that, in fact, for she was a lovely girl. If only she would see that what he offered her was better than anything she could find—even in England, or her dammed Amsterdam.

"I plan to take another ride this afternoon. I would appreciate your companionship."

Marietje lifted her head and looked down the length of the table. Was this it? Would she learn, at the end of the ride, that her time had run out?

Despite appearances that she had abandoned herself to mourning, she had not been idle during her hours alone in her room. She had considered every method of escape. She had studied the slope of the roof below her window and calculated the possibility that she could steal her horse and ride out before any of the soldiers heard her go. And she had rejected each plan as hopeless.

Yet she had not given up. She knew what lay ahead of her if she remained. A life of shame. The very disgrace which her mother so feared that she had begged for death. Yet even now, she knew only vaguely what that disgrace entailed. She had seen the soldier, James, use Anna, and she had realized that this was the thing men did to women. Her observation served only to add to her fear. Anna had screamed with pain. Death, certainly, was better than to face such a horror.

"I think I need to rephrase my invitation. Marietje, I *expect* you to accompany me on a ride this afternoon." There was an edge to Byron's voice that promised no good.

Marietje looked up. "I do not choose to ride."

It appeared for a moment that Byron was ready to shout. He leaned forward in his chair, his hands gripping the arms, his face working in anger. Then, abruptly, he settled back. This was not the time for an argument. Nor did he need fear that her refusal was final. He was the commander. What he wanted, he got.

He rose when she left the table. "I will expect you to be ready in an hour." His tone of voice did not leave space for argument. Nor did she attempt a reply. Holding her head high, she swept from the room.

She did not, however, return to her chambers. Glancing over her shoulder to make certain that she was not followed, she hurried down the long corridor that led to the servants' quarters. Mai heard her coming and stepped out to greet her. "Do you want anything, mistress?"

Marietje shook her head. "No . . . Yes. I need your help. I want one of your dresses."

"Why, Marietje?" Mai studied her mistress's face, and then, aware of what Marietje planned, shook her head. "Oh, no. It will not work. The soldiers know us all. They would see at once that you were only pretending to be a servant so you could get free of the plantation."

Marietje stood in quiet thought. Then, suddenly, she caught Mai's arms. "Then you must bring me a gun. Or a knife. I must be able to defend myself—and if I fail, to end my life."

"Oh, no! Please, mistress. Please. Why do you resist what is pleasant? Men and women were made by Allah to come together. And Commander Scott is a good man. You have said so yourself."

"I did, didn't I?" Marietje tried to remember when she had felt kindness toward the man who controlled her life. "I was wrong. He is a fiend. He's killed everyone. I hate him." Her hands were clenched in fists. "He killed Dirk, too."

"You know that?"

"He told me. Palembang is fallen to the English. Oh, Mai, what shall I do?"

"Accept what the fates have given you. It is the will of Allah."

Marietje pulled free of her servant's hand. "You should not speak of Allah. You know how Papa feels about such heathen beliefs."

"We are not heathens who believe in the one god, Allah. I speak of him now because your father is not here to guide you or to separate you from the proper life of a woman. Submit to what is inevitable. It would not be so if Allah did not intend it."

"I don't know what you're talking about." Marietje stared at Mai, aware that the woman had never spoken her own thoughts before. Always, she had echoed the words of her master—or of Johanna. Now Mai was a stranger—with foreign ideas and foreign beliefs. Maybe it was good that her mother had not lived to see this change.

"You will not help me, then?" Marietje knew the answer without waiting for Mai to speak. She turned abruptly and ran back to the great stairs that led to the sleeping chambers. She wanted to reach the shelter of her room before she began to cry.

The door slammed behind her, and she threw herself down upon her bed. "Mother, please, I need your guidance. Mai will not help me. Please, show me the way." She did not expect an answer, nor did she receive one. Instead, her body shaking with sobs, she sprawled on the bed, waiting.

Waiting for what? For the sort of peace her mother's comforting had always brought her? Her mother could not comfort her now. Resolutely she sat up. She was wasting time. For the next hour, Byron Scott would be tending to his duties, or to the cultivation of the plantation. If she was ever to get away, now was the time.

Blinking away the last of her tears, she walked to her wardrobe. She would have to choose her most durable gown, for she would be in it for a long time. Once she managed to escape the plantation, she would wander until she found refuge—or until death ended her wanderings. One thing she knew. She would not submit to the shame Byron Scott seemed determined to visit upon her.

Trembling with new excitement, she pulled her sturdiest riding gown from its hanger. She draped it over the back of a chair and hurried over to the chest, where Mai always kept her shoes, carefully lined up by pairs. Again, her decision was easily made. The strongest shoes. She could not tell how long her horse would survive in the jungle—or if she would be able to take the little beast with her.

As she removed her morning gown she glanced at her image in the small mirror her father had brought with him from Amsterdam. Her hair was arranged in a neat cascade of curls that bobbed each time she shook her head. A good style—but not suited for a long stay in the jungle. After she was dressed, she would comb it back and tie it like a boy's. The curls would have to stay. She had no time to fuss with them too much.

She paused to consider her undergarments. Were they sufficient for what lay ahead? Did she have any such bits of clothing that were anything but decorative?

The door opened behind her. Mai! After all, the woman could not refuse to help her mistress. Marietje turned, the maid's name on her lips.

The sounds froze before they were uttered. It was not Mai who stood halfway between the bed and the door. It was Commander Byron Scott!

When he saw that she knew he was in her room, he spoke. "How beautiful you are, my dearest."

"Sir! What are you doing in my room? Please, leave immediately, or I will . . ." Her voice trailed off. What would she do? A scream from her lips would go unnoticed—or at least unremarked. She was well aware that the common soldiers left her alone only because they were convinced that she belonged to the commander. If he now chose, belatedly, to take his prize, they would not dare—or want—to interfere.

"Why do you continue to fight the inevitable? Need I speak again of the truths of your life? Your parents are dead. And whether you accept it or not, your lover is dead. But you are far from dead, my sweet. You are a vital woman, in need of the tenderness only a man can provide. Let me comfort you. Let me hold you in my arms and show you that your life has just begun."

As he spoke he moved toward her. She cowered against the bed, her eyes searching the four walls of her room for some hiding place. There was her wardrobe—which he could easily open.

And there was the window.

She turned suddenly and ran toward the opening, her mind racing. Was the fall high enough to kill her? If she threw herself out, would she fall harder, and guarantee her death? She knew as she approached the screened and glassed frame that she would have to try. Her mother had, after all, shown her the way. Death was to be preferred over shame.

She lunged forward, expecting the shock of contact with the glass. But it was not the brittle window that broke her precipitous dash toward eternity. Strong hands caught her shoulders and spun her around. She screamed in fury and tugged to get free, but his hold was too firm. She felt her body crushed against his, felt his lips close over hers, and she knew she was lost.

The violence of her capture did not continue. His lips trailed over her cheeks, resting momentarily on each closed eyelid. He was speaking in a hoarse, low voice that was strange to her, and his hands stroked her, cupping themselves over her buttocks and forcing her close against him.

Only once before had she felt a man's hands on her body—but then the touch had filled her with joy. Now she fought the sensations they aroused. She fought the rising heat that seemed to fill her abdomen. She was aware that her cheeks had grown red and warm, and she struggled to resist the messages of passion that her untutored body understood without a word being spoken.

For one moment she felt the strength of her own nature. She could respond to the caresses—but if she did, she would hate herself forever.

She felt Byron move, and she realized that he had managed somehow to slip out of his breeches and his morning coat. And once more she became aware of his voice, gentle, full of passion, softly persuading her to surrender. "Why do you fight me, my love? A woman as full of passion as you should never resist the touch of love. Come, let me lead you to the bliss that you have longed for. Let me show you that your lover is not the only man who can fill your body with fire."

He lifted her suddenly and stepped toward the bed. "I can love you, my dear, far better than you have ever been loved before. I can take you with me to paradise."

He put her gently on the mattress and stood above her, feasting his eyes on her beauty. All that stood between her and his pleasure was her chemise. He reached down and tore it away.

She lay for a moment, exposed to his view, her firm young breasts standing like finely sculptured hills, topped with rosy red peaks. The curls that covered the entrance to his pleasure were soft and thick, a golden-red hue, like the hair on her head. Her abdomen was firm and flat, as might be expected in a girl who spent many of her waking hours on horseback. And her legs were shapely and long.

"God, how I long to have them wrapped around me!" He bent to touch her, his eyes fastened on her white body.

"No!" She rolled suddenly away, out from under his penetrating gaze. Out to freedom—or to death. Away from the shame that drew her to itself. Away from the fascination of the man-body that towered above her, so much like Dirk's and yet so different.

She stood on the far side of the bed, the quilt clutched in her hands before her, to conceal her nakedness. "Get out of my room! Leave me alone!"

For one moment, Byron's expression showed his surprise. Then he paused, deliberately, and removed the remainder of his clothing. As he moved around the bed he dropped the final pieces to the floor.

She had trapped herself with her move. The bed was too close to the corner of the room. She could try to climb across the mattress, but she knew she would not reach the other side before Byron was there, ready to catch her.

She could crawl under!

No. That way, too, was blocked. Under the bed was the finely made teak box that held most of her covers. Blankets she and her mother had fashioned for her to bring with her to Amsterdam.

These thoughts flew through her mind so quickly she was not aware of making a decision. Yet when she moved, it was swiftly, with no hesitation. She was on the bed, running, while Byron still moved toward the corner where she had first sought shelter. She was on the floor when he had only reached the foot of the bed. And she was halfway to the window before he caught her.

She felt the heat of his flesh against her and he pulled her into his arms. "Don't ever try that again." His teeth were pressed tightly together, and a flush darkened the skin on his face. "If you do not promise me, I will set a guard here, day and night."

He did not permit her to answer. His lips pressed against hers, closing off her sharp protest. She fought wildly to free herself, struggling silently against the inevitable.

His arms were hard and firm, unyielding against her hammering fists. And always, his lips were busy, kissing her hair, her ears, her cheeks. Touching lightly the tip of her nose and then pressing with sudden demand full on her mouth.

Again, he lifted her into his arms. Once more she felt the bed beneath her. But this time he lay beside her, his arms pinning her down, his face pressed close against hers.

"I'll scream." She spit out the words.

"Then scream to your heart's content." He moved his body against hers. "My dear child, there are two ways to take a woman. I would prefer to be gentle. But if this is what you want, I am not averse to a bit of battle. Once in a while, it adds spice to what can become a very mundane act."

He lifted himself quickly. She screamed as he forced her legs apart, screamed again when she felt the hammering inside her body. She fought as he pressed against her, pinning her down to the bed. When he moved, she screamed again, until at last he lifted one hand and held it firmly over her mouth.

Even then, her struggle did not cease. She tried to bite his fingers, tried to push him away. Tried to close her legs so he would be forced to leave her alone. But none of her attempts to stop him had any success. She felt him increase his pace above her, and she lashed out with her hands, tearing at his back with her nails.

And then, unexpectedly, he grew still. The whole weight of his body held her down, and she realized that she was weeping in fury and pain.

He lay for a while without moving. Then slowly, he rolled over and lay beside her. Air rushed in and lapped at the moisture that had formed on her stomach. It cooled the heat of her breasts and sent a shiver through her body. Immediately he put one arm over her to keep her from moving.

Resting on an elbow, he stared down into her face. "I was wrong, wasn't I? You have not had a lover before me."

"Leave me alone! I hate you!" She tried to move away, but he held her firmly. Gently his free arm moved down her body and he touched her legs with a finger. "This is the blood of a virgin." He seemed pensive, and for one moment she thought he might return to the gentle man he had been before. Then he turned to gaze into her eyes. "I am sorry that your first taste of this joy was so unhappy. But you must begin to face what is and cannot be changed. Your fiancé, for that clearly is the truth, is dead. I can guarantee that. You are alone, except for me. And I want very little from you. Only your presence in my bed. Only an end to your fighting. And your promise that you will never again attempt to destroy yourself."

He wiped his finger on the quilt and stroked her abdomen. "I do not make war against women. And a woman as lovely as you deserves more pleasure than you have just received. You must not fight me again, my dear. Give yourself and you will reach heights of ecstasy you have never dreamed existed. I speak from experience. I have had many women, my dear, and the ones who gave me the greatest enjoyment shared the passion with me. You get nothing by fighting except pain."

"I will never surrender to you." She tensed her body, her legs pressed together, and her arms at her sides. "You may take me, since you are my captor. But I will give you no joy. And I promise not to attempt to kill myself again only because I will not tolerate a soldier of yours in my room."

She saw a look of triumph in his eyes, and she spit in his face. "I hate you. I will always hate you. And be warned. I will get free. And if I can, I will kill you." She wondered at her own words. Could she ever kill a man— even a man she hated as much as she hated Byron Scott? She didn't know. But she could see that he was not sure whether or not she meant what she said, and that gave her comfort.

He rose abruptly and began to dress. "I will send your maid to you. She has shown the right willingness to submit to the inevitable. Maybe she can put some sense in your head."

"I don't want to see her. I don't ever want to see her again."

He smiled and stepped from the room. She heard his footsteps move down the hall to the stairs. And then, after what seemed like an eternity, she heard other feet approaching. Mai was coming. When she opened the door, Marietje saw that she was carrying a bowl of warm water.

"I have come to wash you." Mai placed the bowl on the table.

Marietje did not respond. When she felt the warm cloth touch her legs, she jerked away.

"You must not fight him. What happens between a man and woman can give pleasure." Mai dipped the cloth once more into the warm water. This time, Marietje did not push her away.

The water felt good on her legs and between her thighs. It soothed the soreness. With the relief Marietje felt new courage. She had failed to escape, but she would not give up. Before Scott came to her again, she would formulate a plan.

And this time, she would succeed.

Chapter Eight

Dirk Hendrik turned as he reached the first bend in the path and lifted his arm in a final salute. Marietje looked so fragile, sitting atop her horse. Was he wrong to leave her? There had been rumors of fighting between the Dutch and the English, who occupied trading stations in Java and on the peninsula of Cambodia. They owned much of India, too, and had threatened before to extend their empire at the expense of the extensive Dutch holdings.

Then, there was the news that had come from Amsterdam of declared war between the mother country and England. Reason enough for the British East India Company to launch an offensive against the rich Spice Islands.

But would Hans Koenraad urge him to depart if there was any danger ahead? Certainly not! Hans was too cautious a man to risk his daughter's safety. And Hans clearly showed his preference for Dirk as a son-in-law. He acknowledged the responsibility this put upon him. He had to succeed. He had to gain a fortune in Palembang, so that Marietje, his true love, could live her life in the same sheltered surroundings her father had provided since she was born. He would have to build her a big house; he would have to clear land and start his own plantation. For he could never bring her to live in Palembang. Sickness ruled in that city—as it did in most of the trading posts. The heat sickness, he knew, attacked strong men who were not accustomed to the climate. And it seemed to devour women, for they were far too fragile to withstand its onslaught.

He would have to provide Marietje with a great bed draped with fine netting. He would have to be prepared to buy slaves to care for her. She could not be forced to accept a life less protected than that Hans Koenraad had made for her mother.

Yet he knew that in one way the sheltering was not

needed. Marietje was frail, that was true, if compared to Pieter. But she had lived through the heat sickness when she was a child, and now it seemed not to bother her anymore. As he, himself, had done. Dirk remembered those days of weakness and misery with distaste. No wonder strong men succumbed. When the sickness was upon you, you had no wish to live.

He waved once more and spurred his horse. Soon, he knew, he would have to dismount and lead the beast, for the growth of vines overhead would be too thick. But for the time, he would take advantage of the animal and save his own legs.

It was not because of fear for her physical welfare that Marietje needed protection. It was the world that Hans had created for her that could not be disturbed. She had never known unkindness. When she was a small child, she had not felt her father's wrath, even when she was most mischievous. Love had surrounded her at her birth, and it supported her now. All had to be well with Marietje's world, for her father had decreed it.

Hans Koenraad had expressed his feelings about his daughter only once before Dirk spoke to him of his wish to wed her. That had been when she was a child of ten, eager, exploring everything. Then Hans had called Pieter and Dirk to him for special counsel. "Johanna has lived with me since the day we married, and not once has she had to face the unpleasantness of this godforsaken island." He stared at the two lads without smiling. "I have done this for her because I love her. She need not know that beyond us, high up in the mountains, there live men who eat human flesh and who have no wish to share in the prosperity that we have brought to the land."

He nodded toward the house, where Marietje's high voice mingled with the deeper feminine voice of her mother. "They are happy, and they feel safe. You must keep those feelings for my daughter. There will be no stories of cannibals told to frighten her into obedience. She will grow to maturity surrounded by love and compassion. Never, never, are you to cause her alarm or try to alter her vision of this land as a place of peace and beauty. Do you understand?"

Pieter nodded silently, but Dirk had dared one question. "She is never to leave the plantation?"

"I did not say that. Johanna travels with confidence to visit Gerda Johannson. She has even traveled into Panang with me. But I guard her from views of the poverty we sometimes pass, and I keep her from knowledge of the dangers wild animals present. Instead I appoint guardians who travel with her—as I have appointed you to travel with my daughter. Be alert to protect her. Have I made myself clear?"

Dirk had agreed then, since he knew that Hans would remove him from his duties if he did not. Yet his promise worried him. He knew the strengths of Marietje's character, and he knew that she, like her strong mother, was capable of bearing far more unpleasantness than Hans thought. Yet over the years, he had seldom gone directly against his master's command. It had not been his doing that Marietje learned of the savages in the mountains. Only the suddenness of the appearance of the sailor had made it impossible for her to be protected from the dying man's last words.

Pieter and Dirk had done what they could to reassure Marietje at the time. And so far as Dirk knew, Hans Koenraad had never learned that Marietje was party to the incident.

Yet Dirk respected the promise he had made to Hans Koenraad when he took charge of Marietje's welfare. Throughout the eighteen years of his service, he had succeeded in the goal set by his master. Only that once had circumstances caused him to fail. As the forest closed in around him he heard Pieter call an order to the horses. The separation he had prayed would never come was a reality.

He had traveled no more than a half hour when the underbrush forced him to dismount, but it did little to delay his journey, for he had held his horse back to keep it from racing downhill. He was eager to reach his destination, a shelter built by native workmen under his supervision not more than a year before to provide a rest stop for travelers who crossed the island.

He reached the shed just as night fell. Though the month of February was well advanced, no rain had fallen through the day, but as Dirk approached the prepared shelter he felt a quickening of the wind that presaged a storm.

He tied his horse under a camphor tree, removed the saddle, and carried it with him into the hut. Johanna Koenraad had sent him off with a saddlebag filled with good food, and he ate some of it as he sat in the doorway, gazing out at the lush woods.

Though he had been a child when he left the Netherlands, he could still remember the wide, flat lands. He had a vivid memory of the tulips and iris flowers that surrounded every cottage, as well as most of the houses within the city. Yet at times, he wondered what his mother, who, he recalled, loved flowers, would think of the blooms that surrounded him. Orchids hung from the trees and grew wild in the grasslands below. Those, he was certain, any woman would love. The plant that impressed him most was a growth that, like the mistletoe, depended on a host tree for its sustenance. Yet only in that was the resemblance strong, for this plant, called by the settlers a *raffie*, had blooms that reached as much as three feet across. He saw the closed petals of one such flower just over the door of his shelter. In the morning, he knew, it would open to greet the light.

By then, however, if he woke as early as he expected, he would be long on his way. From this point on, the path might be overgrown, for little contact existed between the east and the west coast of this, or any of the other, Spice Islands. That very isolation had been the reason for his choosing Palembang instead of Padang. He was too well known in Padang. All the tradesmen and shippers knew he was the lad who had been taken in by Hans Koenraad. In their minds, he was a servant. Highborn, it was true, but a youngest son, and therefore not to be counted.

In Palembang, he could start afresh. His plans were well made. He knew where, within reach of the Musi River, he could find large stands of camphor and sandalwood trees, both of which were in great demand in the Netherlands. He had money saved to buy flatboats and hire workers. One—maybe two or three—trips inland would give him a cargo that would sell for a fortune in Amsterdam. Sea captains would pay well for his knowledge, enough to start him in the trade. If he played his hand right, he could return to the Koenraad plantation the partner of some established ship owner, for the greatest profit was made by the captain who spent the least time in the disease-ridden port, and most men brought over from Europe could not live long in the damp heat of the swamps.

Dirk, like the natives, was accustomed to the hot weather and the insects. His strength was to be the foundation of his fortune. It stood him in good stead for the length of his journey as well. He reached the Musi River late in the afternoon of his second day of travel. Once more he mounted his horse, riding often through swampland that barely held the beast. Yet he moved quickly, because he knew the terrain. He could thank Hans Koenraad for his skill, for Hans had seen the advantage of contacts in both ports and had sent young Dirk on many exploratory trips across the mountains.

The stink of Palembang reached Dirk's nostrils long before the city came in view. Hans had his own opinion of the settlement. A "hellhole" he called it, and he cursed the stupidity of the traders who discarded their waste into the swamps and even into the river itself. Yet for all of its filth, the city prospered.

Dirk paused at the first house and studied the road ahead. He absentmindedly patted the pocket of his shirt and smiled when he felt the folded paper it contained. A letter from Hans Koenraad to his friend, Bernhard Janset, the man who would open the door to Dirk's own fortune.

A window above him opened, and the round face of a native appeared. Janset's woman. Dirk waved and continued on his way. He would probably meet her later. Now he had work far more important.

The damp earth beneath his horse's hooves gave off a sucking noise each step the animal took. Dirk glanced down at his legs. His trousers were covered with caked dirt and with dust from the hills. Reaching down, he brushed what he could to the ground. Bernhard Janset was not the sort to care about appearances. Yet Dirk's own training as a cabin boy on the ship that had carried him from Europe made him uneasy if he was not decently groomed.

When he was satisfied with his appearance, he moved

on, past a group of houses and a cluster of run-down stores. These, he knew, catered to the settlers. But despite the wealth that went daily through the port, the shopkeepers seemed barely to remain alive. Too many of their customers had their own sources of supply—contacts with captains who transported, at considerable price, those delicacies from Europe that made life in the tropics endurable.

Now he came upon the docks themselves. Here most of the effort had been spent by traders eager to store the cargoes that waited shipment. "Factories," they were called, and they contained large compartments where spices and fine woods would be held. Natives served as workmen in most of the factories, for few white men could labor long in the area without growing sickly. Those Europeans who remained in Palembang doctored themselves regularly with quinine and other exotic medicines they bought from the Chinese merchants who had preceded them.

A ship lay in the harbor, long planks running from the dock onto its decks. A steady line of natives moved up one plank, carrying heavy bundles. They returned to shore by way of the other plank and then, burdened once more, repeated the process. The pace was frantic. High tide would come just before dawn, and only then would the ship be able to clear the bar that blocked the mouth of the river.

Dirk stood for a moment, watching the activity, and then he turned away, walking smartly toward the building. He tied his mount at the railing and continued on foot up the damp wooden stairs into the small, cluttered office that overlooked the dock.

He paused at the door. A man was standing at the window, watching the loading. Evidently he had not heard or seen Dirk's approach. Dirk cleared his throat.

"Come in." The man did not turn as he spoke.

Dirk entered and stopped near the desk that faced the door. Still the man did not turn to look at him.

"You will have to wait. I must see that the loading is completed in time."

"Yes, sir. Thank you." Dirk looked around him. There was only one chair—behind the desk. Evidently anyone who had business with Bernhard Janset was expected to stand. He shrugged and turned his attention to the man himself.

Bernhard Janset in many ways resembled Hans Koenraad, for he, too, was portly, with a belly that proved his wealth—and his susceptibility to gout. His hair was gray, and his features thick and yet at the same time fine—as if age had spoiled a well-carved bust.

He was dressed well, though his coat hung on a hook behind his desk. No sensible man dressed too warmly in this climate. His boots, unlike Dirk's, were brightly polished. His days for tramping into the swamps with native workers were past. Dirk smiled. He had arrived at a good time. Bernhard Janset was in need of a partner.

Once more he cleared his throat. "Sir, I bear a letter from Hans Koenraad."

"Good. Can you handle men?"

"Why, yes, sir."

"Excellent. Let me see. Time is running out. There is a great deal yet to put aboard. And my damn foreman!"

Dirk stepped to Janset's side. He could see that the foreman was losing control of the workmen. Each time a man moved back up the ramp, his steps were slower. At such a speed, the ship would not be loaded until well past the deadline.

Dirk turned on one heel and ran down the steps. He crossed to the foreman. "Are you sick, sir?"

"Aye." The faint smile vanished as soon as it appeared.

"Step aside, then. I will take over." Dirk spoke firmly. The foreman hesitated only a moment. Then he dropped onto a bale and leaned back against the wall of the building.

"Faster!" Dirk spoke in the language of the workers. "Faster!" He picked up a bale and moved into line. The man ahead of him quickened his pace, and those behind him hurried to keep up with his long steps. Sailors took the bundles when they arrived in the hold, for they did not trust landlubbers to balance a ship properly. Dirk hurried back to the dock.

Once more he picked up a bundle, and again he forced the men ahead of him to increase their pace. Now he began to sing a native work song. Its rhythm inspired every man to move more quickly, and its familiar words made the heavy work light. One by one the workmen joined in the chant.

Now the pace quickened of itself. Men swung heavy bundles onto their shoulders and carried them easily, as if the music had a magic power to give strength to tired muscles. Dirk did not once step out of the place he had taken in the line. Each time he reached the shore, he lifted another bundle and returned to the ship. He did not look up at the window, though he knew Bernhard Janset was watching. He did wonder if the proud Dutchman might consider his action not fitting for a supervisor, but he did not let that concern hinder him. A job had to be completed, and Dirk knew that a leader who helped his men got more accomplished than a foreman who relied on shouts and curses.

When the last bundle was stowed away, Dirk stopped beside the foreman. "Have you taken quinine today?"

"Of course. But nothing helps."

"Is there more you must do?"

"The men must be paid."

Dirk raised his eyebrows. "You pay the natives in Dutch coin?"

"No. We give them food. And trinkets. The sultan is paid weekly for their services."

"Where do I find the supplies to give them?"

"There. In that door." The foreman gestured feebly. "One piece for each. No reason to spoil them."

"I understand." Dirk followed the foreman's directions. The native men clustered around him, waiting patiently for their reward. When they were all satisfied, they moved quietly off. Dirk watched them depart. They had smiled as they worked beside him. They were good men. All they needed was some inspiration.

This time, when he reached the door to Bernhard's office, he did not pause. Nor did he stand like a criminal before the dock. He approached the desk where Bernhard was seated and perched easily on one corner. He said nothing, but held the letter out.

Bernhard took the letter, opened it, and, moving closer to the light, began to read. When he looked up, he was smiling. "So you are Dirk Hendrik."

"Yes."

"My friend speaks well of you."

"He has cause. I have served him well."

"You can do what he claims?"

"Yes." Dirk was aware that Bernhard recognized the shortness of his reply. No need to use the polite address of "sir," if one spoke to an equal.

"You have saved my cargo, and possibly my ship. If those sailors had spent one more day in Palembang, they might never have sailed. They lost five men as it is."

"Yes, I know the quickness with which the heat sickness strikes."

"You will not get it?"

"I have had it already. As a child. It does not bother me now."

"We will see. When can you leave?"

"Immediately. I will take the men who loaded the ship. They are good stock."

Bernhard shrugged. "If you wish. They are mine to do with as I will. I will pay their bond to the sultan until you return. But it will be deducted from your share of the profit."

"No. We will share their cost. You profit from their labor, too, even though they will be in my charge."

Bernhard was silent for a moment. Then a thin smile appeared on his lips. "Do you have other expectations?"

"Yes. We can share the expenses evenly—and the profits. That is the way I prefer to work this first time. If we are both satisfied, we can draw up formal agreements. I know that you are desperately in need of my services. Your men are sick or dead. And you can no longer take the journey yourself. I, too, need your assistance. I have no factory where I can store the goods I bring until a ship arrives. Nor have I any contacts with captains who would buy my supplies. So we can help each other. That is, if my friend Hans Koenraad spoke the truth to me."

The smile was broad now. "That he did. And to me as well. He wrote to me before the Christmas season and spoke of you. I understand his praise now. I have not before seen a white man work his men so well."

Dirk rose from the corner of the desk. "Have you another chair? I find this a most inhospitable seat."

"I have a crate. Tomorrow, after you have gone, I will set a native to carving a suitable chair for you."

"Thank you, sir." The respect had returned. Dirk was content. He could work well with this man. And his labors, he knew, would bring prosperity to them both.

Chapter Nine

Dirk was on his way the next morning. He took Lun Kui, the Chinaman in charge of the dock workers, and nine of his best men, and headed upriver in flatboats made especially for transporting spices from inland. Bernhard Janset provided them with rice for the journey, as well as the containers needed for cooking. Meat, if Dirk were to eat any, he would have to kill himself. Of his men, two were Chinese, and carried small pigs for slaughter; the rest were Moslem, with their own food preferences. Each group kept their own kitchen, though before the trip was ended, Dirk ate regularly with the Chinese, who seemed honored by his presence.

Their first target was a stand of native pepper vines, past their fruiting prime, yet certain to still hold many berries that could be harvested for shipment. Pepper was a prime cargo, and worth the search. Yet valuable as pepper might be, there was another goal that Dirk considered more important. With Lun Hsiang, younger brother of the head coolie, Dirk intended to drive up into the highlands of northern Sumatra, where he knew prime wood could be found. They would mark the trees they chose for immediate harvest, and then begin themselves to cut them. Meanwhile, Lun Kui would complete the gathering of the peppercorns, send them into Palembang with yet another brother, and then follow Dirk up into the mountains with the remainder of the workers. All the lumber they harvested would be floated to the coast on one of the rivers that abounded along the entire length of the island.

Yet when all this was accomplished, Dirk's work would not be completed. He would lead the men down and pilot the logs along the coast until they reached the mouth of the Musi River. He estimated that the entire journey would take three months. If he remained on his set schedule, he might be able to make at least three such trips before the

Dutch ship *Wilhelmina* returned for more cargo. The *Margaretha*, which he had helped load, would not be back for another year beyond that. His hopes—and his fortune—hung on how much he sold before the year Hans had given him was ended.

The pepper vines were a disappointment. Proper harvest time, Dirk knew, was before the beginning of the rains, and he had missed that time. Nevertheless he ordered a thorough examination of the vines and recovered enough corns to make the youngest brother's journey worthwhile. But because of the small harvest and the need for an extensive search of all the vines, he did not proceed ahead.

When the last flatboat pushed off downstream, Dirk breathed a sigh of relief. "Kui! Hsiang! Let us move quickly now." He glanced uneasily at the sky. "Maybe we can move up higher and make camp before the evening rain begins."

Lun Kui moved among the men, allocating loads, speaking sharply in the tongue of each man, urging speed. But the heat was heavy over the land, and swift movements were not natural to men born in the villages. When the line of porters finally began to move, Dirk estimated that they had but an hour until sunset.

The woods, silent during the bustle of departure, now came to life around them. Overhead, flying shrews chattered as they followed the procession. A small family of banded leaf monkeys stopped their eating to scream in protest as Dirk invaded their grazing grounds. Birds he could not name fluttered from the brush as he approached. Yet none of these creatures bothered him. They would soon be asleep in their holes. Only one beast threatened the safety of Dirk's small safari. The tiger. This animal, like most of the other predators, hunted by day. Yet there were known cases of men, coming suddenly upon a sleeping family of the animals, being ripped apart by the angry males.

The presence of this danger tempered Dirk's feeling of urgency at first. He led the line of men, aware that they would go only where he had already been. Yet he could feel their reluctance. They walked in silence, though they knew he did not oppose a song to lighten the journey. And when they came to a clearing large enough to hold their camp, they refused absolutely to continue.

Lun Kui moved from group to group until, content that all were soon to eat, he returned to the fire his brother had already set. "You have made for the Dirk man, too?"

"Yes, brother."

"Fine." Lun Kui crossed the clearing to where Dirk stood, staring upward toward the peaks. "We would be most honored if you would accept our hospitality. My foolish brother has cooked too much food for two men."

Dirk looked up. He had been thinking of Marietje. Lun Kui stood silently waiting for some response. Dirk nodded. "Thank you. This lowly person is honored by your invitation." He spoke in his own language, for he had not mastered the Chinese tongue, and he considered the language of the natives unworthy.

Lun Kui and Hsiang ate in silence. They were accustomed to trips into the forest, and they preferred to listen rather than talk, for only a sharp ear could hear the approach of a predator.

Dirk was relieved at the absence of any need for conversation. He ate as his hosts did, smacking his lips at each morsel. As a child, before Hans Koenraad took him in, he had learned much on the wharves. He knew that a quiet eater was rude. Smacking lips and even an occasional belch proved to a Chinese host that the guest was enjoying his meal. He fared less well when Kui produced a pipe, yet he knew that unless he shared at least some of the sweet tobacco, Kui might be offended.

"From my homeland." Kui held the pipe out. "A very high-grade tobacco, sweetened with the juice of oranges."

Dirk breathed a sigh of relief. He had heard that the English captains, always eager to increase their profits, had begun to sell opium in the coastal cities of China, and he had feared that this new smoking material might be what Kui used.

Kui shook his head as Dirk took the pipe. "My brothers and I are honest tradesmen. We work for your countryman because we are still building our own business, but we are not coolies. When you took a burden on your own back yesterday, you showed us that you are as we are. You, too, seek to build your fortune. And you, too, are not afraid to work hard in order that you succeed."

Dirk nodded, aware that he felt new respect for Kui. "I am the youngest of my family. What I earn is all I will have, for my father's estate goes to my oldest brother."

Kui looked surprised. "Ah? So? In China we have a more civilized way. We remain a family, and what belongs to one is shared by all. I am the eldest, and so my brothers follow my lead. But it is my responsibility to see that they are properly rewarded for their efforts. We came here together, for we have long known that there is market for our wares here. We will start a dynasty that will be proud and prosperous. Already I have sent for a wife, for soon—when these journeys of yours are ended—we will no longer need to work for another."

"You will stay with me until the *Wilhelmina* arrives?"

"We have agreed to that. We will keep our contract."

"Good. You are a good man, Kui. May you have nothing but prosperity."

"We have discussed this, Dirk sir. Few men from your land will deal honestly with us. Even the honorable Janset has shown himself not to be above trying to cheat us. When we begin our own business, we would profit much were we to have a man such as you to deal with the white men who buy our wares. Would you consider it?"

Dirk sucked silently on the pipe. Kui had spoken the truth. The tobacco he used was both sweet and pleasant. His countrymen, he knew, would pay a great deal to have such a brew in their pipes. "I can offer something far better. Bernhard Janset has long been searching for a partner who would buy him out and free him to return to Amsterdam. If this journey is successful, I can be that man. And then, if you are willing to work with one as uninformed as I, we could become partners. You would have the factories in which to store your goods, and my countrymen could buy from your stocks."

Kui smiled a tight smile of friendship, his hands clasped together. Then, aware that Dirk's knowledge of people did not extend to a recognition of this as a handshake, he extended his right hand. "My brother, Lun Hsiang, is witness to this agreement. We are henceforth partners, you and I."

They spent much of the evening agreeing upon the fine points of their arrangement. Dirk and Lun Kui were to be equal partners. Each would finance his own projects, but profits would be shared equally. If either partner needed financing and the other was able to provide it, there would be minimal interest paid. And each would care for the other's business matters were either one to be away from Palembang.

Only when all the arrangements had been discussed did Kui refill the pipe and pass it around once more. "Dirk sir." He spoke quietly. "I do not understand. Few of your countrymen would be willing to share a business with a Chinaman. And Janset would never sell his factory to me. Why?"

"Because I cannot always remain in Palembang. I have a woman near Padang . . ."

"Ah, but there are women in Palembang."

"Not like my Marietje. We will be married if I can show that I can care for her. With the business as it now has been arranged, I will have money even when I travel back to see her."

"You are certain that I will not cheat you? Your countrymen do not hold that high an opinion of a Chinaman."

"Nor, I understand, do most Chinese feel respect for us Dutchmen. I have made no bargain with *most* Chinamen. I have formed a partnership with you. I know you, for I have seen you work."

"And I know you." Lun Kui rose. "It will be a good arrangement."

They traveled north along the ridge, stopping to mark trees worthy of cutting. The first stand was large, and Lun Kui set his second brother to the task of supervising the harvest. Soon the sound of axes rang through the woods, and Dirk, content that the chore would be completed, led the way onward.

This time, because there were fewer men in the line, Lun Kui took the position at the end, ready to spur any laggards on. The first day's walk disclosed no other stand equal to the one already being cut down. Once, Dirk saw a grove that appeared to be worthy of his attention, and he left the men waiting on the path while he fought his way through to see.

He returned, exhausted from the struggle. "No. They are young trees, and too far from the river. We would have to chop down half the forest just to get the logs to water." He lifted the burden he had assigned to himself. "Let's go on." He was moving down the path before Lun Kui had all the men on their feet, but he slowed his pace until he heard Kui's reassuring shout. They were on their way once more.

That night they camped in a small clearing, and a man was set to keep the fire burning. Lun Kui had seen the marks of a tiger.

Morning found them all safe. Only after the natives were eating did Lun Kui take Dirk aside. "He was here."

"Who?"

"The tiger. I saw his footsteps. We must stay close together, for he will be waiting to eat anyone who strays from the protection of the line."

Dirk felt a new excitement as he stepped forward to lead the party. He could see that the natives knew of the tiger's presence. They had left a peace offering to the beast, a pig provided to them by Lun Hsiang. The small creature was tied to a stake in the clearing. If the tiger stopped to eat the pig and then rested for a time, they would be safe.

But though they all listened eagerly as they moved along the path, they heard no squeal from the small sacrificial animal. Had the tiger come upon it so quickly it had no time to cry out? Dirk wondered. He moved swiftly forward, but his thoughts were back with Lun Kui. If the tiger was still stalking them, it would strike first at the last man in the line.

The uncertainty affected the spirits of the men that night, and though all were exhausted from their long trek, none objected when Dirk again set an all-night watch. Each man accepted his assignment, and though Dirk woke often, he saw no sign that any of the watchers slept. They knew the fire was all that kept the fearful beast at bay.

In the morning the fire was extinguished, and once more each man walked alone, undefended against a sudden attack.

When they stopped to eat and rest at midday, Lun Kui approached Dirk. "There is unrest among the men. They say that the tiger is the spirit of the forest. They believe he is angry because we are cutting the trees. Unless we can kill him, they will cut no more."

Dirk patted his gun. "Maybe you should carry this. If the animal follows us, he is most apt to strike at you."

Lun Kui shook his head. "I have not fired such a weapon. I will trust the gods to protect me."

But as the day passed, Dirk began to wonder if his concern was wasted. Often when he stopped, fearful that he had heard the footsteps of the tiger on the thick forest floor, he heard only the chattering of the monkeys or the song of some unseen bird. Once he paused to watch a family of orangutans, and though the old male rose when he saw the trespassers into his territory, none made a threatening move.

He listened, after he moved on, to the playful cries of the young orangutans, hoping that any change in their noises might tell him of the tiger's presence.

Was that a warning call he heard? He paused and listened, but he could not be certain. If it was a warning, it was not repeated. He moved forward, still unsatisfied, still weighted down with the worry. Would the men refuse to work when they reached the next productive grove of trees? Was it possible that all of the effort he and Lun Kui were exerting would go to waste?

He slept little that night. Lun Kui studied his face uneasily as they ate. "You worry too much over what you cannot control. What the gods decree you cannot change. Maybe the natives are right. Maybe we are being stalked by the spirit of the forest. We must show him that we are taking only enough trees to satisfy our needs. We must let him see that we will help the forest as well as take from it."

"What help can we be to the forest?" Dirk wondered at his own wisdom to form a partnership with a man who spoke such nonsense. "A forest is just many trees grouped together."

"No, partner, you are wrong." Lun Kui glanced up solemnly. "The forest has its life, as we have ours. When my people dig into the land to plant their grain, they first ask permission of the god of the earth. We, too, must show our respect for the god who rules the woods. I will prepare the proper ceremony when we reach the site of our next cutting."

Dirk shrugged. If Lun Kui wanted it—and if such a ceremony might calm the uneasy natives—it would be well worthwhile. "Maybe you should make your prayers tonight when we camp. You might free us of the tiger." He suppressed a laugh, for he was certain that in this, at least, Lun Kui was as superstitious and ignorant as were the natives.

"You are right, friend. I will say my prayers tonight. We will lose our men unless we can send the tiger on his way."

"Then you hear him, too?"

"No. I hear nothing. None hears him coming. But he is with us." He studied Dirk's set expression. "What harm lies in following my foolishness, if it pleases the natives and sends the tiger on his way?"

Dirk nodded, a smile of understanding banishing his doubt. "Yes, of course, what harm can it do?"

The ceremony was short. Lun Kui brought out some incense sticks from his shoulder bag and set them up before a small altar he constructed from branches of a nearby, isolated sandlewood tree. His prayers were short, and while he said them, the natives stood quietly around him, forming a complete circle.

The campfire was set once more, but Dirk felt certain that the natives slept far better because of Kui's ceremony. He was convinced, when half the night passed without any telltale sign that the tiger was nearby, that Kui had actually succeeded in his intentions.

Morning came with none of the usual warning indications of a tiger's presence. No small animal screamed in fear as it passed. No birds soared suddenly up into the air, flushed by the smooth passage of the speckled beast. When all the bundles were ready for departure, Dirk signaled Lun Kui before he stepped onto the trail. For reasons of his own, he had no wish to admit even to so good a friend that such heathen ceremonies might have value.

Throughout the journey, because it served to remind him of Marietje, Dirk kept the long scarf wound around his waist. Now he took it off and tucked it into his bundle. The heat increased as the day wore on, and the moisture left by the nightly rain hung heavy in the air. Good climate for big trees. Miserable for any human who chose to travel as swiftly as he was going.

He could see the grove for which he searched when, suddenly, he was aware of a small sound. A thud, as if a body had fallen. Alert, he turned and studied the line behind him.

He could see only four of the men. One other—and Lun Kui—were around a bend, and hidden by trees. The first man behind Dirk paused, a look of alarm on his face. "Did you hear something?" Dirk spoke in the man's native tongue without even considering the need.

The man's expression grew strained. "No. I heard nothing. Nothing at all." He stepped forward, but Dirk refused to move.

"Do we stop here?"

"No. Yes. Stop. I must see if all the men are safe." Without waiting to see that the man obeyed, Dirk dropped his bundle and pulled his gun from where he had tucked it. The scarf pulled free, and he caught it to keep it from falling into the dirt of the path. He held it momentarily, and then began to wind it around his arm as he moved past the waiting carriers.

He was running by the time he reached the bend, for now he could hear the silent struggle. The last carrier crouched in terror beside the road, staring transfixed at the tiger.

Lun Kui was poised in the middle of the path, blood streaming from a tear in his leg. Dirk assessed the situation as he moved forward. Evidently the tiger had made some noise as he attacked, enough to warn Kui to leap out of the way. But one of the big claws had caught Kui as he moved away. Now the tiger smelled the blood, and some of the natural caution it normally would have exerted in the presence of men had faded. It did not look at Dirk as he sprinted toward Kui.

Dirk had seen at a glance that he dared not use his

93

weapon until he could get Lun Kui out of the way. Pulling the scarf from his arm he threw it, like a ball, directly into the tiger's face. Distracted, the tiger veered aside, clawing at the roll of wool. "Down!" Dirk shouted the command, and Kui dropped. At that moment, Dirk raised his rifle and fired.

The shot echoed through the mountains like a clap of thunder. The tiger sprang forward, and then, hit by the bullet, fell to the ground. It was over.

Chattering eagerly, the natives gathered around the fallen beast. They examined his claws, studied his teeth. This, they at last informed Dirk, was a man-eating tiger that had troubled the villages for years. They would take its skin with them to prove the prowess of their master. And when he returned to Palembang, he must give the skin to the sultan, for he would gain much favor in so doing.

Dirk nodded. If it was convenient later, he would do as they suggested. Now he had only one concern—Lun Kui.

Lun Kui was sitting up, staring at the animal. "Are you all right? Your leg—can you walk on it?" Dirk stepped beside Kui and bent to look at his injury.

"I'm fine." Kui stood up. Dirk could see him tense as the pain hit, but he did not waver. Instead he pulled himself up to his full height. "I owe you my life. Now it is clear that the gods intend us to be brothers."

Dirk crouched and studied the bloody leg. It was true; Lun Kui was fortunate. Only one claw had touched his leg, tearing a deep gash in the muscle. If he had felt the full weight of the blow, he might not have two legs. "We are brothers." He stood and caught Lun Kui's hand. Kui grasped his elbow with his left hand, and Dirk felt the weight of his body. Clearly Kui was in pain. But his expression was clear and placid.

They made camp just below the grove in which they had been hunting. Kui doctored his own wound, filling it with herbs he gathered from the trees and from the ground. Other than to medicate himself, he showed no concern for his injury. He stood upright on both legs to prepare his food, and he refused to sit until Dirk, too, settled down.

As he ate, Dirk looked up periodically at his companion. It was true, Kui was his friend. He had felt the bond as he moved behind the man when he was asked to speed up the loading of the ship. But what he felt now was greater. This man's life was important to him. Lun Kui was his brother—sealed in the trial of battle with the tiger. Never, even with his own brothers, had he felt such a bonding.

He knew well the Chinese beliefs regarding the rescue of one man by another. The rescued one owed his life—and therefore his service—to the rescuer. And the one who had saved a life had a responsibility as well. He must make the life he saved worth living. They were united in proving that the act of snatching a soul from the gods of the dead had been worthwhile.

Lun Kui led the march when, at last, the final tree was cut and dragged to the water. Now the race would begin. They would travel downstream, first on foot, because of the many falls that interrupted the even flow of the river in the highlands, and then by raft—one made, hopefully, from the very trees they were guiding to the sea.

The job of cutting the wood was over. But more hazards lay ahead. If the lumber reached the coast too much ahead of Dirk and Kui, some passing sailor might recognize it for its true value and take it himself. And even if that did not occur, others might use the wood that floated down. Natives might tow a log in from the river to build a new drum, or to carve a special seat for their chief.

They must move swiftly. They must be prepared to release their logs from any backwater that might catch them. And if they succeeded in their task, they must be prepared to bind the logs together and sail them, like a large raft, along the coast, up the Musi River, to the city of Palembang. Only then would their efforts be rewarded.

Chapter Ten

Dirk leaned against the strong tree branch and watched as two of his men pushed their way through the underbrush to the edge of the river. Lun Kui, standing beside him, nodded his approval. "They will be safe. They know to stay clear of the main force of the water."

Dirk did not reply. He had intended to break this logjam himself, for he hated to risk his men by sending them into danger he was not willing to face. Kui, however, had insisted that Dirk stay out of the water. "If the gods will that a man die, let them take one who is not so important to the future. It matters not to them, as long as they get some soul to bring back to their master."

As usual when Kui began to speak of his strange beliefs, Dirk barely listened. He had no wish to fight with his partner over some foolishness that was important to only one of them. Besides, Dirk was well acquainted with the religion espoused by most of the Chinese merchants who lived in Sumatra. They saw gods in the oddest places—in rocks and soil. In trees and water. Even in the small idols they often carried with them. Yet Dirk was wise enough to recognize that this pagan behavior was not a sign of a primitive mind. He had listened to too many Chinese scholars during his journeys with Hans Koenraad, and he knew that the Chinese culture was far older than that of his own nation. He knew, also, that the Chinese were excellent merchants and traders, getting more than value for what they sold and paying far less than value for anything they chose to purchase. Such men deserved to be humored.

The two natives inched their way to where the logs had formed a blockade that spread entirely across the narrow neck of the river. Dirk, watching, inhaled and held his breath. Now came the danger. If they disturbed the delicate balance of the logs, they could be crushed.

"Good. They're back on shore." Kui spoke softly, and

Dirk realized that he, too, had watched the proceedings with fear for the workers' lives. Now that the men were both safe on solid ground, both Kui and Dirk breathed more easily.

The task, however, was not yet completed. The two men had reached a small formation of rocks and dirt that divided the river at this point into two parts. One passage was far too narrow and shallow for the logs to move down it. The other was wider and deeper. But still the blockage had formed across it and had to be released.

"Careful now." Dirk whispered the words, his eyes focused on the two men who were beginning to push at the logs with the long sticks they had cut before they entered the water. "Keep your balance."

As if they heard him, both men shifted to more steady positions, planting their feet firmly on the rocks. They pushed their rods gingerly among the logs, hunting for that particular place where one log might be tipped over and moved on its way. Dirk felt as if he were with them, feeling here and there, sensing the resistance of most of the logs. Looking for that one log that would move. He knew the danger. As soon as the pileup was released, the logs would tumble onward, moving, for a brief time, more swiftly than the river itself. And during that period, the two men on the rocks would be in their greatest danger, for a log could be pushed toward them and knock them into the raging water.

He saw a small movement in the stationary logs, and he leaned forward. "Careful. You've got it. Now . . ." He braced himself. "Push!"

Both men moved simultaneously, as if they heard his command. Their pressure dislodged a log that bounced forward, down the rapids below. Then, together, they jumped back, to the highest point on the narrow strip of rocky land that served as their only protection from the rush of logs above them. At the same time, they gave a shout of triumph that was echoed by the men still waiting on the shore. Then they crouched down side by side, protecting themselves from the rush of water they had released.

Dirk felt his body relax. They were safe—this time. But

at the next bend? Or when they reached the next white water? He turned toward Kui, his face solemn. "Next time I go with them."

"We shall see. No god expects the head to risk itself to save the feet, for a man can live without both feet, but he will die without his head."

"Yet you seemed to appreciate my working with the men—and with you—at the docks."

"You ran no risk by such a move. These men do not expect you to do their work for them. They appreciate your willingness to share the burden of our supplies, though they do not truly understand your motive. Most white men would consider such an act far below them."

"I am not most white men."

"That I know. You have proven that to us all. But you must learn to maintain your position among your workers. Even the simplest native on Sumatra knows that those above him must be given proper respect. They do not expect their betters to take the same risks demanded of them. If you continue to refrain from acting the part of the head, they will suspect that you are no more than a shoulder, upon which the head rests, and then they will look about them for some other to show the qualities of leader."

Dirk felt a momentary jealousy. "You?"

"No. Not I, for I have already made it clear by my actions that I consider you my superior. Do not shame me now."

Dirk settled back against the tree. Kui knew the natives. What he said carried weight. "What, then, would you have me do?"

"Reward those two men by letting them share the bundles you now carry. It will make them proud that you consider them particularly strong men."

Dirk began to protest but thought better of it. "And then?"

"Nothing else—until we reach the great waters. Then you must sit ahead and direct the paddles. They can work far harder than you expect. You are planning, are you not, to give the tiger skin to the sultan?"

"I suppose I will. Though it is a marvelously beautiful pelt, now that it has been dried."

"Sir Dirk, do not let your own avariciousness interfere with this plan. By giving the tiger skin to the sultan, you will be proving to him that you respect his position. Have you not wondered why the other merchants in Palembang remain so less wealthy than those in Padang?"

"I assume because the spices are easier to ship from Padang."

"No. Because none has ever learned to get the sultan's cooperation. You can do it now, and he will make you rich beyond your wildest imagination."

"A tiger skin is that important to him?"

"This is not an ordinary tiger skin, Sir Dirk. Your men believe that it is the skin of the spirit of the forest. They are certain that as long as you have it, you cannot be harmed by any creature that lives on the island."

"But then, should I not keep it?"

"No. By giving it to the sultan, you spread that protection over all who live under his control." Kui chuckled. "And also, you relieve yourself of the responsibility for any deaths that do occur after you pass the skin on to the sultan. It will be his power that is under suspicion if another tiger rises to take this one's place."

"I had thought to let the men keep the skin for their own uses."

"Never. You killed the beast. The magic is yours." Kui leaped from the branch and gentured toward the water. "We must move on now. The blockage is broken. If we are fortunate, there will be another below, for we cannot keep pace with them through this brush."

"No." Dirk leaped beside his partner and moved toward the path. "I have a mind to send two men ahead at the next rest, so that they are waiting at the river's mouth for our prizes to arrive."

Kui waited until they reached a clearing, through which he could see the water far below. "That is wise. I will go with them."

Dirk considered protesting, but something in Kui's expression silenced him. Instead he signaled the workers to gather, told them all to wait at the next bend in the river, and then resumed the arduous task of chopping his way through the underbrush that edged the river's banks.

It was late afternoon when, at last, Kui headed down with two selected workers. The logjam that had formed had yet to be broken, and by agreement would not be until the following day, thus giving Kui time to locate the next possible point of slowdown. The delay now would be annoying, but it increased the safety of their logs, and in the long run would, Dirk believed, save time as well.

The rains, regular and for the most part heavy, were, Dirk realized, becoming more than a minor irritation to him. Back at the plantation, he had spent little time out in the fields during the monsoon season. Now he seldom felt dry, for even during the brief hours of sunshine, his clothing did not lose its dampness. He smelled of musty decay, and he began to fear that he would succumb to some disease in spite of his natural strength.

Still, he followed the same procedure he had set for himself from the start of his journey. As soon as camp was established he set himself to the task of entering his day's log in his diary. Future trips would be organized on the information he recorded. He glanced back at his earlier entries where he had identified the groves of trees where lumbering was done, the quantities cut, and the quality of each cutting. Noted also were the wildlife encountered, natives they met, and the disposition of both. He was engrossed in this task when a new sound drew his attention.

He was out from under his shelter in a flash, his gun in his hands. "What was that?"

Hsiang looked up from his pot of food. "Gunfire." He moved to the edge of the small clearing. "Below us. We may be able to see from over there."

Together, the two men climbed to a large rock that protruded near the river's edge. They scrambled up, pushing aside wet branches until they reached an observation point, from which they could see all the way down to the sea. Dirk lifted his glass and studied the water, far below.

Two ships seemed locked in battle. Puffs of smoke, issuing from the gun ports, were followed by the sound of firing and the splash of impact. Bracing himself on the rock, Dirk studied both ships. When he lowered his glass, he pursed his lips, deep in thought.

"What is it?" Hsiang could not retain his curiosity.

"A battle." Dirk held out the glass. "Between a Dutch frigate and a British man-of-war."

"Why are they fighting? They've traded side by side for many years."

"I don't know. Maybe it's a feud between two captains, both after the same prize." He looked once more at the distant battle. "We must warn Kui. Maybe we will have to hold up our delivery of lumber until this little fracas is over."

"You think it might extend all the way to Palembang?"

"I don't know. But caution now may avoid the loss of all our lumber later. There are enough hazards to shipping. Why send valuable cargo out to face scuttling by cannon?"

"Shall I go to warn my brother?"

"We'll all go. He will have heard the firing, too, and will not rush into danger. We will not yet alter our plans. Tomorrow will be time enough."

Yet when he lay on his pallet, Dirk found difficult to forget the sight of two ships locked in combat. The last time there had been fighting between Dutch and English, many merchants had lost their fortunes, and damage done to the plantations and factories had never been completely repaired. Was this the beginning of another such conflict?

At last, unable to sleep, he climbed once more to the lookout point and trained his glass on the sea. The Dutch ship was gone. The English ship was limping away to the northwest. Did this mean the fighting was over and his countrymen had won? He could not be certain. This was but one battle. The war, wherever it was being fought—*if* it was being fought—might well take place in some remote area, far from Palembang.

It might take place in Padang! It was the west coast of Sumatra that provided the most cargo headed for Europe. Products from the plantations found their way to many ports. And the climate was easier on the European workmen, too. The swamps that surrounded Palembang made it far more dangerous to the health of foreign traders.

Troubled, he returned to his lean-to and lay down, listening to the throbbing of the jungle. Were there new sounds, like the gunfire he had heard earlier in the day?

Were the English even now attacking Padang? Was Marietje in danger?

He sat up abruptly. He had to know. No fortune, no matter how vast, could compensate him for the loss of Marietje. And if the English had first attacked Padang . . .

He lay down, aware that there was nothing he could do until morning. The sky was beginning to grow light before he finally slept.

Chapter Eleven

"Can you get them to move faster?" Dirk nodded in the direction of the carriers, who pushed their way slowly along the path he and Hsiang were cutting through the forest. The paths used by the natives did not cling so close to the river.

"We are moving amazingly quickly, friend of my brother. We should reach Kui very soon. When one distresses oneself over time, one fights the wind."

"Men have been known to win such battles." Dirk felt annoyed at the ancient proverbs Hsiang seemed always to be quoting. Yet he knew that his impatience was not really with Kui's brother nor with the carriers. What upset him was not knowing what was happening on the plantation. What made him impatient with each small delay along the trail was his knowledge that he was too far from Padang to help if the English attacked, and his realization that the plantation would certainly be taken if the English triumphed.

Would he lose the fortune these logs represented if he abandoned them now and returned to the plantation? And if he found everyone safe, would he regret his decision? He knew Hans Koenraad well, and he recognized that the man scorned unfounded fears. Would he consider Dirk's concern for Marietje's safety—on her father's own plantation—as a simple excuse for abandoning a journey that had proven difficult?

Dirk shook his head. Maybe Hans would accuse him of such cowardliness, but he could disprove any suggestion that he sought excuses to abandon his set plans. And if the plantation was actually in danger, wouldn't Hans appreciate anything Dirk might do to help him?

Dirk hacked at the underbrush savagely. If he met any Englishmen, he would cut them down, too, like vines, and leave them dead on the ground. And if any one of them harmed his Marietje, he would show no mercy.

He worked himself forward in silence, until suddenly he was standing in a small clearing, and Kui was approaching him. "Welcome, partner. I trust you saw the sea battle yesterday."

"Yes. The English. My countrymen won the skirmish."

"Not truly. Both ships were badly disabled. There are others approaching now. Come and see." Kui led the way to another overlook, and soon both men were studying the sea through their glasses. They watched until the fighting ended, once more with both ships badly crippled. Had either won the victory? Were there others fighting along the miles of shoreline? No amount of searching the horizon with their glasses could give them answers to their questions.

Kui was the first to speak as they returned to his campsite. "Did you not say you had a woman in Padang?"

"Yes. Marietje. She lives on a plantation just above the city."

Kui did not speak for some time. When he did, he was looking again toward the distant coastline. "I do not believe it is wise to deliver our lumber to Palembang until we know what has happened there. Our partnership will have no meaning if the English are in control of the city."

Dirk glanced toward his Chinese friend. "You could make another arrangement. Your fortunes need not suffer because the ship that carries your cargo flies another flag."

Kui faced Dirk, his eyes steady. "You forget. You are more than my partner. You are my brother; I owe you my life. A man does not desert his brother because times are hard."

Dirk could not answer. Such loyalty deserved more than thanks. Kui shrugged his shoulders. "You did not believe me before." It was a statement, not a question. "That is not surprising. Foreigners underestimate the feelings of my people."

"Oh, no!" Dirk embraced his friend. "It is not that I doubted you. I have never felt such affection even from my own kin."

"We are kin now." The word sounded strange on Kui's tongue. "Let us find a place—a wide spot in the river nearby—where we can keep the wood until we can return.

Then you must go to Padang. I will take the men and return to Palembang."

"Can we trust them to remain silent about our prize? The English, too, want teak wood and sandalwood."

"They will do as I say. Since I survived the claw of the tiger, they believe I have special powers."

Dirk glanced upward, toward the high ridge that divided the island in half. On the other side Marietje was either unaware of any danger—or . . . He dared not complete the thought. "Shall we start, then? From above, I saw what appeared to be a small lake formed by the river, just below here. We might be able to keep the wood there."

His plan, and his memory of the lake, served to be correct. By the next morning, the logjam at the bend had been released, and the logs were floating safely in the small lake. Kui and Hsiang were directing the workers as they anchored the logs away from the white rapids that bled water off toward the sea.

When the last log was secured, Kui stepped to Dirk's side. "My partner, you must be on your way. You need not worry about the logs. If all is safe in Palembang, I will bring them in and deliver them to Janset. I will tell him you sent me ahead, and you will follow with more valuable treasures. And I will make him understand that you expect a fair division."

Dirk clasped Kui's hand. "You are my friend—and my brother." He glanced at the skyline. "I may be back in time to meet you at the factory. My future father-in-law will have little good to say of a man who lets unnecessary worries take him from his business."

"I will pray to the gods that your worst fears are but dreams." Kui gazed directly into Dirk's eyes. "May the gods watch over your travel."

"May God protect you, too." Dirk smiled. "And may all this be a bad dream."

"I know no other reality. Are you, then, part of my dream?"

"No. For I know none other either." Dirk patted his gun. "Do you wish to take this with you? There are other tigers in the forest."

"I will not need it. But you may want it to defend your

woman." Kui bowed slightly, his hands clasped together. "Travel safely."

"Yes. And you also." Dirk turned and headed for the path they had used during their descent. The forest closed in around him. He was alone.

Behind him, he heard Kui issuing orders to the carriers. Some would return to their villages and stay until sent for. A few would return with him to Palembang. Dirk paused. He had felt alone when he started on his trip from Palembang. Now he knew that as far as his business was concerned, he would never be alone again. His welfare and the success of the Lun brothers were linked. Wherever he might go, his business would be well tended. Shaking his head to rid his thoughts of the past, he turned resolutely toward the high ridge.

As he moved forward he considered what might lie ahead. Most fortunate would be the discovery that his fears were unfounded. Then he would return to Palembang, pick up his venture where he and Kui had abandoned it, and all would be well.

He might find that the English had already taken Padang. Then he could join with the others on the plantation to defend the Koenraad property from the enemy.

Worst of all would be if he discovered that the English had already occupied the plantation. Were that to be the case, he would have to work on the outside, until he devised a method of rescuing his fiancée and her family.

It took him two days to reach the peaks, thanks to the clearing he and Kui had done along the river. When he stood at last on the ridge, Dirk once more drew out his glass and scanned the water far below. A ship rested in a harbor, barely visible through the foliage. Was it Padang he saw? Dirk gazed up at the sky, struggling to get his bearings. Maybe. He would have to walk south along the ridge were he to want certain proof. Or he could begin the hike down, and then, if he were too far north, do his southern traveling on flatter land.

He decided on the latter. He might be able to recognize landmarks sooner and correct his bearings. At the least, he would have a feel of accomplishment, for he would no longer be on the far side of the mountains. Lifting the small bundle of supplies he had taken from the camp, he began the descent.

By nightfall he was far down from the peak, yet in all of his walking, he had not yet seen any familiar signs. There were plantations, yet he dared not approach them openly, for at the first one he had seen, he learned that his worst fears were true. The English were in full occupation. He passed that first plantation silently, keeping well into the forest so as to avoid discovery. But as he approached the second settlement he realized that he could not go on without rest—and possibly some food.

Once more he searched through his knapsack, but he found only crumbs left from his last meal. He had, he realized, been too confident that he would have no trouble reaching the Koenraad home.

He waited until dark to venture into the open, but then he found that the weather was favorable to his concealment. The English soldiers sought shelter from the downpour, and he was free to scavenge without interruption.

He found what he needed with surprising ease. Fruit, piled high for cleansing. Scraps of meat that had been hung out to dry during the day. Like most plantation workers, these on this unknown estate had failed to bring all the dried strips in at nightfall. Dirk filled his knapsack and hurried back into the forest. He passed a shed and considered stopping, but at the last moment his caution took control and he hurried on. If he fell asleep in such an exposed place, he might be discovered and murdered before he woke.

He did not leave the plantation immediately, even after dawn broke. There were things he could learn from watching. He located a thicket and crouched there to wait, aware that for the first time since his apprenticeship with Hans Koenraad, he might have use for his knowledge of English.

He was thinking of Marietje when, suddenly, the silence of the morning was shattered. A soldier appeared at the back door of the main building, a female form draped over his shoulder. He was followed by another soldier. Both appeared to be privates.

"I told you she'd die." The unburdened man spoke first. "Now what'll we say to the commander?"

"That she died. What else. Women ain't too strong 'ere, anyway."

"Well, you're the one what killed 'er. You can bury 'er."

"Just what I'm doin', ain't it? We should'a stayed with the natives. They ain't so weak."

Dirk strained to see, raising his glass carefully, watchful that it not reflect the rays of the morning sun as he lifted it into position. The soldier turned, and Dirk was able at last to see the features of his victim.

It was a face he did not recognize. A young face, almost that of a child. Dirk shuddered, considering what torture the fragile girl might have been subjected to before she died. Then, as the soldier crossed the yard Dirk turned his glass once more to the building itself.

Were there other prisoners within its walls? He listened carefully, but he could hear no sounds of mourning. Most probably this child had been the last of her family—or the womenfolk in her family, at least—to survive. If the soldiers were true to their usual pattern, they would have killed the men first, probably in the heat of a battle.

He realized that the private had dropped his bundle and was beginning to dig. Once more, Dirk turned his glass and studied the land around the new grave. There were many mounds—all fresh. Whatever defense this last victim had had was long gone. "May her soul rest in peace." Dirk barely whispered the prayer. Then, silently, he retreated into the woods. This was no place for him to remain. He could no longer be of any help to the rightful owners, and any delay might guarantee that Marietje would meet the same fate as the girl child he had just seen being buried.

Marietje. He whispered her name as he crept through the woods. How beautiful she was, and how lighthearted. Had her joy in life been destroyed by the rough hand of some English soldier? Was she already dead and buried?

His heart protested at such a thought. No. Marietje could not be dead! He would find her, and save her. And if her home was surrounded with too many Englishmen, he would die in the attempt.

That possibility, too, filled him with anger. She had to be safe. Alive and unharmed. Her father would protect her. And the natives who worked the Koenraad plantation would never desert. They were too well cared for. They had never been mistreated, as had the workers on some of the other fields.

He paused, aware of a movement ahead of him. Had he let himself grow careless? Was his search already at an end?

The forest ahead of him was silent. Unnaturally so. Even the birds seemed afraid to sing. He waited patiently. If there were English soldiers ahead, they would soon appear. They had no reason to be quiet.

Nothing ahead moved. Yet some instinct told Dirk that he was not alone. He listened. Was that a rustle of leaves? There was little wind. Was he being watched? If so, by whom?

His legs began to ache. He was well accustomed to long hikes over land or from one end of the Koenraad plantation to the other. But he was not used to such frozen inactivity. Soon he would have to move. Would he then be shot dead?

Suddenly he lifted his head. He had heard a voice, so soft it could have been a dream. Yet he was sure. Without moving, he spoke. "Where are you, friend?" His words were Dutch. If an Englishman lay in wait for him, he had sealed his fate by speaking. But he did not expect to hear the roar of a gun.

"Go to the river, to your left." The words were spoken so quietly, Dirk could not help but wonder that he could tell it from the rustle of leaves or the distant chattering of a monkey.

Rising slowly, he began to creep forward. His muscles screamed in pain as he inched along, but he forced himself to move slowly. Was he followed? He couldn't be sure. The wind stirred the leaves around him. A bird screamed as he passed. He could not be sure that he was alone—or accompanied.

The river appeared ahead, and he paused. Now was the

moment when he had to decide. If he stepped into the clearing, he would be in danger. It might be his last conscious act.

But it might also serve to put him in contact with the unknown voice that had directed him to this spot. With a sudden resolve, he stood up and stepped forward. The leaves parted as he pushed ahead, and then he stood exposed.

"Welcome." The voice seemed changed. Deeper, and more sure. A man stepped out from the forest ahead and approached. He was dressed in worn clothing, wet from the last rain. Over his shoulder he carried a gun, and Dirk could see that his belt contained ammunition. His powder horn hung from his belt. In the dimness of the clearing, Dirk could barely make out his features. "Welcome. It is good to find another man to join our cause." He stepped forward. "I am Bernhard Herman. My factory was taken a month ago. I did not know there was a settlement above the one over there." He gestured toward the plantation where Dirk had seen the dead child.

"I come from Palembang." Dirk caught the man's outstretched hand. "I am Dirk Hendrik. Before"—he gestured toward the English occupied lands—"I worked on the Koenraad plantation, just above Padang."

"Oh, so you are from the north. My factory is in Bintuhan."

So he had crossed the divide south of Penang. Dirk adjusted his internal map with a feeling of disappointment. He would have a long way to travel before he reached the Koenraad plantation. "Then the English might not be as far north as Padang?"

"The English are everywhere. I will confess I did not expect them when I heard news that they are still fighting their American colonies. But I was wrong. They want to own the world. They have killed my wife and my son. I will die happy only when I avenge my family."

"Are there others with you?"

"Come. I'll show you." Bernhard turned and led the way through the underbrush. He moved as a tiger moves, stalking its prey. Dirk followed as well he could, for his companion paid no heed to him.

Abruptly they came upon a native village. Dirk stared in

surprise. The men who approached them were not natives. Like Bernhard they wore torn clothing and carried rifles and powder horns.

Bernhard greeted them without smiling. "I have brought a new fighter. His home is farther north. Koen, you can tell him what you know of Padang."

As Koen talked, what little hope Dirk had for Marietje's safety faded. The English had set up headquarters in Padang—or nearby. The commander of the entire invading force was there. "You can do no better than to join us." Koen concluded. "I saw the plantations around Padang. They have all been looted. As for the women, they are either dead or they wish they were. They have no wish to see us again, after the shame to which they have been subjected."

"You can desert your wife when she needs you the most?"

"No." Koen looked suddenly very old. "My woman needs me no longer. I tried to rescue her, but she"—his jaw tightened at the memory—"she had already taken her own life. That is why I say what I do. Our women are proud. They do not want to live with shame and disgrace."

"You are wrong!" Bernhard stepped between the two men. "We will continue to fight to save our women. And we will succeed. Come inside. You may be able to help us with our plans."

Their first action served to satisfy Dirk's frustration. With careful planning, they located a road much traveled by small contingents of English and waylaid the first such contingent to pass. They used no guns, for the sound of firing might have called attention to their presence. Yet when they returned to the village, each man had a new gun and ammunition.

Dirk placed his prize next to the others and picked up his own weapon. Maybe, in time, he would forget the look of surprise on the face of his victim. Maybe. He had never killed a man before. Then he thought of Marietje, and any regret he had vanished. She was in danger—maybe killed herself. If he had to, he would single-handedly take revenge for her life. He wasted no more time in idle regrets. There were other soldiers who would pass. More plans to be laid.

His head high, he turned and headed for the hut that had been designated as headquarters for this motley band. The worst had happened. The English had taken over the island. But he was not through fighting. And now he had comrades who would stand beside him in the battles that lay ahead.

Chapter Twelve

"You will love England." Byron Scott lay back on the bed, perspiration still wetting his chest. "It's so green. Like an emerald set in a blue field. Rich with beauty. Not like this land at all."

Marietje wanted to push him out of her bed. In the weeks that had passed since his first taking of her, he had come to her often. At first, he had tried to charm her out of her tight control. His caresses, gentle and full of desire, had tested Marietje's resolve. But, in the end, she had won. She made it clear that she would submit to Byron Scott, but she would not enjoy his presence.

Yet for all of her success, she felt no triumph, for each time he lay beside her, she knew her own weakness. Her mother had had the courage to beg for death. She had no such strength. Her greatest sorrow lay in her knowledge that with each encounter, her ability to conceal her own responses diminished. Despite her vows, she was growing to enjoy the touch of Byron's hand on her stomach, the soft caress of his fingers on her breasts. Her body seemed unconcerned with the identity of the man who brought it pleasure. It responded with passion to Byron's touch, and she hated herself more each time he approached her.

Had she forgotten Dick Hendrik? As Byron spoke of his longing for his homeland she struggled to bring the vision of Dirk's face before her. For a moment, she thought she had failed, and then the vision flashed into her mind. His dark, curly hair. His strong face, filled with love and kindness. His strong young body, firm and muscular. Not at all like the body of Byron Scott. Byron was an old man, with too much fat, and skin leathered from the rays of the sun.

"You can still think of him?" Byron's voice was filled with a mixture of anger and sadness. "I have come to love you, little Marietje, and you still think of a man who is long rotted in his grave?"

She winced at his description. Was it true? Was Dirk killed? "Are you certain he is dead?"

"I have told you, haven't I? The entire island is ours." He raised himself on one elbow and leaned over her, the fingers of his free hand gently stroking her face. "My dear one. Can you not see that your life here is over? What have you to stay for? You have told me yourself that even had your father lived, the plantation would go to your brother. Your lover is dead. And you have a new lover—me. I can give you a good life, my child. I will take you home to England. You will have a house of your own—and servants to command. You will have a carriage and a coachman. And I will come to you and love you."

She remained silent. She had heard all his promises before. She knew only too well that one promise was never made. She would not go to England as Byron Scott's wife, for he already had a wife and children in Sussex. She would be his mistress. His toy. A plaything with which he amused himself during his visits to London.

She felt Byron's touch, and she struggled to understand her own thoughts. Would she be satisfied to marry this man were he available to her? She wanted to say no. She wished fervently that she had the strength to reject him outright, to push him away from her bed and to destroy herself now that he had overpowered her. Why had she lost that power?

She knew the reason. Deep in her heart she believed that he told her the truth about Palembang. She was alone. Dirk was dead.

She stirred, and Byron kissed her shoulder. "My dearest Marietje. The day will come when you will love me. I will devote my life to that cause. And then, once more, we will ride together to the secret lake and make love in the bower."

She gazed at him in surprise. This was the first time he had mentioned the present. Always, before, he spoke of the dim future, when he would take her to England. And always, he kept her well within the confines of the house and its garden.

He lay back, leaving one hand to rest on her hip. The pressure felt good, even though she knew she should hate it. "Do you not miss your rides across the countryside? Can you not understand that I hate to deprive you of such pleasure?"

"Yet you keep me here. If you love me, you—"

"Do not tell me what I would do if I loved you, for you seem incapable of love." He spoke harshly for the first time. Then immediately he was filled with regret. "Forgive me, my dear. I know you have been sorely tried. It is just that I am so very fond of you, and it saddens me to see you still unhappy."

"You have destroyed my happiness."

His laugh was gentle. "Oh, my sweet, you are so very young. Happiness cannot be so easily ruined. I do not deny that you have lost much in these past months. But we all lose both mother and father. That is part of life. And as for your unnamed lover—your fiancé—do you believe that you are the first to be deprived of a first love's embrace? Most women learn to love from one man and then expand that love with another. That, too, is part of life."

"I do not wish it to be part of mine. I wish I had my mother's courage."

"Your mother chose death over submission to an animal. I cannot deny that many of my men treat women most cruelly. But you have been showered with affection and kindness. I have not used you badly, nor will I ever. Why do you reject my love?"

Why, indeed? Marietje felt the hard core of her hatred begin to fade. Was it Byron Scott who roused her anger—or fate? "You are certain that every man in Palembang was killed?" Her voice broke as she spoke. It was not easy to confirm the death of her young love.

"Absolutely sure. My dear, there is no denying the truth. England has won the Spice Islands. I regret that your youthful dreams have been victim to our success, but I cannot take full responsibility for what has happened. Had your men fought better, it might be I who lay buried."

"My father was a good man."

"Had I known he was your father, I would have saved his life, even at the cost of my own." It was a harmless deceit. Byron knew that his chance to control and enjoy Marietje depended on her triple loss. Besides, Hans Koenraad was dead. There was no harm in pretending that he, too, regretted what had transpired.

She lay quietly, considering what she had heard. When at last she spoke, it was softly, as if she were thinking aloud. "I will try. There is nothing more for me to do."

He smiled in silent triumph. "You will not regret your decision, my love. For you are my love. Now show me that you are willing to try." He leaned over her and kissed her full on the lips.

This time she succeeded in controlling her reaction. She forced herself to respond as he wished, with a semblance of inner passion. And all the time she pretended the ecstasy of desire, she repeated silently to herself a promise she had made. It is only for a while. Until he trusts me again. Only by letting him think I have succumbed to his charms will I ever be free. The thought supported her, giving her reason for the stirrings she felt within her as she lay in his arms.

As he moved above her, filling her with his desire, she remembered again the sweet strong body of Dirk Hendrik. She would never hold him in her arms. Why had she let him put her off, when he wanted her as much as she had wanted him? Why?

The heat of Byron's body overwhelmed her, and she gasped. The fire he lit within her swelled upward, wiping out her ability to think. This was what her body wanted. It moved of its own accord, pushing upward to meet the thrusts of her passionate companion. Her lips parted, searching upward for his, and, when they could not find their goal, rested on the hardness of his chest. With a rush her resolve faded, leaving nothing but an awareness of an incredible delight that built up and up until, at last, she exploded in release and ecstasy.

When he lay again beside her, he was smiling. She waited for his words of triumph, but he said nothing. Instead, silently, he kissed her still-damp breasts and then slipped from the bed. She watched as he dressed, expecting any moment that he would boast of his conquest. Still he remained silent. Only when he was fully dressed did he show any awareness of her rapt attention.

"I will be back tonight. I regret the need to spend time in Padang."

She grasped at the words. "You still go there weekly?"

Now he laughed. "You do not have other relatives you want me to locate, do you?"

"No." She felt her body shaking, and she knew the memory of his ardor—and of her own response—would not quickly fade. "I—just wondered."

"Well, I do. Actually it has been cleaned up again. Maybe, if you continue—as you are doing now—you can drive with me. It would be good for you to get out again."

"Yes." She wanted to say more, but before she could gather her thoughts, he was gone.

She lay staring at the closed door. Had she really felt the emotions she released this last time he took her?

"No! I cannot respond with affection for a man who forces himself upon me. I hate him! I hate him!" She was only too aware of the force that lay behind her words. Once they had flowed from her heart. Now she was no longer sure. How could she hate a man who tried as hard as Byron Scott did to please her? How could she hate the only man who had roused her passion to fulfillment? How could she hate the man who protected her as once her father had done?

"I hate him anyway!" She was aware of her own uncertainty, and she felt a rush of shame. She realized that her hands were moving down her body, caressing her own breasts, resting gently on the mound of her belly, and she shuddered. "Mother, please forgive me. And help me. I cannot accept with warmth the man who caused your death."

He came to her again that night, long after she was asleep, and gently kissed her on the nape of her neck. She stirred. "Dirk?"

For one moment, Byron drew back. Then, with a smile, he pushed his way under the light sheet that covered her. "Yes, Marietje."

She turned, still asleep, and drew him to her. Her body was warm from sleep, and he felt more than saw that her nightgown had pulled up around her shoulders. He did not bother to remove it.

"Oh, Dirk, thank God you've come." She was still asleep, he realized, but she was gradually waking up. Soon she would know that it was not Dirk who lay beside her.

But the dreaminess with which she first responded to his presence did not vanish. She clung to him as she never did when she was fully conscious, and he reveled in her passion. When ecstasy threatened to overwhelm her, it was Dirk's name she spoke. Byron learned quickly that as he responded to that name, he added to her own delight—and to his. And it was with joy that he saw her full sensitivity increase.

Was she now no longer deaming? If she was awake, she did not admit it. The passion she kept under rein was now overflowing, flooding her body, released to swell and ebb and swell again until, at last, she seemed to explode in wild abandon. Yet even then, she called the name of her dead lover.

When she grew quiet, he withdrew slowly, covering her quickly so as not to wake her with the chill night air. He lay for a time listening to her steady breathing. Had she known it was he who came to her as she slept? Had she called Dirk's name only out of an unwillingness to relinquish her lost love?

Could a woman respond with such ardor while yet lost in dreams? He could find no answer. When she continued to breathe softly, he once more left her bed and returned across the wide hallway to his own. When morning came, he did not mention his nocturnal visit, but he could not fail to see that for the first time since her imprisonment, Marietje was lighthearted.

"I am glad you feel better this morning." He saw no reason to suggest that he had anything to do with her good humor. "I have decided that you should be permitted some liberty. Certainly, as long as one of my men goes with you, you can visit the graves of your parents once more. I think I have been treating you badly without realizing it. How can I expect you to love a man who keeps you locked in your room?"

"How, indeed?" Marietje seemed lost in some private memory.

Byron pretended total unawareness of her improved humor. "Exactly. So I have decided, as I say, to improve matters. I regret that it is not safe to take you into Padang at the moment. But possibly by next week—certainly by next week—the trouble will be over. If I am to convince you of the importance of your leaving with me when I return to England, I need to start by showing you that not all Englishmen are beasts."

"Thank you." Marietje clearly had not heard much of what Byron said, but he did not care. He knew the secret of pleasing her now. Give her the chance to pretend that it was another who held her in his arms, and she dropped the cold reserve she clutched so close during the earlier hours of the evening.

The rest of breakfast was eaten in silence. When Byron rose and announced that he had to depart, Marietje nodded absentmindedly. She let him kiss her cheek without quarrel, and she watched him leave the room without further comment. Her thoughts were on her marvelous dream.

Dirk had come to her as she slept. She was certain of that, for his presence had been so real. And this time he had not resisted her clinging embrace. He had left her sated with passion long before dawn.

She smiled at the departing figure of Byron Scott. He could confine her or let her ride free. He could kill her parents and separate her from her servants. But he could not invade her dreams.

A shiver of doubt brought a chill to her euphoria. Then, with a toss of her head, she dismissed the vagrant thought. Her visitation was as she believed it to be! It had to be that way. Dirk had come to her—somehow—to tell her of his love, and to let her know that he was still alive. But could his spirit leave her feeling so fulfilled? Had Scott taken advantage of her fantasy?

Frightened, she pushed the possibility aside. She would not think of such things. Dirk *had* come to her. He would come again.

That night Byron appeared, as usual, at her bedroom door just as she was bathing. He stood watching her sponge the perspiration from her body, and when she rose from the tub, he dropped into a chair to watch her dry herself and complete her preparation for bed. "You are very beautiful, my dear one. More beautiful than ever. You seem so full of joy tonight. Is it that you look forward at last to my presence in your bed?"

Marietje's expression froze. "No. I will never look forward to your forcing yourself on me. Never."

His smile did not fade. "Maybe we can change that. I still dream that I may soon convince you of my sincerity. I will be going home soon. Maybe before another year has passed. I do not want to leave you behind, where you will be unprotected."

He was sincere, she knew that. Why was it so hard for her to accept him?

Why did she need to accept him? Dirk would come and rescue her. Her dream had proven that. All she had to do was wait. Wait—and endure the routine of Byron's presence in her bed.

It was, she knew, a routine she could survive. He seldom expected the response she had unwillingly given him the night before. Only occasionally did he try to kiss her lips, for she usually responded by tightening her body to show her resistance. He knew she held back her responses as he lay beside her—and he seemed willing to let it be so. Yet only yesterday he had talked of greater trust between them, and of giving her more freedom.

She reached for her nightgown, and he held up his hand. "No. Leave it off. I wish to enjoy your beauty a bit longer."

Docilely, she let the garment fall back onto the chair where Mai had put it. She felt mixed emotions when Byron treated her in this manner. Foremost was her anger and shame. He gazed at her as one would look on a slave. Yet she felt pride that he found her so attractive. And she wondered, always, if she could use his infatuation with her to some advantage.

That thought always put her into a quandary. She knew nothing of the art of intrigue. Her father had carefully taught her to be forthright in her dealings with all people, even with her servants. Yet she had seen women who had no difficulty using subtle ploys to bend men to their wills. And for the first time in her life, she wished she had that power.

"Come here, my sweet." Byron held out one hand to catch hers as she approached. "Let me carry you to your bed." He rose and swept her off her feet. As he moved across the room he bent over her and kissed her forehead, planting his lips at the point where her eyebrows and her nose met.

She felt a surge of emotion at his touch. This was where her ghostly visitor had kissed her during her wonderful dream. And then the control she had fought for returned. She would fight her own desires whenever this man came to her; she knew that now. But at last she had the power to resist. Dirk's presence in her dreams gave her that strength.

Byron put her on the bed, and then, his eyes fixed on her face, he slowly removed his clothing. When he was nude, he slipped in beside her, pushing aside the netting that protected her from insects, and then letting it fall into place behind him. He propped himself on his elbow and studied her face. "You are very beautiful, Marietje. I have grown to love you, as I did not expect to love any woman again."

She opened her eyes and met his gaze. This was his usual approach. He would speak of the past, of England, and then he would take her. Maybe she could delay his attack. "Is your daughter yet grown?"

He seemed surprised at the question. "My daughter? Yes, I think she is. I do not see my children very often." His expression grew pensive, and he seemed to be looking far into the distance.

Encouraged, Marietje continued. "Tell me again about England."

Byron talked slowly, as if it were an effort to bring back the memories. Yet his pictures were of a beloved land—an island like Sumatra, yet so different. He stroked her body as he spoke, but with each sentence the demand of his touch seemed to diminish.

Marietje grew drowsy. His voice was low and steady, with a slight rise when he spoke of something or someone he held dear. Like a lullaby.

"Forgive me, my sweet, you are far too tired to listen to an old man talk." She felt his hand touch her briefly between the legs, as if in promise of delights to come, and she tensed. But there was no assault. His hand moved on, cupping her breast, and then he kissed her. She held herself ready, prepared to resist.

"Good night, my love. May your dreams be sweet." He was moving now. Marietje prepared herself, but he did not touch her again. She looked up in surprise to see him standing beside the bed. Was he actually going to leave her?

He stood beside her in silence, and then he turned and padded softly from the room. She wanted to enjoy her triumph, but she was far too tired. Tomorrow, she promised herself, she would find an explanation for his strange behavior. Now she would enjoy the pleasure of falling asleep alone. Maybe she would dream her dream again.

She had delayed her prayers while Scott was with her, and now she folded her hands over her breasts. Most of what she said each night was routine, little prayers she had been taught as a child. But she ended each with a prayer for guidance. Was this, she asked, what God intended her life to be? An eternity of being half aware, of feeling no appreciation of the present or anticipation for what was to come?

She knew she behaved at times as if she had lost all reason for living. She moved through the day without enthusiasm. She ate food without relishing its taste. She saw each daily sunrise without joy. And she greeted each nightfall with quiet acceptance. Occasionally she would remember how she had been in the past, and she would want to weep. But tears would not come. Only when, in her dreams, Dirk came to comfort her, did she feel any real emotion.

No wonder, she thought, she looked forward to another visit. But would that be enough for her for the rest of her life? Silently she prayed one more prayer—that God would take her soon so she could be with Dirk forever.

She felt his nearness first. Her dreams reached out to touch him as he approached her bed. "Dirk?" It was the voice of her dreams that spoke—and answered.

"Marietje, my dearest." He moved as he spoke, and she felt him touch her body. His hands closed over the firm mounds of her breasts, and she felt his fingers caress her nipples, drawing them into taut sensitivity.

Her lips parted, searching for his. She pressed upward against his hands, wanting more—relishing the waiting as much as she would savor the culmination.

His lips brushed her lightly and then moved down to the small of her neck, touching her with love, stirring life into the body she had willed to be cold. Her arms reached up and caught his shoulders. The strong, manly shoulders she had never held in life. "Oh, Dirk." All the longing of her loneliness was in that sigh. "Take me, please, take me."

He moved at her command, rising above her and fitting himself into her body. She greeted him with rapture, pulling him close, Pressing against him when, at last, he began to move within her. This was what she lived to feel. This, and nothing else. If God would permit her lover to visit her like this for the rest of her life, she would be content.

And then her thoughts became jumbled. He was moving more quickly, and she moved with him to ecstasy. The flames grew within her, building, ever building until she wondered if she could endure the force of her passion. And then, like floodgates opening, the explosions began. She was helpless in the power of her own sensations.

Helpless—and suddenly aware. Above her, within her, she could feel the pulsations of her midnight lover. His entire body seemed wracked with spasms like those that left her helpless and sated. But something was wrong. She was awake—and her dream lover had not disappeared.

Terrified, she opened her eyes, and knew that she had been betrayed. Byron Scott lay over her, his face strained with the force of his passion, his head up so that in the dim light of the moon she could clearly see his face.

She screamed and pushed him away, kicking and twisting until she was free of his weight. As she landed on the floor she knew the full extent of his perfidy. It was he who had come in the dark, returning after leaving her to sleep. It was he who had tricked her into responses she had wanted to share with only one man—a man he had killed.

She felt the cool air against her body, and she shivered. "I hate you. How could you do this to me?"

He propped himself up on one arm. Even in the dim light, she could see that he was surprised. "What have I done, my dear? I have brought you the love you needed, but would not accept from me when you knew who I was. I have released your passionate nature. I cannot be upset that you know now. You would have to have learned the truth eventually. Marietje, you are a woman filled with passion and fire. You are too rich in love's best qualities to be allowed to languish unawakened. What was I to do? Let you grow into an embittered woman who hated love?"

"You had no right to deceive me. Wasn't it enough that you could take me whenever you wished? Did you have to do . . . this?" She could not describe what had happened. She could still feel the passion within her, pulling her toward him. She would never let this happen again, of that she was certain, even if her body rebelled. She could not live with herself, knowing that she had been so foully mistreated.

He was on his feet beside her now, touching her shoulders, pulling her close. She felt the warmth of his skin against hers, and she knew he had won. Her body had learned to love. Its need for fulfillment was too strong now for her to resist.

Yet resist she must. Resist, and fight to be free. For with a sudden insight she knew that he had done more than betray her trust. He had lied to her as well. He had insisted that Dirk was dead, and she had believed him. But how could he be so certain? Did he know Dirk so he could recognize his body? No. Did any of his soldiers? No. If, in fact, Palembang had fallen to the English, that still would not prove Dirk was dead. And what proof had Byron Scott offered her of the conquest of the city beyond the mountains?

None. He had woven a net to keep her close to him. And had she not learned of his perfidy, he would have managed to persuade her to do his will, to leave Sumatra with him and spend the rest of her life as his mistress in London.

She felt a great trembling overcome her. How close she had come to total destruction! She knew, suddenly, that there were worse fates than the one her mother had died to avoid. Far more terrible than suffering the unwanted assault on her body was this insidious control of her mind. She had almost been persuaded to voluntarily enter into a life of servitude. Byron Scott had taken away all of her hope—and offered her a life of shame in its stead. He had used her longing for Dirk to get from her what she would never have given him voluntarily.

"Get out." She pushed him away, pulling up a corner of the sheet to cover her nakedness. "Leave me alone. I hate you."

He smiled gently as he backed away. "Of course, my sweet. You need time to collect your thoughts, to understand. I would have told you eventually, To be quite honest, I feared each time we were together that you would wake and—do what you now are doing. Maybe I was wrong to let this happen. But I did it out of love. You are too beautiful a young woman to be denied the thrill and ecstasy of passion."

"With Dirk. Not with you. You're an old man. You killed my father and mother. I hate you." She felt the tears welling in her eyes, and she fought them back, praying that she could hold on until she was alone. Her fingernails dug into the palms of her hands as she fought for control. And then he was gone.

His last words rang in her ears. "Sleep on it, my dear. Is it so terrible to be loved with honest passion? Do you really regret that I have awakened the woman within you? You are a beautiful, feminine creature. You deserve to be loved. I am not ashamed of what I have done, for I know that you will thank me some day."

When she heard the door close, Marietje threw herself on her bed and abandoned herself to her tears. "I want to die." She uttered the words as a prayer. "I'll never be able to enjoy life again."

Even as she spoke, she was aware of the warmth his body had left behind. Why, she wondered, had she failed to recognize him in her sleep? He had lain with her before when she was wide-awake, hating the nearness that he forced upon her. Why had she accepted him with such eagerness once she fell asleep?

She knew the answer. Because she needed what he offered her. Because even the anger she felt when he forced himself upon her was not enough to dispel the stirrings of passion he aroused. Because her need exceeded her anger. And because she had joined in his deception. She had convinced herself that the nightly visitations were not real when evidence existed to prove her wrong. She had blamed the damp sheets on her own release, and ignored the presence of visible proof that the visitor who stirred her was not a spirit, but a real, virile male.

And now she could pretend no longer. Maybe, she thought, the only answer was to anger him so that he ended her life.

Even as she considered the possibility of such an action she knew she could not do that. This awakening had made her aware of more than Byron Scott's perfidy. It also forced her to realize that Dirk might still be alive. And if he were, she had to find him.

Slowly she moved from her bed to the window. In the moonlight, she could see the raindrops still glistening on the leaves. The night air was clean and fresh, filled with the fragrance of hidden flowers. Was Dirk hiding somewhere, too? Was he even now lying in the forest above her, praying for some sign that she was still alive?

She turned her attention to the grove of trees where her parents lay buried. Pieter was there, too, and Pieter had died trying to save her and her mother. "I betrayed you, Pieter. I almost let him win, in spite of all you did."

She stared into the night, aware that Pieter would not blame her, whatever she did. He loved her unselfishly, accepting Dirk's right to claim her as a bride.

"Forgive me, Pieter. I really didn't know. And I thought I was alone." She knew that was true. She had thought she was alone. But now she also knew that she had been wrong. Her parents had given her strength of will and courage. Dirk and Pieter had given her a special kind of love. And with all that, she could fight for her own independence. She could keep Scott from her bed until the day when she devised her escape.

Once more she looked into the deep forest. "Wait for me, my darling. I will get free. If you're really dead, I will join you in heaven. And if you are alive . . ." She did not finish her thought. In the back of her mind a new fear was growing. What if she found Dirk and he could not fill the place vacated by her nocturnal lover?

Impatiently she brushed the fear aside. Dirk loved her. Of that she was certain. And she loved him. Turning back to her bed, she cursed the wisdom that brought her such unnatural doubts.

Chapter Thirteen

She remembered her vows when the morning sunlight touched her pillow and brought her back to consciousness. Pretend. Let Byron Scott believe that he had at last won her over. For only then would he allow her the freedom she would need if she were to effect her escape.

She was smiling shyly when she entered the bright dining room, and she paused at the door to inhale the fragrances that came from the kitchen. "How delicious everything tastes." She glanced at Byron as she spoke. Was she too happy now? Would he suspect that she was deceiving him, as he had deceived her?

Her fears vanished when she saw his face. He rose with a new spring in his step and crossed the room to her side. "Ah! My dearest! So night has brought its healing. I prayed that your fears and anger would vanish, and God has granted my wish."

She prayed for forgiveness as she spoke, for she knew she sinned when she lied. "I cannot fight you any longer. Not after"—she paused coquettishly—"what happened last night. I should have recognized you." A tension deep within her increased, for what she felt she now had to say was by far her greatest deception. "I think I knew all along, but did not want to admit it."

His smile broadened. This was what he had longed to hear. Taking her arm, he escorted her to her seat and drew back her chair. "You will never regret this, my sweet." He gave a small laugh as he settled in his own chair. "Odd. I came to the East searching for treasure. I never dreamed that the jewel I would find would be made of warm flesh and blood."

For one moment Marietje felt a tug of regret. Was it fair for her to lead him on in this manner? She was building up his hopes when she knew she would destroy them as soon as she could find a way to escape.

Then the weakness passed. He had not hesitated to deceive her when he thought it would be to his advantage. She was only giving him back what he had already offered her.

For a while she ate in silence. Then she steeled herself for her next lie. Shaking her head to let the golden-blond curls bounce seductively, she said, "I thought we might ride out to the arbor." As she spoke she lowered her head, hiding her eyes. Surely, she thought, he would discern her duplicity.

His response told her he was completely taken in. He rose slightly from his seat, as if to approach her, and fell back with a laugh of pure delight. "Then it's true. You would not want to return there with me were you not willing to accept my proposal. I know how deeply you felt that place to be part of your . . ." He paused, hesitating, no doubt, to mention the unseen rival whom he had finally conquered. Then he seemed to reconsider. "You have let him go at last, and I am thankful. A woman as filled with promise as you should not let herself be bound to the dead past."

Marietje winced inwardly, but she did not let the smile on her lips waver. "Can we go today? It would mean so much to me."

"Of course we will go." He saw that the maid was entering with the next course, and he signaled her to serve Marietje first. "As soon as I have completed the little business I cannot delay. Shall we plan to leave here at noon?"

Marietje considered. All she hoped to accomplish on this outing would easily be done before the rains started. For the success of her plans, she intended to spend at least a week playing the devoted mistress. She had to allay any doubts Byron Scott might have regarding her loyalty to him. This was the first, and most meaningful, step. It would be followed by other, similar outings, during which she would appear to let him in on all of her secrets, to include him in all her plans.

And then, when he trusted her completely, she would make her getaway. She would have only one chance. She knew that. If he caught her and brought her back, he would never believe her again, for he would know, as she did, that she was no longer the innocent child she had been when he first arrived.

The ride to the arbor, her first since she had rejected his offers of a new home in England, was filled with bittersweet memories. Field hands were straggling in from the noonday rest as she and Byron mounted and headed away from the mansion. She waved at one man whose face she recognized, and he nodded back, his expression calm and pleasant, as if nothing had changed in his life. Then the buildings were behind her, and she spurred her horse into a canter.

Byron easily drew abreast. "The sun smiles on our ride, my sweet. The whole world is glad that you have seen the wisdom of my offer." He leaned over and planted a quick kiss on her hand. "You have made me so very happy, my dear. You will never regret your decision. I promise you that."

She decided that an answer was not needed. Instead she leaned forward, tightening the grip of her legs on the small hook of her sidesaddle. She whispered a command to her horse, and he sprang forward.

With a cry of delight, Byron joined in the race. At first he took the lead, but then she realized that he held his mount back, waiting for her to reach his side. When she was half a length ahead, he kept pace with her, and it was thus they reached their goal. Laughing with pleasure, like a youth blessed by the presence of his first love, Byron leaped to the ground and prepared to help Marietje dismount. She slid down, catching her slipper in the stirrup formed by his hands and then dropping lightly to the ground. She felt his arms move around her, and she realized with a sinking feeling that her body wanted what lay ahead. He kissed her, and she gave her natural responses free rein. What she had to do now could not be accomplished if she held back. He would know. *He* had not been asleep during those nocturnal hours of bliss.

When he kissed the small of her neck, she closed her eyes. Dirk. She had to think of Dirk. She dared not look down on the darker hair that covered Byron Scott's head, for she would see the gray hairs that told her that he was her father's age. He tugged lightly at her bodice, and she bent to loosen it. As the lacings fell away his fingers crept in, teasing the rosy tip of her breasts, stirring her passions up.

A shudder shook her body, and he lifted his head. "Come, my love." He took her hand and led her into the bower.

The sun had been warm on her hair; now she felt the cooler gentleness of the shadows made by the vines above her softly caressing her skin. A leaf caught a strand of her hair and stroked it lightly, like some fairy fingers, urging her to abandon herself to passion.

"Oh, Marietje." Byron's voice was thick with emotion. "I am so thankful that you know my love now and can admit your response. I took little pleasure in playing the role of another." She felt his fingers fumble with the buttons that ran up the back of her gown. "You are so beautiful." He kissed her shoulder as the dress fell away. "Like a gem, a ray of golden sunlight. My finding you has made all these lonely years worthwhile."

Her gown slid down from her arms and fell in soft folds at her feet. She felt its caress as it moved over her hips, felt it touch the smoothness of her thighs, and she knew she was ready for what lay ahead. She tried to remember why it was so important that she let him have his way with her, and she could not. All she knew was the heat of her body, the nearness of his fingers to her most intimate parts. All she felt was a growing desire to be held closer, to feel his masculine presence. *Later*. With a sigh she put aside her thoughts. She would remember later—when her passion was spent.

He stepped away from her now, swiftly removing his own clothing. It fell about him unheeded, and for a brief moment she wondered at the sight they would make when they returned, their garments soiled from the dirt, her hair disheveled, and his eyes filled with triumph. And then he stepped close once more, and she thought no more.

Her lips sought his now, feverishly, clinging to him as to the breath of life. Her own arms, idle before, now began to move up to pull him closer. But they could not rest quietly on his shoulders when her desire was so strong.

Her fingers wandered down his back, over his shoulders, teased for a moment the dark hairs of his chest, and then moved under his arms and down his hips. He was thicker than Dirk, that her consciousness told her, but her body did not care. He knew when to kiss and when to caress. He knew the places in her body that even she, in her childhood days of exploration, had never found.

He shifted slightly, and she felt him push against her, demanding entry into her body. Eager now, she lifted herself up and bent her hips forward to let him in. And when she felt him slip through the narrow opening, she caught at his hips with her hands and held him close. What wonderful new charms he had for her enjoyment.

He caught at her thighs with his hands, lifted her up, holding her against him, and moved slowly toward the ledge that was formed by an outjutting stone. And then he was seated, holding her on his lap, kissing her breasts, moving slowly, as if he relished each change in sensation as deeply as she did herself.

Throwing her head back, Marietje abandoned herself to her ecstasy. She shook with her entire body when he kissed her neck, and she felt her trembling echoed in his arms. She had heard a bird singing somewhere above them before, but now she heard nothing but the beating of her own heart, and the cries of delight that escaped unbidden from her parted lips.

She felt his pace quicken, and she moved with him, eager now for the culmination of her longing. And then, with a wild shout, he lifted her up, clutching her to him with such force that she no longer had any need to hold him herself. She found herself pressed down on the ground, the full weight of his body holding her still.

She had no wish to move, only to keep him there, close to her, until her passion was spent, and he lay quiet above her. She heard his cry and wondered at the high voice that echoed it. The high cry of passion rose again, and she knew, suddenly, that it was her voice—her passion—her ecstasy.

"Oh, my love, I have wanted this ever since that day when we first found this place." Byron's voice broke through her fantasy, and she tensed. It was Dirk she had loved. Only Dirk. Dirk she wanted—here and for the rest of her life. Would she ever share this wonder with him? Was she doomed to hold him close only in the arms of this stranger, this Englishman who had forced himself into her life?

With a rush, her consciousness returned. For one moment she felt a glow of triumph. She had done what she had to do. He would trust her now. He would let her move freely about, as she had not done since the arrival of the English. Now at last she could escape.

He felt her tightness, and he raised his head. "Marietje? Have I hurt you?"

She recovered the power to speak—and to think. "No, Byron, I'm fine. I never knew . . . it . . . could be like this. My mother never—"

"Mothers seldom do. Someday, my dear, I will speak of my thoughts on that matter. Now it can wait. Are you cold?"

She had to think before she could answer. "No . . ." She realized that her answer was wrong. Her back was cold, and she could feel coolness creeping in where his body no longer touched hers. "Yes."

He rose, and she felt the dampness on her body where the heat of his was removed. He stood for a moment above her, naked, unashamed of the slight paunch that marred the manliness of his body. And for a moment, she knew that she was capable of heresy. Seeing her lover-captor, she knew that if she complied with his demands, she would not be sad. She could, if she let herself, learn to love this foreigner. She could forget his age, forget even what he had done to her parents.

A rush of shame wiped the errant thoughts from her heart. Never! This man was her enemy. He had shown her pleasure—but he had introduced her to shame as well. She could never betray her mother and father, betray Pieter's love, forget Dirk—just because another man had shown he could stir her passion. Now, at last, she remembered why she had needed to let him take her in this place. It was so her freedom would be restored. So she could escape. She remembered that she had thought of this once, only a few moments earlier, and it had given her comfort.

133

She rose, brushing at her back to remove the dirt that clung to her body. The ground was damp, as everyplace was during the season of rains. Byron was picking up his garments and pulling them on.

When he saw her move, he paused and fetched her dress and her chemise. He had remarked long ago that he was glad she wore no girdles that disfigured her body, and she had not dared to put one on since that date. Now, once more, she was thankful that she wore light clothing. She took her dress and held it up, searching for signs of soil. It was surprisingly clean, and so she pulled it on and began to struggle with the buttons. He let her work on them alone until he was completely finished, and then he pushed her hands aside and closed the rest of her dress. As he fastened the last buttons at her neck she relaced the bodice, remembering that he had unlaced it while they stood outside the bower. Had a native seen them?

She laughed lightly. Why, she wondered, would that matter? The natives, like Mai, had such an open attitude toward love.

It was then, as she stood ready to depart, that she knew why she should not have permitted this at all. If Dirk were watching! If he had seen her let this man open her bodice, would he wait longer? Would he care to rescue a girl who willingly accepted the caresses of her captor? She blanched at the thought. Why had she been so careless?

"It's begun to rain." Byron took her arm. "We must hurry." She felt herself led out of the shelter, and she glanced upward toward the hills. Was Dirk there, cursing her for a traitor? She stopped, uncertain for a moment as to what she should do. What good would it be, she wondered, if she managed to get free, only to find that Dirk no longer wanted her?

"Come, my love, my dearest." Byron propelled her forward. "I, too, hate to leave this quiet place." He caught her suddenly and held her close, his lips touching each eyelid, and then moving down to her full lips. She was caught unawares, unable to resist, and then she was lifted up and placed on her horse.

She sat passively as Byron mounted his horse. Now, for certain, her life was ended. If Dirk had come to rescue her—and if he had seen this interlude—he would care for her no longer. She felt her tears well up and spill onto her cheeks as she turned away, guiding her horse along the soggy ground back to the house. Ages ago, when she had begun this ride, so confident that it would provide her with the key to her freedom, she had hoped she would return before the rain came and wet her fine riding gown. Now she was thankful for the moisture, for Byron, who glanced over at her again and again, could not see that the wet that stained her cheeks came from her broken heart.

Chapter Fourteen

"Marietje?" Mai stood at the bedroom door, unsure of her welcome.

Marietje looked up from her desk. She had been sitting all morning, ever since Scott left for the day's activities, considering her next move. "I do not need you, Mai. I have learned to care for myself." She hoped the reproof inherent in her words would make her servant ashamed of how badly she had neglected her duties.

"I know that, mistress." Mai stepped forward. "I came to bring you news."

Marietje lifted her head, her eyes wide. "News? What news? Have reinforcements arrived to win back our land?"

A strange smile flitted across Mai's face. Sad, and yet understanding. "No. I bring news of Master Dirk."

Marietje was on her feet. "Dirk?"

"My cousin has arrived from Palembang. He brings news from there that may be of interest to you."

"Yes, yes. Of course it is of interest to me. What has he told you of Dirk?"

Mai seemed determined now to torment her mistress. "My cousin has been a long time on the road. He left Palembang when the fighting between the English and your people was only starting. He could not travel quickly because of the rains and the jungle creatures that seemed especially upset by the heavy flooding."

"Yes, I'm sure he had problems. What about Dirk?"

"He had first to go south to Tandjungkarang Telukbetung to let his father know that he was well and prospering. And then, of course, he stayed for the festivities."

Marietje realized she would learn nothing by showing her impatience. "Festivities?"

"My cousin's sister was married, and his brother had a son. The family is very proud."

136

"How fine for them." Marietje wondered if she could wait until Mai was willing to deliver her news.

"Master Dirk is alive."

Marietje stared at Mai, too startled by the sudden announcement to respond. How like the girl to take her unawares, to throw her off balance in this manner.

"My cousin told me that he was not in Palembang when the English arrived."

"But he was going there. Tell me, please, Mai, where has he gone? Does your cousin know?"

"Master Dirk left on a long journey shortly after he reached Palembang. He took many men and went in search of fine woods for trade."

"You have brought me no good news." Marietje felt tears of frustration fill her eyes. "If he was gone when the English arrived, then he would return without knowing that he was walking into the hands of the enemy."

"So it might seem. But my cousin spoke to Lun Hsiang just before he crossed the mountains, and Lun Hsiang told him that Master Dirk had departed for Padang."

"Padang? When? He is here then?" The memory of her visit to the bower flashed in Marietje's mind. She had been right, then, in suspecting that Dirk might be watching. With a small cry of despair, she dropped back onto her chair. "Oh, Mai, I'm lost!"

Some of the old gentleness returned to Mai's face. She crossed the room swiftly and rested a hand on Marietje's shoulder. "Why should you fear? You have done nothing wrong."

Marietje looked up, a faint hint of pride in her eyes. "I know that. What I have done I did so that I might escape. But will Dirk understand? What if he . . . ?" She did not complete her question. She could not admit to Mai that she had submitted to Byron Scott. Not after all she had said about resistance. "Does your cousin know where Dirk is now?"

"He has heard that Master Dirk is near Bengkulu, with a band of Dutchmen who are determined to win back this land."

Marietje glanced quickly at her companion. How disinterested Mai seemed in the entire conflict. "Surely you care who wins, do you not? The English are invaders. . . ." She paused, acutely aware of Mai's eyes. They were filled with amusement, and anger.

"And what, I ask, were your people? Or mine? We have all invaded Sumatra, and each in turn, as we settle in, feels that the next one is destroying all that is good. Your father was an honest man. He treated his workers fairly. But your father was not like the other men from your country. And even he saw no evil in making slaves of the men and women whose lands he stole."

Marietje felt her face redden. "My father stole nothing! He . . ." She saw the smile on Mai's lips, and she stopped. Was Mai right, after all? She would have to think about that more—later. "You are sure Dirk is still in Bengkulu?"

"No. But that is where he was last seen. There will be a big fight in Padang."

Marietje blanched. "Dirk may be killed! Oh, Mai, I must stop him. Help me, please."

"No." Mai drew back, once more the quiet servant. "You would be killed."

"No. I'll be careful. But I must stop him. Will you take a message for me?"

Mai shook her head.

"Then will you at least promise not to interfere? If I am killed, maybe Dirk will understand how much I loved him."

"Death cannot prove love. Only in life can a woman show her innermost heart."

"That's not true." Marietje restrained herself with effort. "Will you promise not to interfere, to say nothing of what I plan?"

Mai seemed to consider. "Yes, I promise. I would not want it known that I could not persuade you to abandon your foolishness."

Marietje sighed. "A poor reason for faithfulness. But if that is how you feel . . ." She searched Mai's face for some sign of real affection. Instead all she saw was a cool look of equality. They were the same, Marietje knew that. All that separated them was the rank of the men they favored. Marietje's man was the commander. "Well, it is better than nothing. Thank you." Mai turned and started to

138

leave the room. "Oh!" Marietje held out a hand as if to restrain her. "Thank you for bringing me the news about Dirk. I have prayed for his safety."

Mai turned. Now some of the kindness that had been so essential a part of their relationship seemed to return. She lifted her hand as if in benediction. "Be careful, little Marietje. For a woman, honor may be of far less value than life."

She was gone before Marietje could answer, but Mai's words rang in her ears. Were they true? Was her life more important to her than her honor? She shook her head, and the movement turned into a shudder. No! Never! She had compromised herself, but not by her own choice. Byron Scott had forced her, had tricked her into compliance. But if she stayed now? If she made no effort to leave after learning that Dirk was alive? *Then* she would deserve no respect, for she would have betrayed herself.

With sudden resolve, she rose and picked out her sturdiest riding dress and shoes. She donned them quickly and stood before her mirror. Did she have what she would need? She studied the dark green of the gown and felt its material. Strong. But was it sturdy enough to stand up against brambles and branches that might tug at it as she rode through the forest?

She decided it would do, mostly because she had few really sturdy gowns. She had never expected to have to leave her home in this manner. Automatically she patted her curls. Should she bring a brush? What about cleaning herself? Should she also bring soap, and . . . She burst into quiet laughter. Such foolishness! She could bring nothing, except maybe, a bit of food and an oiled cloth to protect her against the rain. She pulled the packet from her closet. This was something her father had insisted that she have, even though he seldom let her step outside when it rained. Now she was thankful. During the winter months, rainfall was heavy.

She was at the door when she paused. She could not rush out clutching the oiled cloth without causing comment. Since that day in the bower, she found her movements unrestricted, but she was still aware that she was watched.

She returned to her wardrobe and drew out a packet of

ribbons. First she tied one around the oiled cloth, making it tight. Then, adding another ribbon to the knot, she measured off a length that would put the packet near her knees if the end of the ribbon was tied around her waist. Lifting her skirt, she fastened the ribbons. The packet bounced heavily against her knees when she tried to walk, and she twisted it around so it hung at her side. This time she found walking easier.

With a small smile of satisfaction, she stepped into the hallway and descended the stairs. Now she could proceed. And if her plans went well, she would sleep this night far from the amorous Byron Scott.

Byron looked up from his desk when she entered the study. "Riding?"

She nodded.

"I wish I could attend you. But I must go into Padang this afternoon." He rose and drew her into his arms. "Do not stay out too long, my dear. The rains can be nasty."

She turned slightly to keep the packet from hitting against him. "I will be careful. How long will you be gone?"

"Unfortunately, at least overnight. I will miss you."

"And I will miss you." She did not look up as she spoke, for she feared he might recognize her for a liar. When she felt his arms move, she stepped free. "Goodbye, Byron."

His eyes widened. "I will not be gone long, my dear." Once more he drew her close, and this time she feared he could not fail to feel the packet hanging from her waist. "How wonderful it is to have your trust and love. I feared, for a while, that I would never feel your full passion except when you thought I was another."

She felt a small regret that she quickly squelched. This was no time for looking back. She was off to find Dirk.

As she waited for her horse to be brought to the door she thought about what Byron Scott had said. He was, she acknowledged, a strange man, a combination of gentleness and cruelty. He had forced himself upon her, and yet he had wanted more than her compliance. He had wanted her love. She realized with a sudden insight that, in a way, he had won even that. For though she told herself that she hated him, she knew it was not quite the truth. He was a man—the enemy. He took no more than any member of a conquering army might expect. But he had been gentle with her—and he had awakened her to love. She would remember him with kindness, even when she cursed him for what he had done to her family.

A stable boy appeared around the corner of the house, leading her mount. She took a step down to meet him. And at that moment a movement behind her drew her attention. Mai stood at the door, a basket in her hand. "Cook made you some lunch. In case you ride farther than you expect."

Marietje took the basket, aware that it seemed unusually heavy. But before she could ask Mai what it contained, the girl was gone.

Byron was at the study window, and as Marietje rode past he waved. She lifted her hand in a farewell salute, struggling within herself to suppress a sadness she had not expected to feel. Then the curtains closed, and he was gone.

She fought with her own emotions as she rode away. Byron Scott had hurt her badly when his men killed her father and mother. But could she hold him responsible for acts that were perpetrated when he was not present? He had taken her against her will. She remembered that painful time with a shudder. And he had tricked her into exposing her vulnerability.

The memory of that night when she had realized his perfidy dried her tears and brought a flush of anger to her cheeks. Why was she sad to leave such a man? Strengthened by her anger, she urged her horse to a gallop, and soon she found herself on the gravel road that led from the plantation down to Padang.

She felt a momentary surprise. No one had challenged her passage. Where were the soldiers who usually guarded the gate? Safe now in the shelter of the brush that edged the highway, she paused and looked back. A high, feminine laugh drew her attention. From behind a shed her father had built to house feed for the work animals, a young native woman emerged, followed by a half-naked soldier. Had it been planned to give her passage?

Now she remembered the basket Mai had given her, and

she opened it a crack. Inside were a few fruits, some toast, and under them a piece of batik cloth and a small waistcoat that was worn by the native women. Mai had given this to her so she would have a change of clothing! She cared, after all! It was possible that this diversion that opened the gates for her exit had also been prepared by her friend.

Marietje took only a moment to consider this possibility, and then she turned her horse's head up toward the mountains. If others had contributed to her escape, she owed them some effort. She could not descend to Padang, for she knew the English soldiers were there. Nor did she dare to attempt to contact any of the other plantations. She would have to hide away, high in the hills, and wait for Dirk to find her.

As she moved northward she considered what place might best serve as her sanctuary. Had Byron not found the bower she would have headed there. But there were other places she had visited with Dirk and Pieter. Places she had spoken about with longing. Where, outside the plantation, would Dirk look for her?

Only one place came to her mind. Her mother had had a favorite servant, a gentle little native woman who came from a village far up the mountains, near Danau Manindaju. A year ago, the woman, whom her mother had called Flower, had returned to her village to care for her ailing mother. Upon her departure, she had invited Marietje to visit her. Dirk and Pieter had both been amused at the invitation, but Marietje had scolded them, and announced that if she ever got tired of their company, that was where she would go.

Would Dirk remember that conversation? If he loved her, he would. And if he did not love her, at least she would be safe among people who cared for her.

Once more she urged her horse into a gallop. She leaned forward, aware that the road that had been kept clear by her father and the other plantation owners was now overgrown with vines that trailed down from the trees and clawed at her hair as she passed. She had traveled some distance before she heard the sound of horses ahead, and she drew rein. Dared she risk an encounter with a group of soldiers? She decided she did not, and she turned her horse toward the woods.

She was well hidden when the band of English soldiers passed. They moved slowly, impeded by a carriage that seemed filled to capacity. Was there, she wondered, some officer of higher rank than Byron Scott? The carriage came abreast of her hiding place, and she caught a glimpse of women inside. They sat quietly, as if afraid to talk. And the soldiers kept them well surrounded. She recognized only one, an elderly neighbor from one of the few plantations that had been cleared above her father's. Then the carriage was past, and the sound of the horsemen grew faint.

When she felt certain that the road was empty, she resumed her journey. But now she no longer dared to gallop, for she knew she could not risk coming upon other soldiers without warning.

By sunset, she was high in the mountains. Her oiled cloth had served her well, for even though the rain had been heavy, she was still dry. The pieces of fruit Mai had used to hide the native dress served as Marietje's lunch.

Now, she realized, came the true test of her resolve. Never before had she been in the forest alone after dark. Around her, the noises of awakening predators sent shivers of fear up her back. A tiger, far in the distance, roared his challenge to some unseen enemy. Above her head, monkeys chattered noisily as they settled down to sleep. If only she, like they, could climb in the trees to find safety!

A vine tugged at her hair, and she jerked free with a cry of alarm. She dared not travel far through the forest, no matter how dangerous the road might be. Maybe, in the morning, she would find the path that Flower had told her led from the highway up the mountain to the village. Had she already gone too far? Frightened and tired, she gazed about her with growing distress. And then she knew what she had to do.

Directing her horse into the shelter of the brush that edged the highway, she sought out a thicket that would hide her, at least during the dark of night. She jumped down then and tied her reins to the brush. Her horse would sleep on his feet, and she would take her rest on his back.

She used the oiled cloth to shelter her from night rain and from any creatures that might descend on her from the trees. To make certain that she did not slip off while she slept, she tied herself to the saddle with the ribbons she had used to conceal the oiled cloth. And then, too exhausted to feel her earlier fear, she closed her eyes.

Her prayer was short. "Dear God, save me from the forest, and from the wild beasts. And lead me to Flower." She paused. There was so much help she needed. "Save Dirk, and bring him to me. Amen." She could not say more. Alone, surrounded by wild animals and in danger of discovery by the English, she dared not ask for anything but her safety—and the safety of Dirk Hendrik. If they could survive and find each other, she would never ask for another thing again.

In her fitful sleep, she dreamed of chases and captures. Fortunately, at least for her rest, she was not tormented by images of creatures that might harm her. She did not hear the rhinoceros thunder past, nor did she feel the presence of the python that hung nearby in the tree. It saw her, and it stirred, moving slowly closer, gliding so silently that even the horse did not hear its approach.

Chapter Fifteen

Dirk shifted uneasily, aware of an insect crawling up his leg. In the weeks that had passed since his meeting with Bernhard he had learned much about the tactics used by the small band of fighters. They dared not make a frontal attack, so they fought like the savages, surreptitiously, striking and vanishing into the brush. When they approached a plantation house, they moved cautiously, searching for the enemy.

They lay now, buried in the underbrush, watching the activities below them. The plantation was not one Dirk knew, yet it resembled the Koenraads' place so closely that his heart ached.

"They aren't here." The man hidden beside Dirk spoke slowly, trying to understand what he saw.

"Maybe they've been locked inside. We can't be sure they're gone." He did not add the words "or dead." That would have been too cruel.

His companion had no such compunction. "They've killed them!"

"No!" Dirk put out a hand to stop his friend from firing at the nearest soldier. "Look! Two women."

"My God!" The gun was lowered. "My Henriette." He raised up and studied the two figures. "And Emilie."

Dirk watched as the two women descended the steps and walked across the roadway to where a carriage waited. Both seemed well. They walked firmly, their heads high. The carriage was open, and Dirk could see the faces of the two women as they took their seats. The younger looked up at the house and spoke quietly to her companion. The other followed her glance and then bent her head.

"Is it possible they haven't been harmed?" Ben put down the glass Dirk had lent him. "They seem willing to go wherever it is they are being taken."

An officer—Dirk thought a lieutenant—appeared at the

door. A horse was led to where he waited, and he mounted. He spoke loudly as he directed his mount to a place beside the carriage. "March! We've a long ride ahead."

The older woman seemed to be studying the underbrush that edged the plantation. Did she suspect her husband might be near? As the lieutenant approached she called out. "Sir? Please, can you tell me how long we will remain in Padang?" Her voice carried easily to where Dirk and Ben lay hidden.

The lieutenant laughed lightly, glancing over his shoulder at his men. "No, madam. You will remain until a ship arrives to carry you home. We do not carry on a war with women."

The older woman glanced again toward the brush. Dirk considered the strange interchange. What was she trying to tell them? And what did the lieutenant mean about a ship arriving for the women? Ben seemed ready to leap out from the shelter of the underbrush, and Dirk caught at his shoulder to keep him from disclosing his hiding place. Then the woman looked away and began to speak softly to her companion. And now Dirk could see that the speaker had been the mother, Henriette, and that she was reassuring her daughter Emilie. Any laughter or seeming lightheartedness was caused by their wish to keep up their courage.

For the officer's sly smile had told Dirk the misery that lay ahead for the women. They were being brought to Padang for the convenience of the troops. He leaned close to Ben. "Have you any other women in your household?"

"Yes. Another daughter." His body stiffened. "Look! I see her, up there in that window." He pointed.

The girl was not easy to locate. Sunlight reflected from most of the windows, making visibility difficult. But he could see a faint outline just above the carriage. A window was lifted, and a figure leaned out. Even from a distance, Dirk could see that this girl was by far the prettiest of the three women. She was not quite as plump, and her features were more refined. Not one of the three was as lovely as his Marietje. Yet this one was obviously to be kept at the plantation for the pleasure of the few men who would

146

remain to manage the native workmen. The other two would end their lives in a brothel in Padang.

Unless he and his friends could interfere. Once more Dirk glanced to where Jan, the appointed leader of his band, sat watching. Would they move now, and save the women? If they began to fire, would the women's lives be endangered? Why did none of the women protest their fate?

Dirk saw the reason for the apathetic farewells as the woman in the upper window leaned forward. Behind her, a man stood with a gun aimed at the two women in the carriage. It was easy to see that she had been warned that if she acted in any way contrary to his wishes, he would shoot her mother and sister. "The bastards!" He muttered the curse under his breath.

Now it was Ben who held up a restraining hand. "We must be patient. It is a long way to Padang, and they evidently plan to stop at every plantation along the way. Our time will come." He moved silently toward the brush behind which Jan crouched. Next to the leader, a young man knelt, his gun cradled on his arm. Dirk moved closer to listen.

Ben spoke quietly as he reached the young man. "Son, you must stay and help your sister. Save her if you can. But do not leave her at the mercy of that English beast."

"Yes, father." The lad's brow was furrowed as he spoke, and Dirk felt certain that he would at all costs avoid killing his sister, even though that was clearly the alternative his father gave him. Ben turned to Jan. "I'm going now."

"Good. You'd better go, too, Dirk." Jan nodded toward the clearing. "They're not quite ready to leave. We must watch their passage. Now that we know their intentions, we must not lose contact with them."

The carriage had not yet arrived when Dirk and Ben reached the next plantation, but it soon pulled in, and as the English soldiers tended to the horses, the women vanished into the house. A rustle in the brush told Dirk that Jan and his men had also arrived.

Ben watched the scene before them with angry impatience. A steady stream of soldiers entered and left the house, and he visualized them violating his wife and daughter. Yet there were no lights upstairs, as there had been when the women first arrived.

A movement drew Dirk's attention and he turned, his gun ready. Jan held up a hand. The signal was clear. Gunfire would draw attention to them. And then Chris stepped from the underbrush. "Father." He approached Ben. "I bring a message from Caroline."

"You talked to her and did not save her?"

"She would not come with me."

"In God's name, why not?"

"She says she is hostage to assure her mother and sister's safety." Chris hurried on. "She told me that mother and Emilie are on their way to Padang to be shipped back to Holland."

"She believes that?"

"They have given her their word. If she stayed and accepted the attentions of the officer in charge."

"You should have killed her." Ben's face contorted in anger. "Surely you do not believe what they have told her?"

"No. But Caroline is convinced. She won't come with me until she hears that mother and sister are both safely on board the ship for home."

"Are they fools?" Ben spoke harshly, his jaw tight. "Can they honestly think that they are to be set free? Can't they see that they are simply being deceived, so they will go willingly to Padang?"

"But why bring them all to Padang? Are there no soldiers located at Bintuhan and Bengkulu?" Dirk was thoughtful.

"Maybe there are new men landing at Padang. Men who are not yet exhausted by the heat and the swamps." Ben gestured toward the plantation. "It's clear they want no harm to come to the fields. They tend the coffee trees and the spices with as much care as I ever did."

"I think there's more than that to this move." Jan stepped beside his comrades. "They do not want us to fight them on this land, for they fear damage to the crops that will reward them for this invasion. As for Padang"—he paused and stared pensively ahead—"I cannot be absolutely certain they do not mean what they say. It is troublesome to care for females, especially when you are at war. If most of the women are brought to one city, more can be done to provide them with what they need—or demand.''

"They will dare to demand things of the army that has conquered them?"

Jan laughed wryly. "I expect nothing less of them. Our women are brave, and very strong. They can take hardships our British friends cannot dream of. And they have their own way of fighting."

Dirk did not respond. He was thinking of Marietje; small, delicate Marietje, who had not the courage to kill an insect, even if it bit her. How, he wondered, could she stand up to men such as this?

The next plantation seemed deserted, except for a few soldiers and the usual number of native workmen, many of whom seemed unaffected by the change in foremen directing their labors. As Jan studied the almost-abandoned house some of his scouts brought a youth they'd found. His name was Gunn, and he steadfastedly kept his face averted from the plantation that so fascinated his companions. When he spoke, his voice was thick with bitterness.

"They killed them all. My mother, my sisters, even the women servants. They seemed to like killing women. And I prayed for death to come quickly, for the men were animals.

"Your father?"

"Dead too. He tried to fight them off when they came. But the natives deserted him, and . . ." The young lad did not finish his sentence. Instead he looked upward at the hills. "I was too far away. I was hunting a tiger that had been bothering the native village. Pater was afraid it might next attack our laborers. When I got here, it was all over. I watched from here as they buried . . . the bodies." He was close to tears, but his anger gave him strength to continue. "I vowed then that I would be revenged on them. I didn't dream that I would have help."

Jan shrugged, his expression solemn. "I can't promise to help you. But I can use your assistance. We believe that the men are bringing the women to Padang to draw us out.

They do not want to fight on valuable farmland. Nor do we. So we plan to follow them until we reach Padang."

He glanced toward the plantation. "If we are right, they will leave a few soldiers to put this land in order and get the slaves back to work. They might leave one of the women here. And depending on the number of men who remain, it might be possible to save the woman at least. Much can be lost if a season passes without proper cultivation of the land. So for the present, we must leave the English to do what we cannot do."

"And you will leave the women to be subjected to their demands?"

"They tell the women that unless they do as they are told, those going to Padang will be killed. And the women seem to think that they are being shipped home."

Dirk shifted uneasily. He could not comfortably put up with Jan's decision to leave the English unmolested just because they seemed willing to tend to the crops. And most of all, he worried about Marietje. Was she the victim of some cruel soldier? Had she already been taken to Padang? The vision of Caroline waving farewell to her mother and sister haunted his thoughts. If Marietje were told that her mother would be safe if she consented to stay with some English officer, would she, like Caroline, comply?

Dirk could wait no longer to learn of her fate. "Jan?"

Jan turned. "Yes?"

"Would it not be wise for some of us to go ahead? Mayhap we could warn some of the women and help them escape before the English reached them."

"That I doubt. What scouts I have sent ahead tell me the English control the entire island. However . . ." He studied Dirk's set features. "You say you come from the Padang area?"

"Yes. The Koenraad plantation is just up the hill from the town."

"I remember." Jan was silent for a moment, thinking. "You understand, do you not, that every man is important? If you get killed, you risk more than your own life. We must have numbers by the time we reach Padang, or we will never succeed in freeing our women."

"Yes, I know, but—"

150

"We can accept no buts. Your life means a lot for our future victory. But there is more than that at stake. If the English even suspect that we have a growing army forming to fight them, they will crush us before we are strong enough to resist them. Our success lies in secrecy."

"Yes. I see that. But if I go ahead, I will be alone. How can I expose your group, even if I am caught?"

"You can be tortured. You must understand, now it is the greater number who matter. Do not let yourself be captured."

"I will not." Dirk was growing impatient. "Nor will I kill English soldiers whose disappearance might lead the English to suspect some organized resistance. And if I fail to save my Marietje, my death will be welcome."

"Damn it, man!" Jan was clearly angry. "You must not let yourself be killed, no matter what happens to your woman. Are you any different from Chris, who had to leave his sister in the hands of the English? We must bide our time, and we must work together. If you do not understand that, it might be best for you to stay here, where you cannot get into trouble."

Dirk restrained his fury. His fists clenched, but he did not let his anger reach his voice. "I'm sorry. It is easy for a man to lose his reason when he considers what is happening to the women he loves. But you are right. I will be caution itself."

"That's better." Jan was placated. "Watch yourself. And keep your ear to the ground. We will need you again."

"Aye." Dirk thought of Hans Koenraad. He used "aye" so often. Then he pushed memories aside. Armed with his gun, a horn of powder, and a bag of shot, he headed away from the silent camp. He felt reasonably safe about traveling at night. The English seemed willing to stay indoors after darkness fell.

For the first time since he met the small band of dispossessed landowners, he felt lighthearted and free. He had been wrong to think he would do well to align himself with others. Alone, he could travel quickly. And he alone knew the Koenraad plantation well enough to rescue any women kept captive there. Cautiously he moved toward the dirt road that served as the only line of communication between the many plantations.

It was empty. He stepped out of the woods and stood for a moment listening. The noises of the forest were all around. Monkeys, disturbed in their sleep, chattered quietly in the trees above him. A small creature dashed across the narrow trail, and somewhere behind him, Dirk heard the leaves rustle. Predators were on the hunt. But he was not in danger of becoming prey.

Boldly he stepped forward, his gun slung over his shoulder. What a relief, after days of creeping through the brush! He threw back his head. The urge to sing was great, for he was on his way to save Marietje. But he kept silent, and soon he was plodding along, mindful always of the sounds about him. Ready to hide if he suspected that English soldiers might be ahead.

He stopped that night just short of the outskirts of Bengkulu. Here, he knew, there would be few if any women who needed his consideration. Bengkulu was a small village—little more. Dutchmen with women to care for did not choose to remain near the coast, where the air was bad and disease rampant. The rain seemed heavier than usual, penetrating even the thicket in which he took refuge. At last, soaked and tired, he ventured close enough to the town to find a shed that seemed unoccupied. Crawling behind some ancient crates that had not been moved for years, he fell asleep.

The sun was shining when he awoke. Had he lost his mind, he wondered, to seek rest in the middle of a British encampment?

The tramp of feet passing by caused him to freeze. Would they find him, and end his life before he even had a chance to look for Marietje? A command rang out. The stamping of feet outside his place of concealment told him that the soldiers were only drilling. Cautiously he settled back. He had no choice but to wait until the activity moved to some other section of town.

"Have you heard the news?" The voice seemed to issue from the wall of the small hut. Dirk waited for more. Evidently two junior officers stood just outside his hiding place.

"You mean about the women? They're being brought down from the plantations. Damn good, too. A man gets tired of a black partner."

Dirk understood enough of the English language to feel a surge of anger. So Jan had been right. The women were heading for brothels, not for a ship that would take them to safety.

"Jack was killed last night."

"Those damn Dutchmen! Jack had a family, you know."

"I've been ordered inland."

"Be careful. Might help to have eyes in the back of your head. Don't any Dutchmen know how to stand up and fight like men?"

The last sentence faded until Dirk could hear no more. He closed his eyes and contemplated what he had learned. For one thing, he knew now that there were many of his countrymen still alive and free, all fighting the English wherever they could be found. Many of them might refuse to join Jan, but they would be valuable anyway, for every Englishman killed in ambush was one less to fight when the final battle began.

And then there was confirmation of his worst fears for the women. For the first time since his departure from the east side of the island, Dirk faced the possibility that Marietje might no longer be alive. Or worse—that she might be at this very moment sharing the bed of some lieutenant.

His jaw tightened at the thought. And then, startled at a new thought, he sat up. Was it truly a fate worse than death? What if he found Marietje and learned that she was no longer the innocent virgin he had left behind? Could he love her still?

He should not. He understood that. A woman besmirched was a woman ruined. Old Hans Koenraad would prefer to see his daughter dead than so disgraced.

But did he, Dirk Hendrik, want her dead if she had been forced to submit to some lusty English officer—or, maybe, a common soldier? Again, he considered his emotions. He felt the pressure of anger mixed with indescribable longing. Could he endure the knowledge that she had been held in another man's arms, even if he knew that she had done so under duress?

For one moment, the conditioning of his class threatened to overpower his love for Marietje. He was of noble blood. His father was a peer of the kingdom. Then, tantalizingly, Marietje's delicate form filled his thoughts. He loved her. More than life itself, more than all the traditions that deemed a woman soiled if she knew any man other than her chosen mate, more than honor or his good name, he loved her.

Why, then, was he wasting time in sleep? Why was he not on the road, hurrying onward to rescue her from whatever danger assailed her?

Once more he turned his attention to the noises outside his shelter. They had died away, until once more he could hear the chatter of the monkeys in the trees and the songs of passing birds. Maybe, if he were cautious, he could make his escape from his haven.

He moved carefully from behind the crates to the small door. Once, he could see, this had been a native hut, and at some time in the past it had been utilized for the storage of empty boxes. Now it was neglected, the containers left to rot. He peered around the open doorframe. The clearing, as far as he could see, was empty. And darkness was coming on fast.

Nevertheless, he moved cautiously. Now that he knew how he felt about Marietje, he wanted nothing to stop him from his planned rescue. Shouldering his gun, he moved silently toward the sheltering woods.

A bullet whistled over his head, and he broke into a run. The next bullet was closer, and he glanced over his shoulder to see where his assailant was located. One lone soldier stood near another shack. He had been cleaning and loading a number of guns, and he was firing them, one at a time, as quickly as he could put one down and pick another up.

Dirk made one massive effort and dove into the woods. As the underbrush closed in around him he heard another bullet whine past his ear. He rolled and sat up. Now he could see that more men were joining his single opponent. They were running into the clearing, grabbing guns and beginning to fire in his direction. Clutching his gun close, he pushed his way through the thicket until he reached a narrow path that he recognized as one of the thousands made by wild animals. They snaked through the jungle, always leading to a stream or a small watering hole. The English, not accustomed to the jungle, might not be aware of such a tiny highway.

The narrow path gave him room for greater speed. He dared not waste time by looking back, for he felt certain that at least some of the men were pursuing him. And so he ran on until, at last, the blanket of darkness hid even the nearby trees from view. He was safe. He paused to listen.

At first all he could hear were the usual jungle noises. And then, suddenly, he heard a twig snap. He froze. No wild animal would walk so carelessly. Nor would a native. Someone was behind him in the night, and only if he were willing to take the time and the risk could he determine if it was friend, foe—or wild beast.

Chapter Sixteen

The path widened. Ahead a small lake glistened in the moonlight. Dirk hesitated only a moment. Nocturnal animals would soon fill the air with their cries. And then the rains would come. He glanced back into the darkness of the woods. Maybe his pursuer was only an animal, after all—not chasing him at all, but only heading for water. Afraid to pass another creature on the same errand.

He listened, but heard no noise. Green eyes glowed in the woods, and a tiger roared nearby. The birds above him, settling down to rest, grew abnormally quiet. Was it the tiger that had frightened them? Or was there something else?

Quietly Dirk moved back along the path he had just traversed. He hugged the underbrush, careful to avoid any possibility of being seen by someone hiding ahead.

A rush just ahead threw him suddenly against the vines, and he caught frantically for some hold to keep him from being dragged back to the lake. A one-horned rhinoceros seemed unaware of his presence as it thundered forward. It snorted as it reached the water, and then grew quiet. Dirk waited without moving for any other mammoth beasts to pass him by. But the forest, temporarily sent into a turmoil, once more settled into normal chattering. Dirk held his place, waiting for whatever had been following him to give itself away.

There was no unnatural sound. Cautiously he moved up the path, ever attentive to each side of the forest. But he could find nothing that might lead him to his pursuer.

Frustrated at last, he turned and moved back toward the lake. He would have to remain on the alert, even when he slept. Abruptly he reached a decision. He would continue to move forward, even during the rain. Maybe he could outdistance whoever it was who followed him.

He skirted the small lake, though he watched with interest the playful infants who seemed unaware of the danger that always surrounded a watering hole. Once he and Marietje had watched baby tiger cubs at play, and he had been forced to restrain her, for she had wanted desperately to take one home for a pet.

Marietje loved baby animals. Once he had dreamed that she would someday love a baby of his.

Was such a dream impossible now? Would she care to be his wife—if he found her? Would she even believe him if he told her he wanted her to marry him, no matter what might have happened to her while he was gone?

For the hundredth time he brushed the thought aside. There was nothing to be gained by such worries. All that mattered was that he find her and save her from further misery. When she was safe once more there would be time for him to speak of his love.

He came to the business road unexpectedly. The narrow path he had been traveling sloped down abruptly, and his foot slid in the wet earth, almost throwing him onto the highway. Catching a branch for support, he sat down to break his fall. This was, he could see, a road that led from Bengkulu up to the plantations. In the daytime, it might be filled with English soldiers. Now it seemed totally empty. This, he knew, would be a good time to get past such a possible danger.

But when he reached the middle of the road, he paused. A stream of water flowed around his feet, but he was barely aware of his discomfort. What drew his attention was an eddy just below him. The road seemed to branch. If this was near the coastal road, he could save many hours of discomfort—and reach Marietje possibly before another week was past. Slipping and sliding, he let the water carry him down to where the separation occurred.

He was across the narrow road now, and facing the coastal passage. Congratulating himself on his good fortune, he caught at a low branch that hung over the road and steadied himself. He pulled at a stick, but it would not break loose. Another was less stubborn. It came away in his hands easily, almost throwing him into the mud that filled the road.

Did he dare keep to the highway? His foot slid as he

moved forward. Would he make any better time in this mire? He braced himself with his walking stick and took a step forward. He knew these roads very well indeed. Within minutes after the rain ended for the night the water would run off, leaving a soggy highway, but one far more easy to traverse than the muddy trails that led through the woods. Some effort had gone into the construction of the highway. Slaves had carried stones down to make a surface that would be usable throughout the year. An advantage now for the English. But one that could benefit him, as well.

Seeking the high side of the road, he was able to find more even footing, and as he had expected, his struggle to move swiftly was eased. Once again, he felt the surge of optimism. Everything would be well, once he found Marietje. In the light of such an outlook, even the rain seemed less of a bother.

He came upon the soldiers with no warning. There were two, struggling with a cart that had become mired at the side of the road. Leaping up into the underbrush, he approached cautiously.

"Damn this beast! Can he not pull one little cart out of a small mud sink?" The soldier who spoke kicked at the offending wheel. Dirk could see that the man was covered with mud from head to foot, evidently from unsuccessful attempts to pull the cart back onto the highway.

"We must stop. This poor beast is near dead." A young man held the halter of the struggling horse. He, too, was black with mud, and soaked to the skin.

Dirk held his breath. Here were English soldiers—alone. Even Jan had agreed that such men could be killed without alerting the English army to the possibility of an organized attack. As for himself, Dirk was certain that a sudden ending of any attacks on the English would alarm the officers in charge far more than if they continued as they had ever since the invasion.

He raised his rifle and took aim at the man fighting the wheel. This, he felt certain, was the man to hit first, for the other would be forced to contend with a frightened horse and would have no time to shoot back. Even so, he would have to reload quickly.

Suddenly from somewhere beside him one shot rang out. The man with the horse fell to the ground. Immediately Dirk pulled his trigger. The second man, bent over the wheel, fell before he had time to realize what was happening.

Dirk waited. A rustle in the underbrush beside him told him where his unknown assistant was hiding. Loudly, so as to be heard over the rain, Dirk called his thanks. The movement of the leaves increased, and abruptly a lad of about fifteen stepped into view. He held his gun at the ready, aimed directly at Dirk's head. "Friend?" He spoke Dutch. Dirk stood up, so he, too, was exposed.

"Friend. Is your family close?"

"My family is dead. My brothers and I got away." He lowered his gun and gestured toward the horse, who now stood docilely. "The horse is yours. We dare not keep any here." He stepped closer. "You go to Padang?"

"Yes. You have heard of our plan?"

"Yes."

"You and your brothers must join us. We can use all the guns was can get."

"No. There is nothing waiting for us in Padang. We live now to avenge our mother's death. And when the English are gone, we must be ready to take over the plantation once more."

Dirk considered. "Your brothers are children?"

"Younger than I, yes." He moved toward the cart. "You may have the horse. I must have the food that is in the cart."

Dirk patted his shoulder bag. "I have no need for more food. But I appreciate the mount. It is far to Padang, and the road is difficult."

"You may not be able to keep him. It is not easy to hide a horse."

Dirk laughed. "You are very right. But I shall let that concern me when a problem arises. Thank you now, for your aid. And success in your battle."

The lad smiled a quick tight smile. "And to you, sir. God go with you."

As Dirk continued on, sitting now on the bare back of the rescued horse, he considered the plight of the boy and his young brothers. Had he been wrong to leave them?

They were but children. Like the children he and Marietje might someday have—if they survived this terror.

The thought of Marietje gave him his answer. He had no reason to interfere in the boys' lives, and since the lad he had met seemed both capable and sure of himself, the brothers were probably better off where they were. For certain, adding children to his party could only delay his journey, and increase the chances of his being caught. Satisfied that he had done the only possible thing under the circumstances, he turned his attention to what lay ahead.

He felt the smoothness of the muscles of the horse beneath him, and he reached down to pat the beast's neck. What a find! With a mount, he could reach the Koenraad plantation in a matter of four days or so. On foot, he could be on the trail for more than two weeks. Pleased, he urged the animal into a trot.

His action had been ill advised. One moment he was riding high on the animal's back. The next he lay sprawled on the road, and the horse was screaming in agony.

"Damn!" Dirk pulled himself up and reached for the horse's halter. He could see the problem. The children had dug more than one hole in the road, and the poor beast had caught his foot. Now his leg was broken.

The horse lay quiet now, his big eyes focused on Dirk's face. "Sorry, old boy." Dirk pulled his gun from over his shoulder and aimed it at the hore's head. "Sorry." He pulled the trigger. When the noise died away, he turned without looking at the dead animal. Never, even when there were many horses available, had he liked to destroy a good beast. Now, when he needed the mount more than he had ever needed one before, the act pained him even more.

He sat at the side of the road, out of sight of the carcass, and reloaded his gun. Then he resumed his journey. How far had he traveled before the horse was hurt? Not more than a mile. Fate, it seemed, was determined to make his journey difficult. Yet, though he had reason to be concerned with his own safety, it was not of that he thought as he moved along. Try as he would, he could not banish the vision of the trusting eyes of the injured beast from his mind.

He managed to cover no more than five miles before

light appeared in the sky. The rain stopped, and the road began to drain. Travel would be easier, but not for him. He could not risk being seen by Englishmen. Feeling terribly depressed, he headed for the cover of the forest. Maybe, he hoped, he would do better during his next night's journey.

He woke at noon. A light shower had dampened his shirt, and now a wind chilled him. The sound of a carriage drew his attention. Cautiously he approached the road. A different carriage—and different women. Yet they, like Christopher's mother and sister, seemed content to be moved from their homes. Dirk tried to hear what was being said by the English soldiers who escorted the carriage, but he failed. Yet he felt reasonably certain that these women, too, were being taken to Padang, and that they believed they were on their way back to the Netherlands.

Or did they? He recalled once more the actions of the two women whom Ben identified as his wife and daughter. They had, it was true, gone peacefully with the English soldiers. Yet he could not believe they were fools enough to really think they would be freed.

And then there was the silence during that one stop when he and Ben had watched from above the plantation house and seen men enter and leave. Both he and Ben had suspected what might be taking place in the upstairs rooms. But there had been no outcry, no sounds of protest from the women. Why were they so docile?

What would make Marietje docile to such mistreatment? Only one thing! She would put up with anything, he was sure, to save her father and mother. What would the English have to offer the women in exchange for their surrender?

The answer was clear. Only one prize would seem worth such a sacrifice—the lives of their men! The English did not care what falsehoods they uttered, as long as they got their way. By persuading the women to come to Padang peacefully, they were drawing all the Dutchmen on the island toward that city. The women knew that, but they believed that their husbands and sons and lovers would be captured and exiled with them. It was the only explanation of what was going on that made any sense at all. The women believed that for their cooperation they were to be given their own lives, and the lives of their loved ones.

Dirk smiled wryly. He knew the few Dutch women who lived in Sumatra. They were brave, courageous, strong people. They loved their homeland. And many lived in Sumatra only because that was where their men had brought them. They had no love for the tropical wilderness. They had, most of them, lost children to the fevers, and sisters and friends to sicknesses unknown in the cool, crisp climate of Holland. It would be easy for the English to use the natural longing of the women against them.

And against the men whom they loved. He quickened his pace. Marietje needed him now. How could he reach her before she, too, was caught in the web of intrigue?

He traveled now with a dull persistence that kept his fears at bay. He dared not consider Marietje's dangers until he was close enough to help her. His own perils were too great. More than once he crouched beneath some broad-leafed vine as soldiers tramped past, searching for their enemies. More than once he hid and watched yet another carriage begin the long journey to Padang. And each time, as he resumed his journey, it was with renewed vigor. He had to reach Marietje. He had to save her. His life would be worthless if he did not succeed.

He ran out of food after a week of walking. But though this did cause him additional delay, he felt in no danger of starving. Wild fruit grew all through the jungle. Nuts were abundant. And though some of the food grew beyond his reach, enough could be found within a short distance of the ground to supply his needs. It was the time he resented, for he had to devote some of his waking hours to gathering food that would keep up his strength, leaving him less safe time for travel.

Too impatient to endure the delay, Dirk began to spend extra hours pushing his way through the forest. And at last, after two tiring weeks of forced marches, he found himself approaching familiar ground. Like a horse heading for the barn at the end of a long journey, he quickened his pace. And in his eagerness, he grew careless.

He still traveled by night, yet now, with the Koenraad plantation so close, he did not let the coming of dawn end his forward push. He was within five miles, he estimated, of the road that led up to the Koenraad plantation. He would stop when he reached that turnoff.

Maybe it was his fatigue, or maybe it was his preoccupation with what lay ahead, that caused him to be unaware of the sound of hoofbeats behind him. All he knew was that a soldier on horseback was upon him before he could raise his gun.

All that saved him was surprise, for the horseman was as unprepared for the encounter as was Dirk. He drew his horse up, almost spilling himself in the process, and turned to face the bedraggled man who had already regained his senses and was running toward him with fire in his eyes.

Dirk, recognizing immediately the impossibility of escape, determined that his best defense was to attack. So he headed toward the horse, shouting loudly to keep the beast upset. He grabbed the reins of the animal and tried to pull the rider to the ground.

But by this time the soldier had also recovered, and he resisted the sudden tug on his arm. He could not draw his gun from its place behind him, but he felt certain that he could at least get free of his assailant's grip. And then he would kill the man.

Dirk was determined not to let this happen. Once more he tugged at the man's arm, but at the last moment, he did not actually exert any force. The soldier, leaning back to avoid being dislodged, now fell backward, his leg swinging out as he struggled to regain his balance.

This was what Dirk had hoped would happen. Grabbing the man's foot, he pulled it from the stirrup and pushed upward. Helpless, the soldier toppled. Immediately Dirk slapped the rump of the horse, sending it on its way. Now at least the battle was even. Crouching slightly, he prepared for the fight.

In doing so, he knew he was violating Jan's orders. This man had to die. But Dirk was not a soldier. He had learned that he could shoot from a distance and see his victim fall. But he could not shoot a man in cold blood, as he had been forced to shoot the injured horse.

The soldier was on his feet now, recovered from his fall and ready to continue the fight. He roared as he faced

Dirk, filled with anger at his upset, and aware of his disadvantage. In losing his horse, he had also lost his weapon.

"A bit of luck. It will not last." The soldier spoke as he bounced lightly before Dirk, like a boxer waiting for his opponent to show his weakness.

Dirk noted the uniform. This was not a mere militiaman. He was preparing to wrestle with a Lieutenant. And one who seemed to be intent upon delivering the packet that still hung from his shoulder.

"I deal in more than luck." Dirk forgot his fatigue in the excitement of the struggle.

"Truly. You had best prepare for your death. Unless you have another trick up your sleeve, for I shall surely kill you."

Dirk did not bother to answer. Bracing himself, he prepared to respond to the man's attack.

The expected lunge did not come. A shot rang out somewhere in the forest nearby, and the man dropped to the ground; a hole in his chest had ended his life. Too shocked to move quickly, Dirk stared at the body before him. This was the second time he had been assisted by a stranger. Was the lad he had met weeks before still following him?

Suddenly he felt his arm grabbed. He turned in alarm to face this new assailant, but he was not able to move in his own defense. He struggled as he felt himself pulled from the road into the forest. A man, bearded as he was, pushed him roughly to the ground. "No time to run. We'll just have to hope they don't search too well." The voice was gruff, almost angry, but the expression of the speaker was kindly. "A good trick, that. Not many men can unseat a rider without a horse of his own."

"Who are you? Why did you shoot him?"

"Why? Man, do you want to be killed? Or captured?"

Dirk shook his head. He understood the man's action now. A moment longer spent in man-to-man wrestling, and the fight would have been over. For the horse had served as messenger to the soldiers in Padang. A platoon was on its way out to rescue the lost rider, or to find his assailants.

Dirk felt a chill of anticipation as the sounds of the approaching soldiers grew louder. This, he knew, might be the end of his journey. But if he had to die, he would take as many men as possible with him. That was the least he could do for Jan—and for Marietje.

Chapter Seventeen

In the days that followed, Dirk stayed close to his new friend. He met more men, banded together like those who followed Ben to accomplish what no one could do alone. He was impatient to move on, yet he knew it was important that he know more about the organized defenses of his land before he started on alone toward the Koenraad plantation.

"There, to the left. Someone's hiding." Andrew spoke quietly. "Stay still. I'll use our signal."

Dirk nodded, his eyes fastened on the place where he had moments before seen a branch move. Beside him, his companion let out a low whistle like that of one of the rarer woodland birds. Then they waited.

There was no response. Andrew bent his head close to Dirk's. "It is not one of ours. But I doubt it is an Englishman. They see no reason for hiding."

"Another recruit, then?"

"Maybe. Let us hope it is not another child. Far too many have been orphaned in this fighting." Andrew stood up. "Friend?" He spoke in Dutch.

The branch stirred once more, and a broad-shouldered man appeared. "Friend." He spoke Dutch, too, in a thick guttural voice that brought Dirk to his feet.

"Frans! Frans Johannson!" He plowed forward through the underbrush until he stood beside his neighbor. "I feared that all the plantations here had been wiped out."

"Nay, selectively destroyed." Frans's voice was filled with bitterness. "The British are careful to save the crops and the natives who care for them. They captured my plantation while I was away, clearing ground for new trees. I think they murdered my family."

"You saw them?"

"Nay. I crept back into the empty house after the British had departed. God knows why they did not remain.

And there was no one. My wife was gone—and my son. The British do not take captives. I think Gerda and Willem were shot as they tried to escape into the forest. I searched for them, but so far I have not found them." His jaw tightened. "But I will. I will not leave their bodies to be food for the wild animals."

Dirk contemplated the fate of his neighbor's family. Gerda had been heavy with child. She could not run far from the guns of the enemy. Willem might have escaped, if he did not try to help his mother. Dirk shook his head. Frans was right. They were both dead. Willem would not desert his mother if she were in need.

"Have you news of Hans Koenraad and his family?" Dirk felt an uneasiness in the pit of his stomach as he waited for an answer.

"Dead. All dead. I myself saw Hans fall when the British arrived in Padang, and my foreman witnessed the slaughter of Johanna and Marietja." Frans shook his head from side to side as he spoke. "Everyone is dead. There is nothing left for us but revenge."

Revenge. Dirk felt a protest rising in his breast, and he knew that he would never accept the word of another regarding the fate of Marietje. "Did your man see their bodies? All of them? What about Pieter?"

"I'm sure he is dead, too. My man saw it all."

"Did he say he saw Marietje?" Dirk could not add the word *die*. There was something too final about it.

"Why do you press me so? See for yourself, if you do not believe my word!"

"I will. Forgive me, neighbor, but that is something I have to do." Dirk turned to Andrew. "Frans is a good man and an excellent fighter."

"Good. You speak as if you think he should replace you. You are not coming with me?"

"No. I cannot." Dirk glanced up the hillside toward the Koenraad plantation. "I must see for myself what has happened. If she is alive . . ." He did not finish his sentence. What, he wondered, would he do if he found Marietje alive? Could he rescue her from the plantation and ask her to live in the forest, without protection from wild beasts and rainfall?

"You will join us later?" Andrew seemed reluctant to let Dirk go.

"Yes." Dirk turned to Frans. "You know the mill, up the river from Padang?"

Frans nodded.

"I will meet you there in a week. If I survive. And I will continue the search for the bodies of your loved ones."

Frans smiled faintly. "I pray God that you succeed where I have not. I cannot bear the thought that my wife . . ." His voice broke, and he grew quiet.

Dirk caught his shoulder in one hand and held it firmly. "Do not despair. Have you considered that they might be alive, and hiding?"

"Aye. But I gave up that hope long ago. Gerda was near her time. How could she survive? And Willem is but a lad. . . ."

Dirk did not wish to hear again the tale of misery. "Nevertheless, I will search for them." He took Andrew's hand and shook it. "Good-bye for now. I promise I will return."

He turned without further words, and headed upward, pushing his way cautiously through the underbrush. How easy it would be, he thought, were he able to use the highway. But that road belonged to the English. To venture out upon it would mean certain death.

The Johannson plantation lay immediately above him, and he headed in its direction. Frans had said the English did not remain in the great mansion he had built for his young wife. Was it possible the building was still empty? If so, he might use it as a place to rest, and to bring Marietje to when he rescued her. Turning in the direction of the buildings, he resumed his slow pace forward.

He paused as he reached a cave that had once been used by the Johannson family to preserve foodstuffs. Carved deep into the earth by nature, it had been widened and made more accessible by Frans himself, and had, in fact, served as shelter for the busy farmer during his first days in Sumatra, before he brought his bride from Holland. Long ago, the entrance had been boarded up, to keep little Willem from losing himself in its many lower chambers.

Had Frans looked in this cave for his family? He made no mention of such a shelter. It was possible, Dirk realized, that in his despair, Frans had forgotten this natural hideaway. "I owe it to my neighbor to look here before I go on. I told him I would watch for his family." Dirk realized, with a start, that he had spoken aloud, and he paused, waiting and listening, to be certain he had not attracted British attention.

The woods seemed quite normal. A few chattering monkeys, a bird or two flitting down from the tops of the tall trees to nests closer to the ground. The buzz that seemed never to stop, and which grew louder at sunrise and sunset.

Reassured, Dirk headed for the mouth of the cave. At first glance it appeared to be boarded up as tightly as ever, and for a moment, Dirk considered proceeding without further investigation. He was, after all, heading north to save Marietje, not to locate bodies of the dead.

He took another step, and paused. The framework of the barricade was loose. Someone had pulled the boards away and then carefully propped them back up. He moved to the right and peered inside, but he could not penetrate the darkness. Yet something held him there. What? He glanced down at the rough dirt underfoot and knew. The rain should have turned the dirt into a smooth surface. Someone had scraped the earth. Again the question. Why?

He smiled. To eliminate footprints. A foolish need, since each night the dirt was wiped clean of marks by the rainfall. Yet wouldn't a child, and a distraught woman expecting to deliver a baby, be apt to make such a mistake of judgment?

He grasped the boards and pulled them loose. When he was inside the cave opening, he reached down and pulled them back and reached out to wipe away his telltale steps. Then he turned and moved cautiously into the darkness. "Willem? Gerda? It's I, Dirk Hendrik."

"Dirk?" The voice was feminine, and shaking with fear.

"Yes." He stood still, waiting for directions.

In the dimness that his eyes could now begin to penetrate, two figures appeared. One he recognized as Willem

Johannson. The other was Gerda. It was the woman who spoke first. "Dirk, thank God someone has come. We are almost out of food."

He stepped forward and caught her arm. "Are you all right? The child . . . ?"

"My time has not yet come. Willem has taken good care of us."

"Thank God." Dirk looked frantically about for a place for them to sit. The rains had begun, and he felt a strange comfort in the knowledge that his footsteps were now totally obliterated. "Frans has searched for you. He is with some others now, readying an attack on Padang."

"He's alive? Thank God. Willem, your papa is alive!"

The lad smiled faintly, but he continued to say nothing.

Dirk turned back to the woman. "I do not recommend that you try to reach him. Below us, the countryside is overrun with English soldiers. Is there anyplace where you can go to deliver your child. This cave is far too dank."

The lad spoke at last, his voice low, as if he feared he might be overheard. "We were heading for the native village just above our plantation. My old nursemaid lives there. Mother says she is a good midwife."

Dirk met the boy's gaze. In the darkness, the fear in the lad's eyes could still be discerned. Was it fear for his own safety?

"I chose to stop here. Mother cannot walk that long a distance, and I cannot carry her. I was going to find the village and bring Kala here."

"You can't stay here, especially after the baby is born. This is far too close to the plantation houses. If the English return, you are certain to be discovered."

The lad tensed. "I'll kill anyone who tries to come in."

"Like you killed me? Don't you see? You cannot guard this entrance day and night." Dirk looked again at the pregnant woman. She was small, almost fragile. "I'll carry your mother. Do you know the way to the village?"

For the first time since his arrival, Dirk saw Willem smile a true smile. "Yes." The lad moved toward the entrance. "We can be there before daybreak if we leave now."

"Then let us be gone." Dirk bent and lifted Gerda up

with one smooth movement. Even carrying the child, she was light. Then he followed Willem through the opening out into the rain.

They moved swiftly, daring to take the road because they knew that in the rain the Englishmen would seek shelter. Dirk moved carefully, aware that his feet found little beneath them that was not slippery with mud. Once, he almost fell, and he threw one arm out to brace himself. And then one of his feet hit a rock, and he was on solid ground once more. Ahead of him, Willem turned and reached out to help. But the danger was over quickly, and they went on their way.

When they came opposite the Koenraad plantation, Dirk paused once more. This was his objective. Here lay the goal of his long search. Was Marietje sleeping now, inside the quiet plantation, safe from the rain and from the marauding Englishmen?

Ahead of him, Willem realized that Dirk had stopped. He turned and spoke in a whisper. "Hurry. The rain is almost ended."

Dirk knew the danger. With the end of the rain would come the morning. And they would not be safe on the road after dawn.

"Maybe she is safe, after all. We made our escape, and I am clumsy with my baby. Marietje is young and strong."

Dirk shook himself and moved forward once more. It was embarrassing to think that the woman he carried could so easily read his thoughts. Yet it was also comforting to know that she could still offer him encouragement. "We had better move into the woods. It is growing light."

He spoke to the lad, and Willem moved as if obeying a command. As the brush closed over them Dirk turned for one last look at the plantation where he had spent his youth.

At that moment, a shot rang out. Instinctively Dirk bent forward, as if to protect his burden from the bullet. He felt the blow of the missile, but at first his body did not respond to the wound. He moved forward, barely aware of his action, until he was out of sight of the road and far from view of the plantation he had called home. And then, gently, so as not to hurt Gerda, he sank to the ground.

He was barely aware of Willem rushing to his side, but he felt the cool touch of a small hand on his forehead. Then a rag was tied over his head, half covering his eyes. He reached up to brush it away. "What happened?"

"You've been hit on the forehead. I think the bullet just grazed you." It was Gerda's voice, and her cool hand that soothed him.

He turned to Willem, who hovered nearby. "How much farther do we have to go?"

The lad leaned close, as if he were afraid he would not be heard. "The village is very close. Just ahead. I'll go for help."

"Who shot me? Was it an Englishman?"

"No." Again, Gerda spoke. "I saw him run as you turned. It was one of the Koenraads' workmen. Frightened, I suppose. And unacquainted with a rifle. I wonder how he got his hands on such a weapon?"

Dirk felt a surge of hope. Maybe, even if the British had occupied the plantation, they were not in total control. He turned to Willem. "Go. I'm not sure I can stay conscious until you return, and your mother has no other protection." Had he finished the last sentence? He wasn't certain. His head was spinning wildly.

Vaguely he saw the lad turn and run up the path. He tried to focus on Gerda Johannson, but she seemed to fade before his eyes. Was the night really growing darker? What had happened to the dawn? He tried to brush the film from his eyes, and his fingers touched blood. A sharp pain shot through his head, and the darkness closed in.

Chapter Eighteen

"Look! He's awake!" The voice was soft; a native woman, Dirk was certain. So he was safe in the village, in spite of his wound. He wondered who had carried him the rest of the distance. And then the thought vanished. His head ached painfully, and his eyes stung.

He opened them and looked about. This was a typical native village, with neat homes made of palms and branches from the forest. Everything seemed spotless, yet he could see that he rested on a small pad directly on the mud floor. The idea came to him that the women must work constantly to keep dust out of their dwellings and to maintain the high level of cleanliness that seemed so typical of all their villages.

A pale light filtered in through an open window, illuminating the small, almost circular room. He lay against a wall that was decorated with woven palms. Across from him sat a woman, weaving a piece of cloth from a pile of thread she had obviously spun herself. She was looking at him now, with large, dark eyes filled with unfathomable sorrows. She smiled when she met his eyes and spoke again. "Willem. Your friend is awake."

Willem appeared in the doorway, momentarily closing off some of the filtered light. He approached Dirk's side and paused. "Mother and I have been praying for you. I am thankful you are awake again."

Dirk mustered his energies and braced himself on one arm. "How long have I been asleep?"

"Not long. We reached here yesterday. I have a baby sister."

"Already?" Dirk glanced about. Where was Gerda?

Willem answered his unvoiced question. "She's in the women's hut." His voice dropped. "Kala isn't sure she will live."

"Your mother?"

"No." He tried to smile at Dirk's mistake and failed. "My sister. I wish there was a minister here. She should be baptized."

Dirk considered the problem. He pushed himself up into a sitting position. "I was a witness at your baptism. Maybe we can do it ourselves."

Willem smiled. He held out a hand to help Dirk rise and stepped beside him as they moved away from the pad. When they reached the door, he paused. "Thank you, Kala. You are a good nurse. I wish you could save my sister, too."

"I wish I could, too." Dirk felt a momentary surprise at Kala's perfect Dutch. "She is very weak. You will be sick, too, master, unless you stay in bed. It is easy for the heat sickness to come when the body is not strong."

Dirk turned. "I'll be back. But I have to see Gerda and the baby."

He was not permitted into the women's house. When he persisted, Gerda was brought to the door. She held the infant close against her breast, and she showed no shame that Dirk should see her so exposed.

He glanced at the baby, and his heart ached. It was so frail! So tiny! The strain had brought Gerda to delivery before her time. Would it live?

Gerda held the baby out toward him. "Do you know the words of the Scriptures? She must not die without the redeeming water."

He took the child and cradled it in his arms. "I know them. What name do you wish to give her?"

"Henriette." Gerda sank back onto her litter, but her eyes did not leave the child. "Willem, get Dirk Hendrik some water."

When Willem held up the vessel of water, Dirk dipped his fingers in it and touched the child's head once. "I baptize you, Henriette Johannson, in the name of the Father .. ." He dipped his hand again and brought it to the infant's head for the second time. ". . . and the Son . . ." Again, he repeated the gesture. ". . . and the Holy Ghost. Amen." He placed the infant in her mother's arms and knelt beside the litter. "I think we should say the Lord's Prayer."

Willem knelt beside him, and the three began to recite the well-known phrases. When Dirk opened his eyes and raised his head, he realized that some of the natives had joined them. Not surprising, he knew. Frans Johannson felt it was important to teach the story of God to the natives who worked for him.

As she rose Kala tugged at Dirk's arm. "Now you go to bed. Tomorrow, maybe, you will be strong enough to travel."

Dirk let himself be led back to the hut. He lay down with a feeling of relief. Kala was right. He was not yet ready to move on.

Each day he tried to rise, and though he usually succeeded in getting up, he found that his endurance was limited. He could walk to the women's hut and visit Gerda. He could wonder each time that the baby still lived. But then he would be overcome with a great weakness, and he would return to his own bed and his own healing.

He counted the days with impatience, breathing a sigh of relief when, on the seventh day, he was able to remain up without dizziness. When he spoke to Gerda he found his optimism increasing. She was better, too, and the baby showed signs of progressing. Maybe if they could get to other Dutch women who could care for them properly, they would both survive.

Dirk glanced at Willem, who stood beside his mother with an expression of eagerness he had not shown in the past week. "It looks as if we can leave. But where do you think to go now?"

"You said Papa was alive. I had hoped we might go and stay with him."

" 'Tis a strain being the only man in the family, isn't it?" Dirk's smile was sympathetic. "But how do you expect to travel all the way to the coast? And how are we to find your father? I had a meeting planned, but this"—he touched his forehead—"has kept me from keeping my bargain. He might be anywhere."

"You found him once, didn't you?"

"By accident. I can't promise that I can do that again."

"But I can. When Papa and I used to ride into Padang,

we stopped for lunch at a small bay below our plantation. If we go there, Papa will find us."

Dirk turned to Gerda. "You want to take such a risk?"

"It is not a risk. I can travel now, and I will care for Henriette. We must join my husband. He still thinks we are dead."

"It is not what I would advise. Why don't you stay here, where you are safe, and I will find him and tell him you are alive. Then if he thinks you will be better off with him, he can send for you, or come for you himself."

"I do not want him risking his life to bring us where we can go by ourselves. If you do not escort us, we will make the trip alone."

Dirk looked into Gerda's eyes and bowed his head. She would not be dissuaded. He could see that. "Shall we leave now?"

"That would be nice. But I suspect you would prefer to wait until sunset."

"Will the baby not be harmed if we travel in the rain?"

"Kala has provided palm leaves to shelter her. And I will carry her against my body, as the native women do. Their children seem to endure the rains with no problem."

"Yes, but they do not suffer from the heat sickness, either."

Gerda hesitated only a moment. "She will be all right. We must go."

They departed after sunset, before the rains began. As they moved along the narrow footpath the natives used to travel from the village to the Johannson plantation, Dirk considered his position. He still had only one goal—to rescue Marietje. Yet here he was again, escorting other people to safety. Would he ever be free to consider his own desires? As they passed the plantation that had been home for Willem since his birth, Dirk turned to the lad. "I think the house is empty. Are there some foodstuffs or clothing you wish to salvage?"

Willem glanced at his mother. "Mama? Shall I get some blankets for the baby?"

"Yes. And a bedroll for us. I will look for food."

It seemed strange to Dirk to find the kitchen empty. He stood at the door while Gerda searched the cupboards, and

176

he glanced nervously toward the back stairs, which Willem had taken up to the second floor. When he heard the sound of footsteps, he straightened up and moved toward the doorway, ready to attack if a British soldier appeared.

Willem pushed his way into the kitchen, pulling an armload of blankets behind him. "I tried to carry them, but they're too heavy."

Dirk laughed. "You think we can carry them through the forest?"

Willem looked abashed. He glanced toward his mother, who had stopped her search, and was studying him with a small smile on her lips. "Did I take too many, Mama?"

"Yes, little Willem, you took too much. But I thank you, anyway. It shows me that you love your mother and your little sister."

"Oh, yes." Willem looked disappointed. "Can we take any blankets at all?"

"Yes." Gerda stepped forward and pulled one blanket free from the others. It was smaller and lighter. It had come from Willem's bed. "Will you let your sister use your blanket?"

"She can have anything I have, Mama." Willem reached out and took the infant hands in his own. "She will live, won't she?"

"That is in God's hands. All we can do is try to keep her warm. I thank the Lord that my milk has begun to flow, for she will not go hungry." Gerda turned to Dirk. "Shall we go on. This is painful. I wonder if we will ever be a happy family living in peace in our own home again."

"We must. Either that, or we will all be dead."

Night travel downhill proved far easier than Dirk had expected it to be. They risked using the road, though they stayed close to the side so they could hide quickly if they heard anyone ahead of them. When they reached the clearing from which they could see the ocean, Dirk paused. How could he decide which way to go? Where were the men hiding? Near Padang? Closer to Bengkulu?

"We will go this way." Gerda found a narrow path that led off from the road. "It will take us to the coast."

"When I planned to meet Frans, we set to get together

at the old mill, to the right from here. I think you should go there."

Gerda glanced in the direction Dirk pointed. Then she turned back toward the ocean. "No. He might have planned to stay there to meet you. But we will be safe at Willem's hideaway. I know. Frans built a shed there so he and the boy would find shelter when they went to town. We have food there, and a place for us to sleep. You may go to the mill if you wish. If you meet Frans, tell him where we have gone."

Dirk studied the tiny woman. Very clearly, her weakness before the delivery of the baby was over. She felt in charge, for she still considered Dirk to be more like another child than her equal. For a moment Dirk cursed his youth, and then he paused. He probably was no younger than Gerda, herself. His handicap was not his youth, but that he had been a servant at Hans Koenraad's plantation, while Gerda was the wife of a plantation owner.

He considered the dangers that lay ahead, and his own impatience to get about the business of saving Marietje. "You will take precautions?" She nodded. He pursed his lips. "No, I still cannot allow you to go by yourself. I will see that you are settled in your shelter, and then I will set out to find my Marietje."

"If you insist." Gerda resumed the journey. Willem moved ahead, and Dirk fell in behind.

When they reached the coast, the sun was rising, painting the sky with rich golds and deep purples. The shed stood where Gerda had said it would be, and when she unlocked it with a large key Willem took from his pocket, Dirk saw that it contained two narrow cots and a cabinet.

He stood at the door and watched as Gerda settled into one bed and began to nurse the infant. Willem stood just inside the cabin, as if preparing to bid a welcome guest farewell.

"You will be careful?" Dirk glanced at the woman. "You must not let your mother be captured."

"I will take care of her. What reason would they have to come here?"

"Who knows? I cannot predict what the British will do." He stepped outside. "Keep a lookout. I will try to send your father to you." He turned quickly and strode away. Before he passed from sight of the cabin, he turned. Willem still stood watching him. He waved, and moved away. What a strange world it is we live in, he thought. That a child should be given so great a responsibility.

He glanced down at the path, and stopped. In the soft dirt, his footsteps would serve as a guide to anyone seeking fugitives. With a groan, he turned and traced his steps until he reached the edge of the grassland where the cabin stood. From that point on, the wind and the grasses themselves served to obliterate the trail.

He turned and searched the forest until he found a branch that might serve his need. Then he once more returned to the path and resumed his journey. However, now he traveled backward, scraping the stick behind him over the dirt to obliterate the indentations that had been made by his shoes, and those of Gerda and Willem. When he reached the clearing where they had turned from the road, he moved from one path's head to the next, repeating his scraping action. If a British soldier should seek to follow them, he would have trouble deciding which path to take.

A ray of sunshine touched his shoulder, and Dirk paused. He was risking capture now, for the British would be on the move soon. With one final glance at his handiwork, Dirk pushed himself into the woods, seeking a shelter where he might rest.

He located a strong tree with wide, overhung branches, and he settled on the lowest branch. He might be able to sleep there all day if he was fortunate. And then, at nightfall, he could resume his quest. He would have to retrace his steps until he reached the Koenraad plantation. And then?

He decided not to let himself plan too much for the future. What he did when he arrived at his destination would depend on what he found. If Marietje was alive . . .

He clung to the thought. She had to be alive. His own life would be worthless without her.

Chapter Nineteen

Marietje woke with a start. She had no time to consider what disturbed her, for her movement upon awakening set the horse in motion. Clawing for the reins, she fought to stay in the saddle.

Abruptly her protection was torn from her, as a low-hanging branch caught at her oiled cloth and held it. She emerged, suddenly, into the dim light of morning. The snake, poised above her, barely moved, and she was out of danger without even realizing that it existed.

Yet her risks were not ended. She caught the reins and tugged, bringing the horse to a stop. She was hungry, and barely rested. Her back ached from the unnatural position in which she had slept. And she felt desolate and alone. What had possessed her? Why had she left the safety of the plantation to die in the forest?

The image of Dirk's face invaded her thoughts, and with it came awareness of her predicament. She had run from Byron Scott because she could not endure the thought of remaining in his power. She needed to find Dirk—if not to be united with him, at least to see for herself that he was alive.

What direction had she been heading in when she stopped to sleep? Was she above the plantation or below it? She opened the basket Mai had given her and began to nibble on a piece of toast. It was hard and dry, but it tasted sweet, and it reminded her of her childhood, when she had been given such rusks as special treats. The taste reminded her of Pieter and Dirk and days long past.

The memory of Pieter's death returned, bringing with it a dull ache. She was awake, and once more aware of her dilemma. The British were everywhere. Where had she been heading?

To Flower's village. But now a new fear assailed her. The Tobas Indians, the cannibals she had learned to fear though she had never seen them, lived to the north, too. What if she missed Flower's village and continued on until she was captured by savages?

Another doubt assailed her, and she drew rein. What if Dirk did not remember Flower's offer of refuge? Could she be certain he would ever come to find her? Was it not possible for her to reach the village and then never dare to leave it again? Deep in the jungle, she would never know when the Englishmen were defeated.

If she did not go to Flower, then where should she hide?

Dirk might look for her in the bower. She considered that thought for a moment, and then rejected it. Byron would go there, too, if only to recall what had transpired between them.

Could she find another plantation where the English had not yet arrived? Byron had said little about the other Dutch families spread over the island. The cities would surely be overrun by the enemy. But the plantations were scattered. The Johannsons lived above her, somewhat to the south. She would go there.

She felt shame at her own cowardice, yet she knew she could not ride toward the cannibal villages. Dirk had said they were far to the north and up the mountain. But how far north? She dared not risk the possibility of losing her way and being captured by such a terrible tribe.

Her horse shifted restlessly, and she tugged on the reins. To reach the Johannson plantation, she would have to cross the road. Had she time, before the English ventured out?

She had to back her horse up into the small clearing where she had spent the night before she could turn him around. The animal seemed uneasy, shying away from the open area. Leaning close to the filly's ear, she urged her on.

It was then the snake moved. The horse saw the motion and panicked. With a snort, it plunged forward, onto the road. Marietje caught at the animal's mane and held on. She was far down the road before she managed to stop the precipitous flight.

When she once more held her filly in control, she paused to listen. Was it possible the English soldiers had not heard all this commotion? The road was empty.

Carefully she turned her horse's head until once more she was moving up the hill. Maybe there was hope, after all. She would search until she found Dirk, and she would make him understand what had happened to her. She had to. All of her father's hopes and plans depended upon her marrying and remaining on the plantation.

The thought brought a sad smile to her lips. Her father had never acknowledged what both she and her mother had known from the day her brother left for Holland. Johan Koenraad had no intentions of returning to the Spice Islands. He preferred the sea to the life of a farmer.

Hans had refused to accept that decision, and believed that Johan would soon take his place as his heir. At least, that was what Marietje had believed. Now, remembering how her father had guided Dirk through his proposal, she wondered. Maybe he had known that he would have to depend on Dirk to give him heirs and to take over control of the plantation when he was gone.

"Look what we have here!" The voice jarred Marietje into awareness of her surroundings. Two soldiers on horseback blocked her way. "How do you think this one escaped? And with a horse." The voice continued. "I thought we had caught them all."

Marietje moved swiftly. Sliding from her horse, she pushed her way into the underbrush that lined the road. She was too frightened for reason. She did not think that the men could do as she did and together catch her again. All she knew was that she had to try to get away.

But it was not easy for her to push through the brush. Her skirt caught on the first rough branches, and she was held as if in a trap. The soldier who had remained silent slid from his mount and moved swiftly to her side. Her feeble attempt to escape was over.

"She's very pretty." Her captor spoke at last. His eyes roved from her face to her breasts, and on down her body. "And she's young. It will be a pleasure to try her out."

"Not now, Bill. Not now. We're already late getting back, and you know how the captain can get. Who knows? She might be just what we need to turn his wrath aside."

" 'Tis a shame to waste such beauty on that old rascal."

"Don't let him hear you say that. He fancies himself quite a gentleman."

"Well, I suppose you are right." Marietje felt herself propelled back to where her horse stood. Strong arms caught her around the waist and lifted her up into the saddle. When her horse was turned back, the officer who held the reins led her forward until she was between him and his companion. Then he pushed the reins into her hands and mounted his own horse. She knew he had no reason to fear that she might try to escape. There was no way she could break free of their convoy.

Her captors moved along the narrow dirt road that wound its way down to the coast. When she passed her home, she felt surprise, for these men made no attempt to deliver her to Byron Scott. For a moment, she considered telling them that Scott would be searching for her, but at the last moment she held her peace. If he did realize she had been trying to run away, wouldn't he have her killed? At least these men were allowing her to live. And they were not attacking her either. Besides, they were talking between themselves, moving side by side, with the man closest to her holding on to the reins of her horse as well as to his.

No sooner was the Koenraad plantation out of sight, however, than she regretted her silence. At least she knew what to expect from Scott. And he was considerate, even though he had deceived her. Then the memory of her shame seared her thoughts, and she turned her head away from the estate that had once been hers. She hated Scott. She would never let him capture her again. She would die first.

"You got any friends out there in the woods?" The soldier closest to her spoke suddenly, startling her out of her reverie.

"No."

"No husband or brother or father?"

"No." She wished he would be quiet.

"Too bad." He turned toward his companion. "She ain't no use to the captain then. We might as well enjoy her ourselves."

The other man seemed annoyed. "Mind your tongue. How do you know she ain't lying?" He raised his voice and addressed Marietje. "We don't plan to harm you, miss. We'll just bring you to Padang. Got a ship there will take you and a lot more women back to Europe. You'd like to go home, wouldn't you?"

She caught herself before she answered that she was already home. That she knew no allegiance to Holland, except that her parents loved it. "Yes. I suppose I would."

"Well, then, you should thank us for finding you. You could have been killed by some wild beast. Now you get to go home, and just because we happened to run into you. You're a lucky woman, that you are. Ain't she, Bill?"

Bill nodded. "Luckier than she knows, Jack. We're the sort that keeps our women happy."

"I said enough!" Jack's voice rose in anger. He leaned forward and spoke to Marietje. "You'll be safe in Padang. And you'll be heading for home before you know it." The last was said at top volume, as if he wanted to be sure that anyone hiding along the road would be certain to hear.

Marietje did not answer. She was too busy trying to decide what he meant by his actions. He was trying to tell his message not to her but to any men who might be listening. Why? The cold truth of his intentions burst upon her with a shock. He wanted the men to follow. Was it so she could be the innocent dupe who led her own to ambush? He spoke of other women. Were they also being used to lure whatever remained of Dutch resistance into a trap?

She had no time to find answers to her questions. They were approaching Padang. She realized that she was very tired, that her legs were sore from being too long in the saddle. Her head ached, and her back still felt as if it were permanently bent out of shape. Perversely she also wondered about how she looked after a night in the forest. She would be meeting other women. Would they hate her because she gave in to Byron Scott?

Would they even know of her shame? She had no answer, and so she forced herself to be patient. She stared straight ahead as she moved through the streets, praying that she would not meet Byron Scott, for she suddenly remembered that he had said he was going into town. If the women were to be shipped to Holland, maybe she should go. Dirk would hear that she had gone.

No! She felt the shock of her response. He would not necessarily know she had gone to safety. And, besides, she had no wish to leave Sumatra. It was her home. But did she want to return, even temporarily, to Byron Scott?

That, too, was unacceptable. For the time being, she would remain wherever the men took her, for if they spoke the truth, other women waited there. But she would not give up hope of escape. This time when she was on her own, she would go directly to Flower's village.

"Look what we caught!" Bill spoke loudly. "She was heading for the mountains. Do you think that's where the men have gone?"

"The men are here." A surly guard barely looked at Marietje. "They killed my brother last night. His horse came racing to the barracks, and when we headed out, we found him lying facedown in the road, shot in the back. Damn the cowards!"

Bill patted the man on his shoulder, but he made no reply. Then he took Marietje's arm and led her into the inn.

The building was small in structure, as such establishments go, but Marietje was not aware of its limitations. To her it seemed large—double the size at least of her father's plantation home. She had passed it on her rare visits to Padang but never entered its door, for it was a man's world. The rooms were often rented by ships' officers seeking a few days of relaxation before returning to Europe. Occasionally a landowner who had no city dwelling of his own would put up at the inn while handling the sale of his produce. Marietje had heard rumors that the inn even housed prostitutes who served the sailors, and at times, the landowners themselves. Now it was crowded with women. Each room held two women, but none of them rushed out to greet Marietje as she arrived. They stood well within their doorways, watching as she was led along the hallway. And many, as she passed, held their hands over their faces, as if to prevent her from recognizing them. Those whose faces she could see had a look of despair that brought tears to her eyes.

At what appeared to be an empty room, Bill stopped. He pushed her inside and stood looking at her. "Bill! We can come back! You know we've got to report to the captain!" Jack's voice brought him out of his reverie. He stepped forward and caught Marietje in his arms. She struggled furiously, but his hold was too tight.

"I'll be back, lovey! You ain't seen the last of Bill Jonas." Suddenly she was hitting against empty air. He was hurrying away, back to the door that led to the street.

Overcome with despair, Marietje turned and ran to the bed. Throwing herself on it, she abandoned herself to her grief. She knew now that she should have tried harder to escape. While she had the chance. How could she get out of this prison?

She had no doubt as to what Bill meant when he said he'd return. Nor did she fail to get the message in the dull faces and shamed behavior of the women she had seen as she was led to her room. These women had all suffered the same indignities visited upon her by Scott. Maybe the English did intend to send them back to Holland. But until the ship came to carry them home, they would be used as if they were common whores.

A hand rested on her shoulder, and she jerked away. Immediately the hand was removed, and a voice broke the stillness. "Marietje, I'm sorry I startled you. But I need your help. My baby . . ."

Marietje turned and looked into the face of a friend. Gerda Johannson was not much older than Dirk, though she was a married woman with a child. Marietje glanced around the room. She saw then that she had not been alone when she entered. In one corner, crouching low as to avoid too much notice, was young Willem, and in his arms he held an infant.

Marietje brushed her tears aside and rose. "So your baby was born! How happy Frans will be."

Gerda shook her head. "He has no cause for joy. My baby is dying." She took the infant from Willem's arms and cradled it to her breast. "I have tried to get her to eat. Oh, Marietje, she's going to die."

Marietje bent over the baby. Its lips were closed, and its skin was white. She touched it gently and drew her fingers back. "She is gone already, Gerda. She will not eat."

"No!" Gerda pulled away, as if to hide her dead child

from sight. "She can't be dead! Willem has taken such good care of her!"

"She is beyond care. God has her in his arms." Marietje was terribly aware of her own helplessness.

Willem approached the two women. He held out his arms and Gerda relinquished her hold on the baby. He returned to the corner and picked up a blanket which he tossed onto the floor. He lay the tiny body on it and rolled it up. When he rose, the dead infant was hidden from view. "Marietje is right, mother. My sister is dead. But she was baptized. Her soul is in heaven." The words were meant to comfort, but they brought tears to all three.

Marietje caught Gerda in her arms and cradled her as they both sank onto the bed. Willem laid the bundle on the foot of the bed and sat close to his mother, his arms around her waist.

When their tears were spent, Gerda pulled free of the embraces. Her eyes seemed strangely wild. "I will kill them." Her voice was low and filled with hate. "The next one who comes here will die."

"Mother, no!" Willem threw himself against his mother. "You promised. You said you'd do whatever you had to to stay alive. Mother, I need you! Papa needs you! If you live, you can give Papa another baby. You said so yourself!"

"No. I want no child of Frans Johannson to grow in a body that has been defiled. You are his son. You are pure and good. But another child to come from me would be filled with sin. God took your sister because I am not worthy to raise her. The milk from my breasts is poisoned by hate and lust."

Marietje listened in horror, but she had little time to spend in confusion. A noise at the door drew her attention. The man who appeared there wasted no time in introductions. He crossed the room and grabbed at Gerda's arm. Only after he moved with her toward the bed they had just abandoned, and on which the body of the infant still lay, did Marietje realize that Gerda, with one quick movement, had pushed herself in front, so she would be certain to be the one chosen for what lay ahead.

As Marietje and Willem watched in horror the man tore Gerda's gown from her and threw her onto the bed. The bedroll, with the infant inside, rolled onto the floor, and Willem rushed to pick it up. But Gerda seemed only aware of the man who was already pressing himself upon her. She gasped as she felt his weight, and then her hands moved up to his neck. She seemed unaware that he was taking what he came to get. All of her strength and effort went into tightening her fingers around his throat.

And then, suddenly, he rose with a shout. "You bitch! You damn bitch!" He reached for his pistol and fired before either Marietje or Willem could cry out. The shot echoed in the small room, and Gerda fell dead.

For a moment, the soldier seemed stunned by his own action. Then, with a grunt, he pushed the body to the floor. He stared for a moment at Marietje, and then moved to the doorway. "Here!" His shout startled Marietje. "Come here and remove this garbage."

Two natives arrived. At the soldier's direction, they carried Gerda's body away. As they headed for the door Willem moved quickly and placed the body of the baby in her mother's arms. Then he stepped back and watched in silence as they were carried out.

The soldier turned once more to Marietje. "Come here, pretty one. I didn't want that slut, anyway."

Marietje saw Willem tense and then slump to the floor. He had been witness to other such attacks. Maybe he had been prepared for what took place.

She had no time to ask him, for he crawled into the corner and curled up, his head protected by his arms. She felt the soldier grab her wrist and pull her to him. It was starting . . . the horror she had feared. The misery she had been protected from when she stayed with Byron Scott.

As she was forced to the bed she knew with a searing certainty that she had made the wrong choice. She should have called out to Scott for help as she was ushered past the plantation. Now it was too late. She would have to endure what lay ahead until the day came when she, like Gerda, could stand it no longer.

Chapter Twenty

"Maybe mother was right. We should kill them." Willem stood next to the bed, stroking Marietje's cheeks. "They'll kill you, like they killed my mother."

Marietje opened her eyes. When had she lost awareness of what happened to her? She made a feeble attempt to recall all that had occurred since Gerda was taken away, but what came to her was too painful. She had been in the room barely an hour, and she had seen her friend's baby lie dead. She had seen her friend shot. And she had been forcefully taken. She met Willem's eyes. How had the child survived all this tragedy? It was his sister, his mother.

She forced a smile, but he did not respond. "I could steal a knife when they bring us our food."

She was aware now, fully awake. "And could you thrust the blade into a living man? I would sooner die myself."

A look of fright distorted his features. "Don't! Please, don't. You're the only one I have now."

"And what then do you propose that we do?"

"Mother and I were planning to escape, but she feared the baby might . . ." His voice broke. Their worst fears had been realized. When he continued, his voice was husky. "We were going to climb out the window at night and run back to the village." For a moment, there seemed to be more hope in his voice. "We could do that still."

Marietje considered all she had seen as she passed through the town. British soldiers and sailors were everywhere. No one could succeed in such a plan.

But had Gerda expected to reach safety? Or had she thought that by attempting such an escape, she could be certain that when she died, Willem would not remain, to be brutalized by the cruel men who held her captive?

She closed her eyes. What torture for a mother!

Willem tugged at her shoulder. "Are you all right? Can't you get up?"

"Oh, yes." Marietje sat, aware that the recent attack had left her sore as well as angry. "When do they feed us?" In spite of having eaten little, she was not hungry. Yet food might distract the lad from his sorrows.

"Soon." Willem moved to the window and looked out. He drew back in alarm. "There's another man coming. On horseback."

Marietje thought only of the child. "He might not come in here, Willem. There are many other women."

"He's a commander." Willem moved back toward the corner.

"A commander?" Marietje raced across the room to the window and looked out. With a cry of relief, she began to hammer on the pane. It was Byron Scott.

He seemed, at first, to pay no attention to her pounding. He spoke to the orderly, gesturing toward his horse's left hind leg. Then he turned to leave. He was, she could see, not going to enter the inn at all. His business was in another building across the dirt road.

Frantically, she hammered harder. "Byron! Help me!"

With a frown, he turned in the direction of her pounding. She could see that he was remarking on the strangeness of the Dutch women, who seemed to court the attentions of their captors. And then their eyes met. He stared at her for a moment and turned to the orderly. He seemed angry, and very impatient. Marietje sighed with relief as he stormed off in the direction of the inn door.

He would be in her room soon, that she was certain. What would she tell him? If she admitted she was trying to escape, he might leave her where she was. Willem stirred and watched her in silence as she pondered. When she broke into a smile, he smiled back.

At that moment, her door was thrown open again. This time, however, it was Byron Scott who entered. He strode across the room and swept her into his arms. "Marietje! My dear, how did you get here? I've had everyone out searching for you."

She drew on the tears she had not shed for Gerda. "I got lost." Her voice sounded choked, and she felt his arms tighten around her shoulders. "I was trying to get to the arbor." She felt his reaction to her words, and she knew he would believe anything she told him. "And I got lost. I had to sleep in the woods, and I was so frightened. And then, this morning, two men came and found me. I thought they were going to bring me back home—but they brought me here, instead."

"Oh, my darling! Sweet little Marietje! I've been so worried." He turned her in his arms and moved toward the door. "Come with me. This is no place for you." He seemed to remember suddenly, and he continued. "You have already told me you have no fondness for Holland. You belong with me, now."

She noticed how his voice grew louder as he spoke, and she felt a sudden revulsion. He was part of the deception. He knew that the women who occupied these cheerless rooms would never leave Sumatra. Yet he continued the pretense. *I hate him. More than ever.* She let the reality of her thoughts comfort her. She hated Byron Scott, but she would use him to save herself, and Willem.

She stopped before they reached the door. "Byron, I want to take Willem with me."

"Willem? Who is Willem?"

She turned and beckoned the boy to come to her side. "This is Willem. His mother was"—her voice dropped—"killed this morning. He's the son of a friend. His family is all dead."

Byron stared at the lad. Willem cowered against Marietje's skirt, as if he wished to disappear. Yet she could see defiance in his dark eyes, and she prayed he would remain quiet and allow her to save him. She reached down and caught one of his hands in hers and held it tightly.

"Please, may I take him with me? He's only a child."

"Children can be a great deal of trouble. Surely he can stay with someone else here."

"He has no one else. I can use him as a companion, when you are unable to ride with me. If he had been with me last night, I might not have been kidnapped by the soldiers."

Byron stared pensively out the window. She watched him closely, aware that Willem's life hung in the balance.

Gathering her courage, she made one more attempt. "Please. I've grown very attached to him."

Byron smiled. "Well, if it pleases you, he can come along." He turned to the soldier who had escorted him to the room. "Before we leave, I wish to speak with your captain."

"Yes, sir!" The soldier seemed all military now. Not at all the way he had been on the long ride down to Padang. He turned abruptly and led the way down the hallway to the front door. Marietje followed, clutching Willem to her side. Behind them, Byron Scott moved stiffly. In spite of her worry, Marietje smiled. It was like Byron Scott to keep his dignity in the most unlikely of surroundings.

In the great entryway, where a small desk was the only remaining proof that this had once been a legitimate inn, Byron paused and touched Marietje's arm. "Wait here. And do not let the boy run around. I have no time to waste hunting for him."

Marietje nodded. She watched in silence as Byron followed the soldier into a small anteroom. As the door closed behind him she became aware that she and Willem were not alone. Soldiers moved past, each pausing long enough to leer at her. One even attempted to grab her to him, but she drew back, clutching Willem close to her side. "Be careful!" Her voice was sharp. "I'm Commander Scott's woman."

She felt Willem jerk, and for a moment she feared that he might break free of her hold and run, an act that would have meant certain death for the lad. When he felt the firmness of her grip, he relaxed. But when she gazed down into his eyes, she saw the same hostility he had shown to Byron earlier. "Willem? It isn't what you think. This is just a way to free us, that's all."

He did not reply. But when she tried to get him to smile, he turned his head away. She had no time, however, to speak to the lad. Byron's angry voice reverberated through the closed door, and then, suddenly, he burst back into the entryway. He caught Marietje's arm and pushed her toward the street.

As they emerged he spoke quietly to her. "The captain says you tried to run away from his men."

She was prepared for his doubting tone. "Of course. They were strangers, and they carried guns. And one of them threatened to . . ." She did not continue. She could feel Byron's anger turning once more against his underlings.

But she felt no change of heart in Willem. The lad stood beside her until a carriage arrived, and then he leaped ahead of her into a seat. When Byron Scott sat next to him, across from where Marietje sat, he moved closer to the man. And for the first time since their meeting, Byron actually saw the boy. He studied the upturned face in silence for a moment, and then he smiled. "Well, lad, you seem a spirited sort. Do you speak English?"

"Yes, sir." Willem's voice was a bit too sharp.

"Good! Do you like to ride horseback?"

"Yes, sir."

Byron raised his eyebrows. "Well, then. Would you like to run errands for me?"

"Oh, yes, sir." Willem did not look in Marietje's direction.

"Good!" Byron turned to Marietje. "It appears your boy is more interested in soldiering than in becoming a lady's maid. I think I'll use him myself. You'll just have to accept Mai."

"I don't want Mai. I want Willem."

"Maybe we should leave that up to the boy." Byron turned to Willem. "What say you, lad?"

"I'd like to work with you, sir. If you please."

Byron seemed actually delighted. "I do please." He turned to Marietje. "You got along without him before. And I can use him well. He will release a soldier for more important duties."

Marietje looked across at Willem, but the lad still would not meet her eyes. Why, she wondered, was he willing to work for a man who had frightened him such a short time ago? What now made him unwilling to speak to her, when before he had sought her out for protection and comfort? Silently she promised herself that when they were once more alone she would question Willem further.

They reached the plantation amid a flurry of activity. Soldiers were returning from their daily search for the isolated bands of men who still harassed them. As they passed the carriage they saluted Byron, and those who thought they were not noticed leered at Marietje. One man, a sergeant, detached himself from his command and rode beside the carriage. "Sir!"

Byron leaned out his window. "Yes? Can't it wait until you give your report?"

"Yes, sir." The man still rode beside the open window. "No, sir." He leaned down, as if attempting to keep his information a secret from the other passengers. "We've located them."

"Oh? Nearby?"

"No, sir. I mean rather, sir."

"You are not going to attack? You know my orders. Wipe them out."

"Yes, sir. I thought we should return there in the morning. They forage at night, sir."

"True." Byron seemed to be considering options. Then, with a nod, he settled back in the carriage. "Maybe tomorrow I'll go with you. Carry on."

The sergeant saluted and moved ahead. Byron smiled across at Marietje, but he made no explanation of the conversation he had just concluded.

"Have you eaten?" Byron caught Marietje's elbow and helped her up the steps to the great front door. It seemed to her she was seeing that beautifully carved wood for the first time since her father died. He had designed the pattern himself and had hired native craftsmen to carve the figures that alternated with clear squares. Each carved section depicted a separate phase in the formation of the Koenraad plantation, beginning with the top square, which showed a fourteen-year-old Hans, seeing the island for the first time, as cabin boy on a schooner from out of Amsterdam. The bottom square showed him with his family, and in the background the coffee trees that had made him a wealthy man.

The door swung open, and Byron waited as she stepped into the hallway. At the foot of the steps, he paused. "I will leave you now, my dear. If you want food, speak to the cook. I regret that I must return to Padang tonight. Finding you, and returning you to your home, superseded my duties. I must return to them now. But I will be back, and we will celebrate your return tomorrow." He leaned forward and kissed her lips.

His gesture served to comfort her. She forgot, momentarily, that she had run away to avoid further contact with this man. All she could think of was how terrible her life would have been had he not found her. If she had not been standing at the window when he appeared. She shuddered. Her life would have been over. Now she was tired, and thankful that she would not have to contend with his lovemaking. All she wanted to do was sleep.

He stepped back, saluted lightly, and headed back toward the door. His footsteps sounded hollow on the fine tile her father had brought over from India. She had closed her eyes when he kissed her. Now she opened them. Willem was hurrying behind him. She reached out one hand to stop the boy, but he was too fast.

At the door, Byron paused, aware of the boy for the first time. He glanced down, and Marietje saw that he was pleased with Willem's show of loyalty. "Not you, lad. Not this time. Tonight you may rest, too. I will find duties for you tomorrow, when I return."

"You are going to Padang? Sir, the soldiers took my mother and sister away just a bit before you came. If I went with you, I might find them." His eyes were pleading. "Please?"

The look of approval faded, to be replaced by anger. Byron glanced toward Marietje. "I told you he would be trouble." His voice was hard. "We have no need for more women here, nor for a little girl. I have extended my kindness as far as I will. You wanted him here. You must make him behave."

Marietje was at Willem's side, protecting him from the wrath in Byron's voice. "He did not mean what you think. His mother and sister are both dead. All he wanted was to bring their bodies back for burial."

"God, no!" Byron pushed aside the orderly who stood ready to open the door and grabbed the handle himself. He swung it open and slammed it closed behind him.

Marietje dropped to her knees beside the lad, but he showed no inclination to cry. He stood stiffly, his face set, staring at the place where Byron Scott had been.

"I'm sorry." Marietje took the small body in her arms, trying to warm it, trying to soften the grief that held it so tight in its grip. "Willem, you must not give up. He will be more understanding after I speak with him."

"You do more than speak with him. You . . ." Willem held himself tightly, unwilling to give in to her embrace. "You know him. You didn't fight, like some of the women did, and you didn't run away, like Mama and I did. You wanted to come here."

"Of course I did." She realized that the servants, and some of the soldiers, were watching them, and she paused. What she had to say to Willem was not for others' ears. "Come. I'll show you where you can sleep. Are you hungry?"

He shook his head, but she ignored his response. Before she headed upstairs, she stepped into the kitchen. She ordered food, told the maid to bring it to her room when it was ready, and then she took Willem's hand and led him out. When they reached her room, she drew him inside and locked the door.

He stood where she left him, refusing to be part of this house which he felt was occupied by traitors and the enemy. And she knew, as she returned to his side, that she would have trouble explaining her actions to him.

But explain them she must. She knew that. She was back in the same prison she had fought to escape, and now she knew it was better than any other shelter she could find—at least for the time. Yet Willem's presence might serve to bring her to Dirk. If he would accept her and her seeming fondness for a British officer.

She pulled him over to a love seat near the window and sat at his side. "Willem, you must try to understand. I do not like this"—she gestured to indicate her situation—"any more than I liked being at the inn. But I was caught and brought here. My mother is dead, too. Killed by Byron Scott's men. I hate him, but I cannot fight him or escape from him by myself. I tried. That was how I came to be brought to the inn."

She saw that he was at least listening, though she could not tell whether he understood her predicament at all. "Now I'm glad it happened, for if I had not been there to take you away, you would have been made a slave, and killed, in time, as your mother and sister were killed. At least your father has you."

"My father has nothing. Dirk Hendrik said he was alive. We were going to meet him. We were waiting at the cabin for him to come. But the English came instead. Mother and . . . I think he is dead, too."

"Don't be so certain." She could barely continue, for her heart had responded to the name of her lover. She wanted desperately to ask about him, to hear his name again. But she knew she could not think of herself until Willem was calmed. "Did you hear what the sergeant said to Commander Scott as we rode in?"

Willem nodded. But once more he seemed unwilling to speak.

"I think they have located one of the men's hideouts. If we do not warn Dirk and your father, they may be captured." She did not add "or killed." That, she felt, would be too harsh, after all Willem had been through.

He seemed to yield somewhat. "You want to warn them? I thought . . ."

"You were wrong. Yes, I know Commander Scott, and he . . . is fond . . . of me. But I love Dirk Hendrik. And I hate the British. They killed my mother and my father. And they killed Pieter."

Willem knew Pieter. His eyes widened and then narrowed to slits. "I could go to warn them."

She felt a flow of relief. It was risky, but it was necessary. "I don't know where you should go. Do you?"

"No. Not exactly." He seemed to shrink, as if even the slightest discouragement was too much to bear. Then he straightened up again. "Dirk spoke to me of the mill. I'd look there."

She chewed lightly on her lower lip. Convincing Willem to help her had been easier than she expected. But how was she to get him out safely? If he tried to sneak away, he would surely be shot. She glanced down, and her gaze rested on a brooch that had belonged to her mother. She had pinned it on her dress when she rode away. "Jewelry!" She rose to her feet, filled with a new excitement. "Is there any way you could find some of your mother's jewelry?"

He looked at her in surprise. "We hid it in the cave."

"Does that mean you could get it now?"

"Yes. Why? How does that help my father?"

"It will get you away from here." There was a knock on the door as she spoke, and she hurried to unlock it. A native maid entered with a tray of food. Spiced rice and peanuts, and saffron-seasoned vegetables. She placed the tray on a table and departed.

"Come and eat. I'll tell you what you must do." Willem did not rise. "Hurry! You will need the food for strength. And you must return here before Commander Scott gets back from Padang."

Willem rose. She could see that he still was suspicious of her.

"I'll persuade the guards at the gate to let you go and get your mother's jewelry. I'll tell them you don't want it lost, and that I have persuaded you to give it to Commander Scott for safekeeping."

"He'll steal it. Why should I give it to him?"

"So you can get out to warn your father. It is worth a few pieces of jewelry to keep your father alive?"

"Yes. If he isn't dead, too."

"We must believe that he is alive. And we must warn him."

Some of the suspicion left Willem's eyes. "All right. I'll go."

She felt the relief, like a blanket, shield her from her fears. She had eaten little. But Willem had cleaned his plate. "Are you ready?" She dared not consider how much she was entrusting to a child of ten. All she knew was that he was her only hope. Before they reached the door that led to the hall, she knelt and embraced him. "God guide you. And keep you safe. Tell Dirk . . ." The lad waited in silence. "Tell Dirk that I am alive. And hurry back." She drew the boy close. "And be careful. There are few English out in the dark. But there are animals, and . . ."

Willem was growing impatient. "I'll be careful." He opened the door and led the way downstairs.

Convincing the sergeant to let Willem go to find his mother's jewels was easier than Marietje had expected. He was still suffering from the rebuke he had received when she seemed to be lost. And he knew the commander's fondness for precious gems. He looked down at the boy as he spoke, but he made sure that only Marietje heard his words. "I'll send him through the gate, and I'll tell the guards to let him back in if he returns. But he had better be back here before dawn, for if he is not here when the commander arrives, I'll say he tried to run away, and we shot him."

"He'll be back." Marietje knelt beside Willem. "Be sure you're back before dawn, even if you don't find the jewels." She hoped he understood her, for it was of his father and Dirk she spoke.

He nodded and she rose. Together they walked to the gate. The sergeant spoke to the guard, and Willem was signaled on. He was visible for a few moments, and then he vanished into the woods. Just as he disappeared from sight, a soldier detached himself from the others at the gate and followed him.

Marietje stopped short of giving herself away. Yet all of her instincts were to scream a warning to Willem. Instead she turned and walked slowly back to the house. She had sent the boy to his death, she knew that now. And in all probability, she had also provided the English with a chance to flush out more of the Dutchmen who harassed them. Maybe, as a result of her action, Dirk and Frans Johannson would both be killed.

When she reached her room, she threw herself on her bed and cried herself to sleep.

Chapter Twenty-One

"Damn it, man, you should never have left them! What right had you to leave my wife alone when she needed you so?" Frans Johannson's face was red, as it always became when he was angry or prepared to do battle. Dirk had seen him in this state often in the past, for Frans did not share Hans Koenraad's sympathy for the natives, unless they accepted his religion and showed proper respect for his God. Now his wrath was directed at Dirk. "How could you entrust a woman's safety to a child of ten?"

Dirk remained quiet. What answer could he give that had not already been said? Gerda had been so definite. She had shown the sort of confidence he had hoped he would find in Marietje, when—and if—he found her again. And even now, he was taking time from his own search because of Gerda and her two children. "You do me an injustice. I left them in a place your wife was certain would be safe, and I came straight to you. As quickly as was possible, seeing that our appointed meeting had passed."

"Aye, you are right, my friend." The anger was gone, and only sadness remained. Frans stepped into the small cabin and pushed through the debris. Whoever had come to take Gerda and her two children away had taken the time to search for any valuables that might be stored in secret places in the small hideaway. "Forgive me. I know you did all you could. It is not you I rail against, but a fate that has taken my family from me." For a moment, it appeared that Frans's firm control might break, and Dirk felt a rush of embarrassment for the bereaved man.

"They have been taken to Padang." Frans did not ask a question. It was a certainty they both admitted. "I must try to save them." He had picked up a ribbon that had once graced Gerda's hair, and he pushed it into his pocket as he turned away. "We must waste no more time in mourning."

Dirk followed in silence. Frans spoke to himself, not to

any other. And his actions showed that he heeded his own advice. Dirk moved silently behind him, alert for the presence of any stray Englishman who might attack. But aside from the natural noises of the night forest, the air was still. The rains would soon begin, and then travel would be safer. The English sought shelter against inclement nature.

At the mill, Frans paused. "Thank you, my friend, for all you have done to help me. I know your concern for my loved ones has kept you from your own search." He caught Dirk's arms and drew him close. Dirk returned the embrace, aware that this was as close as Frans Johannson could come to exhibiting openly his own grief, or his concern for another.

But this show of forgiveness on Frans's part did little to free Dirk of his own feeling of responsibility for Gerda's fate. "I cannot forget that it was I who saw her alive last. I never should have left her. You are right."

"No, my friend." Frans had overcome his own anger. "I know my Gerda. She is a strong-willed woman. *Was* a strong willed woman. I controlled her only because I was her husband. Away from me, she would accept no other authority." He looked up, a light of hope once more in his eyes. "God forgive me; I spoke of her just now as if she were dead. Pray the Lord we reach her before it is too late."

At the outskirts of Padang, the two men halted. In the darkness, they could be reasonably sure of remaining undetected, yet they would need to be cautious. Dirk crouched low beside Frans, studying the scene spread out before him. The sentries stood disconsolately, trying as much as possible to stay under the shelter of palms. For the rain had begun, whispering softly among the leaves. Soon its force would increase, and then, Dirk felt certain, the sentries would retreat to drier posts. Only then would it be safe for him to enter the city.

His back was wet, and rivulets of water ran over his face before the sentries moved. After a pause to reconnoiter, Dirk rose and stepped out of the protection of the forest. "We can go now. I think they're keeping the women at the inn."

They approached the large structure from the rear, for even in the rain, soldiers were moving through the streets. A dim light from the kitchen spilled out, forming a square of gold in the frame of blackness. Dirk and Frans stepped carefully around the light, aware of sounds coming from the building that told them many soldiers were entertaining themselves at the expense of the fine Dutch women they had captured.

"Damn redcoats!" Frans spoke under his breath. "I hope they all rot in hell."

"They will." Dirk whispered. "They are paving the way at this very moment." He reached the wall of the house, and he crouched under a half-open window. After a moment of listening, he stood up and peered over the sill. The room was empty. He ducked and moved to the next window. Just as he raised his head a light appeared in the room, and he crouched, waiting silently to be certain he was not seen.

"My God! No!" The moan of agony spun Dirk around. He found himself staring at Frans, who was bent low over what appeared to be a half-completed grave. The hole was shallow, with a mound of dirt beside it, and lying on the ground beside the hole was a body.

With a nervous glance at the windows, Dirk moved to his friend's side. "What is it . . . ?" He caught his breath. No need to question Frans. The still form on the ground was Gerda Johannson. Her eyes were closed, as if she were sleeping. Beside her, a roll of blanket lay covered with mud. Frans touched his hand to the dead woman's belly, and then, with another moan, he caught the roll in his arms and unfolded the covers. The infant was clearly dead, too. Maybe it had died before Gerda, for it seemed more waxlike. Dirk crouched helplessly as Frans cradled the tiny form in his arms and rocked back and forth, unmindful of the rain that soaked his clothes, that sponged the dirt from the infant's pale cheeks.

Slowly the rocking ceased. "We must take them with us. I cannot let my wife lie in such polluted ground."

Dirk did not answer. Instead he bent and lifted Gerda's body, remarking as he had once before on how frail she was. With an uneasy glance back at the inn, he moved across the yard. Frans paused a moment, and then he followed. Dirk knew without looking that his friend had wrapped the infant back in the blanket.

They moved swiftly now, barely aware of the burdens they bore. When they reached the mill, Dirk paused. "Let us bury them here. Willem was with them when I left them. Maybe, since I spoke of the mill in his presence, he will come here if he is free."

"He cannot be. Would he stand idle and let his mother and baby sister die?"

"No. Maybe not. Unless he was not captured. He might yet be hunting for them, as we were." Dirk entered the old mill house and returned with a shovel. He found a large tree that seemed to shelter the land around it, and there he began to dig. Occasionally he glanced at Gerda's body, which he had carefully placed out of the rain to wait completion of the grave.

Frans made as if to assist Dirk, but he could not put the tiny burden down, and so at last he sat beside his dead wife, rocking the infant and singing a hymn of lament in a quiet voice.

The ground was soft and easy to work. When Dirk had a deep enough hole dug, he laid the shovel aside and went to his friend's side. "It is ready. Come. I'll help you put them to rest." He bent and lifted Gerda's body from the ground. Cradling it on one arm, he helped Frans rise to his feet. Then together they walked to the side of the grave.

"She is baptized." Dirk spoke quietly. "Her name is Henriette."

"Henriette." On Frans's rough tongue it sounded like a caress. "Little Henriette. May God grant you joy in heaven."

When both bodies lay in the grave, Frans knelt on the damp earth, his hands folded. He prayed long and loudly, daring the English to hear him. But Dirk felt no fear for their safety. The rain was making a noise of its own that muffled all the noises coming from the forest.

Then with a sigh Frans rose and pulled the shovel from Dirk's hands. The first dirt landed on the blanket, and he stood staring at it as if transfixed. Dirk pried the handle from him and pushed him away from the grave. "Wait by the tree, Frans. I will do this for you.'' He watched until Frans was too far away to see the dirt fall, and then he resumed the task of burial. Only when the grave was filled and he had stamped the dirt down as best he could did he join his friend.

Frans stood silently, staring out into the rain. An occasional drop of water, spilled from the leaves overhead, caught him on the head, trailing its way over his face and mingling with his tears. When he saw Dirk approach, he seemed to return to life. "I will find the man who did that, and kill him."

"My friend, I know your distress. But Henriette was sickly from birth. We baptized her because we feared she could not survive."

"Had she been born in our own bed she would now live. Had the doctor come and . . ." Frans angrily brushed a tear from his cheek. "I have wept enough. Now I will fight. Come. I'll show you where we are camped." He did not look back, even when he reached the shelter of the forest.

When they reached the cave in which the men were sheltered, he paused. "There will be no one here, of course. The rain is our friend."

Dirk barely heard Frans's words. He was thinking of the path they had left leading directly to their hiding place. "I must go back. I did nothing to obscure our tracks."

"The rain will do that. By morning the ground will be smooth."

"Nevertheless, I think I will return. And then I will be on my way. I have yet to learn what has happened to my Marietje."

"Then you are not staying with us?"

"Not yet. I may return as you have, with a sad knowledge. But go I must, for I cannot live with the uncertainty."

"Aye. I understand. I will tell the others you will be back."

"Yes. Thank you. On the way, I think I will see if your house is still vacant. It might serve as a place to hide our women as we release them."

"If we can release any." Frans seemed drained of hope.

"But yes, see what you can, and decide. I had forgotten the cave. It might serve others, as it did my wife."

Dirk nodded. "Maybe, when the others from the south join us, we will be saved the need to search for hiding places for our loved ones. If we do it right, we could push the English back into the sea."

"A faint hope, my friend." Frans turned and headed for the road. His heart was filled with anger and hate. Dirk knew that Frans would find no rest until he had taken at least one life in payment for his Gerda and little Henriette.

Alone at last, Dirk moved swiftly back to the mill. He wanted to cover the grave with brush, to further hide it from the English, and from the wild beasts that roamed the forest. He worked quickly, aware that much of the night was gone, chopping branches from low-hanging trees and tearing up underbrush and dragging it to where the slight mound told of recent digging.

He was on his second trip from the woods when he saw a movement at the corner of the mill pond. Immediately alert, he paused, ready to fight or flee.

"Dirk?" The voice was high, yet it had a sound of maturity that it had not possessed the last time he heard it.

"Willem! Thank God *you're* alive, at least."

At the sound of his voice, the boy ran forward. He paused a few feet from Dirk, as if afraid to come closer for fear that he might be embraced, as if he were still a child. From his safe distance, he extended his hand. "What do you hear, friend?"

Dirk repressed an impulse to laugh. The words sounded so strange when spoken by a child. "I am . . ." He realized suddenly that the boy might not know his mother and sister were dead.

"My mother is killed, and my sister, too. They were taken from me at the inn."

"Then you were there? Your father will want to speak to you. He mourns greatly that he was not nearby to save your mother the indignity of her death." Dirk wanted to hold out his arms to let Willem find comfort, but he sensed that the boy's strength came from a fragile source. And he needed now to be a man, not a child.

"She died fighting them, Dirk Hendrik. Not like Marietje."

A chill shook Dirk. "Then Marietje is dead, too?"

"No. More's the sorrow. She found an officer who has made her his ward. She is safe. But she is a traitor."

"You know this for certain?" Dirk stared at Willem in disbelief. "You have seen her?"

"I left her barely an hour ago. After . . . after my mother and sister died, she saw a British commander and called to him for help. She said she got lost and was taken to the inn by some soldiers. He seemed very glad to see her, and he brought us both to the Koenraad plantation."

"You say she went there voluntarily?"

"No. She went eagerly." The scorn in the lad's voice was enough to make his high-pitched child's speech seem almost mature.

"I cannot believe it."

"Nevertheless, it is true."

Dirk was silent, lost in thought. Could he take the lad's word in so important a matter? "How is it that you are here? Did you manage to escape without trying to take her with you?"

"No." Willem seemed unwilling to accept any responsibility for Marietje. "She helped me get out. I must be back before dawn."

"Go back? Why? Your father needs you beside him now."

"No." Dirk heard the single word, and he knew that for Willem, the days of childhood were over. Ten years old, and a man. "If father tries to keep me here, I will not see him."

Dirk frowned. "If you are not here to see your father, and if you did not run away to escape the British, then why are you here?"

"To give warning. The British have found your hiding place. I—we—heard the commander order an attack for tomorrow."

"Ah!" Dirk's eyebrows went up. Maybe they would have to hide in the mountains after all. But not yet. First, they would move to other caves, climb trees, do anything

206

that would permit them to remain close to Padang. "You must go and tell your father."

The boy drew back. "No. I must get back to the plantation." He seemed ready to depart, and then abruptly he paused. "I have made myself liked by the commander. If I stay near him, I can give you more information. Do you come here often?"

"No. Your father and I buried your mother and little Henriette under that brush."

"You found them?" Again, for a moment, Dirk saw the child that still hid beneath Willem's veneer of maturity. "Thank God!"

"Yes, and thank your father, too. You must let him know you're alive."

"I must not delay too long . . ." By his hesitancy, Willem showed his need.

"Come. I'll make certain you return to the plantation on time." He sought out the barely visible path and headed toward the cave where he had left Frans. "You are sure Marietje is alive?"

"Yes."

"I will not believe she is a traitor until I have proof for myself. Tell her I have come to save her. She loves me."

Dirk stood to the side as they entered the clearing. He had thought Frans was on his way to Padang to find English soldiers on whom to vent his rage. There was little chance that he had returned. Yet there he sat, close to the cave's entrance, his head buried in his hands. Had he returned because he recognized his own risk? A man so recently deprived of his wife and child needed some time to control his grief. He would help no one if all he did was to get himself captured.

Frans looked up, his hand moving automatically toward his rifle. When he saw Willem, he leaped to his feet and ran toward the boy. "Willem! God be praised!"

The child-look returned to Willem's face as he ran forward. For one moment, he was the boy of ten, safe in his father's comforting arms. And then abruptly he drew away. "I'm glad to see you father."

Frans's eyebrows went up. "Father? What has happened to 'Papa'?"

"Please, Father. I have a message. Commander Byron Scott has located your hideaway. I have come to warn you and the other men to move before it is too late."

Frans turned a questioning glance toward Dirk. But he spared the child the indignity of asking for confirmation of his message. Dirk could see it was not easy for Frans to play his son's game. "How did you learn of this, Willem?"

"I have convinced the commander that I will make him a good errand boy. He need not know that I share his messages with you."

Frans's eyes gleamed with new pride. "You are a good soldier, Willem. Your mother would be proud of you."

"Thank you, sir." Willem seemed ready to embrace his father once more, but then he thought better of it. "I must get back. I am glad I saw you. And I am thankful that you found Mama and Henriette."

For a moment the boy's eyes met those of his father. Dirk watched them in silence. They deserved that much privacy, at least.

"Good-bye, then." Willem turned before either Frans or Dirk could stop him. As he vanished into the forest a new burst of rain pelted the ground. He was gone. It was hard for Dirk to believe that he had been there at all.

Chapter Twenty-Two

Marietje sat up suddenly, wide-awake and wondering what it was that woke her. The night was still, for the rain had at last stopped. In the distance, she could hear the forest beasts. Dawn would come very quickly now. And . . .

Willem! Was he back? Struggling to repress a growing anxiety, she rose and hurried to the room that had once been Mai's. She pushed the door ajar, and paused. The boy sat on the edge of his bed, struggling to remove clothing soaked by the night rains. He looked up as she entered.

"I didn't want to wake you."

"I'm thankful you are back. Did you find them?"

"Yes. My father is among them. He found my mother and Henriette."

"Thank God. I hated to leave them."

"You did? It did not seem that you cared."

Marietje felt the sting of his words. Where, she wondered, was the friendly child she had met at the cave? Was he gone forever? "I understand that it helps you to be strong if you feel anger. And if I am to be the brunt of your strength, then so be it. You delivered your message?"

"Yes. To my father, and to Dirk Hendrik." He watched her closely as he spoke.

"Dirk? You spoke to him?"

"I met him at the mill. Yes. I spoke to him."

"What did he say?" Marietje felt her irritation increase. Did the lad expect her to beg for every bit of news?

"He said he wanted me to tell you he would rescue you."

She felt a glow of relief. He loved her still. And then doubt once more obscured her happiness. Could he possibly know all she had been through? And if he did, would he understand? "Is that all he said?"

"He said you loved him."

She felt the cruelty of his words. If Dirk said she loved him and made no mention of his love for her, maybe it was to warn her that he could not accept a woman who had been despoiled by another. And if this was his message, did she want him to find her? "He said nothing else?"

"He thanked me for the warning and said they would move to safety."

"He said nothing of when or how he would free me?"

"I did not ask him. I had more important news."

"Yes." She turned away. Nothing that had passed between Willem and Dirk had served to change the boy's mind regarding her. He still was sure she was a traitor. Had he convinced Dirk of that, too? "Did Dirk say he would rescue me after you told him that I was under Commander Scott's protection?"

He thought for a moment. "Yes. I'm very tired, and the commander will expect me to be on duty when he arrives."

"You plan to work for him? After you met your father?"

"Yes. I can learn more as Commander Scott's errand boy that will be of use to my father."

"He agreed to let you do this?" She stared at Willem in surprise. She had always considered Frans Johannson an unfeeling man. If this were true, then he was worse than she had believed him to be.

"I did not ask him. We all have duties, when our work is to free our country." He had succeeded in loosing his shoes, and he placed them quietly on the floor. He turned from her and removed his wet clothing, and then, without looking back at her, he climbed into his bed.

For one moment, he appeared as he once had been—a child. And then his expression tightened. "Good night."

"Good night." She closed the door quietly behind her. He would have little enough time for sleep, if what he believed about Commander Scott was true. All she could hope was that enough work had to be done and duties attended to after Byron Scott's arrival, so that Willem would get at least a few hours of sleep.

There was a tap on her door as she approached her bed. "Yes?"

"It's I. Byron. Are you still in bed?"

She glanced down at her gown. It was rumpled from the

210

night, and a quick look in the mirror told her that her hair was in equal disarray. "No. I will open to you in a moment. I'm . . ." She laughed, hoping that it appeared she was embarrassed. "I'll be there in a moment."

There was no reply. Quickly she tugged at the buttons of her dress, feeling them pop open. She tore the dress off and almost threw it in the wardrobe. From under her pillow, she drew her nightgown and pulled it over her head. She needed do nothing to her hair. He would understand it being tousled after the night's sleep. She was almost at the door when she thought of the chamber pot. She returned to the bed and drew it out, carrying it to the door that led to Willem's room. From a shelf she drew a cloth cover and draped it over the pot. And then, once more, she headed for the hall door.

She pulled it open. "Byron! You look exhausted. Have you had a difficult night?" She touched his sleeve. "You're wet."

"To the bone. I've ordered a bath sent up. It would comfort me greatly to have you share my bed, at least until I am asleep. I swear, I did not know the rain here would feel so cold."

"You're tired, that's all." She found herself hoping he would catch the heat sickness, but she dared not show her dislike at being pushed once more into his arms.

"Aye, maybe you're right. Ah, here comes the tub." He stepped into the room as two men approached, carrying the large wooden tub Marietje's father had had carved for him by native craftsmen. Like the front door, it was decorated with carvings depicting life on the plantation. The inside of the tub had been coated many times with grease, so that it was almost waterproof. Yet it was necessary to place it on a rug that would absorb any water that might spill during a bath. She directed the men to the window. The sky was light now, and the sun was already warming the air.

Byron made no attempt to hide himself as he disrobed. He dropped each item of his clothing onto a chair, and at last he stepped naked into the tub. Marietje sat nearby, trying to keep her eyes from the body of this man who showed such rudeness. Yet she could not completely ignore his presence. As he stood knee-deep in the hot water, waiting for one of the servants to pour another pot of water over his body, she watched surreptitiously. How well she knew that body. The strength of his arms. The tenderness of his fingers as he stroked her. The force of his desire when he was aroused to passion.

There had been a time when she thought she would know only one man so intimately. Dirk Hendrik. She had dreamed of seeing his firm thighs, his strong, flat stomach. She had dreamed of feeling *his* arms around her. Dreamed of the day when she would discover the wonderful secrets of love in his embrace. Now that could never be. She was not the innocent child he had loved. She was aware now of her own body's fire, of the passion that welled within her at the touch of probing fingers. She knew the object of her longing.

Could she lie passive in Dirk's arms, waiting for him to teach her the meaning of his love? She knew the answer. How often had Byron awakened that perverse nature in her that pushed all consideration of propriety aside and demanded satisfaction? How often had she become the aggressor, clawing for fulfillment?

She felt a blush of shame that was lost in the old longing. Would he finish his bath and leave her? Or was this titillation a prelude to what she knew they both desired? Ashamed of her own responses, she turned away and buried her face in her hands. She was lost. She knew that now. Maybe Willem was right, after all. Maybe she was so devoted to what Byron Scott gave her that she could never again trust her pledge of loyalty.

She felt his gaze upon her, and she turned, both hating and longing to meet his eyes. He smiled when he saw her tears. "You worried for my safety? Oh, my little Marietje, what a gem you are! Come. I wish to hold you."

She frowned in dismay. "But I am in my nightdress."

His smiled broadened. "Then take it off."

She hesitated a moment, and then she reached up and released the buttons at her neck. She pushed the garment down over her shoulders, letting it fall in soft folds at her feet. Her eyes were on Byron's face, and she saw his expression change as she bared herself. He might be tired, but he was lusty, too.

"Climb in beside me." Byron spoke softly. "I wish to caress your soft skin."

She lifted one foot and slid it into the water. He caught her ankle and brought her toes to his lips. For a moment she teetered, and then she caught at the edge of the tub for balance. How strange the sensation was! Never had she felt such a sensitivity in her foot before. By the time his tongue moved up her leg, she could think of nothing but her need to close the gap between them. Yet he kept her from her goal. He seemed to relish each new part of her body as it came against his lips, drinking in her fragrance. Building her passion—and his own.

She knew the extent of her shame when, at last, he drew her down into the water, fitting his body into hers as she knelt over him. She could think of nothing but the sweet warmth of their blending. She could see nothing but his eyes, burning into hers. She could feel nothing but the growing force of her passion. Closing her eyes, she threw her head back and moaned with pleasure. He caught her shoulders and supported her, leaving her free to push against him. And then, leaning forward, he caught the nipples of her breasts, one at a time, between his lips. She felt the teasing of his tongue, felt the fire grown within her, and then she exploded in a sudden outflow of passion. She knew she was calling out. She had done that before. Yet she was not aware of making a sound.

Slowly the fire within her cooled, and with it came the hate that always waited to shame her. She should not let this man reach her. She should hold him off, fight against his caress. But she knew she could not. She opened her eyes slowly, hating to see the day that started with such a betrayal of all she had known and loved in the past. She had let her passion be expressed in the very tub her father had used to cleanse himself before the Sabbath. She had polluted the sign of cleanliness through lust. Would she ever have the courage to destroy herself, as she had already destroyed all that was sacred to her?

She saw the movement then, and her eyes widened. Willem stood for a moment in the open doorway between their rooms. His eyes were filled with hate—and disgust. When he saw that she had seen him, he vanished, closing the door silently behind him.

With a cry, Marietje fell forward, resting her head on Byron's shoulder. There was no hope for her now. She knew that. Willem would convince Dirk of her perfidy. And then Dirk would certainly have no use for her.

Gently Byron rose, lifting Marietje into his arms. He signaled to a slave, of whose presence Marietje had been unaware, and a sheet was draped over his shoulders. He caught it up with one hand and wrapped it around them both, enclosing them in a soft cocoon. She felt him move across the floor, felt herself being lowered onto the bed. But her mind would not accept the reality of what was happening to her. Her life, she knew, was over. It mattered not at all whether she stayed with Byron or ran away. She would never again feel the love that Dirk had once offered her.

How long ago had it been that she had first entered the bower with Dirk? Not even a year had passed since that day when she had felt her life begin. Had the British not come, she would still be waiting for Dirk to complete his service in Palembang. She and her mother would have been busy sewing her wedding gown. But the British had changed everything. Now her life was ended. All that remained was shame—and regret.

"It's working, little Marietje. They're following their women, as I said they would. If we can keep the fighting confined to the area around Padang, we can save the spices. They must wonder by now why we haven't raided their hiding places. Yet they stay nearby. When the *Bonnie Elizabeth* docks, we will end the fight. One day will be all it will take to kill them all."

Marietje was suddenly awake, alert to what Byron was saying. More soldiers were coming! She had thought of the Dutchmen who lay hidden around Padang as brilliant hunters, slowly eliminating the British army. But they had been duped. The British knew where they were and planned to kill them all. She remained quiet. He could not suspect the extent of her interest. "What a pretty name, the *Bonnie Elizabeth*. It sounds like a pleasure barge. When it comes, can we sail on it around the island? Papa once told me that one could see the volcanoes of Burma and the tall volcanoes on the northernmost part of Sumatra, if one made such a circuit."

"I don't know about Burma, but it is true that you can see the volcanoes of Sumatra from the water. I have heard warnings that they might erupt—someday." He hurried on, as if concerned that he might have frightened her. "It is a beautiful voyage. Yet, my love, the Elizabeth is far too large for us to use in that manner. It is a troop ship, barren of most comforts. Yet . . ." He stroked her nearest breast with his fingers. "Yet we might find it a delightful interlude, after the fighting is over. It will be here soon after the rains end for the season, so the weather will be good for such a pleasure jaunt. Did I tell you that I saw the King of Siam take just such a cruise in a barge? He lay with his newest concubine, in the center of the deck, served by slaves, and his boat was powered by a hundred oarsmen, slaves from India and from Sumatra. When he tired of eating, he amused himself with his woman under the shelter of a red canopy. I have dreamed, at times, of enjoying just such an afternoon. Strange, my love, that you, too, should have such fantasies."

She waited to answer until she could collect her thoughts. So the boatload of reinforcements would come with the spring. If the Dutch could end the English control before that time, they could greet the ship with cannon and destroy her before the troops came ashore.

"You're tired, too, I see that." Byron nuzzled his face against her shoulder. "Forgive me for disturbing you with any thought but that of love. Good night, my sweet." He dismissed the slave with a wave of his arm, and then abruptly he was asleep.

Marietje lay quietly until she heard his even breathing turn to a gentle snore. Then cautiously, she slipped from his embrace, pausing when he stirred. At last she stood beside the bed. Byron lay sprawled on the coverlet, for already it was too hot for covers. His nakedness did not excite her now, nor did it fill her with revulsion. He was a man, nothing more. Good sometimes, cruel at others. He assumed that his dream was hers, too, and that was her salvation. For though she hated herself for her inability to say no him, she realized that her very compliance made her seem more trustworthy to him. And it was because he felt he could trust her that he spoke of his plans.

She was in the garden when, at last, Willem awoke. She saw the lad hurry from the kitchen, and she called out to him. "Willem! Come here. I have something to tell you."

He paused, his face a mask. Was he angry? Disgusted? Afraid? She could not tell. "I have nothing to say to a traitor."

She suppressed her anger. What else could she expect him to think? Before the British invaded the island, he had been a child, unaware that men and women coupled in lust. And when he did learn of such behavior, it was at the inn, where the men were hated and cruel, and where the women, like his mother, fought against the unwelcome attacks. How else should he judge her except as a traitor? Did she not enjoy the touch of the enemy? Had she not voluntarily gone with Byron Scott? In Willem's eyes, she was damned. Yet she had to convince him that her message was true.

He approached slowly, making no attempt to conceal his distrust. "What have you to say to me?"

For one brash moment, she considered trying to explain to this child what he had seen. But before he reached her, she knew the folly of such a plan. "I have learned something that must be brought to your father immediately. Can you go out again tonight?"

She could see him hesitate. "What can you say that my father would want to hear?" His voice was expressionless, but his eyes were filled with anger.

"I could tell them that they must attack soon, for a ship with reinforcements is on its way here from England. Its name is the *Bonnie Elizabeth*, and it is due in by spring."

"You want me to tell my father and Dirk Hendrik that?"

"Yes. Please, Willem. I know you hate me, and I understand why. But you must believe that I still want the British to leave this land. Will you go?"

He considered, like an old man weighing the relative importance of several alternatives. "All right. I will go.

When I brought the jewelry to the sergeant, I told him there was more, but that I would have to search a bit for it, since the rains had washed out my place markers. He believed me. This way I can get . . ." He paused, and she knew he thought he was telling too much to a traitor. "I will go tonight." He turned then and ran across the garden. She saw him again, later in the day, but he did not bother to look in her direction.

Chapter Twenty-Three

"You're back again?" Dirk held his gun ready. If Willem had been followed, he would be ready.

"Yes."

"Your message last night was wrong. There was no attack."

"I know. I do not know why. I heard Commander Scott order one. I swear that I did."

"You're too young to swear. Yet I believe you. The English are up to something. Tell me, how did you get away then, and now?"

"I have told a sergeant that I know where my mother's jewels are hidden. He lets me out to find them. I think he plans to give them to the commander."

"Yes." Dirk laughed a cold laugh, free of any hint of humor. "I have heard and seen the English penchant for looting." He lowered his rifle. Evidently the lad had not been followed. "Your father is with a raiding party."

"That's all right. I did not come to see him."

Dirk felt the hardness in the boy's voice, and he winced. If war did nothing else, it destroyed the children. He thought of the young boy he had met on the road from Bengkulu. He and his younger brothers were probably seasoned killers by now. What kind of lives would they lead—even if the war ended, and they were free once more? Would they be able to forget the men they had slain? Would young Willem be able to put behind him the vision of his mother, dying of a gunshot wound after being viciously raped by a lustful, rough soldier?

"You wanted to see me?" Dirk's eyes widened. Was it good that the boy seemed to want to avoid his father?

"Yes. You gave me a message to deliver. I have an answer for you."

Dirk felt his heart beat more wildly. An answer from Marietje? Was she waiting for him to come for her?

"It was she who sent word of the reinforcements. She learned of them, she said, during the night. You should not trust her. She is a traitor. She begged Commander Scott to take her from the inn, and she went with him willingly. And I have seen them . . ."

"Enough!" Dirk was startled by the fierceness of his emotions. "I forbid you to say more!"

The child continued as if he had not heard. ". . . together, and she enjoyed it. She does not wait for you, Dirk Hendrik. She never has waited for you. She belongs to the Englishman. It is what she wants. I have heard him speak of bringing her to England with him when he retires."

Dirk moved forward without any awareness of his action. He caught the boy's shoulders and shook them. "Stop! You must not speak of Marietje like that! She is good, I tell you! She loves Sumatra! She is not a traitor!" He heard an echo of his desperate cries, and he stopped.

What was he doing? Why was he standing in the middle of the forest, shaking a neighbor child as if he wished to kill him? As suddenly as he had grabbed the boy, he released him. With a sob, he stepped back, his fists clenched. He had to control his anger, and his despair. He had to.

Shaking from the force of his emotion, he clenched and unclenched his fists. His breath sent shudders through his body. It could not be true. He would not allow it to be true.

Yet . . . As his emotions calmed, his thinking ability returned. If it were not true, why would the boy say it? He knew Marietje from the past. They had been friends. How often the lad had ridden over to the Koenraad plantation to spend an afternoon with Marietje and Pieter. *And me.* Willem knew long before the British came that Dirk and Marietje planned to marry. What else but a need to speak the truth would inspire him to make such a declaration regarding her traitorous behavior?

As the anger faded, a new emotion overwhelmed Dirk. He considered Willem's words. "I have seen them . . ." What had Willem seen? Overcome by jealousy, Dirk longed to hear every detail. Yet he had closed that door already. He could not ask Willem to speak now, when moments before he had threatened the child if he said another word.

Yet the torment of uncertainty seemed even more painful than the reality of knowledge. Would he hurt less if he knew all that had transpired? Would the sure knowledge of her pleasure in Scott's arms hurt more or less than the picture drawn by his imagination?

Willem seemed to sense that Dirk was growing calm once more. "I must find some trinkets to bring back. I will be working for Commander Scott as his messenger boy. I'll be back with more news when I get it." He turned and was gone, as if afraid to remain longer in the presence of an angry man.

Dirk stared at the place where the child had stood. A thought had brought a ray of hope to his troubled heart, and now he could not let it go until he pursued it to its logical conclusion. How odd it was that Willem should be free to wander around at night, when he was supposedly the captive of the commander. Was it possible that the boy—not Marietje—was the traitor? How easy it would be for the lad to get away if the English wanted him to contact his father! And how easy to feed him stories that he would believe just in order to cause the Dutch defenders inconvenience!

If only some of the things the boy said were true, how would the small bands of landowners know which to believe? He and Frans and the others would have to act as if every bit of information were true. They would move unnecessarily, tire themselves out with hiding. And they would neglect the important task of eating away at the British defenses.

If the boy was delivering some untruths mixed with some honest reporting of British plans, he must be unaware of the difference between the two. So he was not actually a traitor, only a dupe.

But what about Marietje? The thought of her in another man's arms burned at his consciousness. How he hated any man who knew her charms! Yet once, when the possibility was still only something he thought he ought to explore, he had decided that he could love her even if she had been raped by a lust-filled soldier. Was it any different, now that the man had a name?

Ruefully, he admitted that there was a great difference. The first time he considered the possibility of Marietje being forced to submit to some conquering soldier, he had not really believed it would happen. Now he knew it to be true. She was a virgin no longer. Another man had performed the pleasurable duty in his stead. He felt an emptiness that threatened to tear at his very soul. "I'll kill him. If she submitted willingly, as Willem claims, he deserves even more to die." He recognized, deep within himself, the ridiculousness of his anger. But that knowledge did not help his mind to clear. All the passion he had held back, all the times he had wanted to hold her and had not because of her innocence, came back now to taunt him. What a fool he had been! Maybe, if she had not been a virgin, the Englishman would not have found her so to his liking.

"Dirk! We missed you. It was a good night. I saw at least ten men fall this trip, and more at the hands of others." Frans appeared where, sometime before, his son had stood. But Frans's face was wreathed in a smile, and his hand was stretched out in friendship.

"Willem was here. He said that the British expect a ship of reinforcements before spring."

Frans showed no surprise that his son had not waited to see him. "Reinforcements, eh? By spring."

"Yes. But he seemed uncertain as to whether the news was the truth. I think it is not, and the British want to lure us out before we are ready to battle. Maybe they have learned of the many groups that are converging on Padang, and they want to kill us off before others arrive to help us."

" 'Tis a possibility. At any rate, it is something we need not act on right away. Did you not say you wished to rescue your Marietje?"

Dirk felt the question as one would feel a slap in the face. Was Frans, now, challenging him to prove the loyalty of his woman? "Yes." He hoped Frans would not notice the uncertainty in his voice.

"Well, then, why don't you reconnoiter? You must make careful plans, for we have few men to risk saving one woman when so many are beyond our help."

Dirk knew Frans spoke of his wife and of the many others who lay dead. In a way, their hopes hung on

Marietje's rescue, too. For she represented to them all the women who now suffered under British domination. If she were rescued, all of their spirits would rise.

"I'll go now, then." Dirk dared say no more. How could he hint to his friends that he had cause to doubt Marietje's loyalty? It would be like telling them that their wives and fiancées had shared her appreciation of the British treatment.

"I'll tell Ben." Frans patted Dirk's shoulder as he passed. "Good luck. We'll be ready when you want help."

Alone, Dirk headed toward the plantation. Rescuing Marietje's loyalty? It would be like telling them that their have to be attempted in daylight, when most of the soldiers were on the roads. But to do so, he would first have to see how things lay. Then the next time Willem came for more jewelry and to deliver more information, he could transmit all the plans to Marietje.

Yet what if in telling her, he exposed his friends to capture—or death? Could he trust her not to deliver them into the hands of the enemy?

Angrily he pushed the thought from his mind. How insidious lies and accusations could be! They undermined trust, even before any proof could be found that they were true.

I have to trust her—as she must trust me. If we love each other we should have faith. He felt the emptiness in his own heart as he uttered the words. He should have faith, yet he had none. How easily it was destroyed!

His mind was filled with confusion as he moved through the forest, and at last he found himself on a promontory overlooking the plantation. He had traveled there before with Pieter and Marietje, and the three of them had picnicked on an escarpment. He patted his back where his glass hung. With it, he would be able to see what went on at the house. And he could see for himself how Marietje took her confinement.

Moving carefully, so his glass remained in the shadows where it would not reflect the sunlight and draw attention to him, he lay down and began to search the gardens that surrounded the plantation house. Now that he had reached the ledge, he would remain in its shelter until nightfall, dozing if he felt tired, so that he could make the return journey to his friends after dark. He had all day to watch. Plenty of time to prove to himself that Marietje remained true to him in her heart, even though her body might for a time belong to another.

Slowly he moved the glass across the garden area, past the great house. The sun was barely risen. He could see the soldiers changing guard, and the slaves moving out to the fields. He wondered, briefly, if their new masters treated them with the same kindness Hans Koenraad had shown.

A door opened, and Byron Scott stepped into the sunlight, followed by Willem. Dirk studied the lad closely, wishing he could be closer so he could recognize the expression on the boy's face. Was the child the one who had succumbed to the charm of the Englishman? It was not inconceivable. The man had much to warrant admiration. He was a powerful person, in command of all the forces the English had landed on Sumatra. At his command, men hurried to their deaths. Why shouldn't a child find him fascinating?

Yet Willem seemed too intent upon providing his father with information. Dirk paused in his thinking. Too intent. That was the secret. Maybe it was Willem, after all, whom he should mistrust. He resumed his contemplation of the boy.

Now he noted certain characteristics he had not seen before. The boy held himself stiffly, as if he hated to touch anything around him. He seemed always on guard. Didn't Scott see that behavior, too?

Dirk looked at Scott. No. The commander was far too involved in his own thoughts to pay that much attention to a child. He called out, and though Dirk could not hear his voice, he realized that Byron Scott was waiting for something.

Once more the door opened, and this time Marietje appeared. She was dressed in a riding gown, and she carried a small crop in in her hand. As she moved toward him Scott signaled for a groom to bring the horses.

Dirk was not aware of the groom or even of Willem. His glass moved from Marietje's face to that of the commander. Both were diffused with an inner glow. She reached Scott's side and held out her hand, but he pushed it aside, pulling her instead into his arms.

Did she struggle? Dirk looked for some sign of resistance. A pressure of her hand against his chest. A turn of her head. Anything to prove to his willing heart that she did not like what was happening to her. But he saw nothing. She seemed to float into Scott's arms, and she remained there until he released her. Then, still, she clung to his arm and let him lift her up into the saddle.

With a curse, Dirk hammered his fist on the rock beside his glass. Willem was right. Marietje had no wish to leave Scott. He had no right to risk the lives of his friends to rescue a woman who no longer cared for her freedom.

He knew he ought to go, but instead he returned to his glass. He watched as Scott and Marietje left the plantation house and headed toward the northwest. Out to survey the workers? They rode close together, talking as they moved along. Once more the sting of anger mixed with jealousy blurred his vision. If she truly wanted to escape from this man, she would have little to say to him. If he in any way forced her to do his bidding, she would be unable to conceal her resentment. Marietje was such a transparent child. Open, easy to read. He could not believe that in a few months she could become a woman capable of concealing her emotions for the sake of some stronger goal.

Was this the behavior of a woman who wanted to be rescued? Not at all! Willem was right.

Dirk followed Marietje with his glass until he realized with a shock that she was leading the way to the bower. To his secret place! She was taking her lover to a place made sacred by her love for . . . *For me!* Again he hammered his fist against the stone, and he paid no heed when he tore his skin and began to bleed. *That place is ours! How dare she . . . ?*

He wanted to cry, but his anger was too great. Lying out of sight, he was seeing proof of her infidelity. Over and over he repeated his curse. *Damn her for a faithless bitch! I can understand her being forced to submit—but Willem is right, she goes with this man of her own free will.*

Still the torment of jealousy would not let him put down

his glass. He watched as they entered the bower, waiting in agony, wondering if she were giving herself to this vile Englishman even as the glass wavered, searching for some crevice through which he could see.

He breathed a sigh of relief and increased anger when the two emerged. Marietje's hair was in disarray, but what he noticed was how brightly she moved, how high she held her head. Was this the stance of a woman shamed? No. Willem was right. Marietje had betrayed his trust. She belonged now to the enemy.

Unable to endure the torment any longer, Dirk rose and moved back from the cliff's edge. He had seen more than he wished. More than he could ever forget. He had gambled on her innocence and her loyalty to him—and he had lost.

He moved without caution, too angry to care for his own safety. Yet some perverse guide protected him, even when he approached the lower lands, where the soldiers were apt to travel. He stumbled on, clenching and unclenching his fists, cursing under his breath, glancing over his shoulder, as if he were followed by a demon.

And then abruptly, his stumbling advance ended.

"Halt!" The cry rang out, freezing Dirk in his tracks. In one second all of his carelessness flashed before him. It was, he knew, his fault that he was now in danger. He had forgotten to be careful.

Yet, though his response was to blame himself for his predicament, his reactions were those of a fighting man. Automatically he leaped toward the woods and threw himself into the brush. A bullet whistled over his head as he dove, but he paid it little heed. Spinning as he landed, he brought his own gun up, ready for firing.

The battle was short. He had come upon three soldiers, pushing a cart loaded with flour, found at some plantation up the hill. The first he killed with one shot. The next managed to duck one bullet and caught the next. Meanwhile Dirk had moved from his first place of concealment, loading and shooting as he ran, so the third man was confused as to his whereabouts. Before he had a chance to direct his aim in the right place, Dirk fired one more shot. The man dropped, his gun falling from his hands.

Cautiously Dirk stepped onto the road. He picked up the three rifles, removed the powder horns from the soldiers' shoulders and tucked them all on the cart, next to the sack of flour. Then, without a look back at the dead, he continued down the road. He paused at a bend. If he had a uniform, he could continue the rest of the way with less danger. Once more he returned to the dead soldiers.

When he moved on again, he was dressed in a red jacket. He carried his rifle over his back, with a powder horn hanging at his side. The boots he had taken were tight, and his feet complained with each step, but he persevered without any indication that he was in pain. Once he passed two soldiers who called out and asked if he needed help, but he shook his head and answered "No." He moved on before they had time to ask any more questions.

At the narrow path that led into the forest close to where his friends lay hidden, he whistled and waited. When no one responded, he moved into the woods, leaving the cart alone. There he removed his headdress and the red coat. This time his signal was answered. Frans appeared. "Dirk! I thought you were an Englishman!"

"I was. I have a sack of flour on the road. Help me pull it up."

Frans caught one handle of the wagon and tugged. Dirk pulled on the other. Slowly at first, and then with a sudden rush, the cart was lifted from the road and into the brush. They tugged harder, until the cart was hidden. Then Frans lifted the heavy bag and shifted it onto his shoulders. "Better not leave the cart here. It'll point directly to our shelter."

"Yes. I thought of that. I think if I get it back onto the road I can push it so it will roll downhill. It should travel some distance before it stops."

"Good." The bag was heavy, Dirk could see, for Frans was bent low. "I'm glad you're back. When you return, we'll talk about rescuing your Marietje and my son."

Dirk nodded. He was thankful, suddenly, that he was not required to answer. It would be difficult. How could he tell his friend that both Marietje and Willem were probably working with—not against—the enemy?

He turned a bend. Ahead the road slanted steeply. Giving the cart a shove, he aimed it downward. It bounced away, gaining speed as it moved. Satisfied that he had disposed of the cart safely, Dirk stepped into the forest. He had gone in search of his woman. Well, at least he had not come back empty-handed.

Chapter Twenty-Four

"Willem?" Marietje looked up as the lad stepped into her room. Would he smile at her this time? Was there, in his eyes, any sign of understanding, of forgiveness? For the thousandth time, she berated herself for her failure to lock the door that separated her room from his. If he had not seen her in the tub with Scott, he might have been persuaded that she was submitting to her captor against her will. Now she was certain he would never accept her explanation.

How could a child of ten going on eleven recognize the subtleties of adult relationships? How could he ever understand that she had to give herself completely to Byron Scott or he would sense her holding back and know that she was not loyal to him? How would she make it clear to a child who still saw life as a fight between pure good and pure evil that far too often the two lines were confused? There was no way. Marietje knew that. Yet she hoped. For Willem saw Dirk regularly. What Willem said had to carry weight among the men, even though he was a child.

Was it Willem's distrust of her that kept Dirk from his promised rescue attempt? She searched the past days for some other sign, some other cause for Dirk's delay. Long ago, or so it seemed, she had feared he might have been watching her as she entered the bower with Byron. Had that fear at last become a reality?

She had not wanted to go to the bower, not after she learned that Dirk was near. But Scott had insisted. He had been so open to her after that morning in the tub. And to him the bower, their coming together in the primitive surroundings of nature, seemed to have special meaning.

"Willem. Please come here. I must deliver a message to Dirk."

"Like the message about the reinforcements?" Willem studied her coldly. He was in charge of their relationship, for he felt he knew her to be a traitor. "All other news we have gathered say this is not so."

She repressed the urge to argue. "If I was wrong, it was an honest mistake. Byr—Commander Scott told me during a . . . period of confidence."

Willem, too, seemed eager to avoid any open conflict. "What is your message this time?"

"Ask Dirk whether he still carries my scarf."

"Your scarf? Why should he carry a scarf?"

"Please, I can't explain, but he will understand—if my love still is meaningful to him."

Willem pursed his lips. *Like an old man,* Marietje thought. *He will not be eleven until next month, and he is already an old man. This is the crime of war—that it destroys our children.*

And then, sometimes, the children destroy us.

She was aware that she feared the child who stood before her. If he wished, he could destroy any love Dirk had left for her. Because she knew Dirk would not endure a traitor.

Willem seemed unmoved by her emotion. "I'll ask him. But I'm sure he has thrown it away. I have never seen a scarf in his possession." He turned and was gone before she could think of any further words to say that might tell Dirk of her love.

Filled with sadness, she moved toward the window. She heard the great door below open, and she knew Willem was on his way. And then a sudden terror possessed her. It was still day! He should wait for the protection of nightfall! She ran to the window and looked out. Below, she saw Willem surrounded by four soldiers. Scott stood on the front stoop, issuing some order. She could not hear the words, but she had no doubt of their meaning. Willem had been caught. He was being sent now to his execution.

She rushed to the door, her thoughts tumbling about. She had to do something. But what?

Before she could reach it, the door to the hall burst open and Scott appeared. She saw his clenched fists, and she braced herself for a blow. It was over.

She dared to look at his face, and what she saw stopped

her in her steps. There was some anger, that she could see, but it was pain that shone in his eyes.

"Why, Marietje? Why did you betray me?"

She responded to his cry with new strength. She was dead, whatever she said. Now, at last, was the time for truth. "Did you think I loved you? How could you? You killed my mother and father. You have murdered my people. Can you still expect me to forget all you have done?" She gained strength as she spoke. "Well, you are wrong. I do not love you. I hate you, Byron Scott. With all my soul and body I hate you and all you stand for. I am a loyal subject of my native land. I am a Dutchwoman! I detest all things English. And I despise you! You took my innocence and turned it into . . ." Her voice broke. The memory of her ecstasy as she moved in his arms was more than she could repress, even in anger. ". . . into shame!"

Spurred by her emotions, she warmed to the fate she was certain awaited her. He would kill her now. He would have to. To save his honor. And she would welcome death. Dirk loved her no longer. Life held nothing for her. "I have pretended. Every time you took me, I played at my responses. I let you think you had won me over, and I joyed in the power I had over you. Do you believe that you could win a woman with your love? You made me laugh!" She saw that she had struck a sore spot, and she hurried on. "Yes, laugh! Do you know how ridiculous you are? An old man, thinking he has gained the love of a young woman! Old—and foolish!" The scorn in her voice was real. It was easy to feed her own anger with her hatred and thus forget the reality of his love for her.

"Did you really believe I wanted to go with you to England? If I did, I would find myself another man. A young man, capable of satisfying me." Even as she spoke she wondered at all she was saying. Had she really thought such thoughts about this man? Was she really the horrible, lusty whore she made herself out to be?

Yes. If Dirk had trusted her, if he had kept faith with her, she could have continued to see the inner core of purity that held her soul above the contamination of her surroundings. But Dirk had abandoned her. He did not love her. She knew that, even without an answer to her question about the scarf. And if he loved her no more, then she was all that she seemed to be in Willem's eyes. A whore. A traitor.

No, not a traitor. She would die an honorable death, and prove her loyalty. Dirk would learn of it and be sorry. Her death would prove her innocence—and her undying love for him.

She wanted nothing now but to anger Byron until he could control his rage no longer. She could see the color rising to his cheeks. She could see his fists clenching. She could see the fire in his eyes flaring to life.

"You destroyed me, Byron Scott. I will destroy you. I hate you. I pray every night that you will die in your sleep. I pray that your blessed ship filled with reinforcements will sink, and all of them drown. And I know the lie you have told the women in Padang. They know, too, and they join in my cursing. You have turned us all into whores. But we will win in the end. Our men will kill you all. And those who are not killed with bullets or sword will die of the plague."

He seemed not to hear her words. His mouth worked, as if he was ready to speak, but no words came. Until suddenly he was galvanized into action. "Silence!" His cry deafened her. "Silence, bitch!" He raised his hand and caught her arm, pulling her to him. She felt his arms close around her, crushing her with their force. His face was inches away, and she suddenly felt an overwhelming fear. Did he intend to throw her from the window? She had hoped he would draw his gun and shoot her. Hoped for a quick end to her torment. What did he have in store for her, if not what she wanted?

His lips crushed hers with a force she had not felt before. She felt his hardness against her, and she knew with a sudden horror that he would never set her free. He released his hold and caught her gown with one hand, pulling it from her body. He spoke through his teeth, his face set in anger. "You hate me? I don't believe it! You laughed at my lovemaking? Liar!"

He swept her off her feet and threw her onto the bed. "Laugh now! Show me how you laugh!" He was on her with a force so strong she thought for a moment he would crush her bones. She struggled to free herself, and he cuffed her ear with a blow that set her head reeling.

Subdued at last, she submitted to his assault. She felt his fingers tear at her breasts, and she cried out in pain. Was this what he thought she wanted? To be taken by force? She hammered against his chest, trying to push him away. But her struggles seemed only to rouse him to greater fury. Yet she continued to fight.

Suddenly he rose and lifted her from the bed. With one movement he twisted her and threw her back on the mattress, this time with her face buried deep in the blankets. She felt her skin tear as he forced himself into her body, and she screamed. Yet he did not diminish the force of his assault. She tried to struggle, but each movement she made only increased her pain, and then darkness closed in. The pain was still there, the hurt of his thrusts still tore her apart, but the edge of her awareness was gone.

She awoke in a room filled with shadows. Somewhere, someone stirred, and she tensed with fear. Footsteps came toward her. Would it start again? Could she endure more torture?

"Marietje?" Mai spoke quietly, her face a mask of concern. "I'm glad you're awake. I thought he had killed you."

"I wish he had." Why, she wondered, did it hurt when she talked. "Is he gone?"

"Yes." Mai stroked Marietje's forehead with cool, smooth fingers. "Did he not say he had to go into Padang?"

Marietje searched her memory, but all she could find was pain. "I don't know. I must get away. He won't kill me. I know that now. He'll take me with him. I want to die here in Sumatra."

"You mustn't speak of dying. Why did you fight him? Has he not been good to you?"

"Willem! He knows about Willem! I have to get to Dirk."

Mai did not answer. She seemed lost in thought.

"Don't you hear me? I must get word to Dirk. Byron is going to kill Willem."

"I'll deliver the message." Mai spoke quietly. "Where shall I go to find him?"

Marietje stared at Mai's face. Was she speaking the truth? Or would she take the information and give it to the soldiers so they could kill all the men? "No. You must help me to get away." Marietje forced her legs to move to the edge of the bed. She cried out as she sat up, but she did not abandon her plan. She had to get dressed, and she had to go. Now. Before Willem was killed. He was a child. Whatever he thought of her, he deserved the chance to live.

She moved cautiously across the room to her wardrobe. Mai followed slowly. "Well? Are you going to help me? You can say I forced you, if you want. You helped me once. Help me now. For the sake of the boy." She could see that she had found Mai's point of greatest sensitivity. Mai, like all of her countrymen, loved children. Native babies were coddled and loved by every member of the village. And a person who harmed a child was considered a terrible criminal.

"I cannot give you food."

"That doesn't matter." Marietje still hurt when she moved, but her new feeling of purpose seemed to deaden the pain. "Help me dress." She paused, suddenly alarmed. "Are you certain Byron has gone to Padang?"

"Yes." She pulled out a plain gown and helped Marietje put it on. "You will have to go on foot. The soldiers guard the horses."

Marietje dared not answer. She needed all her strength to stay on her feet and to walk. She could barely lift her legs to let Mai pull on her shoes and lace them up. Yet she had to go now. It was the only hope she had to save Willem.

They descended to the kitchen by way of the servants' stairs, pausing often to let Marietje rest. By the time they reached the servants' door that led to the garden, Mai seemed hesitant to continue. Marietje leaned against the doorframe. "You must get me some laudanum. Just a small amount. To kill the pain."

Mai hesitated a moment, and then she was gone. She returned silently, a small packet in her hand. "Do not take more than you need. Sometimes the spirits visit one who eats of this medicine."

Marietje suppressed a growing impatience. She had never learned much about the beliefs of the natives who lived on the island. They seemed so confused. Some, she knew, followed the Moslem belief in Allah, though they were not, so her father had told her, like the natives of Arabia. Others—the Chinese—seemed to worship their ancestors. But there were other, smaller groups. Mai once spoke of Allah. Did Moslems believe in spirits?

It didn't matter. Marietje took the packet and tore it open. Was this the medicine she had requested? Laudanum was a liquid. She had seen her mother use it. But she had no time to question her maid. She took a small bite and wrapped the rest, tucking it into her bodice. A new warmth flooded her body.

With a nod to Mai, she descended the steps. For safety, Mai would remain behind, to keep anyone from looking in Marietje's room and discovering that she was gone.

A sound from the stables drew Marietje up short. She stood for a moment, undecided, and then she hurried on. The horses were restless. Spring was coming. The rains were not as heavy as they had been even a week before. Would the grooms set to guard them let the big stallion mate with her delicate mare?

She shook her head at her wandering thoughts. Did it matter? Did anything matter anymore, other than ridding the island of the hated English?

She moved carefully, for even though the medicine had subdued her aches, she still felt a stiffness in her legs. Yet for all her clumsiness, she moved unnoticed. The soldiers were busy—or sleeping. They had no reason to suspect that she would be out of her bed.

She did not head for the gates. Instead she crossed the barnyard and hurried toward the rows of coffee trees. They would offer her shelter as she ran for safety. If she could run. She tested her legs and was surprised to find that they seemed strong again. Whatever the medicine was that Mai had given her, it worked.

As she left the clearing she glanced back at the house. In the moonlight, the white walls seemed stark and cold. Yet once it had sheltered a family in love. She wished suddenly that she could set it afire. How could she ever live there again, with the memory of Byron Scott's cruelty filling its rooms?

A cloud concealed the moon, and she turned toward the woods. God only knew if she was already too late. In her concern for Willem, she was able to forget that she would soon come face-to-face with Dirk Hendrik. The medicine helped to soften her anxiety, as it controlled her pain. But it was her worry for the safety of a boy who had shown his dislike of her that kept her going.

As she reached the forest the moon burst from its cloud covering. This promised to be a clear night. The first since the monsoon season began. She searched the underbrush for some sign of a trail and saw one almost immediately. Was this a sign that her search would be a success? She dared not pursue the probability. Already the medicine that kept her injury from interfering with her movement was affecting her mind. She felt light-headed, as if she were floating over the rough pathway.

Only one thought remained clear. She had to find Dirk. And she had to warn him of Willem's danger. The boy had to be saved. For somehow, in her confused, pain-filled thoughts, he stood as a symbol of her honor. If Willem died, she was lost. But if he could be saved . . . Stumbling, she moved forward into the forest.

Chapter Twenty-Five

"They're out tonight." There was surprise in Frans's voice as he gestured toward the road. Dirk, close behind him, rose up to see what sort of Englishmen would be out after sunset.

The road was clear, but the sound of movement upon it was growing louder. "Are they searching for something?"

Both men stood quietly, listening. Just around the bend above them someone was beating the brush. An English voice issued a string of curses. "You know what the commander will do if we let him get away."

Dirk crept closer, with Frans at his side. They paused abruptly. Ahead of them were two soldiers. One had penetrated the underbrush by about fifteen feet, and he stood still, hitting at the branches that served to conceal his vision. Dirk and Frans crouched low. It was only by chance that they had entered the English soldier's range of vision at a time when he was far more concerned with his own comfort than with the search that had brought him into the forest.

A voice from the road caused him to spin around. "Ben boy! Can you hear me?"

"I hear you, Sergeant."

"Can you see where he went?"

"No." The soldier made a feeble attempt to look under the covering of leaves, but he did not turn around.

"Come out then."

Ben boy pushed his way back to the road. Dirk could see that the man had hacked his way in, and he left by the same path. These men were not used to forest fighting. They seemed unaware that animals made the only paths that could be followed easily.

"Who are they hunting for?" Frans dared to whisper the question as he heard Ben boy join his fellows.

"Maybe we'd better find out." Dirk crept closer. Now

he could see four men, three of them common soldiers, the fourth a sergeant. They were standing in the middle of the road, as if afraid to get too close to the underbrush. The sergeant was staring at a spot in the forest about twenty feet from where Dirk was hiding. The other three men were trying to be quiet. One scuffed at his boots with the point of a great knife. Evidently, Dirk decided, he had been the one to enter the forest. The other two leaned on their rifles, pretending an interest in the dirt on their leggings.

The sergeant cleared his throat. "He won't go back."

Dirk saw the three soldiers look up, and though none spoke, he sensed their surprise at the sergeant's words.

"Stupid! He can't go back. He knows we've been ordered to kill him."

"Damn brat. What made him suspicious?" It was Ben boy who spoke.

"Have we gone with him before when he went off on one of his 'errands'?" The sergeant didn't wait for an answer. "But it doesn't matter. We just have to stick together. We'll tell the commander the job's done."

The four men gazed at each other, bound suddenly by the daring of their conspiracy. Then one of the two with guns spoke. "Can't do that if I ain't fired a shot."

"Then fire, idiot!" The sergeant's voice seemed to grow tight and higher as he spoke. "Damn it! Fire off a few shots, both of you. Maybe you'll get him, after all."

As if on command, the two men raised their rifles and aimed straight into the forest. As the rifle shots resounded, stirring up a cacophony of response from the beasts of the forest, Dirk crept back to where Frans was waiting. "They're hunting for Willem. I don't know why. But I think he got away. By now, he might be safe at the camp."

"Willem?" Frans's voice showed his alarm. "How do you know? Why are they shooting?"

"So they can tell the commander that they killed him. I think that for some reason they did not follow his instructions to the letter. Maybe when we find him, we'll know why."

Under cover of the forest noises, Dirk and Frans moved swiftly back into the woods. Frans led the way, and Dirk wondered at the speed with which the man traversed the trails. He had been one who barely knew of their existence when he first joined the band.

When they reached the old native village they had chosen as headquarters, both men paused. Willem sat in the shadow of the largest hut. The moonlight bathed the village in a eerie light, and Willem seemed like a ghost of some earlier occupant. He had tied leaves around his head, like a crown, and he was half hidden under a mound of grasses that served to give the village a vacant look.

Frans stepped into the moonlight. "Willem? It's all right, lad. They aren't hunting for you."

The boy hesitated for a moment and then moved from his shelter. As he advanced he removed the odd headdress with which he had concealed himself once he had broken free of his captors. Now Dirk could see that the boy had other leaves tied on his arms and legs. A method of camouflage used by the natives on a hunt for food.

"Come here, lad. I thank God you escaped." Frans held out his arms to receive his son. But Willem approached like a soldier, his back straight, his head high.

When he reached the two men, he saluted. "Reporting for duty, Dirk Hendrik. I'm sorry I am no longer qualified for the work you assigned me."

"Assigned him?" Frans turned to Dirk. "What assignment did you give my son?"

"None you were not aware of. You agreed that he should go back and serve as our eyes and ears at the British headquarters."

"He has reported to you?"

"It was his choice."

For a moment, Frans stared at Dirk with unconcealed anger. Then he turned to his son. "Why, lad? Why not to me?"

The boy did not change his position. Like a soldier on duty, he stood erect, his head high. "Dirk Hendrik . . ." He seemed unable to continue. "You treat me like a child, Father."

"But you *are* a child!"

The boy drew back. "I do a man's job."

Frans looked into his son's face. Gradually the anger

and hurt faded. "Forgive me, Willem. You're all I have left. And it is hard for me to forget that you were a child, before the English came. You still are, in age. Maybe I do not want to see that your mother's death has changed you."

The boy did not respond. At mention of his mother, he winced, but he did not break down, as his father seemed to be doing. He stood dry-eyed and erect, waiting for the emotion of this reunion to pass.

Dirk stepped forward. "Why were they trying to kill you?"

"I was betrayed." Willem looked directly at Dirk as he spoke. "By Marietje."

"Marietje?" Dirk knew he showed his hurt in that one word. He glanced at Frans, a new understanding in his heart. Frans had lost the little boy he loved. Though Willem lived, he would never return to the innocence that had made him so charming before the British invasion. And he, Dirk, had lost Marietje.

True, she, like Willem, was still alive. But she was not his anymore. She had changed her allegiance from him to the English commander. He had seen proof of it himself. Still, it pained him to hear confirmation of her betrayal from another's lips.

"Tell us what happened."

"I made the mistake of telling her my plans. She asked me to deliver a message to you."

"A message?" In spite of his knowledge of her perfidy, he could not keep his emotions under full control.

The boy did not continue. "What was it?" Dirk hated himself for his curiosity.

"Nothing important. She wanted me to ask you if you still had her scarf." He paused. "I should have known it was just a way of getting me to admit aloud that I could contact you. When I left her room, Commander Scott came out of my room." He paused. "They're next to each other. And he went with me down the steps. He kept me a prisoner until his soldiers arrived, and then he told them to take me to the woods and kill me. He said they should make it appear an accident, if there was any danger he and Marietje might come upon my body when they went riding.

239

I think he wanted them to leave me where I'd be found later." He spoke without emotion of his own death, and Dirk remembered that the boy had seen his mother and infant sister die.

This time Frans moved before Willem could avoid him. Catching the child's shoulders, he pulled him close and held him firmly. "Dear God! That she would try to destroy my whole family!" The pain in his voice seemed to trigger a response in the lad. Abruptly the tight control broke. His arms went around his father's waist, and he began to sob.

Frans bent and lifted the boy in his arms. Cradling the child, he headed for the hut that served as his home.

Dirk watched them go without protesting. He remembered Frans's stern control before the English arrived. He had demanded obedience from his son, but he had never been known to give love. Even Gerda had been forced to live by strict standards. They were a Christian family in the middle of a heathen land. Frans had never permitted a native to work near his wife or child unless she or he was first baptized. His love, if he felt any had been expressed in rules and stern discipline.

Maybe one thing had come out of this fight that was good. Frans showed warm affection for his son. Maybe that very love would help the boy to recover from the horrors he had endured. The two vanished into the hut. Dirk was alone.

He stared for a time at the hut where Frans and Willem sat together as they had never been together before. Father and son. He had dreamed that he and Marietje would have children. Dreamed that he would have a son of his own whom he could love and teach the ways of man. Now he had nothing.

His shoulders sagging, he turned and moved up one of the overgrown paths that led from the hidden village. Why was he continuing to fight? His goal had turned to dust. Marietje had betrayed his love in another's arms.

A small voice within him reminded him that once he had decided that he would love her still—even if he found that she had been forced to submit to the enemy. At the reminder, a harsh laugh brought him to a halt. How full of irony life could be! He had thought that the worst thing that could happen to Marietje was physical defilement. He had tormented himself with visions of her in the arms of some British soldier.

But she had not been attacked by a rough enlisted man. She had become the darling of the commander of the invading forces. And she had turned from her own people. He had seen that for himself. No one had forced her to greet the commander with such a show of affection. No one, surely, had forced her to reveal to another man the location of the bower that held such importance in her relationship with him.

How he had misjudged her! He had thought she would be true to him no matter what might happen to her. He repeated again his decision of so long ago. "I could have loved her still, even if she was no longer virgin. I know I could have. But only if she remained true to me in her heart. She has shown me that her heart has no constancy in it."

He paused. Had she hurt him so badly that he now was losing his sanity? When, in the past, had he talked aloud to himself? When had he wandered off, away from his appointed duty, to think of her?

Many times—but as a lad. He had never neglected his duty even when he wanted her the most. Nor had he ever considered seriously an act that might bring shame on her. She showed no such consideration for herself.

What he wanted was to forget her. To put her from his mind as she had removed herself from his presence. Yet in this one small task he had been a failure. Everything reminded him of her. A sudden rain brought visions of the bower and her sweet embrace. The promise in her eyes and voice. The innocence of her trust.

A shadow moved ahead of him, and he stopped. Had one of the Englishmen followed him after all? If one, then more could follow. Unless this one was killed before he could expose them. He raised his gun and took aim.

"Please! Don't shoot me."

His finger froze on the trigger. Was this another dream? "Marietje?"

"Thank God! Oh, Dirk, I prayed so that I'd find you."

She moved swiftly from the shadow into his arms. He saw her approach with a mixture of emotions. Here she was, in the flesh, where he could confront her with her deceit. Why did he not speak out? Why did his arms move upward to receive her?

Or was this a dream, too, like all the others? He felt her body press against his, and he abandoned himself to the joy of her touch. A moment's diversion. She would vanish, as she had so often before, and he would continue on his walk.

But she did not fade away. She clung to him with arms that felt real, and her lips touched him on the chin. This was more than a dream.

This was real! He stepped back, a look of horror on his face. "Marietje! You aren't a dream. It's really you?"

"I had to come away. I was afraid he'd kill me."

"As he tried to kill Willem?"

Her face showed her surprise. "Willem? You know about Willem?"

"Yes, I know it all. You betrayed him. He told us."

"Betrayed him?" She seemed to be searching her memory. As if she were drugged, or half asleep. Then her expression changed. Her eyes widened, and she stared at Dirk with something akin to terror. "I did. Yes, I betrayed him. But I did not intend to. You must believe me. I had to know . . ." She lowered her head, as if ashamed to meet his gaze.

"Why have you come? Why don't you go back to your lover? Isn't it enough that you have tried to bring about the death of a child? The only family left to an old friend? Must you come now and torture me, as well? I have seen you in the bower. I know. You cannot pretend to me that you have suffered under this lover of yours. And Willem has told me, too, though it sickened me to think that you had lost all modesty. Go back to him. Leave me alone."

She stood before him, her hands at her sides. He had not touched her, though he had been tempted to push her, maybe even hit her, his anger at her was so intense. Was she ill? A wave of concern threatened to wipe out his anger, and he forced it away.

It was then he saw that she was weeping. She stood

alone, unmoving, tears streaming down her cheeks. She seemed ready to speak, but no sound came from her lips. And then, slowly, as if every movement brought her pain, she turned and headed for the road.

An uncontrollable passion forced him into action. He could not let her go without learning from her own lips the truth of her betrayal. She had already admitted to her responsibility for Willem's brush with death. He had to hear her renounce his love. That pain, cruel as it would be, would at last free him of her memory. "Yes!" His voice was harsh. "Go back to your lover. I know now that you never loved me. All you thought about was yourself."

She stopped, her back to him. Her voice sounded muffled. By tears? Did she still possess enough decency to recognize the shame of her behavior?

"I have always loved you. I will love you when I die."

"You show it poorly. It is not usual that a woman express her love for one man in another man's arms."

She seemed to wilt under his words. Had she truly grown smaller? Her answer was so faint he had to strain to hear. "I knew you would not understand. But God will prove my honor. I had no choice—then. Now, thank God, I have the strength to die."

"You seem very much alive, however." He felt shock at his own words. Did he really want to see her dead? Part of him, he knew, answered yes to that question. But there was still a place deep within his heart that cried out in protest.

She did not turn around. "Good-bye, Dirk Hendrik. Someday, I pray, you will know how much I loved you."

Fury at the daring of her words galvanized him into action. His right arm shot out and he caught her shoulder, spinning her around. The cloth of her dress was weak; it was, he realized, a dress he had seen before. With a rush the memory returned. She had worn it the day they had declared their love in the bower.

Why had she worn that gown! Fury possessed him. Was it not bad enough that she taunted him with her lies? Did she have to dress to torment him, too? "Has your lover sent you here?" He tugged at the dress, wanting desperately to tear it from her body. She had no right to wear a gown that had once been a sign of her purity! Better that she return naked to her English lover!

The gown ripped in his hands, but she made no attempt to stop him. She was willing, it seemed, to take any punishment he wished to inflict.

And she deserved so much more than he would be able to give. His anger was restrained, he knew, by the memory of what she had once been.

The dress fell from her shoulders, and now at last she bent to catch it as it drooped around her breasts. The bright moonlight illuminated her ivory skin.

Over her left shoulder, a dark, ugly bruise was visible. Startled, he pulled her closer and slid the other sleeve down. That arm, too, was dark with bruises. Horrified, he forced the gown from her shoulder and let it fall to the ground. She winced as he grabbed her, and cried out, like a fawn caught in a trap.

He barely heard her cry. He was staring in horror at her body. It was covered with bruises down to the waist. "Take off your undergarment." He spoke in such commanding a tone she dared not disobey.

She did not look up as she removed her last clothing. He had already told her of his disgust for her. She seemed to feel that there was no disgrace she could not endure. Her face was devoid of expression. Her jaw held tightly closed.

Naked, at last, she stood before him. He moved slowly, aware of the terrible bruises she had uncovered. They were fresh, for he could see scabbing where her skin had been torn.

"Dear God, forgive me!" His prayer was whispered, but she heard it, and a spark of hope returned to her eyes.

"Has he done this to you?"

She spoke now, her voice hollow. "I tried to get him to kill me, but he wouldn't. I don't want to live without your love."

A frown wrinkled his brow. "I do not understand. You seemed so willing." He saw the spark die, and he hurried on. "I was watching last week. I saw you ride with him to the bower." The agony in his voice was heartrending. "Marietje, why there?"

She sobbed, but she seemed at first unable to respond.

"He discovered it. I thought I could help, give information to Willem that would be of value, if he liked and trusted me." She paused. "Did he tell you that a ship is coming with reinforcements?"

"Yes. It has not arrived yet." He saw her head droop, and he spoke more gently. "Is it possible he has made up tales to deceive us, knowing you were in contact with us?"

"I don't know. I think not. He was very angry when he heard me give a message to Willem. That was when . . ." She paused. "I must go back. If he finds me gone, he will come hunting for me. I know it. And he will find you and kill you all." She reached for her clothing. He had not touched her since she undressed. Now he reached out and caught her hand.

"No. Not yet. I must put something on your injuries." He felt the softness of her skin, and the last bit of barrier he had built against her vanished. He opened his arms, as Frans had opened his to his son.

With a sigh, she crept to him. She trembled as he pulled her close, but she did not draw back. His hands stroked the parts of her body that were unharmed. The expanse between her shoulders. The small of her back, above her sore buttocks. She whimpered in appreciation. Was it only pity he felt for her? He rested her head on his shoulder, a new feeling of wonder possessing him. If he felt pity, had his love—his passion—gone forever?

She spoke without moving. "Mai has promised to keep my absence from the soldiers. By . . . Scott went to Padang. Maybe to prepare for the arrival of the soldiers. I don't know. Until he returns, I am safe here."

"How long will he be gone?"

"He said a week. I must return before it is over."

"Then you will stay with me now?"

"If you will let me."

He did not answer. Instead he lifted her up in his arms, as Frans had lifted Willem. He bent and caught her gown between his fingers, and she took it and draped it over her nakedness. Then carefully, so she would not be hurt by the underbrush, he headed for the village. He, too, had a hut. And now he would not be alone.

Chapter Twenty-Six

"How beautiful you look."

Marietje opened her eyes and stared up at Dirk. Had he actually spoken such kind words to her? She moved cautiously, aware that some of the pain had left her body. "Dirk?"

"Yes?" He bent closer. "You've been asleep for two days. And I think you still need more rest. It's all right. One of our men is watching Padang. He'll let us know when Byron Scott begins his journey back to the plantation."

She wondered, in a hazy way, why Dirk was so willing to allow her to return to a man who had hurt her so badly, but she did not have the strength to ask. She felt his hand close over hers, and the comfort of his touch lulled her back to sleep.

When she woke again, the tiny hut was dark. "Dirk?" She felt a momentary fear that he would be gone.

"I'm here, Marietje." He touched her cheek with his fingers. "I won't leave you."

She moved her legs and discovered that much of the soreness was gone. "What day is it?" She struggled to sit, aware that though there was a delay, her muscles did respond.

"Thursday. You have been resting for two days. How do you feel?"

She felt tears trickle down her cheeks. Did she hear a hint of concern in his voice? "Better. Thank you. My arms don't feel quite so sore."

"I've been massaging you. It is a technique I learned from my friend, Lun Kui. If you rub bruises, they fade more quickly, and the pain goes away faster."

She blushed. Her legs felt better, too. Had he rubbed her there, too? Timidly she touched her inner thigh with her fingers. The pain was definitely gone. "Is it raining?"

"No, my dear. The monsoons are over. We have moved

farther into the forest, for the English might be more daring in their search for us."

Her eyes widened. "They are nearby?"

"No. We have guards. Willem has been asking to see you."

She felt herself grow tense. "Willem? I don't . . ."

"I've told him what you have been through, and why you came here. I think he is sorry he misjudged you." Dirk smiled. "He's a child. You cannot expect him to always make the right judgments. You remember, don't you, that he came to us when they shot at him?"

She searched her memory. Yes, she had known Willem was safe. "Did they hurt him?"

"No. Only frightened him a bit. He is with his father now. The ship has been sighted near Palembang."

"How?"

"How have we learned of it? My friend Lun Kui again. He sent a man after me and arranged for drum signals to convey messages. We learned of the ship only yesterday." He saw that she wanted to sit, and he put an arm under her shoulders. "We are prepared, thanks to your warning. The men from the south have joined us here. On Sunday our attack begins."

"Sunday?" Her father had objected to her working, or even riding, on the Sabbath.

"We must. The English, like us, seem less on guard on the Sabbath. So we must attack when their guard is most down."

She blanched. "You plan to attack Padang?"

"Yes."

"And the plantations?"

"Only the Koenraad plantation. The commander has kept his headquarters there."

"No. You mustn't. My father and mother are buried there." She felt her panic rise. "My father's farm must not be burned."

He was solemn. "I will do what I can. But our victory must come first."

"Yes." She sat quietly, resting against his shoulder. How comforting his touch was! How strong he seemed! "I'm sorry I have been such trouble."

"You are no trouble. Marietje, I have learned something wonderful during these days while you were so sick."

She half turned so she could see his face in the pale moonlight. There was so much she wanted to say. So many explanations she wanted to make. But she could not put the words together. All she could do was sit quietly, waiting for him to declare an end to their engagement.

Why, she wondered, was she so certain that was what was on his mind? Did she really wonder? No. She knew that he could not love her as he had before after seeing her as she had been when she arrived. He sympathized with her, maybe. But sympathy was not love. In a strange unhappy way, it forced love out the door.

"I don't want to . . . I don't need to hear it. I understand . . . A man wants mo—"

"I do not know about any other man. I know only how I feel." He leaned back, letting her rest beside him. "Marietje, remember when I asked your father for the right to marry you?"

It was coming now. She knew it. Why couldn't he wait? Maybe, in the fight that lay ahead, he would be killed. Did he have to leave her with the knowledge that his love for her had died? "Please, Dirk. Tell me later."

"No. I must tell you now." He moved suddenly, his lips covering hers.

She had no explanation for his unexpected move except, maybe, that he was saying good-bye to the past. Yet she could not ignore the message his lips were sending. She felt something akin to an ache as her body responded, and suddenly a terrible fear seemed to overwhelm her. Her arms moved up, pushing him away.

He retreated enough to relieve her panic. "You must let me, Marietje. You have been hurt badly. But if we are to have a life together, we must together fight the demon of fear that holds you so firmly. Did you know that while you were asleep, as I cared for you, you spoke my name? Yet when I touched you, you winced and drew away, as if you feared I might do you harm. He was cruel to you, but I will never be."

She shook her head. "I do not want your pity. I would

sooner live my life alone than marry a man who came to me with compassion void of love.''

"You think I have no love?" He retained the distance that seemed to help her to remain calm. "I thought maybe that was true, myself—for a time." He touched her lips with a finger. "Be patient, little Marietje, and let me talk."

She gazed into his eyes, and for the first time in what seemed to her to be ages, she felt a glimmer of hope. Then she pushed it away. All hope could do now was increase her pain later.

"I thought, for a while, that you had abandoned your own people and turned your loyalty to England. It hurt me, for I love our land. Sumatra must remain Dutch. While I thought these thoughts, I think I wanted to hate you." She drew back, but he continued without allowing her to interrupt. "I could not. All I felt was a terrible emptiness, for I thought I had lost you."

She felt a wave of anger. "What did you think happened to me? Why would you care if you lost a woman who had become a whore?"

He tensed. "Never call yourself that again! I know what a whore is, and you are not such a creature." She was shaking her head, angry at his self-deception. "I know now that you remained true to me even when Commander Scott forced you to accept him in your bed."

"No." Her voice had a dull sound. He would never understand. She was certain of that now. But she knew she could not stay near him without trying to explain, even if her words forced him away. "That is not how it was. Not after the first times." She tried to remember how she had come to accept Byron as her lover. He had tricked her, she remembered that. Haltingly she continued. "I tried to fight him at first. But he was so strong. And then I began to have dreams."

She spoke of her nighttime visits with a phantom lover she had thought was Dirk Hendrik. "I thought it was you. Truly I did. And then, one night . . ." She buried her face in her hands.

"Have you had such dreams since then?"

"Not the same. He was taking me as I slept. He tricked

me into wanting him—into liking what he did. And then . . ." Once more she hid her face. "Please, Dirk, I can't stand much more. Let me go. I do not deserve even your pity."

"You no longer have my pity. But you do have my love, and my admiration. You know that many of the women have been taken to Padang?"

"Yes, I was there with Willem and Gerda—and little Henriette. That was when I brought Willem with me."

"He told us. I believe you saved his life then. And the information you have sent us through him may save many of our lives. If the reinforcements came without our being aware, they could have trapped us all."

She was silent. Was this the only way they could feel comfortable together, when they spoke of battles and fighting?

He seemed to sense her change of attitude. She felt him move closer to her, and something about the touch of his trousers against her skin comforted her. He would not hurry her.

His arm moved behind her. "Will you sleep with me now?" He smiled as he spoke. "When I tried to lie beside you before, you pushed me away. May I stay with you now?"

She nodded, feeling a small fear begin in her abdomen. Would he take more, now that she had permitted this small move of reconciliation?

She got her answer quickly. He lay down, without removing even his shirt. She sat for a moment, and then let herself slide in beside him. To her surprise, she found his closeness comforting. Was it his willingness to remain dressed? She faced the truth. Scott's cruel assault had shaken her far more than she had realized. Her mind and heart needed to heal, for the scars there were deeper than any her body had endured.

At first she lay tense, holding a distance between herself and Dirk. But when he made no move to touch her more than he already was, she began to relax. When she heard his breathing become steady, she let herself drop asleep.

For the first time since the terror of Scott's attack, her dreams were devoid of violence. She was a child again, playing with Dirk and Pieter in the field behind the house, where neat rows of coffee trees now stood. She smiled in her sleep as in memory she raced after her two friends, heading for a mound where they had discovered baby field mice. She had watched them for a long time, wanting desperately to pick them up, but afraid that their mother would bite her.

Dirk stirred, and her dream changed. She was fifteen, watching Dirk and Pieter direct the planting of a new grove of trees. For the two boys, this was a step up—from nursemaid to foreman, and they were so very proud of their new status. Yet even then, Pieter deferred to Dirk, and Dirk took the lead—a natural director. Born an aristocrat.

She was jealous of their new authority, and at last she rode her horse into the field, temporarily disrupting the work. Pieter had stepped back as she rode forward, but Dirk would not accept such lack of respect from a mere girl. With a sudden leap he caught her reins and slowed her horse to a trot. Then he was up behind her, taking control, returning her to the plantation house, where she belonged.

Toward morning, her dreams changed again. She was in the bower, and Dirk was beside her. She felt the stirring of passion that had made that first awareness of her love so exciting, and she moaned lightly. Her hands, until that time kept well to herself, moved closer to Dirk.

He woke at her touch. "Marietje?"

Her eyes opened. She felt protected by the warmth of sleep, and yet she could not deny the feelings that seemed to grow as she met Dirk's dark eyes. "Dirk? I . . . ." She became aware of where her hands were, and she pulled them back. "I'm sorry. I didn't mean to . . ."

"Maybe it means that you would dare to try. If I let you decide what can be done."

She stared at him in silence, not comprehending his meaning. Some part of her wanted him to touch her, to pull her into his arms and prove that her long-ago fear was meaningless. Yet a far more recent fright pushed him away. She lay frozen, waiting for him to assert his masculine right, knowing that when he did, she would hate him as she hated Byron Scott.

When he remained still, she felt a strange ease. He spoke quietly. "I know now, Marietje. I have never stopped loving you."

She felt a chill shake her body. "I thought you hated me. I thought I could never make you understand."

"You were a soldier, too. You sent us information that no one else could have unearthed. You and Willem. Each in your own way. I have learned much about the English. They put the prizes of war far ahead of any victory. I have seen a platoon of soldiers back off from a fight with us when they discovered some plantation that had not yet been looted. And they would prefer to spend an hour with a woman rather than do battle."

She laughed lightly at the picture. Yet it was true. Even the officers seemed to judge the importance of a victory by the gold and valuables they were able to steal.

He smiled back, and his dark eyes seemed to sparkle with humor. Still he made no move to touch her. She lay for a time beside him, feeling a growing awareness of his nearness. Her fingers felt as if some inner fire were warming them. They seemed to move of themselves.

When she touched him, he started, but immediately he grew quiet again. Waiting, fearful that he might consider her next action approval for an assault of his own, she spread her hand over his stomach. Beneath the heavy cloth of his breeches, she felt the familiar swell.

She drew back, timidly, but he made no move to draw her on. Comforted and reassured, she fumbled with the buttons that held the garment firmly in place. She could hear his breathing grow heavier, but still he lay quiet, passive under her probing.

Encouraged, she opened the buttons. When she moved to push his trousers down over his hips, he lifted up slightly and then lay down, waiting for her next move. She leaned over and kissed his lips. "I love you, Dirk."

"I love you. Enough to go away anytime you wish. Even now—if this frightens you."

She shook her head. The fear she had expected did not rise to stand between her and her lover. Would it crash down upon her if he were to abandon his passive acceptance of her tremulous touch?

She moved her hand, testing him. He remained quiet. Yet she could feel his passion growing. "You would leave me now—even now—if I asked you to do so?"

"Even now. I want your love, Marietje, not your fear and obedience. I want to live my life with you, until the day I die. I cannot live happily in the presence of terror."

She smiled and kissed his lips once more. She could feel the fire growing within her, and she felt no fright. Quietly she removed her gown and lay down beside him, sensitive to the rough weave of his shirt, the firmness of his body against her naked skin. She tingled with an awareness of ecstasy to come.

Later, lying in his arms, their bodies bathed in sweat, their hearts beating with the force of their passion, she could not remember how she had moved from her timid approach to the full excitement and tender susceptibility of love. But the transition had been made, and she had felt no uneasiness. She knew she cried out; she could hear her voice and she knew it to be hers. She thought once that she should feel pain, since she had been so recently hurt, but there was no agony to the love she shared.

He moved—but at her will. He kissed—with her consent and desire. He penetrated and probed into the depth of her heart, it seemed, and she only cried to feel him further within her, to hold him forever. She moved to stir his passion—and hers increased tenfold. She held back to tease him—and felt, herself, the torment of love unfulfilled. And then, with a cry of delight, she clasped him close, reveling in his nearness, in his presence within her. Knowing that all of her fears were unfounded. Dirk Hendrik was her man. She was his woman. Nothing that had transpired while they were apart could change the full truth of their love.

When she lay at last exhausted beside him, she felt a smile brighten her face. "I love you, Dirk Hendrik. Will you be my husband?"

He laughed at the reversal of their roles. "My father has given his consent. Will you marry me now? God does not approve of love like ours without the consent of the church."

She sat up, chuckling. "Silly! We have no priest here!"

"There is Frans. I baptized his daughter. Surely he will see us properly wed."

"But I have nothing to wear." As she finished speaking he began to laugh, and soon she joined him, laughing at the pleasure of knowing he loved her, laughing at the odd picture he painted, of Frans Johannson speaking the holy words that would bind them before God.

Then she suddenly grew solemn. "I must go back. If I am not there when Commander Scott returns, Mai will be killed. She can keep the soldiers from my room, pretending that I am affected with some illness. But Byron Scott will force his way in, and kill her when he sees that I am gone."

He studied her face without smiling. "Yes." He spoke very quietly, as if he wished he did not have to say the words. "You must go, if her life is at stake. But I will go with you. I cannot let you out of my sight again. Nor can I trust you to the mercy of the English commander. I must go with you, or I cannot let you go."

She felt the fear return. "If you come, you will be killed."

He laughed. "Do you plan to walk in through the gate, past guards, announcing that you have been out for a stroll? If you can slip into the house without attracting notice, can I not, too?"

The smile returned to her lips. "Yes. I had not thought beyond my need to save Mai. We can go in together and bring her to safety before Byron returns." She frowned. "Have we time? How long have I been sick?"

"Two days. You said he would be in Padang for a week. We are rallying forces around the city. It is possible that your commander will not return to the plantation. Still, we will go, in case he escapes our net."

She thought of the soldiers in the city. There were many. Could a few Dutch landowners triumph over a large, well-armed force? Would the fighting endanger the women at the inn?

A mosquito landed on his hand and he slapped it, brushing it to the ground. "Maybe, if God is with us, we will need to expend little ammunition against the English army. The heat has returned. How many Englishmen can resist the heat sickness, when it attacks them?"

"They will have quinine."

"Pray God they do not have enough." He rose, pulling her to her feet. "Let's go. I will wait to make you my wife until we can stand in your father's chapel, as he would have had us do. And until I have made the fortune he expects a man worthy of his daughter to possess."

She shook her head. "I will wait, for I know mother would understand, and father would prefer it. But not while you go back to Palembang. When you marry me, you will become master of my father's plantation."

He shook his head, smiling. "I can see that you are independent in more than I had imagined. But I will not battle with you now on so trivial a matter." He saw her shake her head, and he continued. "No, not trivial—except when compared with the importance of saving Mai. There is enough night left. If we hurry . . ." He dressed as he spoke, watching her cover her fair body with her gown. He could still see some scars from her ordeal, and he knew that he wanted Byron Scott to be alive . . . so he could kill him.

Chapter Twenty-Seven

"Mai?" Marietje tapped lightly on the door that separated her room from the room set aside for her companion. Willem had used it, but he would not return. Mai had promised to return to her accustomed place, to keep others from learning of her mistress's absence.

The door opened. Mai was dressed in her native garment—the long straight skirt and the bare torso. Marietje smiled. How much lovelier Mai looked this way than with her high breasts hidden under a tight shirtwaist. Yet her father had found such nakedness offensive.

"Are you ready to go?" Marietje barely waited for an answer. She led the way across the room to the hallway. "Dirk is with me. He wants us to get away before dawn."

"I cannot go." Mai had not moved from the doorway. "The house is full of sick men who need my help."

"But you must! If you stay here after I go, Commander Scott will know you helped me escape, and he will kill you."

"Commander Scott is here now."

A panic threatened to send Marietje rushing down the steps to where she knew Dirk waited in the stable. She gazed at her maid in confusion. "He knows I am gone, and he did not harm you?"

"He does not know. He was carried in yesterday, on a litter. The heat sickness came over him while he was in Padang."

"Did he ask for me?"

"He has asked for no one. He was not conscious when he arrived."

Marietje caught at the doorframe to steady herself. Why, she wondered, did she feel pity for a man who had treated her so poorly? "I should be happy that he is sick." She spoke more to herself than Mai, but the words did not banish her sadness. Now, when she stood on the brink of a new future with Dirk, she did not want to waste her energy in sympathy for a man she had vowed to hate. But she could not control her reactions.

"Where is he? Take me to him." She waited until Mai stepped into the hall. Then she followed. If Byron Scott was sick, he deserved at least one more visit from her before she left him. Just one. She had to know if he would survive.

At the door to his room, she paused again. What would she say to this man who had been so heartless the last time they were together? Could she face him at all? She turned away. No. How could she show concern for his health when she still felt the bruises he had put on her body?

"He may want your forgiveness. He thinks he is dying." Mai stood immobile, waiting for Marietje to decide what she was going to do.

"I don't know if I can give it to him. All I can remember is the pain he gave me." As she finished speaking she tried to recall that terrible moment, but the vision would not come at her bidding. Instead her thoughts centered on a more tender moment. She was in the bower. Could she honestly claim that he had hurt her then? Could she pretend that he had always been cruel to her? Which stood stronger in her memory—the pain or the earlier pleasure? Was there not enough compassion within her to permit her to see him and give him comfort on his dying bed?

Mai pushed the door open. Marietje stared inside. Byron Scott lay on the bed that had once held her mother and father. She realized with a start that she had not been in the room since they died.

It had changed considerably. The thick brocade curtains her mother had ordered from a special merchant in Amsterdam had been taken down. In their stead, a small casement curtain hung over the glass, blocking vision but not light. The lounge on which her mother had often rested was gone, and in its place was a desk brought up from the study.

The room seemed bare—more like a monk's cell than the residence of the officer who directed all the English forces. There was a feeling of loneliness about the room she had never felt when her parents were alive. Then it had been warm and welcoming—like her mother's arms.

The bed was the same, with the same draping netting her father insisted upon to protect against insects. A foolishness, some neighbors had said, but her father had always insisted that the netting saved his family from some of the diseases that afflicted many other colonists.

Byron Scott appeared not to bother with the netting, however. It hung useless over the head of the bed, more like a shroud, waiting to be draped over a corpse. And Byron himself lay beneath it.

She started at the sight of his face. A week ago he had been strong and healthy, strong enough to cause her much pain, and to leave scars she would never lose. Now his wrist was thin, his hand bony and weak. He lay with his eyes closed, but she sensed he was awake. He was breathing heavily. She could hear him all the way across the room.

He stirred, aware of a new presence. "Marietje?" His voice seemed far away. "Marietje?" His eyes opened, and he turned his head to look at her. "Thank God you are better." His thin arm stretched out, beckoning her to come to him.

She stood immobile, held by some unrecognized fear. Death lay on her parents' bed. Could she approach without falling under its sway?

"Forgive me, Marietje. I had no right to ask for your love. Not this soon. Not while we yet stayed within sight of your mother's grave. I should have been patient." He coughed. She could see that he was already exhausted from the effort of speaking.

Released from her fear by pity for this poor ghost of the man she had known, she stepped closer. Now she knew there had been a short time after Mai told her of his sickness when she had prayed he was already dead. A time when she had rejoiced at the thought that he was cut down by a power greater than himself. But seeing him wiped out those hateful thoughts. She saw only that he was a man—sick and alone. She forgot his anger and remembered only the pleasure he had given her and the love he had offered.

Could he be at fault because she had refused his proffered gift?

"Will you sit with me?" His voice seemed weaker.

Marietje glanced at Mai. Had she spoken of Dirk, waiting in the stable? The night was over. He would fear for her life and risk his own to save her.

"She has not eaten since she recovered." Mai spoke up before Marietje could respond. "I would like to feed her first. A little, at least, to keep up her strength."

A shadow passed over Byron's face. "Yes, of course. She must not grow sick because of me. I have harmed her enough."

Before he could change his mind, Mai caught Marietje's arm and led her from the room.

They moved swiftly to the kitchen, past soldiers who seemed no stronger than their commander. The men who had accompanied Byron to Padang. The sickness there must be out of control.

The cook smiled when Marietje entered the kitchen. A new man. Not the one who had served her father and mother for so many years. "Sri Gdang"—she hesitated to continue—"is he dead?"

Mai smiled. "No. He is back in his village. He had no wish to serve a man who killed your parents. When you escaped, he followed. When he saw you were safe with Dirk Hendrik, he went on to his own family."

Marietje shook her head. She had felt so alone as she wandered through the woods, searching for Dirk and Frans Johannson. Yet she had never been alone at all. Her father's love, expressed through the devotion of his servants, still surrounded her.

"Mai, can you forgive me for judging you? I didn't understand."

"We will never be the same. I do not need your forgiveness, nor you mine. We do what we have to do, and for reasons that matter only to ourselves." Mai's smile softened her words. "One does not expect a child to behave like a woman."

"I was a child, wasn't I? Even though I was grown enough to plan to wed." Marietje stopped, aware again of her reason for needing a time alone with Mai. "Can the cook speak Dutch?"

"No. He is new from the village."

"I had no time to tell you before. Dirk is waiting for me to bring you out. He does not know that Byron is here. If I do not go out to him, he will try to rescue us, and he will be killed." She felt her panic rise as she voiced the danger that confronted him. "Mai, if I must go now to stay with Byron, you must bring a message to Dirk for me."

Mai nodded, her voice low. "Will he be patient? The commander is dying. Can Dirk Hendrik wait?"

"Will he be safe? The soldiers spend much of their time in the stables."

"He knows the plantation. He will find a place of concealment."

Mai's encouraging words comforted Marietje. Yet she felt a growing uneasiness. Dirk would have to wait all day. His risk would be extended until darkness, when she could escape and join him. With Mai. Even with the change of events, she was determined to take Mai with her.

The dish the new cook set before Marietje had a delicious smell. She took a fork and began to eat. Then she put her fork down. "Please. Try to find a way to let him know we are safe. I cannot return to Byron's room until I know I will not endanger Dirk by so doing."

When Mai was gone, Marietje ate slowly. The new cook seemed fascinated by her, as natives who had not seen foreigners often were. He smiled at her each time he brought her a new dish, and he seemed to find some excuse to watch her as she ate. She smiled back—but nervously. She was aware of Byron, lying on his bed at the head of the stairs, waiting for her to return. She felt the presence of the soldiers, some as sick as their commander, who tried to keep their posts, and who succeeded only in giving the plantation home an air of decay and defeat.

Had Mai managed to deliver her message to Dirk? The question brought a wry smile to her lips. How many times had she been at the mercy of some messenger? Friendly, certainly—but an outsider, unable to convey the full concern inherent in her message.

Willem had delivered her messages to Dirk, but in so

doing he had almost succeeded in convincing Dirk she was a traitor. And now Mai. Would she succeed in explaining to Dirk why, after all their plans for a quick departure from the plantation, she felt a need to remain? Could he possibly understand, after all that had happened between them?

She half rose. She would have to find Dirk herself. He deserved more than a message.

The vision of Byron Scott, laid low by sickness, flashed before her, and she dropped back into her chair. She could not leave him now. He was too ill. He could not last much longer. And he was so alone.

The kitchen door was pushed open, and Mai stepped inside. Marietje forced herself to wait until the slender girl sat at her side. Her eyes asked the question.

"I found four soldiers in the stalls, cleaning them. So I stood talking with them for a while. I told them you were better and might want to ride later. And I told them you were going to stay with the commander, because he was so sick. I spoke very loudly. If Dirk Hendrik is hiding in the stable, he will have heard—and he will wait."

Marietje felt a crushing disappointment. Would such a terse bit of information satisfy Dirk? She feared not. He might still foolishly rush the house, determined to save her. And she could do nothing to stop him.

Mai sat quietly, expecting approval for her effort. Marietje nodded. "I pray God he understands and does nothing foolish." She caught Mai's hand. "You will come with me tonight?" She recognized the same hesitancy that had kept Mai at her post the last time. "They will know you helped me get away, and they will kill you. You cannot stay here. Don't you see that?"

"If the commander is dead, then I will go. He is a good man, Marietje. Like your father."

Marietje's love for her parents rose in protest. No one was like her father! He was a great man, a kind, loving man.

But he, too, had been known to show violent anger when pushed too far. He had been strict with her when she was a child. She had seen him punish Pieter and Dirk when they let their youthful ebullience lead them—and her—into situations Hans Koenraad considered dangerous.

Was Byron Scott so different from that? She recalled the night when he had turned on her in anger. Had she not asked for his treatment? Had she not taunted him, half hoping he would kill her?

A distant sound drew her attention. A shot? She lifted her head, listening. The noise was repeated. Gunfire. Far away, yet close enough for her to hear it. From the direction of the gate.

"Dirk!" She clutched Mai's hand. "I had forgotten. He told the others that if we did not return by dawn, they should attack." She closed her eyes. "Dear God save him."

The food had lost its charm. Placing her fork on the dish, she rose and hurried into the hallway. The sounds seemed louder and more frequent. There was a battle going on somewhere nearby. Was Dirk one of the combatants? Clasping her hands, she prayed for his safety. "Oh, Mai, we should have gone when he expected us to. If he is killed . . ." She dared not finish her sentence. If Dirk was killed in battle, she would have no reason to live.

"Marietje!" The cry came from upstairs. It was a call for help, a cry of agony, a confession of fears no soldier dared admit. It galvanized Marietje into action. Turning, she ran to the staircase. She lifted her skirt and ran up, passing the guards who sat so weakly without noticing that they had left their posts.

The door to Byron's room was ajar, and Marietje moved swiftly to his bedside. He saw her coming and held out his hand, a wan smile on his lips. "Thank you. I thought you had left me again."

Her eyes widened in alarm. "You knew I was gone?"

"I suspected it. Mai would let no one in the room. Yet I prayed you would come back. Whatever the reason, I wanted you here, beside me, when I died."

She fought back her tears. "You aren't dying, Byron. You're far too strong a man to let the heat sickness triumph." She knew she was speaking words not natural to her, and she felt a growing awkwardness. Could she, if she said the right things, keep him from dying? "I am much better. I was wrong to taunt you as I did."

"No. You must not blame yourself. I loved you, Marietje. I truly loved you. Far more than I have ever loved another woman."

She thought of his wife, of whom he spoke so seldom, and she knew she could not hold back her tears. "Your wife . . . Your children . . ."

"They mean little to me. I barely know my son, and my daughter was born after I left for Sumatra. You are real to me, Marietje. I could foresee happiness with you. I wanted it so. A soldier has little to show for his years of service." He gestured toward the wardrobe. "Oh, he has uniforms, and bits of those things he thinks are valuable. But the finest silk is no comfort when one is dying. And old age is barren if all that surrounds it is gold. With you, little Marietje, I saw a vision of love I had never seen before. I wanted it for myself."

He paused, his breath coming slowly, as if each intake of air was a struggle. She squeezed his hand gently, afraid she might break it, and yet aware of how short a time had passed since he was the strong one—and she at his mercy.

"I know now that was unfair of me. A pure child like you . . ." He closed his eyes, exhausted by the effort of speaking. "I knew all along that you loved another, though I did not know his name. Now I know you are no longer mine. I can see it in your eyes. Was it . . . what happened between us that killed your affection for me?"

She could not answer. Had he forgotten all she said to him? Had he forgotten, too, that he came to her in anger, aware of Willem's spying? Did he not remember that he had sent Willem into the woods and ordered his soldiers to follow and kill the boy? Had the confrontation between her and this strange Englishman faded from his memory? What was it he wanted her to forgive—if not the beating he had given her?

He seemed unaware of her silence. "I should not have brought you to the bower. I know that now. It belonged to him, didn't it? I didn't want to see that. I wanted it to be ours, the secret hideaway where I at last won your heart.

But I knew even then that I had possessed only your body."

He was silent for a while, and the sound of gunfire was heard again. A wild look came to his eyes, and he sat up. "My sword! Orderly! Bring me my sword! I must go to battle!"

Marietje tried to hold his hand in hers, but he drew it free and threw back the covers. He threw one leg over the edge of the bed. "Where is my uniform? Orderly! My boots!" As he spoke his features seemed to set. His mouth clamped shut. He clawed the air with one hand, finally catching Marietje's fingers in his. And then he fell back. She moved with him, listening for his breath. His chest was still.

With a sob, she lifted his head and rested it on her lap. She perched precariously on the edge of the bed, his body twisted by his fall, half on the bed and half pulling toward the floor. Mai approached, lifted his leg and put it back under the covers. She held Byron's shoulder while Marietje settled farther back, and then she stepped back. "There are others that have died, too."

Marietje looked up, her eyes filled with pain. "I care not about the others! Oh, Mai, why is life so cruel?"

Mai did not respond. Quietly she turned and left the room. And as she disappeared Marietje abandoned herself to her grief.

It was as if all the sorrow she had held back was at last released. Had she wept when her father died? She could not remember. But some of her tears were for him. Had she felt the terrible truth of her mother's death? Not until now, when she sat with her killer's head on her lap.

Pieter had gone to his grave unmourned. But she cried for him now, recalling all the times he had helped her, all the fun she had shared with him—and with Dirk.

She cried for Dirk, too, and for herself. She wept when she recalled the beauty and happiness that had once been part of her father's life—and her own. The plantation had been a place of hope and love. Now it was filled with sickness and despair.

Gently she closed Byron's eyes. Had he ever known peace until his death? He had clutched at her as a man reaches for help when he feels that he is alone. He had deceived himself into believing that she loved him. All because he needed love so very much. Could she hate him for that?

She shook her head. She could not even hate him now for the pain he had inflicted upon her. He had been, that terrible night, a man fighting against a truth he could not endure. And she had not seen his need. She had thrown her hatred for him in his face, hoping he would end her life. Instead it was his life that was over. An empty life, a soldier's life.

She thought again of her father. He had built a good home in Sumatra. He had earned the respect and love of his servants. He had been affectionate to his wife and loving to his daughter. He had taken two orphan lads in and given them a home. If he had been given the opportunity to examine his life before he was killed, he must have felt a satisfaction.

Her mother, too, had shared happiness with others. When she went to her grave, she left behind memories of love and caring. She had given freely of her energies and her love—and though she died a violent death, she did not die alone.

Even Pieter had done much in his young life to keep his memory alive in those who loved him. And he died after giving the greatest gift he could give to the woman who had taken him in.

Did Byron Scott have any such memories? He had fought side by side with many men before he reached his position of authority. Had he felt friendship for any of his comrades? He had a wife and two children somewhere in England. Yet he had told her he felt no affection for them at all. They were strangers. And he was still alone. In all of his life, he had known only war.

War for land, war for gold and spices. War for loot. He had had many women, of that she was sure. Had he ever felt affection for any before he met her? If she could find them, would one of them, his wife included, feel sorry at his death?

She had no wish to face the answer. His haunted,

hungry eyes had told her more than she wanted to know of the emptiness of his life.

Gently she rested his head on his pillow. She straightened his limbs, folding his hands over his chest. And then she knelt beside his bed and began to repeat the Lord's Prayer. Of all the dead she had known, this one man was the most in need of her intercessions.

Chapter Twenty-Eight

Dirk stepped into the shadows of the hayloft, watching Marietje slip silently across the barnyard. They were committed now. He would have to wait for her return and pray that she accomplished her errand safely. It did not occur to him to question her need to save her servant. He had learned the same respect for the natives she had been taught by her father. Mai had risked her life to help Marietje find him. They owed the girl something for that.

As Marietje slipped in through the door that led to the kitchen, he settled back. The wait might be long. He had no way of knowing how difficult it would be for Marietje to reach her room without being seen by the soldiers. There was the servants' staircase. If she remembered, and if she was lucky, she might avoid any confrontation she could not explain. They had discussed her approach before she left him. He prayed she would be careful.

He closed his eyes. Had he ever felt rested? He could not remember. All he knew now was nights of attacking the resting British soldiers and days of intermittent sleep, disturbed by any suspicion that their hideaway had been discovered.

He considered the manner in which they had to carry on their attack. Disgraceful, that was how it seemed to him. He had a deep need to face his enemy directly. Yet he knew that he and his companions would lose such an encounter. They had too few guns, and not enough ammunition. And there were so few of them compared to the English forces. Their only hope lay in surprise attacks.

He was not a good soldier. He knew that now more forcefully than he had ever known it before. When as a child he had left the ship and sought shelter in Hans Koenraad's home, he had already admitted to the deep hatred for the cruelty he had seen on shipboard. Fate had provided him with a reason for leaving the service. He, like so many of his shipmates, was affected by the heat sickness. Johanna Koenraad had volunteered to nurse him, and so he had been moved from the ship to the plantation. And when the ship sailed, early because of the captain's need to save some of his crew from the death that surrounded them, he was left behind. Yet he would not have left the ship on his own. He would have endured, and probably died, as so many of his shipmates had.

In Hans Koenraad he found the kind, reasonable leadership that fit his own temperament. Was it Hans's example that had helped him reach an understanding of Marietje's relationship with the English commander? He had not considered that possibility before, but he instinctively knew it to be right. Hans Koenraad had been a truly noble man, kind to his servants, loving to his family, and with the ability to extend his protection to strangers without demanding anything of them—not even their thanks.

But Dirk knew that he had cause to thank his dead master. It had been Hans's idea to have the boy sign as his indentured servant, not so there could be more demanded of him, but so he could not be legally taken back aboard any ship again against his will. The papers had been signed and put aside, and young Dirk Hendrik had found a family who loved him. He had given years of devotion to Hans Koenraad, and all of them had been deserved.

He jolted awake. Had he slept long? Why had Marietje not returned? His fear for her safety brought his mind to total awareness. He seemed to hear the sounds of the stable more clearly. The morning songs of the birds were fresh and loud in his ears. A door opened below, and he crawled quietly to the edge of the loft and peered down.

Four soldiers entered, carrying brooms and shovels for cleaning the stalls. They bantered between them, working with as little speed as possible. Obviously they had no taste for the work they had been assigned.

The door opened again, and Mai entered. Dirk caught his breath. Would Marietje follow, and fall into the soldiers' hands? Why were the women exhibiting so little caution?

The soldiers stopped their work, clearly relieved to have some excuse to move out of the stalls. "Mai, you're here early. Is the commander better?"

Mai shook her head. "No. He thinks he is dying. He's sent for Marietje, and she has gone in to him. I have seen him. He will not live long now."

"If I know the bastard, he'll send us out to find a battle, so he can be killed like a soldier, with a bullet. He never had the stomach for dying in bed."

Dirk pulled back and lay listening to the two men talk. Was it true? If so, Marietje had arrived just in time to save Mai. But what, now, would happen to Marietje. Why would a man who had mistreated a woman as Commander Scott had abused Marietje ask to see her again?

A cold chill seemed to take possession of Dirk. Could it be that Scott intended to murder her? He had tried once.

He half rose, and then dropped quietly down again. He would be of no help if he moved without thinking. Below him, two of the soldiers had resumed their unsavory task. They would have to be first. If he were to rescue Marietje before it was too late, he would have to overcome his hatred of killing. "For Marietje." He whispered the words, hoping they would give him the power to do what lay ahead. But the sound of her name brought visions of summer, of beauty and smiles. He thought of her lovely face and knew he could not kill in her name.

He cursed his own weakness. Byron Scott, he knew, would not hesitate to kill him. Nor would the soldiers working in the stalls. If they knew he was hiding above them, they would shoot at him without any uneasiness. Why was he so different a man? Did this prove he did not deserve her love?

He contemplated the thought. She had shown no admiration for Byron Scott's soldierly nature. When she spoke warmly of him at all, it was when she told of how he cared for her. It seemed important to her that he had not been on the plantation when her mother and Pieter were killed.

Dirk lifted his head in alarm. Shooting! Quickly he crawled to the loft window and peered out. The sun was high in the sky. He had promised Frans Johannson that he would return with Marietje before the sun lifted above the horizon. And they had agreed to wait with the assault until then.

They had complied with their part of the pact. But he had failed in his.

A wisp of smoke rose from the area of the plantation gates. They were making a frontal attack—a good way to move when they knew the enemy was weakened. But where had word come to Frans to that effect?

Below him, the soldiers heard the gunfire and dropped their pitchforks. Grabbing their guns from where they leaned against the wall, they hurried out. The stables grew quiet, except for the sound of horses eating and the occasional thump of a hoof hitting the strong wooden floor.

Dirk inched his way down. The stables and their environs were empty of human life. He stood for a moment, seeing the half-cleaned stalls and remembering how spotless they always were when Hans Koenraad lived. One of the horses neighed, and he stroked her head. "Quiet, girl. It's all right." He reached into the feed bin and drew out a bucket of grain. Rare in this climate, and hard to come by. But Hans Koenraad had always wanted the best for his animals. Soon the feed would be gone.

He pushed the door ajar and peered across to the kitchen of the big house. The room appeared empty. Inhaling deeply, he stepped out into the open.

He was halfway across the yard when a shot rang out. He felt the bullet hit his shoulder and he dove for the ground. The gunfire did not continue. He moved a hand, hoping to regain his feet, and another bullet grazed his leg.

He had little time to act, he knew, before his opponent could reload his rifle and be ready for another shot. With a grunt, he rolled over, pushing his way into the shelter of the barn. He had not achieved anything by his daring. Unless he wished to risk another bullet, he would have to remain where he was.

He lay for a time, waiting for another bullet to hit. No more shots rang out from the house. But the shooting that had started in the distance was coming nearer. He could hear some shouts, as men began to pour out of the dairy house, which had been turned into quarters for the foot soldiers. Instinctively Dirk crawled into the shelter of some bales of straw. The voices drew nearer, and he raised himself up to see.

The men who were assembling before him were far removed from the smart, military men who had first invaded the plantation. Three were in such poor shape he wondered they could hold their rifles. The rest were wan. They moved sluggishly. He knew the symptoms. The heat sickness. It had affected more than Byron Scott. His entire army was rotting from its ravages.

Yet the men were willing to fight. Maybe they knew the danger that faced them. Maybe they realized that the plan to draw the few plantation owners to Padang had worked against them. For the Dutch landowners were accustomed to the insufferable heat and the insects that plagued the English. They were angry, too. Angry at the English for what had been done to their lands, and for the indignity that the conquerors had visited upon their women.

Dirk prodded at his shoulder. A little more than a flesh wound. He would be fine once the bullet was removed. He reached for his rifle and realized with a start that he had left it where he fell—in the middle of the yard.

He watched the men, his breath suspended. Would one of them see his gun? It was a miracle he had not been killed by the gunman and left to rot where he fell. Would his unknown assailant inform this platoon of men that there was an enemy nearby?

There was no sound from the house. The men formed lines and stood at attention, waiting orders. "Men! The fight lies ahead!" The call was given by some officer just out of Dirk's line of vision. A sword was held aloft, and the plantoon moved forward. Dirk could see that at least one of the men was using his last bit of energy just to stay erect. Nature was fighting on the side of his people.

When they were out of sight, Dirk rose and stepped boldly into the clearing. This time there was no gunfire. He crossed the yard and stood for a moment on the steps leading to the kitchen door.

He had mounted the first step when a new sound drew his attention. Somewhere between the house and the road a cannon had been set up, and the loud retort told him that a cannonball had been fired toward his companions. Another would follow, and another, until all his friends were dead.

Unless the cannon could be silenced.

He stepped down and began to creep around the house, pausing at each corner to peer around it. The cannon was not in sight.

Another roar told him that the men who handled the gun were still capable of quick action. He watched as the ball soared on its way. Now he knew where the cannon was concealed. What Dirk did not know was how many other officers and men remained in the house. Were they suffering from the same heat sickness that had incapacitated their commander? He studied the empty windows only a moment before reaching his decision. If the men inside were able-bodied, they would be out fighting.

Turning, he considered the approaches before him. The cannon was mounted under the great tree on the mound where Hans Koenraad had built a small chapel and near which he had buried the ill-fated nursemaids who had been unable to survive the Sumatran climate. The white picket fence, so reminiscent of places in Holland where Dirk had lived as a small boy, had been torn down, or maybe broken by the movement of the cannon. A line of soldiers was formed around the artillery, protecting it and the men who fired it from bullets. When a man fell, the others closed rank until a new man could move in to take his place. Dirk considered his chances of reaching the cannoneers without himself being killed. There was, he had to admit, no possibility of success.

Unless he could approach from the rear.

He looked to his left, where the most recent groves of coffee trees were bursting with blossoms. If he could reach them safely, he could circle around. The formation of the soldiers told him they were not expecting an attack from behind.

He moved cautiously until he turned the corner, out of sight of the men who guarded the cannon. Clutching his rifle, he sprinted across the open area, diving under the low-hanging branches of the coffee trees. Now he moved with more dispatch. When he was sure he had gone well beyond the danger area, he began to move to his right. He crept low, careful not to disturb the branches of the trees, until he could see the chapel ahead of him.

The cannon fired again, and during the confusion caused

by the noise of firing he raced from the protection of the trees to shelter behind the chapel. He considered entering the building, for from the one window above the narrow doorway he would have a good view of the cannon. But once he was in the small building his movements would be restricted. He could not kill all the soldiers at once, and those who survived would find him easy prey.

Leaning against the wall of the chapel, he aimed at the chief gunner. His bullet hit, and the man fell dead. Immediately Dirk moved, settling at last behind a tree some distance from the chapel. The direction of the firing told him he had moved quickly enough. This first time at least, no one had seen him rush across the open area.

Now, however, his position was far more precarious. The guards were alert. They faced an enemy near enough for them to defend themselves against him. Nevertheless, he had to continue his attack. The cannon had to be silenced. Keeping as close to the tree as possible, he took aim again.

At that moment, a shot rang out from far to his left. Someone was firing from the barn! Not at him, but at the cannon. At least one of his comrades had come to his rescue.

The red-coated English soldiers turned toward the new source of gunfire with practiced ease. Under fire, and without an officer to command then, they followed the pattern of defense that worked so well in the fight with the French. The first line of men knelt. Behind them, a second line stood with their rifles trained ahead. And behind them were reinforcements, ready to fill any position that fell vacant. For Dirk and his unseen helper, the Englishmen made a perfect target.

Again, Dirk raised his rifle. His bullet found its mark, and another man fell to the ground. His place was taken immediately by another, but Dirk could see that the supply of reinforcements was not endless.

At that moment, another shot rang out, this time from the grove of coffee trees. Another Englishman fell. Dirk, from his position, could see that the men were becoming confused. Their impenetrable line was not effective against random attacks by an enemy they could not see. They fired quickly, backing up to be replaced by others whose guns were ready. But the new line took its casualties.

Now Dirk realized that he had not been alone in his plan to still the great cannon. He tried to count the number of allies he had, but the firing was too quick. The men from Bengkulu had arrived in time.

Before Dirk could reload, one of the British soldiers held up his rifle high over his head. Tied to its muzzle was a white kerchief. He stared at it in disbelief. It was not expected. All he had heard of the English army led him to believe they would prefer death to surrender.

A voice rang out from behind the barn. "Throw down your guns and stand apart from each other!"

The English soldiers seemed confused. They moved a little, but they maintained their body cover of the cannon.

The voice called out again, and this time Dirk recognized it. Frans Johannson. "I will count to five. If you are not unarmed and standing apart by then, we will fire."

The sound of his count filled the stillness. "One! Two! Three."

At that moment, the redcoats broke ranks. The muzzle of the cannon appeared, aimed directly at the barn. Dirk did not wait for the next count. He fired quickly, and the gunner fell. Now there was gunfire coming from every tree. An English soldier grabbed the torch and brought it to the cannon, but he failed to make contact. Someone to Dirk's left stopped him with a bullet.

In the confusion that followed, Dirk was sure of only one thing. The cannon was out of commission. Every time some soldier tried to reach it, he was killed. Until, at last, the gun stood exposed. The battle was over.

With a whoop, Dirk's companions ran from behind their hiding places. Dirk watched them move down the road. There was still some activity near the gate. Soon the Englishmen would find themselves attacked from the rear.

When the last of his companions was gone, Dirk stepped from his tree. He would join them later, for the fight was not yet ended. Padang was under attack, too. The battle would continue until that city fell. And then, when the shipful of reinforcements and ammunition arrived, the Dutch defenders would be ready. They would even have cannon with which to return the fire from the ship.

Frans Johannson was among the last men to leave the site of their victory. He waved at Dirk. "Is she safe?"

"I don't know. I go now to find her."

Frans crossed the open area, stepping aside to avoid the dead. "I stayed to give you help."

"Thank you. You came just in time."

"We waited until we knew where you were. We have no wish to fire on our own."

They had reached the kitchen door, and Dirk pushed it open. Inside, huddled against the far wall, was a native he did not know. One of the many the British had found to replace the loyal servants who had deserted when they took over. Dirk spoke in the man's native tongue. "It's over now. You're safe again."

As he and Frans headed for the hallway he saw the native rise and run out of the house. *Maybe*, Dirk thought, *we can persuade them to come back when peace is restored*.

Dirk and Frans entered the hallway with their guns ready. No one opposed them. On the steps, a red-coated soldier sprawled, too sick to lift his head. Beside him, his rifle lay. He had not even tried to load it. Dirk felt an odd mixture of regret and satisfaction. Clearly all the able-bodied men had responded to the first shots and run to defend the plantation. That gave him a feeling of being in control. They had performed as he expected them to.

But the sight of the sick soldier gave him no pleasure. He saw only that the man was barely beyond childhood. He saw the empty face and the haunted eyes, and he felt pity. There was nothing he could do.

Frans moved more quickly. Raising his rifle, he shot the man. Dirk looked at him in surprise mixed with anger, but he did not respond with an expression of regret. "I would do as much for my horse. I see no honor in a slow death."

Dirk nodded. Frans was right. Who now could say that the lad did not die fighting?

They moved up the stairs two at a time. At the head, Dirk gestured toward Marietje's room. Frans stood guard while Dirk pushed the door open. The room was empty.

With a cry of alarm, Dirk crossed the hall to the door

that led to the room which had once been Hans Koenraad's. Mai had said Byron Scott was sick and had sent for Marietje. He should have known she would be too softhearted to refuse him.

They pushed the door open together, their guns ready. It appeared that the room was empty. Through the open window Dirk could hear the sound of occasional gunfire. Soon the fighting would end and his men would be on their way to Padang.

Alert, he moved toward the bed.

It was then he saw her. Marietje knelt beside the bed, her hands folded, her head resting on the coverlet. She looked up as he approached. "Dirk! Thank God you are safe."

"You were praying for our victory?" His glance swept the bed, and he realized that a thin form lay under the cover. Scott. Dirk frowned. There was no coercion here. Scott was clearly unable to force Marietje to stay beside him.

Marietje saw him look, and she reached out and stroked the still hand. "He's dead, Dirk. He was so repentant. He begged for forgiveness, and I could not hold my anger. I thought of the nursemaids who died so far from their homes. He reminded me of them. He has a family, too, but it was to me he turned for comfort."

Dirk felt his anger rise. "Is this how you act as soon as you leave me? Did you mean any of what you said? If he beat you as you claimed, how can you have sympathy for him now?"

She felt a confusion that threatened to bring tears to her eyes. "What is the matter with my sympathy? Dirk, I told you, he's dead. He died alone, far from his people. Do you feel no pity for him?"

"Pity? Why should I feel pity for a man who stole what was rightly mine? Why should you comfort him when you tell me he harmed you?" He studied her in silence, aware that he felt a resentment of Byron Scott that must be voiced. "Marietje, I hate him. I cannot understand that you do not, too." His eyes narrowed. "Unless you lied to me. Unless he never hurt you. Tell me, was it some other soldier who attacked you so brutally? And why, when you were hurt, did you run to me and not to him?" He gestured toward the still face of Byron Scott.

Marietje tried to respond, but words would not come easily. She had been right before. Dirk could not forgive her for what had been done to her.

He saw her silence and continued. "You loved him, didn't you? Tell me the truth—at least once. Admit that you loved him."

She shook her head, strangely aware of her curls bouncing against her neck. "No. I never loved him." As she spoke she knew she was lying. There were so many kinds of love, and she had once thought there was but one. "I mean . . ." She saw his expression darken, and she hurried on. "I love many people, Dirk. I loved my mother and father, but not in the same way as I loved Pieter." She saw Dirk frown, and she felt her own anger growing. "Don't act as if that was wrong. You loved Pieter, too."

"Yes, but man-to-man. Not—"

"Women can love men in that way, too. I never felt for Pieter the kind of love I have for you. But I did love him. And I suppose you are right. In a strange way, I loved Byron Scott."

A look of triumph brought Dirk's head erect. "There! At last you are not lying! Did he teach you to dissemble, my dear? Is that where you learned to hide your thoughts and speak only what you thought was wanted?"

"Don't put words into my mouth, Dirk Hendrik! I am not a child anymore!"

"How well I know that!" His look brought a blush to her cheeks. "No child would know the skills you exhibited last night."

Tears of frustration welled in her eyes, and she forced them back. "Why do you insist upon misunderstanding me?" His face remained set, and he did not respond. "Maybe, in a way, I did lie to you. But it was because I did not understand myself. When I left you to find Mai, I thought I hated Byron. I could think of nothing but the pain he inflicted. But when I saw him dying and heard his penitence, I knew I could not hate him. I can only pity him." She rose and stood across from Dirk, the body of

277

Byron Scott lying between them. "As I pity you. For you cannot understand."

He stared at her in silence. Gradually his eyes widened, yet he said nothing. When he did speak, his voice was oddly quiet. "You pity me?"

"Yes, if you cannot understand that when one loves, one learns to understand. I know now that Pieter loved me, maybe as much as you did. But he understood that he could not speak of his feelings, and so he accepted what he could. Byron Scott was good to me in many ways. He helped me find my father's body, and he buried Papa and my mother with proper respect. He was gentle to me while I mourned."

"But he took you against your will." Once more, Dirk's eyes narrowed. "Or *was* it forced upon you?"

"Yes!" She stamped her foot in anger. "Yes, he forced me! But he was gentle, too, and I believe he felt affection for me. He tried to make me want him."

"Then I was right? It was not Byron Scott who hurt you?"

"You are wrong. It was Byron. But I tried to get him to kill me. I taunted him. I knew you did not love me anymore, and I saw no reason for living. But even then, he could not kill me. His rage made him hurt me, that's true. But he was so repentant. I know he did not want to do me harm."

"Then you did not fight him—except that one last time?"

"No." She could see that some of Dirk's anger was fading. "I fought him when first he took me, and every time he came to me. But I could not win such a battle. Each time, when he left me, I felt the shame—and the hate. For him—and for my own weakness." The tears she had been holding back could be stemmed no longer. Annoyed with this further sign of her frailty, she brushed them aside.

He studied her for a moment in silence. "Do you love him now?"

"Oh, Dirk, can you not understand? I have never loved any man as I love you. I never will. But I pity Byron Scott, and in a way I do love him. I cannot forget that he did many kind things. Can you feel for me and see how it could be thus?"

For the first time since his entry into the room, Dirk glanced to where Frans stood in silence, near the window. Once Frans had thought love could only be expressed through discipline. But the fighting—and his suffering—had changed him. He thought of the other men who fought beside him. They were hoping to rescue women who had been forced to put up with many assaults from more than one stranger. Yet most spoke of forgiveness and love.

And then, as if for the first time he understood his own self-deceptions, he met Marietje's eyes. "I thought I could never kill any man, yet I have caused many Englishmen to die."

She felt a spark of hope. "You are not proud of your prowess as a soldier?"

He shook his head. "No. Yet I will go on killing until Sumatra is free again." He smiled faintly. "That is more than is asked of you. Your days of submission to what you do not want are over."

She smiled, and her eyes lit up with a deep joy. He knew the meaning of what she had said!

He stepped around the bed and moved to her side. Yet he did not touch her. Instead he stood before her, his hands at his sides. "I think we must learn to understand each other, my dear, and to forgive. I feel no compassion for this man." He gestured toward the bed. "Nor for any of the men I have killed. They are my enemy. Can you forgive me for that? Can you understand that the only regret I have upon seeing Byron Scott dead comes from my need to kill him. I am helpless now. In a way, he has won."

She waited in silence for him to continue.

He caught one of her hands and held it. "I know you want me to feel the sympathy and understanding that fills your heart. But I cannot." He turned her hand in his and brought it to his lips. "Yet I want you to feel as you do. I know that now. A woman without such charities would be a poor mother and a worse wife."

"Then you do understand?"

"No. I am jealous of that man"—he nodded toward the

bed—"because you cry for him. I cannot help the way I feel."

"He is dead, Dirk. And he died alone."

"No. You were with him. I may die in the fighting to come—and I will be alone."

A look of distress overwhelmed her. "Oh, no! You cannot be killed! I need you."

"As you needed Byron Scott?"

"No. He needed me. I see that now. I was goodness he longed for. Love he had never had. And I was innocence. I think that is why he grew so angry when I taunted him. He had no wish to hear such words from my lips."

Dirk smiled at last. "Nor would I. But you have not answered me. Can you forgive me for still hating my enemy?"

"Yes. If you can forgive me. Maybe you can't believe me when I say I never loved Byron Scott as I love you, but it is the truth. Pity and love are not the same. But I can promise that my heart remained true to you. Can you take me for a wife, knowing another man has violated my body?"

He took her in his arms, looking down into her gentle eyes. He loved her, he knew that. He had loved her all the time, even when he burst into the room and saw her kneeling at the bedside of his enemy. "Let this be the end to our self-reproach. We are neither of us as we once were. Yet we have been fighting a battle, and the war is not over. Soldiers are loyal to their cause when they fight, and when peace comes, they do not reproach each other for deeds performed in the heat of combat. You cannot hold a gun, yet in your way you fought a good fight."

He drew her close, and she could feel the acceptance that had at first been withheld. "Your fight is over, little Marietje. Come. I will help you bury this man, and then maybe Frans will marry us. The chapel is still standing. I think your father would want us to say our vows there."

Together they turned to Frans. He had been standing to one side, waiting for some solution to their conflict, and now he approached, smiling. "I'm glad you have settled that. I feared, for a time, that you would begin your own fight, and we would never again have peace on Sumatra."

The grave was easily dug, for the ground was soft from the recent rains. Marietje chose the site, below the graves Byron had ordered dug for her parents and for Pieter. And then the three entered the tiny chapel. Dirk took her hands and held them between his as Frans recited the ceremony.

"Before God, I pronounce you man and wife." He touched their shoulders. "May you live long together in peace."

As they approached the small entryway Frans spoke. "Will you live here, after the English are routed?"

Dirk looked down at Marietje. "Can you build a life here, after what you have endured?"

She smiled. "This house was built by my father—in love. It is my home. There is no place I would wish to go." She met Dirk's eyes. "Our love will wash away all this unhappiness."

"Then the answer is yes." Dirk turned to Frans. "Though I will travel to Palembang occasionally. I have a partner there who will need my help in setting up the factory. We will have to rebuild our trade as well as our lives."

"Good!" Frans picked up the gun he had left inside the doorway. "Then I will leave you now. Join us soon, Dirk. We need every gun we can find." He caught Dirk in an embrace and then was on his way.

Marietje watched him move down the road until at last he was out of sight. Then she turned to Dirk. "Will you be able to stop the reinforcements from landing?"

"We will try."

"Could you not dress in these English uniforms and lure them ashore north of Padang? Then you could trap them as they landed."

"We cannot take prisoners, Marietje. We have no way to keep them." He saw her disappointment. She had been hoping for a way to avoid more bloodshed. "But nevertheless, it is a sound idea." He caught her around the shoulders and led her into the sunlight. "And I have another. After I am gone, you must prepare this house to receive the women as we free them. They will need your comfort and understanding more than Byron Scott ever did."

She smiled up into his face. How strange it was to know that her childhood was over—that she was a woman capable of giving help to others. Like her mother had been. "I'll be ready for them. I am thankful there is something I can do."

"There is much you can do. When the war is over, there will be much to heal." He chuckled softly. "Oh, my little Marietje, I can see you will want to be part of everything I do, and I do not regret that. This is a land where strong people are needed. It's strange. Once I thought of you as frail and helpless. Now I know you are stronger than I am—for you can be hurt and still feel love." He turned suddenly and caught her in his arms. "I do love you, Marietje."

"I love you, too, Dirk." She reached up and kissed him. "Will you help me prepare the rooms for the women?"

He laughed and lifted her up. He felt how light she was and marveled at the strength that she possessed. "Maybe, my dear. But not now. Now is our time to be together. Now is the time for love."